THE
TROJAN
CONSPIRACY

ERIK SAMDAHL

ISBN: 0692329447
ISBN-13: 978-0692329443

Cover and layout by Bryan Swan

www.eriksamdahl.com

To my mom, who has urged me to pursue my passion for writing for as long as I can remember.

PROLOGUE

SHE SMILED AT the man she was going to kill.

He grinned lazily back at her, other intentions on his mind.

"I'll get you another," the man glanced over his shoulder to catch the eye of the dutiful waiter whom he had no doubt tipped well to keep the drinks flowing. As he turned back around, his beady eyes lingered on her cleavage. After several drinks, any sense of discretion had left him.

"I don't know," she said with a faint southern twang. The woman with blond hair leaned forward and gently placed her hand on his leg. "I'm starting to feel tipsy. I'm such a lightweight."

Before she could protest further, the waiter, a young man in crisp khaki shorts and a white cotton shirt, appeared with another stiff margarita for her and whiskey sour for him.

"You are so bad," she locked eyes with him over the rim of her glass. "Can I at least pay for this round?"

"I've got it," the man reclined in his wicker seat, his shirt parting to reveal a clump of sweaty chest hair. His name was Gerard. Fitting, for a weasel with slicked-back hair and greasy gray whiskers.

"Aw, thanks," she purred. "Billy's so cheap, he'd probably make me pay my own way. He's no gentleman like you."

Tonight, she was Charlotte, a young, 23-year-old girl looking for her big break in the modeling industry. She was here on vacation with her reluctant boyfriend, who was in their hotel room puking into a toilet. Billy—everyone else called him Will—didn't like the thought of her becoming a model, nor did he like traveling. He just wanted to go back to the U.S. of A., but she wanted to see the outside world for the first time in her life. She wanted to learn and experience everything. *Everything*.

That is what she had told Gerard, anyway.

Of course, Billy, or Bill, or William didn't exist. Nor did her interest in modeling. In fact, Charlotte didn't exist.

"I can't possibly think of anything better than being here right now with you," Gerard raised his glass, though she knew he was thinking of at least one thing he'd rather be doing with her right now.

"It's so peaceful. Most everyone has already left," Charlotte finally broke eye contact with him and looked around. "It feels so early."

It wasn't early. The outdoor bar was slowly emptying. A few hotel guests still lingered, sipping wine against the rail that separated them from the black abyss beyond. The hotel, a sprawling white paradise embedded into the craggy rocks of the coastline, glowed under the star-splashed sky. The grand terrace, like the hotel, sat perched on the edge of a cliff.

Charlotte rose from her seat and strode to the railing just a few meters away. Out of the corner of her eye she saw a beefy islander stir, his massive frame bulging against a sweat-stained T-shirt. The bodyguard didn't look concerned. He had no reason to be. His employer was relaxing at an upscale hotel on the Venezuela coast and she was a blonde in a bikini and sarong with nowhere to hide a weapon. The bodyguard was also drunk.

"It's so beautiful," she said when she sensed Gerard arrive beside her. "You can't see the ocean at all."

The smallest of breezes soared up the sea cliffs, gently slipping through the humid air that was just as cloying as it had been at high noon. She barely noticed it. Her attention was fixated on Gerard.

"It's one of my favorite resorts in the world for a reason."

"Do you really live here?"

"For the time being," Gerard gloated. "Maybe next week it'll be Cyprus. Or Sri Lanka. It's hard to say what I'll be in the mood for."

"You must be rich," she giggled. "I bet you have an amazing view from your room."

Gerard licked his lips. "It's extraordinary."

"My room is so boring. I don't even have a view."

"That's really unacceptable. Do you want to see mine?"

Charlotte grinned at him, her eyes sparkling. He stared back at her, waiting breathlessly for a response, looking a little too eager. "I don't know... Billy might think... well, what he doesn't know won't hurt him."

She had no desire to spend a minute longer here than required, among the socialites and vacationers and families who scoffed at slow service and complained about sunburns and other silly inconveniences. And she hadn't needed long with Gerard. He'd been sitting alone at his reserved table, gnawing on a bloody steak, watching for drunk college students or local girls who would ignore his pockmarked cheeks for free booze. Within minutes of her sitting down next to him, he would have bought her a yacht if she had asked for one.

Gerard led her to his suite where he'd lived in bliss for the last several weeks, all the while chatting her up about his investment in tech stocks. They were all lies.

"You can wait outside," Gerard told his guard at the door. He must not have been wholly unsuccessful in luring beautiful young women to his room as his protector showed little surprise at her interest in Gerard. The man simply nodded as Gerard urged her inside with a nervous hand at the small of her back. He closed the door behind her without turning on the lights.

The balcony doors were open, the moonlight casting long shadows across the marble floor. Despite a soft breeze, the room was stifling hot.

"Where're you from?" he murmured, his hand caressing her hip.

"Tennessee," Charlotte said as he guided her to the balcony. Off in the corner, she noticed a desk, and on it a closed laptop. This was going to be easier than she had thought.

"Tennessee, a beautiful place," he said automatically. Another lie, she detected. He had never been.

"Yeah, you really like it?" she asked innocently, turning her back to him. The balcony extended beyond the edge of the cliff, a straight drop to the shadows. The warm ocean churned forty vertical meters below, but from above it appeared as nothing more than black glass. During the day, the view must have been spectacular. At night, it felt like the edge of the world.

"I do," he said. "Come here."

She let him draw her close, ignoring the alcohol heavy on his breath. His small, greedy hands coiled around the straps of her bikini top, though he was too drunk to properly untie them. Charlotte leaned towards him innocently and let him kiss her. His tongue flicked down her neck and between her breasts, his hands following suit. She embraced him tightly and pulled him to the bed. He fell on top of her, his head still buried in her chest, and she hastily removed his shirt.

He breathed loudly, sucking in large gasps of humid air as she ran her hands across his oily skin. She flipped him onto his back and climbed on top, her slender body looming over his. He gazed up at her with fascination, aroused.

"I want to do all kinds of things to you, Gerard," she tilted her head toward him. "All kinds of things."

"You can do anything you want, my dear."

It's amazing how fast a man sobers up when he realizes he's gotten himself into serious trouble. When Charlotte's smile faded, as the soft innocence of her expression turned to ice, and as her hands, which had so playfully been teasing him, slid up his chest and coiled around his neck, Gerard knew within seconds that he'd made a horrible miscalculation.

"You've done a bad thing, Gerard," Charlotte, who was no longer Charlotte, said, her southern accent gone.

"Who are you?" he blurted out, though the volume of his voice was choked by her tightening fingers. He gasped, trying to take in a full breath of air. She wouldn't let him. He scratched at her arms, but his pathetic attempts at escape didn't faze her. She stared down at him, her eyes cold and face expressionless.

"You know what this is about," the woman glanced over her shoulder at the desk.

"That computer over there. Does it have what I'm looking for on it?"

"I don't know what…" he squeaked, but she responded by striking him hard across the face. Gerard's nose ruptured and blood splattered across the white pillows. He tried to scream, but she retightened her grip on his throat, allowing him just enough air to croak out a response.

"It's on there," he said after the initial shock had worn off. "It's all on there. But it's too late! I already—"

"Who hired you to do it?" she cut him off again, but this time not with a blow.

"I'm not—"

"You know what I'll do if you don't tell me."

"Fuck you, bitch," his lips curled, revealing blood-soaked teeth. She struck him across the face again and he began to cry silently, his mouth twisted and wide.

"Tell me."

"They'll kill me. They'll—"

"You don't need to worry about what they'll do to you. You need to worry about what I'll do to you."

He coughed up some blood. "Listen, all I did—"

"*All you did?*" she asked contemptuously. "Tell me or I'll beat you to death."

The rodent gave her what she needed, just as she knew he would. He was like so many others, wannabe gangsters who buckled under the slightest pressure. They were reliable for all the wrong reasons.

She looked down at the man. Gerard had relaxed, believing he was safe. But her grip around his neck didn't relax. A moment later, he was dead.

The woman with blond hair climbed off her broken victim, heading straight for the desk. In less than a minute, she deftly cracked the password. As she copied the contents of the laptop to a flash drive she had tucked into her bikini bottoms, she marveled at the tranquility of the room. The only sound was the ocean crashing into the rocks below.

Then, the woman climbed onto the balcony's railing, closed her eyes as she felt the tug of wind on her body and gracefully leapt over the edge.

PART I

JANUARY 6

1

"THEY'RE COMING FOR you."

Christopher Morgan's stomach sank, though the words failed to resonate. He stopped in the middle of the street, ignoring a blistering gust of wind that swirled down the narrow stretch of parked cars and barren trees.

"They know everything about you," the voice in his ear said. "You need to—"

"What?" Morgan pressed the phone closer to his ear, as if that would help him understand any better.

"Listen to me. They're at your place as we speak. Do *not* go home."

His eyes focused on the nondescript brick building fifty yards away. Warmth. Safety. Anonymity. There was a reason he chose this neighborhood. The street was lined with five-story apartment buildings, home to middle class and young couples. Crime was low. Nothing bad happened here.

His heart beating faster, he quickly scanned the familiar street. At first glance, nothing seemed amiss. The block was still, even tranquil. The frigid air kept people indoors; not so much as a bird made a sound. Everything looked as it should. But the façade quickly melted away. Morgan tensed. The white cable van parked suspiciously near the front door to his apartment building, the back windows tinted black. The door across the way sitting slightly ajar. A sliver of movement on the rooftop.

His silence didn't go unnoticed. "You're close, I can tell. Get clear, then call me back."

The line went dead, but Morgan kept the phone to his ear. His heart beat loudly now, so loudly he could barely hear himself think. He had to calm himself.

Laughter. To his left, he observed a young girl, a teenager with a fluffy jacket, ass tight jeans and an ass worthy of them, walking down the sidewalk, chatting on a cell phone in a Hello Kitty case. She entered the corner grocery store and he was once again left in silence.

Morgan started walking again. As he stepped onto the sidewalk, he noticed a homeless man sitting on the ground, wrapping in blankets and mumbling to himself like the pathetic creature he was. Only it wasn't right. Bums never hung around here for very long, and they certainly didn't beg for change on an empty street far from any bustling intersections.

He searched in his jean pockets for some loose change. He put his phone away and approached the bum. As the man extended his hand—only one, his other remaining out of sight—Morgan examined him again. The beard was long and curled, with pieces of garbage tangled in the hair. The man's cheeks were grimy. He smelled of grease. He was the quintessential bum. The perfect bum. Law enforcement.

The man was dead in an instant. Morgan's blow struck the agent across the cheekbone. The man's hands rose to protect himself from the punch that had already fractured his face, revealing a Glock 23. Morgan snapped the man's wrist, retrieved the weapon and dispatched a single bullet into the man's head. The head snapped back with a whoosh of air.

Morgan heard the van doors open. A rush of footsteps. But his attention was on the surrounding buildings. He fired three cover shots at the rooftop where he assumed the snipers were perched—where he would position himself in such a situation—and when he didn't immediately receive a bullet to the chest in return, he figured he'd aimed correctly.

He turned and ran. Knowing he couldn't make the full corner before receiving one in the back, he sidestepped into the grocery store. There was another entrance on the other street, the perfect shortcut to save a few precious seconds. But, as the door jingled closed behind him, he caught movement out of the corner of his eye. A man running toward him from across the street. Gun in hand.

On instinct, he grabbed the closest thing to him—the teenage girl in the fluffy jacket. She screamed loudly. Under any other circumstance Morgan would have loved the situation. He loved to hear women scream.

He swung the trembling girl in front of him, driving his new gun deep between her shoulder blades. Peering over the girl's shoulder, he spotted his assailant.

The man's name was Ryan Harper. Harper was a rising star within the FBI, an already respected agent with limitless career potential. He was smart and stubborn. An adequate adversary.

Ever since he'd shot the senator, Harper had been pursuing him. Aimlessly, but relentlessly. He thought he'd gotten away with it. The FBI had made no progress, given no indication they were onto him. He was convinced they would never catch him. They'd failed so many times in the past. He'd gotten lazy. Complacent. And now, he had just wandered into a death trap.

Morgan surveyed Harper. He studied the young agent, watching his eyes, assessing what he was thinking. Harper did the same, reading his every move.

The grocery store would be surrounded in a matter of seconds, and Morgan didn't have time to play around. Slender and athletic, Harper could easily beat him in a foot race, but as good a shot as he was, Morgan knew Harper was no match for him.

Unlike his adversary, Morgan was willing to do anything to survive.

"Christopher!" Harper barked and stepped forward, sensing what he was about to do.

Morgan pulled the trigger. The girl's screams silenced as she lurched forward, a torrent of blood gushing from the hole in her throat. He pushed the corpse toward the FBI man, but Harper made no attempt to catch her. Instead, he let the already-dead girl collapse to the floor and dove behind the convenience store counter.

Morgan spun toward the door on the other street, but instincts kept him from approaching. The FBI would take him down the moment he stepped outside. They might not even wait that long. Instead, he veered to the right, crashing through an "Employee Only" door to a windowless storage room that smelled of fish. Dim fluorescent lighting flickered overhead. He spotted a gray metal toward the back and went to it, praying that it led somewhere other than a closet.

He found himself in a gray service corridor that was even darker than the room he'd just been in. It appeared to run the length of the block, away from his street and the legion of federal agents who were undoubtedly swarming out of their hiding places. He started running, his feet feeling heavy. The corridor seemed to go on forever, straight and offering no room for cover. He was an open target. He passed a few doors, but they wouldn't take him where he wanted to go; he was focused on the door at the end, up four steps with a faded "Exit" sign taped above.

The door behind him opened. Morgan stopped, took one breath, and fired a single round. The bullet missed, but it came close enough that Harper was forced to retreat. The door closed again, and Morgan knew Harper would be more cautious next time. That would give him a few more precious seconds.

He reached the half-set of stairs and climbed them two steps at a time. He rammed his shoulder against the heavy door, reaching for the doorknob at the same time. The door didn't budge.

"Morgan!" his name echoed down the hallway.

He fumbled with the lock, his sweaty fingers suddenly useless. *Don't panic*, he told himself. He breathed out, vanquishing if only for a moment the effects of adrenaline, and unlocked the door.

A gunshot rang out, much louder than normal given the confined space. A bullet bounced off the step directly beneath his feet, but before Harper could fire again, he was outside, back in the cold and daylight. He emerged on a sidewalk on a street much like his, another stretch of apartment buildings and condominiums.

The sound of a car engine caught his attention. To his right, he spotted his escape: a taxi was stopped in the street, a pregnant mother and small child waiting on the sidewalk with luggage. The driver's side door was open and the cabbie, a Pakistani fellow, was walking around the rear of his vehicle to assist them with their bags.

Morgan shot the man in the head as he approached. To her credit, the woman didn't scream, but she was in too much shock to even move. But he didn't care about her. His cover was blown; all that mattered was escape. He slipped into the car, closed the door and sped away. Only as he turned the corner did he see Agent Harper come into view, a frustrated look on his bloody face.

MORGAN DITCHED THE taxi five miles away. He tossed his blood-soaked jacket in a dumpster, no longer concerned about the cold. He dialed a number and the man answered immediately.

"How the fuck did this happen? How'd they find me?" Morgan asked before the man had a chance to speak. He ran a tight ship and didn't make mistakes. But clearly he'd made one somewhere.

"'Thanks' might be in order," the man said coolly. "We're still trying to figure that out. The FBI received an anonymous tip a few hours ago, but so far no one's been able to pinpoint the source of the call."

"An anonymous tip? Who in hell would that be?" he growled, crossing onto a busier street. He would blend into the crowds and become lost.

"We don't know."

"You have to know, because it sure as hell wasn't me," he said. "Someone on your side."

"No," the man said quickly, almost defensively. "Only the two of us know."

"Curious, don't you think?" Morgan growled, but then the answer came to him. "Patricia."

"Sorry?"

"Nothing," his voice grew faint. Patricia Giddy, that stupid whore, had sold him out. His girlfriend. Or as close to a girlfriend as he allowed. She knew what he did for a living. He didn't like people knowing the truth, but as much as he despised her, he liked having someone around to talk to. Besides, she was a great fuck and didn't know the difference between a Democrat and a Republican, let alone how to betray a man who gave her shiny things and a roof over her head. He never gave her specifics, and had purposely said nothing about this last job, but apparently she'd figured it out and gone to the cops. Stupid bitch.

"Christopher, you need to complete your new assignment today."

"What?" Morgan snapped back to reality. "Are you fucking kidding me? The heat's on. We're done."

"They'll never see it coming, and it's the only way I can assure your safety. Do what we paid you to do and go to the arranged meeting point. You'll be safe there, and it'll give us time to figure out what to do next."

Morgan remained silent, his fists clenched.

"Christopher, is that agreed?"

Morgan frowned. He needed to get away. Disappear. Drop off the grid like before.

But this wasn't like before. He'd shot a senator. Killed his whole family. He needed to get out of the country, out of reach of the feds. It wouldn't be easy. By now, his face would have been distributed to every agency on the western seaboard. Airport security on high alert. The borders shut down.

He hung up.

2

THREE PEOPLE DEAD. One a federal agent.

Erin Kinsley watched the television intently. Anxiously. No one was returning her calls. No one had told her what had happened, who had died.

She should have been there, leading the charge. Instead, she was home with her leg bound in a cast. Left out of the loop, unable to assist in the field. It was a terrible feeling. "One federal agent killed" was all the news had to say. The ominous words repeated over and over in her mind.

But if something had happened to Ryan, John would have called. Whitmore would have called. Someone would have called by now.

She hobbled into the kitchen. The leg no longer hurt, but for a woman as active as she was, and who needed to be active to do her job, it was a daily reminder that she still had over a month to go before she'd be back to full speed. She hunted criminals for a living, but she had been sidelined by an old man who hadn't seen her crossing the street. She'd been lucky, but right now she felt no such way. Delegated to desk duty until she was fully recovered, she felt the walls closing in around her.

Most days she would relish the rare opportunity to hang around her house on a Saturday afternoon, but with her boyfriend, another FBI agent, off leading a massive manhunt, she felt completely out of the loop. Even though she was receiving periodic updates, the silence in between was deafening.

She jumped as the front door swung open and Ryan Harper appeared. His intense gaze went right to her and he smiled, but she could see the frustration in his eyes. She knew him too well to be tricked by his outward calmness.

"Hey," he said in as upbeat tone as he could manage. He looked tired as hell. He'd barely slept in days, and the adrenaline from the phone tip that came in earlier was apparently wearing off. His normally handsome, chiseled face was worn, the muscles in his cheeks sagging from fatigue. He had a bandage over one eyebrow.

"I didn't expect to see you anytime soon," she greeted him warmly as he embraced her. She didn't want him to see that she'd been fearing the worst. He held her for a second, then pecked her on the lips. She smiled, her eyes concerned. "What happened to you?"

"Dodged a bullet, hit a countertop," he said matter-of-factly like he always did. He wasn't one to sugarcoat, except when she asked how she looked in certain dresses. "You heard about Russell?"

"No," she gasped, picturing the agent in her mind. Fortyish, an infectious laugh. She hadn't known him well, but they were all family. When one died, they all felt it.

"It was so sudden. We didn't even have a chance to react. Two civilians died, too. Total cluster."

"What happened out there?" she looked into his brown eyes. They'd found that the sooner they talked about things, no matter how horrible or disturbing, the faster they could get on with their lives. Ryan summarized what had happened, and described Morgan— a man in his mid-forties, slightly stocky but athletic, strong and agile. Graying brown hair, a weathered yet unremarkable face, except for his piercing gray eyes.

"He nearly killed me," Ryan said. "He could've killed many more if he had chosen to. Didn't waste a single bullet."

"So what are you doing home?"

"We've got cops looking everywhere, but he isn't going to be easy to find. John's talking with Morgan's girlfriend. Whitmore sent me home to take a shower, change clothes… see you, of course." He smiled his first genuine smile of the day, and it was enough to distract them from their subject.

"Got any need for a crippled woman?" she asked.

"No, you're pretty useless," he joked.

She smacked him on the arm. He laughed, grabbing her wrist.

"I might get lonely in the shower," he glanced down the hallway toward the bedroom.

"Well, that's too bad, because I can't get my cast wet."

"Hmm," he purred, pulling her close to him once more. She smiled suggestively and let him kiss her on the lips. "What *are* we going to do with you?" His arms coiled around her, and she felt the pull of his body as he guided her into the living room. She let him lead her to the couch, where he lost all balance and toppled onto the cushions, taking her with him. "Sorry I didn't call sooner."

"I'm a tough woman, Agent Harper," she said, running her fingers through his sandy blond hair. "Tougher than you."

"You're the one with the broken leg," he rolled both of them onto their sides. Erin tensed, thinking she was going to go right over the edge of the couch, but he held onto her, keeping her close. "Did I tell you how beautiful you look today?"

Erin rolled her eyes, accepting the compliment even though she knew she didn't look her finest, with her faded tank top and gray shorts, and uncontrolled raven hair pulled back into a loose ponytail.

"Weren't you going to take a shower?" she reminded him.

"The shower can wait," he said, his fingers sliding under the hem of her shirt. Erin closed her eyes, sensing his lips on her neck, softly brushing the surface between her ear and collar bone. She let out a quick breath, and he squeezed her tighter. She arched her head back as his mouth moved under the base of her chin, and she dug her fingernails into his back.

His cell phone rang.

Erin kept her eyes closed as she felt his hands withdraw, his embrace loosen. She could hear Ryan trying to find his cell phone in his jacket, and then the beep as he activated it.

"I have to go," he said after twenty seconds on the phone.

"They find him?"

"No, not yet," he climbed off the couch. Erin remained where she was.

Ryan bent over and kissed her on the cheek, and then said, "I'll see you later today. I love you."

"Love you, too," she said, eyes still closed. She listened to Ryan leave the house. She smiled, looking forward to later today.

Little did she know that she wouldn't see Ryan again that day, or the next, or the day after that.

CHRISTOPHER MORGAN RECLINED in his car seat and sighed as he measured his pulse. He needed to be relaxed for what was to come. The next 24 hours were crucial. Everything needed to be executed perfectly. Every cop and fed in the city were looking for him. If he stayed nearby, he was a dead man. Even if he ran, they would most likely find him. His greatest asset had been his secrecy, his invisibility. No one knew him. No one had even heard of him. Now he was in a shit storm with no way out.

His only ally was his latest client, but how much could he rely on him? Even if it was his own foolishness that had cost him everything, Morgan couldn't trust the man. The guy only had two options: protect him, or kill him. He knew very little about his client, but he knew enough to be dangerous. Too dangerous to be kept alive.

But the client had asked him to continue with his new assignment. For the time being, that provided him a way to survive to see another day.

He laughed at the thought. Here he was, the federal government raining down on him, and he was sitting outside a woman's house in the suburbs.

Morgan looked across the street to see the front door of the beige house open and a man who looked all too familiar emerge. Morgan ground his teeth, his index finger tapping on the pistol laying on the passenger seat. He wanted to kill the man so badly he could taste it. But it wasn't the time or the place. He'd only get protection if he delivered the woman to the cabin, and shooting a federal agent dead on a suburban street was not the best way to ensure that would happen.

Christopher Morgan watched as Ryan Harper climbed into his car and drove away, leaving the beige house unguarded but certainly not empty. Slipping the pistol into his jacket pocket, Morgan climbed out of his car and crossed the street.

3

RYAN HAD ONLY been gone a moment when someone knocked on the front door. Groaning, Erin sat up. She waited, hoping whoever it was would go away, but when the person knocked again, she decided it was best to answer.

"Coming," she shouted, hobbling to her feet once more. She crossed the room and opened the door.

The next few seconds were a blur. Erin heard a smashing sound and she felt herself falling backwards, but she didn't connect the dots until she landed hard on the floor. Looking up, dazed, she could see a stocky man looming over her, silhouetted against the light outside.

The door slammed against the wall, but Erin's attention was focused on the gun the man held in his right hand.

Before she could think, she reacted, kicking out with all her force. Her foot struck solidly against the man's leg, but not enough to snap anything. He grunted, wincing in pain, and she scrambled to her feet. Her broken leg forgotten, adrenaline pulsing through her veins, she went on the offensive and lunged at him, her training triggering on instinct.

Her attacker was strong, and also well-trained. He deflected her attempt to disable him. She grabbed his right wrist and twisted. He shrieked in pain and dropped the gun, but his loss of control only raised his level of intensity. He swung out with his left arm and knocked her halfway across the room. Stunned, she staggered backwards until her back connected painfully with the wooden edge of the couch arm.

The man was already charging at her again, and she knew she wasn't in a good position to fight. She considered going straight for the sliding door in the kitchen— the only other exit—but she didn't have time. Instead, she darted down the hallway, moving as fast as she could. Through the hallway bathroom, she could double back through a second doorway into the kitchen and to outside.

She entered the bathroom and slammed the door shut behind her. She frantically locked it. The lock, while not strong, would preoccupy her assailant for just a moment, and if he was a cocky bastard, maybe he'd try to frighten her for a few minutes before breaking through, all the while she'd already be outside calling for backup.

Her plan didn't work. When she opened the second bathroom door and stepped into the kitchen, her assailant was there to greet her as if he'd read her mind from the beginning. Unable to move or even react to the attack, the fist struck with a deafening blow to her cheek, knocking her sideways. Before she collapsed, however, the man grabbed her by the neck with his left hand and flung her against the wall.

She was running out of options. Her off-duty weapon was in the bedroom, and the closest weapons—a set of knives—were lying scattered on the floor. Her attacker kept her pinned to the wall, his breathing calm, teeth gritted. She grabbed his wrist and attempted to free herself, but he wouldn't let go. Fighting for air, she stared groggily at the man before her, feeling his fingers bore into her throat, watching his blurry fist rise for another strike.

"I've waited for this day, Erin Kinsley," she heard him say. "To feel you, to actually touch your skin, is exciting beyond words."

The last thing she saw before his fist blocked her view were a pair of deadly, gray eyes.

BEFORE ERIN REGAINED full consciousness, she could feel the pain. It was a low throbbing that started just below her temple and ran down to her mouth, a sensation that transformed into a stabbing pain when she tried to stretch her jaw. She could taste blood in her mouth, and feel more caked under her nose.

When she tried to raise her hand to touch her wounds, however, the reality of her situation came rushing back to her. She forced her eyes open—they didn't want to respond—to see her lap, her gray shorts splattered with blood and mud. She was sitting, her arms and legs bound by duct tape to a creaky wooden chair. Her arms were smeared with dirt; it looked like she'd been dragged through the mud.

Erin sucked in an uncomfortable breath of air and then raised her head. She gasped as more pain shot down her spine; her neck felt like it had been run over by a semi truck.

She looked around. She was in a small cabin. She could see a door and window in front of her. The door looked like it might fall from its rusted hinges at the touch of a finger, and the window was so dirty she could hardly see outside. It was obvious no one had inhabited the cabin in quite some time. The walls were gray and infested with mildew. Ivy snaked its way through a hole in the roof. The wooden floor appeared like it would cave in at any second, sagging heavily beneath her feet. The only sign of life was a small candle flickering on the floor in the corner, underneath the window.

"Good morning, sunshine," a man's voice came from behind her. She heard footsteps, and then her chair shook as two heavy hands came down on her shoulders. In her ear, he said: "God, I wish I could have more time with you."

"What do you want?" she asked fiercely, though her voice came out choked and shaky.

"Not what you think," he pulled away from her. Leaving one hand on her shoulder, he circled around so that she could see him. Erin gazed up at the man. He was of average height and stocky, but even through his hooded sweatshirt she could tell he was all muscle. His grayish-brown hair was cut short military-style, which made his neck appear extra thick. His brow was fat and bulging, his chin slightly off center.

And when she connected with his gray eyes, she knew exactly who he was.

"Ah, you recognize me," Christopher Morgan read her expression and smiled. "Your boyfriend's been quite a nuisance today. Nearly killed me. Then again, I nearly killed him. Needless to say, I think I have the upper hand now. I have to admit I've been a bit jealous of him. I've been watching you for quite a while, nearly a month now…" He trailed off, letting her acknowledge what he'd just said. "I know so many things about you, things you probably don't even know yourself. It's amazing what you can learn about someone from afar. Amazing how attracted you get to a person, too."

Erin tensed as the hand that had been on her shoulder dragged across her collar bone and down her chest. Morgan licked his lips as he cupped her breast through the flimsy fabric of her tank top, feeling her elevated heartbeat. He stood closer to her now, his other hand gently brushing away the straps from her shoulder. He grinned, touching the soft skin, first with his fingers, then with his mouth.

She wanted to fight, to yell, to rip a chunk from his neck, but she knew that would only excite him more. Instead, she did nothing, tried not to react. She never imagined something like this would happen to her.

"I've heard you fuck your boyfriend so many times," he growled in her ear. "You want it rough but he won't give it to you. I can tell."

Erin couldn't believe her ears. He'd been watching her for weeks. He'd been listening to her, to them. Christopher Morgan, the man they had been hunting for over a month, had been fifty feet away the entire time.

"I've wanted to taste you," he ran his tongue across her neck. "I've wanted to have you. You're a pretty thing. You try to hide it, but you are one good-looking bitch."

And then, just when she thought it was going to get worse, he pulled away and wiped his mouth with the back of his hand. "I'm not a rapist. I'm many things, but I'm not a rapist. You may be asking for it, but I won't oblige."

For some strange reason, she believed him, and she let out a breath she didn't know she was holding.

"The bad news for you, however," he continued, "is that you're not going to survive the night."

MORGAN PULLED A hunting knife from his pocket, unsheathed it and watched Erin Kinsley's reaction. Her eyes focused on the blade, but still she refused to beg for mercy. She was a tough cookie. She'd be tough until the end.

Erin looked sexy despite the fact that her face was smeared with blood and dirt, one of her eyes was nearly swollen shut and the whole left side of her face was one big black-and-blue bruise. Her dark hair, matched with those sparkling green eyes, were what did it for him. Her athletic body and shapely breasts didn't hurt, either. If he were any other man he'd be indulging in her right now, but he had his rules and he stuck by them.

It was a shame she had to die. But if tonight was his last night, he wasn't going to die alone.

He'd walked into a trap. He'd even seen it coming, but had ignored every instinct that had served him so well for so long. His client had tricked him into going to the cabin with his hostage. The feds should never have had a chance of finding them there. They were in the middle of the fucking woods in northern Oregon. It was when he heard the helicopter that he realized he hadn't found salvation. His client hadn't sent him here to rescue him; he'd sent him here to have him killed. The feds were surrounding the place, and in another hour, at nightfall, they'd move in and it would all be over. Morgan had kidnapped one of their own, and in doing so had guaranteed each and every one of them would have itchy trigger fingers.

His only chance of escape was up and over a series of foothills that rose high behind the cabin, but it would be a two-day hike to another road. By that time, it would be too late. Besides—and his client knew this all too well—that wasn't his style. Morgan would prefer to go down shooting and take as many people with him as he could. Suicidal, perhaps. Homicidal, certainly.

"Your friends are surrounding the place as we speak," he explained to her as he bent down on one knee. He sliced away the duct tape that kept her left leg restrained to the chair and, holding her ankle firmly, began to saw away at the cast. "Waiting for nightfall to make their attack." Hoping to take away his advantage.

"They'll succeed," Kinsley said. "What do you expect to accomplish?"

"I know they'll succeed," he spat back at her, grabbing a big chunk of her cast and tearing it away. Her skin was milk white underneath. "They'll gun me down. Not before I pick off a few of 'em. How's this feel?" He squeezed her shin hard, and Kinsley gasped loudly.

"Still raw," he laughed, and tapped the knife's grip hard against her bone. Tears streamed from her eyes. "I need you to know this is real."

"Why the hell did you bring me here?" she gazed up at him, her eyes still watery.

He didn't know why his client insisted he bring her here. Didn't care. He didn't ask questions like that. Better to lie. "It's simple: you're bait. Your boyfriend wants you safe—looking at that body of yours, I don't blame him—and he's going to come in with a lot of your friends to save the day. Unfortunately for him, I'm going to be waiting to take him and anyone else out with my M40. And as for you, I won't be the one to kill you. They'll be responsible. I've laced this cabin with plastic, and as soon as they open that door right there, this place'll explode like Nagasaki."

Kinsley looked at the door. She was hoping he was lying, but even before she saw the delicate, indiscreet wiring lining the frame—and packets of C4 crammed into rotting gaps in the wood—she knew he was telling the truth. Her friends would be responsible for her death, and she theirs.

"And with that pleasant thought, Agent Erin Kinsley, I hope you have a very pleasant evening." This time, he hit her leg as hard as he could.

Morgan watched her head sag into her chest once more, and then stood up and put the knife back in his pocket. He smiled, his eyes perusing her frame. He knew this would be the last time he would see her in one piece. His time was almost done, but she would die sooner.

4

ERIN ROCKED SIDE to side in her chair, desperately trying to tip it. Break it. Loosen her restraints. Do anything to improve her situation. Yet after what seemed like countless attempts, the chair remained upright. It was hard to breathe with her mouth gagged—Morgan had all but wrapped her head in duct tape after she lost consciousness again—and her body burned under a sea of sweat. She'd wasted valuable minutes, exhaustion and frustration setting in. She wasn't making any progress, and death approached.

It was getting dark, but a candle flickered in the corner, light dancing on the decrepit walls. If Morgan was right, and she believed he was, her colleagues would be advancing on the cabin any minute now. When they did, they'd walk right into Morgan's trap. The cabin would explode and she would die. It wasn't the ending she had foreseen for herself.

She knew what she had to do. Erin planted her bare foot on the wooden floor, her toes wiggling as she let her body settle. Morgan had freed her broken leg. Perhaps he didn't believe she could do it, or perhaps he did and wanted her to suffer the agony of desperation. It didn't matter. She had to do it.

She moved her fractured leg away from the chair; the motion, even with little resistance, made her leg throb deeply. She breathed out, then in, then out again, then in, increasing her respiration until that was all she was thinking about. Then, with all her force, she pressed down on her foot and jerked her upper body away. The pain was excruciating, every bit of force she could muster splintering through her shattered leg. She blacked out. Again.

When she awoke moments later, her cheek was pressed against the cold, warped floor. She lay on her side, one arm and leg pinned underneath the chair, her free leg dangling overhead. She shifted slightly, the pain overwhelming her once again, and to her relief found that one of the chair legs had broken off.

Erin's eyes settled on the piece of wood that had splintered from the chair. The shaft was long, and lying only a few inches from one of her hands. To her delight, a rusted nail protruded diagonally from the piece. It could be enough.

Teeth clenched behind her mouthful of duct tape, Erin urged her body forward, scooting one inch at a time. Each inch sent painful tremors through her body. But she forced herself closer, and soon her fingers were playing with the nail.

Erin began to saw at the duct tape that bound her wrists. The position was awkward, her efforts frustratingly slow. It took three minutes just to pierce the duct tape with the nail, and her sawing motion seemed to glance off the tape without much resolve.

"Come on!" she screamed, though her voice was muffled by the tape. She was crying freely now, the pain no longer sharp but a steady, stifling feeling that ran through her body. The duct tape was cutting into her wrists. Blood was starting to drip onto the floor.

Still, she didn't give up. Her friends would be coming for her soon. Maybe too soon.

NIGHT SETTLED OVER the rolling hills, the last strip of deep blue vanishing on the horizon. The tall pine trees rustled softly under a cool, winter breeze. The moon was out, but clouds were descending, painting the earth with ominous shadows.

Ryan Harper lurked between the trees, his eyes searching the darkness. He ducked under a branch, fingering his Sig Sauer P226 as he went. The climb was slightly uphill, but he barely noticed. He breathed in and out slowly, listening for any peculiar sounds. For Christopher Morgan.

The man was out there somewhere, waiting for them. He was a trained killer. His girlfriend said Morgan brought home phenomenal sums of cash for every job, suggesting high-status, high-risk targets. Based on his earnings alone, he was a premium assassin, a deadly force. Everything about him implied that he was one of the best out there—so good that no one had even known he existed until that morning.

Everything Morgan had done until this point was cool and collected, so why this? He should have run. Should have disappeared like he did so many times before. But he took Erin, an FBI agent, his girlfriend. He'd taken the one person Ryan cared about most. Because of that, Ryan knew Morgan had a death wish.

There was no other way to explain Morgan's actions. They weren't logical; he'd backed himself into a corner. There were a hundred square miles of forest beyond the cabin, but it was a limited space. In time, he'd be squeezed out.

Ryan glanced to the left and just barely made out the silhouette of Agent Jennifer Halsbrooke, who was twenty feet ahead of him. Dressed in full tactical gear—Kevlar vest, helmet, night vision goggles— and possessing a semi-automatic assault rifle, she was a force to be reckoned with. A petite, innocuous woman, when on a mission she was as cold and calculating as the people she pursued.

Beside her, another member of the welcoming party, Alexander Radly, sifted through the trees, looking almost identical to his smaller counterpart. They would be on the front lines of the assault, backed by three other tactical agents. Another ten, a mixture of battle-worthy fighters and secondary field agents, were moving into position. John Lancaster, Ryan's trusted partner of several years, was among them, though he was approaching from the southeast. They were the best of the best, and they were about to unleash hell on Christopher Morgan.

Whatever Morgan's plan was, the FBI's was more straightforward. Morgan had a hostage and he knew the FBI was out there. He was expecting them, waiting for them... They just had to do what they were trained to do: secure the area and squeeze. Even though Morgan was expecting an attack, they could still have the element of surprise. They would take him out before he had the chance to decide what to do with his hostage.

If he hadn't killed Erin already. Morgan was a killer. He was the most wanted man in the country now. He'd already shown he was willing to do anything, and he had to know a hostage wouldn't be enough to get him out of a sticky situation. If anything, Erin would just slow him down.

Ryan paused for a moment, eradicating the thought from his brain. He'd convinced his superior, SAC Rachel Whitmore, that he needed to be on the mission. He *had* to be on the mission. He'd been pursuing Morgan for a month. It had turned personal, and he was one of the best agents the FBI had. Whitmore couldn't deny him.

He was backup—after all, Halsbrooke, Radly and the rest were trained specifically for situations like this—but he needed to be there. Erin's life was in his colleagues' hands, and it was better that way. If presented with an opportunity to get at Morgan, he didn't know how he would act. He wanted to kill him. He wanted to destroy him.

Up ahead, Ryan could see a faint glow. It was the cabin.

"Keep your eyes open," the team leader—a man by the name of Greg Wexler—chirped in his earpiece. "I have a bad feeling about this."

"I'm looping around the cabin," Halsbrooke said. "Radly, you have my back."

"Already got it," Radly said.

"It looks like something is burning inside. I can see it through the window," another assault team member said after a moment.

Ryan crouched behind a bush. He could now see the cabin quite clearly. It was dark, but the moon had emerged from behind its cloud cover. It was a small building, only one room, two at most. The structure was elevated several feet above the ground. Part of the roof was sagging, but still looked as though it could withstand the elements. Three rotting steps led to a small porch, the front door and a window, the clouded glass cracked but intact. A dull orange glow flickered inside.

The cabin sat in the middle of a clearing; there was a good ninety feet of grass and low brush between the porch and tree line, and sixty feet on the other three sides. If Morgan was watching, he would see them coming.

"Report," Wexler asked.

"Clear," came the unanimous response.

"Eyes on the woods. I can picture him sitting around somewhere just waiting for us to walk by."

"If he's still here," Radly said. "Could've cut across to another road by now. He could be miles from here."

"We'll consider that when we need to."

"I'm in position," Halsbrooke said.

"Move in. Be extremely careful. One at a time. We'll watch for movement."

Ryan watched as Halsbrooke, almost on her hands and knees, emerged from the forest and looked around. Ryan tensed, waiting for action. Out in the open, she was more exposed than ever. If Morgan was out there somewhere, he would have no problem killing her now. She wouldn't have time to react. Ryan's heart beat louder than it ever had before. He breathed out, trying to calm himself.

She darted silently across the clearing and stopped at the rear of the cabin. She sank into the shadows, disappearing from sight. Radly joined her a moment later, followed by three more agents.

"Okay," Wexler ordered. "Let's do this."

"I got it," Radly moved to the corner of the cabin. He edged around the side, followed by Halsbrooke, and approached the front porch.

They reached the front of the cabin. Three steps led up to the small porch, but the lowest was missing, long since rotted away. Radly dropped to his knees and scanned the pitch-black area underneath the porch with his infrared. He pulled away a small section of the rotted trellis that ran around the circumference of the cabin and, on his back, vanished from sight. A minute of agonizing silence passed as Radly slowly drilled a small hole in the floor of the cabin and proceeded to feed a small, fiber optic needle lens into the room above.

"One room," Radly said in a faint whisper.

Ryan realized he wasn't breathing. The wait was unbearable.

"Kinsley's in the middle of the room, on the floor." On the floor. "Tied up." Tied up. The words rang repeatedly in his ears, knife strokes to his stomach.

"She alive?" Wexler asked.

"Can't tell," Radly said. "Room is clear."

Radly slid back out of the black abyss as quietly as he'd entered, his night vision goggles now removed. He drew his pistol again. He glanced back at Halsbrooke and motioned that he was going in. Halsbrooke disabled her goggles and relayed the signal to the three other agents standing guard. She motioned them forward and they quickly moved into position at the base of the porch, their rifles aimed away from the cabin, prepared for a flank attack.

Radly slowly applied his weight to the second step. He tested the wood as it bent under his weight, but appeared confident it wouldn't snap. He slowly crept up the stairs, keeping low. The window was now directly above him, the dim light on his back. He paused, waited, and listened for sounds from within. He heard nothing.

"On your back," Halsbrooke said. "Can the deck support us both?"

"Yes," Radly said. "Get ready, guys."

Halsbrooke scrambled up the stairs in one fluid motion and was soon crouched just behind Radly, near the door. She readied her weapon, its heavy barrel angled toward the door. If she wanted to, she could tear the cabin apart with a single magazine.

"Whenever you're ready," Wexler told them. Ryan's heart beat loudly. If Erin was alive, she was only moments away from being rescued.

5

ERIN HEARD THE faint whispers outside, following by groaning wood. The FBI was here, about to break in. Her time was up.

She looked down at her bloody wrist. The duct tape still pinning her to the chair. She'd sawed halfway through her bindings, but couldn't afford to spend any more time on it. She pulled on her wrist, the skin now numb. It didn't give. She stabbed at the tape some more, unable to see through the tears that were running freely down her face. She couldn't remember the last time she'd cried. Now was not the time, she told herself.

More sounds from outside. The whole cabin seemed to moan.

She tried her wrist again, yanking as hard as she could. To her surprise, it tore. Her whole right arm was free. Laughing beneath her gag, she pushed herself onto her back, no longer noticing the pain in her leg.

Elated, she clawed frantically at the duct tape over her mouth. Morgan had bound her so well that she couldn't find the beginning of the tape, and simply pulling it off was out of the question. Sucking deep breaths through her nose, she instead decided to focus her attention on the other leg. Free, she'd be able to hobble to the window and call them off.

The duct tape on her good leg came off within seconds, and she let out another sigh of relief. Both legs unrestrained, she rolled onto her good knee and focused on her other arm, which was still attached to the chair. With more leverage, she didn't even need to remove the duct tape—the chair was so old she was able to break the arm off with one swing against the floor.

Wincing, Erin pushed herself to her feet. She turned toward the door, then froze. She saw motion outside the window. They were coming in. She was too late.

RYAN WATCHED WITH bated breath as his two colleagues rose to their feet, ready to strike. The muted light that flickered through the soiled window cast surreal shadows on Radly and Halsbrooke, their features morphing with every passing second.

"Move in," Wexler ordered. He knew it was trap. They all knew it was a trap. But what could they do? They had to move in. They had to get Erin.

"We're ready. On the count of three. Three, two, one… Now!" Radly kicked the rotting door off its hinges. Radly moved inside the cabin, his gun sweeping the interior. "FBI! FBI! FBI!"

Halsbrooke was right behind him, though she stopped in the doorway. Ryan watched as her gun lowered to her side.

"Confirmed. Clear," Halsbrooke stated into her headset. "Kinsley, what are you doing?"

The words caused Ryan to tip to one side. He had to put a hand down to support himself. He exhaled and then laughed, his head shaking in amazement. Despite everything he'd told himself, he hadn't expected to find her alive. He tried to say something, but his voice was suddenly faint, choked.

"Back!" Radly shouted.

"What?" came Halsbrooke's sudden response.

The intensity of Radly's order made Ryan's hair stand on end. Radly appeared, his hand on Halsbrooke's vest. The man was literally pushing his partner out the door.

"We need to get her out of here," Halsbrooke complained, but Radly shoved her away. She gasped as she lost her balance, fell backwards and hit the railing. The wooden plank snapped instantly and Ryan heard a whoosh of air in his ear as she fell to the ground.

"Radly, what's happening?" Ryan started to ask, but was silenced by a deafening boom. Everything that followed happened in seconds.

Ryan, already in a crouched position a hundred feet away, was forced backwards. The clearing turned from night to day, the sudden light blinding him. A huge fireball hurled into the air, the cabin transformed into nothing more than scorched scrap wood. A wave of heat rushed over Ryan as flames erupted everywhere. Halsbrooke screamed, then nothing.

Four more explosions went off, the edge of the clearing erupting into flames. Men screamed. A tree crashed to the ground, its branches on fire. Ryan found himself on his back, flattened by the concussion. The agent who'd been standing not far in front of him was running off to the left, his body engulfed in white-orange flames. Ryan wanted to help, but a second wave of heat—much more intense than the first—kept him pinned to the ground. The burning agent dropped to his knees and then collapsed entirely.

"Agents down. Agents down. We need backup!" John's voice ringed frantically over the radio. "Halsbrooke, Radly, you okay?"

As fire spiraled into the heavens, Ryan readjusted himself and searched the clearing. The flames were bright and blinding. Billows of black smoke had consumed everything. The serene clearing in the middle of the woods had turned into a war zone. One of the tactical agents who'd been near the cabin when it erupted was lying immobile not far from ground zero; the other two had scrambled for cover, but had been knocked over by the secondary explosions. One was lying on his back, looking dazed, while the other was struggling to push himself to his feet. As for Halsbrooke, Ryan spotted her writhing at the base of the devastated cabin. She was on her hands and knees and clearly in pain, but didn't appear to be on fire. The explosion had blown her helmet off and left her face and caramel hair black.

She pushed herself to a kneeling position, shouting her partner's name as she frantically scanned the area for Radly.

"I'm here," came Radly's voice in Ryan's headset. He sounded weak. Ryan was now near the edge of the clearing. He took another step forward, searching for the man. Radly had been thrown nearly fifty feet to the very edge of the clearing. He was moving slowly, but moving nonetheless.

"You okay?" Halsbrooke's voice crackled over the radio. She rose to her feet and looked in Radly's direction.

"I'm alive," he sat up and flipped his helmet's visor up. He touched his face. "Kinsley…"

Ryan blinked and swallowed hard, his eyes remaining on Radly. He couldn't look back at what was left of the cabin, not now. Everything had happened so fast, his brain hadn't processed what had happened to her. He'd felt nothing when the initial bomb had gone off; he hadn't reacted when Erin had died. She was everything to him, and in an instant she'd been taken away.

Another loud bang snapped him back to attention. A gunshot. A rifle. Ryan watched in horror as Radly's head snapped back. The agent's body slumped to the ground, lifeless.

"Jesus Christ!" Halsbrooke took a step toward her partner, but instinct prevailed. Radly was dead and she was the next target. She turned to move behind the remnants of the cabin. Before she could take two steps, however, her right calf muscle exploded and she collapsed to the ground, screaming.

Ryan reached the edge of the clearing. Halsbrooke was now lying flat on the ground, dragging herself like an infantryman to safety, except there was nowhere for her to hide.

Another gunshot rang out, striking one of the other agents in the neck. He screamed, grabbed his wound and collapsed. The dazed agent was dead a second later, a bullet piercing his skull through his helmet. Ryan heard the *splat* in his earpiece.

Halsbrooke was only fifteen feet away, crawling toward him. Her face streaked with soot and tears, she pulled herself forward with her arms, kicking with her good leg. She was making good progress. Ryan wondered where Wexler was; he hadn't heard his voice since the explosion. Had he been taken out?

Another rifle shot went off, and Halsbrooke stopped moving. Ryan stopped, his hand on a tree. She was dead, and he'd just given away his position.

6

"THERE YOU ARE, you son of a bitch!" Christopher Morgan laughed, shifting his aim from the splattered head of the woman to the silhouette standing on the tree line. Though he couldn't make out any features of the newcomer, he knew it was Harper, and Harper would be the next to die.

The plan had gone brilliantly. While there were certainly dozens of agents moving into the area, he'd caught the FBI off guard. They'd walked right into his trap, and he was picking them off like flies. Kinsley was dead, a waste of a beautiful woman, but the real thrill came from watching bodies jerk to the rhythm of hollow point bullets. He'd nearly gotten off on the sight of the first victim's head splitting in two. The woman agent's had been even more satisfying. There was nothing better than letting a woman know she was going to die, just before, a tease.

But today, he wouldn't accept anything less than Harper lying dead in the woods. The man had ruined his life, and in return he would end his. He brought the dark figure of Ryan Harper into his sights. His index finger coiled around the trigger. Harper shifted behind a tree, his shadow morphing into the rest of the forest. Morgan fired anyway. Careless on his part. The bullet had torn away a chunk of the tree, but he'd also informed Harper that he was the next target. If he'd just waited, been patient, the FBI man would have eventually moved from hiding.

Suddenly, gunfire erupted from the shadows. Off to his left. He couldn't see his new target, but fired anyway. Another stupid mistake. Excitement was getting the better of him, and he'd just given away his position.

RYAN POKED HIS head from behind a tree and scanned the clearing. The intense fire illuminated a vast area, but the dancing flames were so bright and the smoke so thick and black it was hard to determine where one object stopped and another began.

"I'm under fire," came John's voice. "He's somewhere southeast of the cabin."

Ryan heard return fire and recognized it as John's gun. Beneath the cloud of smoke, he saw flashes as his partner fired away. A few seconds later, deeper in the woods, Ryan saw more flashes, but this time from another weapon. That was where Morgan was.

Without hesitation, he rushed across the clearing. Morgan was preoccupied with John, and that would give Ryan time to flank him.

"John, I'm moving in on his position."

"I'm firing blindly," John said.

"Just don't shoot me," Ryan slipped into the low brush and ducked below a branch, waiting for more gunshots. They came, drawing him to Morgan's location. "Aim high, John. Keep him distracted—I'm moving in behind him."

"With pleasure," John said, then fired two more rounds. Ryan, his eyes steady on the place where he'd last seen Morgan, crept forward, waiting for movement. It was hard to see. With the fire still blazing wildly, the forest seemed to change shape with every passing second.

And then he saw him, hunched behind a fallen log, eyes toward John's position. Ryan prepared to fire, but Morgan spotted him. The killer spun and fired, forcing Ryan to the ground. When Ryan looked up, Morgan was nowhere to be seen. He frantically scanned the woods, expecting an attack, but loud footsteps eased his fears. Morgan was retreating.

Ryan raced after him, winding through the woods as quickly as possible. If Morgan was looking to reposition himself, Ryan would take him off guard with a pure blitz.

Moments later, he passed an abandoned Marine-issue rifle. He didn't doubt for a moment the man had other weapons.

"Where are you?" John asked over the radio.

Ryan realized he wasn't quite sure. The forest was darker, the fire no longer penetrating the shadows. "A couple hundred feet from your position. Don't know exactly."

"Pull back," John said. "We know he's here. Let's regroup."

"I'm on him."

"Ryan, don't get lost. If something happens…"

"I'm on him!" Ryan insisted. He wasn't going to let Morgan survive one more minute than he deserved. The man had killed Erin, nearly assassinated a United States senator and had murdered several of his friends. Morgan wouldn't live to see morning.

The ground suddenly rose sharply—he'd hit the base of the 2,000-foot hill that loomed over the area. Ryan kept going, his eyes scanning the area above for movement. His instincts told him Morgan had gone this way, even though the climb was arduous. Ryan found himself scrambling up on all fours in certain parts, the cold ground surprisingly loose beneath his feet.

"Harper!" It was Whitmore. "Stay where you are. That's an order."

Before he could respond, shale beneath Ryan's foot gave way and he collapsed against the hillside. Small rocks tumbled away and into the darkness, and when Ryan collected himself he realized his radio had done the same. He searched desperately in the uneven dirt, but knew the small earpiece was lost.

He was separated from the FBI, alone with Morgan. He suddenly became aware of how silent it was, the forest devoid of sound. The serenity didn't last long.

The tumbling rocks had given away his position. Ryan pressed against the hillside as pistol gunfire rained down from above. He gazed upwards and saw flashes of light coming from the dark forest above him. Bullets tore the surrounding ground to shreds, and dirt and rock pelted him from every angle. All he could do was lie there and hope nothing hit him.

The gunfire stopped, and a moment later he heard Morgan running again. Ryan scrambled up the hill, returning to the sanctuary of the woods. The incline continued. His muscles burned, his breathing was labored, body tired, but he was so close, justice near. Morgan was twenty years older than he; he too had to be tired, if not exhausted. Ryan clawed into the frozen dirt, propelled upwards by an invisible force. The inevitable was approaching, he could feel it.

Ryan suddenly burst into a large grass-and-gravel clearing several hundred feet across. Beyond, the hill rose once more, even steeper than before. Ryan scanned the far perimeter, but he'd lost sight of Morgan. Frustration and panic suddenly set in. He couldn't lose him now.

Then, out of the corner of his eye, he saw a large shape hurtling toward him. Acting on instinct, Ryan took a step back and then lunged, catching Morgan's massive frame around the waist. They both dropped to the ground, but Morgan crushed the handle of his pistol into Ryan's forehead. Morgan reared back for another strike, but Ryan managed to squeeze in a punch of his own. Blood erupted from Morgan's lip, but the assassin continued his assault. This time, more prepared, Ryan deflected the blow and knocked Morgan onto his side.

Ryan bent toward him, ready to strike again, but Morgan grabbed him by the chest and hurtled him onto his back. For a man of his age, Morgan moved with amazing speed and was on his feet before Ryan could even stop rolling. The assassin kicked Ryan's gut ferociously.

"I'm out of ammo, can you believe that?" Morgan prepared to kick Ryan again. Ryan rolled away from him, attempting to separate himself enough to get to his feet. But as soon as he tried, Morgan smashed into him, knocking him down once more. Ryan's gun flew out of his hands, and before he could reach it, Morgan had rushed by him and picked it up. The assassin chuckled, fingering the weapon.

In an instant, Ryan reached down and withdrew the backup pistol he always carried on his ankle. Morgan's smile faded, but the assassin still showed no fear. Ryan pushed himself to his feet and took a step toward him, but Morgan didn't back away.

"Why'd you have to take her?" Ryan asked. It seemed silly to ask this monster anything, but he had to know.

Morgan's smile returned. It was eerie in the darkness, a perfectly wicked grin. Ryan gazed into the assassin's eyes and, for the first time, saw just how deranged he was. This was a man who was prepared to die. Was willing to die. The assassin's plan finally clicked into place for Ryan: he was here to kill, nothing more. Tonight— Erin's death, Radly's death, Halsbrooke's death—had all been nothing more than a notorious goodbye.

"You know, I've broken my record. Never killed more people in one day. Didn't even get paid for a single damn one of them. Hell, I lost money on the whole ordeal."

The man was cornered, and there was nothing stopping him from shooting Ryan. His questions would have to wait.

"Morgan, I don't want to shoot you. Put the gun down." The words were hollow, and Morgan picked up on it.

The assassin threw his head back and laughed. "Of course you want to shoot me! I just turned your girlfriend into a fucking s'more."

EVEN IN THE darkness, Morgan could see the FBI man's face redden with anger. "You're right, Morgan, I do want to kill you. You killed her, you son-of-a-bitch, and you enjoyed it. I'd love to put a bullet in your head right now, but where would that put me? I'd miss out on the satisfaction of seeing you suffer for the rest of your life."

Morgan was impressed. Harper was a smart kid. Despite everything he'd been through, he wasn't going to kill out of rage. At least not without a little coaxing.

"You know, I didn't just kill your girlfriend, Harper. Fucked her first. Repeatedly. That girl cried like there was no tomorrow. Funny enough, there was no tomorrow for her."

Harper didn't move a muscle.

"Think she almost liked it for a few. Said she wasn't getting her fill back home… Needed a real man to ride her hard."

"Morgan, the entire FBI is going to descend upon you in a matter of minutes," Harper ignored him. "Put your gun down and this can all be over."

"I think you're begging for your life, Harper. You begging? I'm not putting my gun down. So maybe you should put yours down instead." All he wanted to see was Ryan's vacant eyes staring up at the black sky, a bullet hole between them. "How 'bout you just let me go? Chase me another day. If you don't, I'm going to kill you then kill a bunch more of your buddies. You're the lawman, but I'm the professional killer. We both know who has the better odds of winning here."

"Put your gun down." Harper was nervous. Could hear it in his voice. Knew he had no leverage, no advantage. "Threats aren't going to work."

"Then I'll just have to shoot you." Before Harper could react, Morgan shot him in the side. Harper groaned in agony and fired back. The shot went wide, the bullet merely grazing Morgan's shoulder. The feeling barely registered with Morgan, as the very thought of Harper in pain excited him beyond belief. Blood was seeping out of the hole in Harper's lower abdomen—just below his Kevlar jacket—and the sound of it splattering against the frozen ground gave Morgan chills. *Splat. Splat. Splat splat.*

He slapped the gun out of Harper's hand. Harper, dazed, watched it bounce along the grass and come to a stop several feet way. The FBI man wavered and dropped to one knee, already becoming lightheaded.

Morgan pressed the steel of Harper's own P226 into his forehead.

"After I kill you, I'm going to reposition and plow down five more of your friends. Just for fun. Using your gun."

Ryan remained still, focused on the pistol.

"No one's around to save you, Harper. Just you and me, and I have the gun."

"Then stop talking and shoot me!"

Morgan smiled, his finger curling around the trigger. In another second Harper would be dead and his goal would be achieved.

Suddenly, a piercing light penetrated to the very back of his skull. Morgan blinked, but couldn't rid himself of the blinding, blue-white light. He looked around and could just barely identify the tree line. He raised his hands to block the light, but his fingers, his palms, his wrists, melted away into the nothingness. What remained of the world spun out of control. A high-pitch buzz resonated in his ears, deafening him.

He saw motion coming toward him, and then nothing at all.

PART II

REBIRTH

7

BLACKNESS SWIRLED, WITH streaks of dark blue. Everything shook violently, the emerging shapes vibrating. Crackling thundered everywhere. A thousand pin drops fell at once, the needles stabbed at his skin, awakening him. It was difficult to breath, but with each desperate gasp of air he lifted a foot and moved forward, unwilling to stop.

Before he could see, he could feel, and the needles—rain drops —stung. He felt submerged in the liquid, and the constant crackling of water striking the trees around him overwhelmed the senses.

Ryan Harper blinked, breathing hard. Rain dripped from his upper lip and down his chin. There were trees everywhere, looming over him, engulfing him. He could hardly see, but the shapes were starting to take form. He saw a branch directly in front of him, but it was too late. It struck him on the jaw and he fell backwards, his body sinking into the muddy ground.

Keep going, he told himself. For some reason he felt as though he had to run, and so he clambered to his feet and kept going. The trees and bushes came into clearer focus. He was in a forest. It was night. It was raining.

He stepped onto a log, applying one foot to the fallen wood. As he leaped back onto the forest floor, his eyes drifted to his body.

He was not wearing pants. In fact, he was wearing nothing at all. He was naked, his exposed body soaked in rain water and splattered with mud and blood. He suddenly got the sense that he'd been running for much longer than he could remember, but he didn't know why or for how long.

Up ahead, Ryan heard a new sound. He stopped and listened. Something unnatural, something that shouldn't be there. It was a low rumbling, a whine. Unnatural but familiar. A car!

Not too far away, he saw the dim shine of headlights come and go. The cry of the engine faded and the sound of the rain returned. A road was nearby. He didn't have to think, to try to explain to himself why he was running through the woods naked. He just had to get to the road. He pushed on, renewed by his discovery.

His hands and feet dug into wet, loose gravel as he scrambled up the embankment to the road. The climb was steep and the gravel gave way with each step, but after what seemed like an eternity he reached the top, his hands clawing desperately at pavement to pull himself to the road's surface. Panting hard, he observed his new location, a country road, freshly paved but lacking streetlights. Still couldn't see the moon.

Ryan heard something behind him. The road brightened. He blinked and turned around. A car was racing toward him, its headlights glaring. He raised his hands in stunned shock, his legs too heavy to move. It was in this moment, as the car screeched to a stop, as his body tensed in preparation for impact, as the rain swirled around him, that he realized he had no idea where he was, or why he was there.

8

THE HALLWAY WAS a blur, a parched white span with no walls or floor or ceiling. There was only the door the doctor was angling for, the guard stationed outside. The guard's head turned to take her in, and for a moment they exchanged gazes, but his face eluded her, a part of the blur. The doctor said something to her, his hand extending toward the door, but she didn't hear his words. She blinked, trying to steady herself. The doctor repeated himself, but again his words were lost on her.

Erin Kinsley approached the door, at once eager and hesitant. Her hand pressed against the doorframe. She paused, staring straight ahead, taking in the grained wood paneling, the first detail she saw clearly since the plane landed twenty-five minutes earlier. She breathed out and leaned forward, looking through the small window into the room beyond.

It was an ordinary hospital room, with two beds, white walls and fluorescent lights. Unlike the hallway, the room was picture clear; she took in every detail, every corner, every object. Her eyes fell on the obsidian window on the far wall, drawn to the heavy rain that pulsed against the glass.

He was sitting on the nearest bed, his back to her, hunched over in his hospital gown. Even without seeing his face she knew it was him. She sucked in a short breath, unable to take her eyes off him. It couldn't be him. It was impossible. It *couldn't* be him.

Erin opened the door and stepped inside. The man, this stranger, didn't bother to look up. She approached him, giving the bed a wide berth, holding onto the belief that he was alive for as long as she could before, inevitably, he would turn and reveal he was someone else. But then, detecting her approach, he looked up and over at her, his drowsy eyes fixating on her legs, her frame, her face.

She froze, unable to believe her eyes. It was *him*, just as she remembered him.

Her lips parted—she wanted to say his name—but still, it couldn't be him. He gazed back at her, his face ashen, recognition not sinking in. And then his eyes widened, more out of shock than delight. As if she were a ghost. His mouth dropped open, his hands, which were resting against the edge of the mattress, tightening around the sheets.

He would later tell her that she shrieked, but she didn't remember. She took a step forward, then another, and finally dropped to her knees in front of him. Her trembling hand caressed his cheek and with her fingertips she felt his hair, that warm spot behind his ears. He looked back at her, tears welling up. He opened his mouth to speak, but she lunged forward and wrapped her arms around him. Her weight pushed him back onto the bed and she fell on top of him. She would never let him go again.

"Where have you been?" she cried, smelling his hair. Pine needles and cheap soap. "Is it really you? It can't be."

"Erin," Ryan croaked, his voice barely audible.

Before he could say more, she kissed him, pressing her lips as hard as she could against his.

When she finally let him breathe again, he still had the same stunned look on his face. "You're…"

She laughed. It wasn't the reaction she had expected from herself—all this time she had spent worrying, and Ryan had been worrying about her. "I'm not dead. I'm not." She lifted her head so she could look him in the eyes. God, he was handsome. "I broke free at the last second. But my mouth was gagged, and I couldn't get to the door in time. I went through a hole in the floor just as the bomb went off. The floor… it was rotted through. It just gave way."

"But…"

"I don't know," she cried once more as her smile widened even further. "I didn't escape unharmed. None of us did." Her smiled faded just as quickly, thinking of her fallen comrades, but Ryan blinked, and she sensed he wanted to discuss something else entirely. "I was damn lucky."

"I don't understand," he stammered, his voice faint. She could tell every word was excruciating, his ravaged throat like sandpaper.

"I don't know how I got out alive, but I did. The real mystery is you. Where've you been?"

He opened his mouth to tell her, but the very question seemed to tear at him. "I don't know," he finally said, shaking his head. "I must've been knocked unconscious or something." He touched the back of his skull, expecting to find a bruise, but there was none.

"Ryan," Erin said, frustrated. After all this time, after all this waiting, she still didn't have an answer. She had Ryan, but no answer. "The doctor—I spoke with him on the plane ride down—he said that aside from some mild hypothermia and dehydration, you're in good shape. You have some cuts and scrapes on your legs, but there's no sign of major trauma or scarring."

"That's good, then."

"No, I don't get it. You don't remember anything?"

He stared at her, unsure what else to say.

"You were running naked through the woods, Ryan." She reached out and touched his hair. "Your hair is as short as it was before." She dragged her fingers across his cheek and chin. "It looks like you shaved a day ago, at most." He looked no different than before. She had had this dream before, many times, but never had she truly expected to see him like this. In such good condition.

He shook his head, confused. She wasn't making any sense to him; she could see it in his eyes. He sat up, half pushing her off him, his mind at work. She watched him studiously as he tried to propel his memory into gear, to make sense of it all. Finally, he turned and looked at her. His gaze was intense, almost disconcerting, but then the intensity faded and his eyes drifted to her legs, then her feet.

"New shoes" she tapped her New Balance tennis shoes together impatiently.

"Your cast..." he said. "I don't understand. Your leg."

Erin gasped, so faint he probably didn't even hear it. It suddenly sank in why he was so confused, so disoriented. It wasn't that he couldn't remember what happened to him earlier tonight—he couldn't remember *any* of it.

"Ryan," she put a hand on his shoulder as he began to hyperventilate. He wasn't one to overreact, but it looked like his chest was compressing. "You don't know?"

"Know what?" he spat, suddenly annoyed. She squeezed the flesh above his collarbone, trying to calm him.

"They didn't tell you?"

"Tell me what?" he shouted, though his words came out as nothing more than a pitiful, painful whimper. He coughed hard, his chest constricting.

"Ryan, I don't know how else to say this: You were missing for six months."

9

ERIN FELT THE pull on her stomach as the private jet lifted off and immediately turned north toward Seattle. Ryan sat silently, his fingers gently curled around the arms of the seat. He looked exhausted, even more so than he had at the hospital, the bags under his eyes adding a decade to his age. His eyes half open, he appeared to be slipping in and out of consciousness, but his chin stayed steady, even as the plane bounced around in the storm.

The doctor had said he was fine, that he was merely tired and a little dehydrated. But Erin was concerned about him. She'd never seen him like this, had never even imagined him in such a state. The thought that he'd never be the same nagged at the back of her mind, a paranoid, selfish idea that she hated herself for. Ryan was alive, and that's all that mattered. Something terrible had happened to him, but he was alive.

He hadn't spoken since the hospital. Stunned by the revelation of his disappearance, he didn't know which question to ask first so had opted to ask none at all. *Six months*, he had to be thinking. The number had to be repeating in his head like nails to a chalkboard.

She took his hand, her fine fingers sliding over his knuckles and curling around his. At first he didn't respond, but then he squeezed back, the reaction electrifying her. Erin took a deep breath and looked away, forcing back tears.

"I couldn't have been gone for six months," he muttered, breaking the silence. She looked back. He hadn't moved, was still staring straight ahead.

"It's impossible to believe, I'm sure," she said quickly, as if she'd been anticipating that he'd say that. "We looked everywhere for you. We scoured every inch of that mountain, but we couldn't find you. You really don't remember anything?"

"No, all right! I don't remember a fucking thing," he snapped. He looked down, embarrassed by the outburst.

"Okay," she said softly. He rarely lost his cool. "What exactly do you remember?"

"I remember…" He had to think about it. Several agonizing seconds later, he turned and looked at her, his brown, magnificent eyes now fully open. "I don't remember. It's all black. I don't remember when I disappeared. It seems to be right there, but the more I think about it the more it escapes me…"

"What's the last thing you remember vividly?"

Ryan scratched his head, aching for things to come back to him. "We went out for dinner. It was Christmas time, and you wore that sexy black dress that you have. We went to Assaggio… you had linguini, I think."

"Jesus. That was weeks earlier. You don't remember anything past that night?"

"No," he shook his head. "Bits and pieces."

"Even later that night?"

"Well, I can guess," Ryan grinned, but Erin wasn't amused. "Anyway, what the hell happened to me? And what happened to you? You said you survived."

Erin was suddenly speechless, shocked. He'd lost nearly seven months of his memory. A little amnesia was one thing; over half a year was another. That indicated serious brain damage.

"Survived what?" he squeezed her hand.

She looked at him. "I thought you remembered. You looked so surprised when you saw me, like you were seeing a ghost."

He shook his head, his eyes wetting. "That's exactly what I felt when I saw you. I can't explain it, but I had this feeling you were dead."

"You would have thought I was dead," Erin took his head in both hands and kissed him on the lips. He didn't resist, but he didn't respond, either. "Christopher Morgan kidnapped me and locked me in a cabin. You were in the assault party that attempted to free me, but when Radly and Halsbrooke opened the door, they triggered the explosives he'd planted. The bomb went off and I had every right to be dead."

"Radly… Halsbrooke?"

"Yes, they're dead. They died trying to save me. Others, too." She didn't want to list the names.

Ryan stared at her blankly, attempting to process the information. He'd been missing for six months and had just learned that two of his friends had been killed. She waited for him to lose it, for his mind and body to just give up, but it never happened. Instead, he gazed into her eyes and said, "Please start from the beginning."

She did. She told him about Christopher Morgan and the chase that had led to the deaths of several FBI agents. She told him how the FBI had lost communication with him and that he and Morgan vanished together shortly thereafter. She told him that the manhunt revealed nothing other than a few footsteps in a grassy field and several empty shells scattered on the hillside.

He didn't remember any of it. Everything after that date where she'd worn that black dress was an empty void. To him, Christopher Morgan didn't exist. She woke up nightly dreaming of him, of those gray, sickening eyes, and Ryan had no memory of the man.

"Christopher Morgan," Ryan said firmly, his voice stronger than it had been earlier. "He must have taken me as a hostage. Drugged me or something."

"We thought that was it at first, but it wasn't. You see—"

"Well, what else could it have been? I'm hunting down some psychopath—" Ryan paused to cough, eyes watering. "—and I'm all by myself, and then disappear for six months… who else could be responsible other than Morgan?"

"It wasn't Morgan," Erin said. "Morgan's body was recovered four months ago."

"He still could've been involved…"

"Perhaps, but that still doesn't answer any questions. How'd he hide you? How'd he drug you? This was no ordinary kidnapping or hostage situation, Ryan. Like I said, we searched everywhere for you—and Morgan. The National Guard was brought in and we combed that forest for weeks. On foot, with a hostage, there is no way Morgan would've gotten out of the grid. But we never found him."

"But he's dead?"

"His body was found by a couple of bird watchers hiking in the back country not far from where you disappeared. He was forty feet up in a tree, and had only been decomposing for a week. It was like someone had just dropped him there—there was no way he could have climbed it."

"Assuming I wasn't lying unconscious for six months," Ryan rubbed his clean-shaven chin, "someone had to have taken me. And if it wasn't Morgan, then it was someone working for Morgan."

"But what possible reason would someone have for taking you? And why let you go now? Why risk it?"

Ryan shook his head. It didn't make any sense to him either.

After a moment of silence, he looked at her out of the corner of his eye, cracking a grin that seemed to brighten his pale face. She couldn't help but smile at the sight of it, but then he spoke and her lips flattened. "Maybe I should be checked for anal probes."

"That's not funny," she grumbled, looking away.

"Alien abduction *is* another theory," Ryan said. "I mean, I disappear in the woods and am returned six months later, in peak physical shape and lacking any memory of past events. Christopher Morgan is found in a tree as if he's been dropped from the sky. *That* makes sense."

"Seriously, not funny."

"Wait," he detected something in her tone. He always could. "Did you actually entertain that idea?" He started to laugh, though it clearly hurt to do so.

"The case had gone cold. And we had to follow all leads, no matter how crazy," she stated firmly, annoyed that he was still laughing. "But you weren't abducted. We have aerial footage from the time you were taken and there weren't any UFO's or any other kind of vehicle that could've taken you from the area."

"Okay, okay," Ryan chuckled, raising his hands in defeat. "Touchy subject."

"I'm just happy you're back, Ryan," Erin said. "Nothing else matters to me right now. I missed you so badly I'm embarrassed to say so." He stared at her, studying her face with renewed alertness. She couldn't help herself any longer. Erin lurched toward him, her hands smothering his face, and she kissed him. Caught off guard, he kissed back, but not with the intensity she was expecting. But it didn't matter. The feel of his cracked lips against hers caused her to melt, and the tears welled up once again.

"Erin," Ryan said after a long moment. She opened her eyes and realized she was still holding his cheeks, but was resting her forehead against his, out of breath.

"When we land, the head of every major agency is going to be waiting for you," she dried her face with her sleeve. "You should rest your voice. You're going to be up for a while."

Ryan squinted, acknowledging what she was saying. "What kind of reception am I going to receive in Seattle?"

She was blunt about it: "Prepare for an interrogation."

10

THE TWIN-ENGINE PLANE touched down at Boeing Field, the nondescript commercial airport in south Seattle. Erin and Ryan were immediately guided to a black SUV. Within a minute, they were headed north toward downtown Seattle. Nearly one in the morning, there were few cars on the freeway. The drive took no more than ten minutes.

Ryan and Erin sat in the back of the vehicle, watching the scenery go by. It wasn't raining, but churning clouds threatened overhead. The very thought of a storm seemed to wipe any color from the area; everything was dark, gray and empty.

The SUV stopped on Seventh Avenue outside of the U.S. District Courthouse.

"So…" Ryan opened his door. "What would happen if I try to run now?"

"That wouldn't help your case, Ryan," Erin didn't appreciate the joke. She followed Ryan onto the sidewalk.

"And what is my case exactly?"

"Listen," Erin put her hand on his shoulder. "Officially, you're not considered an accomplice in any way or form. Unofficially, there are some suspicions. You have supporters, but you have your skeptics, too. This isn't going to go away overnight."

"They think I was working with Morgan? That I helped him kidnap you?" He looked stunned.

"Given the nature of the case, people will entertain just about anything."

"This way," their driver waved to an open set of doors. Erin glanced inside; a panel of men was eagerly waiting in a small courtroom. She recognized the heads of several key agencies, including the CIA and Homeland Security. The men all stared at Ryan, their true emotions masked by the distance. She could feel the intensity, and she could sense Ryan's trepidation.

But, without any visible hesitation, Ryan stepped forward and left her in the hallway.

ERIN WATCHED THE proceedings on a monitor two rooms away, completely unaware that it was past three in the morning. The conference had been going for over two hours, and there were stretches where she became lost in the questions and answers as if it were like any other interrogation. Then, suddenly, she would refocus on Ryan and it would all come back to her once again, that Ryan Harper had returned, that he was alive and he was well. She'd assumed him dead, and yet here he was, the man she loved—still loved—sitting on a chair in a middle of a room with bright lights shining down on him. Every time she thought about this miraculous turn of events, her body seemed to warm, her hair stand on end. It was as if she'd been plugged into a wall socket and an electrical current was running through her body.

Still, it was hard to watch Ryan in his state. The interrogation was taking a toll on him. He was usually a man who could stand up to any kind of punishment—in fact, she'd never seen him encounter a situation he couldn't calmly maneuver his way through—but tonight, Ryan was tired, confused and flustered. The man she watched on the video feed was broken; his responses had started off strong, but as the committee continued to grill him on events he could neither recall nor even fathom, his frustration had gotten the best of him. He now responded in anger, and then, each time, as if realizing how he was presenting himself, would recoil. It was in these moments, when Ryan would retreat, that she saw something she'd never seen before, something she didn't recognize.

"Kinsley," someone said from behind her as a pair of hands came down on her shoulders. The sudden presence of another person startled her and she flinched, twisting around to see who had joined her. For a moment she saw the cold, gray eyes of Christopher Morgan staring at her, but then they flashed away.

"Jesus, Lancaster, you scared me half to death!"

"You looked rather focused," Agent John Lancaster said matter-of-factly. Erin stood up to greet Ryan's former partner, but his attention had already drifted to the monitor. She watched as the man took Ryan Harper in, as his mouth parted slightly, his eyes as wide as she'd ever seen them. John loved Ryan like a brother, if not more like a son, and had been devastated when Ryan had gone missing. He blamed himself for not providing adequate backup for his partner.

John was ten years older than Ryan, a seasoned veteran. He'd taken Ryan under his wing from day one, and the two had formed a strong bond over the years. John was a good agent, but was well aware from early on that his partner was considered to be one of the best up-and-coming agents in the Bureau. They'd been teamed so that Ryan could learn as much as he could as fast as he could, and Ryan soaked everything in at an alarming rate. The two were best friends and made a great team.

"I can't believe he's back," John stated, running a bewildered hand through his thinning hair. His blue eyes shot to her. "He's really back."

The look on John's face was priceless, utmost excitement, complete shock and utter confusion all compacted into a single expression. Erin wondered if she had looked much the same when she'd first seen Ryan alive.

"I can't believe it either," Erin said softly. John returned his attention to the monitor, but Erin, lost in thought, continued to watch him. He had probably been good looking once, but age had not been kind to him. While he remained athletically fit, his face had filled out to the point where one could mistake him for being overweight. His lips had thickened and his nose grown a touch bulbous. His unruly, carroty hair gave him an unintentionally goofy demeanor.

"I would have been here sooner—didn't get your message until half an hour ago. How are things going?"

"They've asked him the same question over and over again for two hours. He's tired, annoyed and there's nothing more they're going to get out of him. At least not today."

"What the hell happened to him?"

Erin told him everything she knew, yet not once did John take his eyes off the monitor. When he asked questions, they were out of the corner of his mouth, as if he didn't want to miss a second of audio from Ryan's interrogation.

"Is he telling the truth?"

Erin didn't respond at first, surprised. Then she said: "Yes, of course he's telling the truth."

John finally shifted his full attention to her. "He disappeared for six months, doesn't remember anything, and is as good as new."

"Yes," Erin said calmly, locking eyes with him. There was a part of her that was surprised that John would question Ryan's integrity so directly, but this is what John did. He questioned assumptions, reality, the status quo. That's what made him so good at his job, his willingness to upend the accepted truth. And the accepted truth, *the* truth, was that Ryan Harper was back, having no memory of where he was or how he escaped. Even John shouldn't question that.

"Okay," John nodded. "But we need to be prepared. Ryan returned for a reason. He didn't escape. Otherwise he'd remember something. So if he didn't escape, then whoever was holding him all this time released him for a reason. Why? Why now? To what purpose? We need to figure out what that purpose is before it presents itself."

His eyes told her that he no longer fully trusted Ryan Harper.

11

RYAN HARPER STARED into the darkness, a void with no end, no beginning. Nothingness. He strained to turn his head, but couldn't. He tried his arms but his body was paralyzed. Even his eyelids refused to react, and he was left looking into blackness.

Suddenly, a light as bright as the sun erupted around him, replacing the darkness with pure white. His eyes burned and began to water, but still he couldn't blink. The light pierced through his eyes and into his skull, the pain intense. Out of nowhere, a black dot appeared. At first it was nothing more than a faint pinprick against the whiteness, but the orb continued to grow until the light had receded completely. Then, suddenly, a corona burst forth around the orb, glowing stronger than any solar eclipse. Ryan found himself drawn to the orb. It continued to grow larger. The blackness turned to gray and its surface began to lose its consistency. Pockets formed, cavities of shadow where none had been before.

It was a face.

A sudden sense of panic swept through him, a tingling that started in his toes and struck his heart a moment later. He tensed, holding his breath. His chest felt heavy, his skin clammy. The face came closer, examining him. It was not a normal face. It was featureless, the skin pale and lacking texture. He wanted to look away but couldn't. He wanted to scream, but only heard silence. His heart was palpitating.

God, he wanted to scream.

A mouth emerged, no more than a black slit. No teeth, no lips, only a faint, dark chasm. The chasm widened, speaking to him. He could discern no words, just an increasingly loud roar, as if wind were rushing through a small space.

He stared into the mouth, awed and frightened at the same time. It was horrifying.

"Ryan!" it shouted. No, the face hadn't said his name. "Ryan!"

He blinked. Everything was bright again, but the face was gone. In its place was another, more comforting vision. Erin was above him, her beautiful raven hair dangling across her face. Her lips were moving, and she looked frightened. Her hands were on his shoulders, shaking him. Someone was screaming.

"Ryan!" she said again, her voice finally syncing with her lips. Ryan blinked once more, and returned to reality. He was the one screaming. His face and body were soaking wet.

He sat up and exhaled. Erin looked him in the eyes, concerned.

"I—I—Just a nightmare," he stammered.

"You never have nightmares. It sounded like you were being torn apart."

"It was horrible," he kept his eyes on her. He was afraid to close them. "There was a face. It was saying something."

"What?"

"I don't know. I couldn't make it out. But the face... it wasn't human. At least I don't think it was human." He embraced her, his hands pressing against her back to keep her close. After what he'd been through, he never wanted to let go. Her body was warm, soft. Comforting. She wrapped her arms around him, squeezing even tighter.

Intoxicated by the scent of Erin's shampoo, Ryan shifted his attention to his surroundings. He was in a normal-looking bedroom, though he didn't recognize it. The bed was queen-size, with lilac bedding. A dresser stood against the far wall. Off to his left, sunlight was beaming through the window, illuminating the entire room.

"How long was I asleep?" he looked away.

Erin, much to his dismay, drew away from his embrace, but she remained kneeling on the bed beside him. "About thirty hours."

"Really?"

"You'd been sleeping soundly up until now. The doctor said it was best that we just let you rest. Clearly you needed it."

"And where are we?"

"You're at my condo. In Green Lake."

"What happened to our house?"

Erin forced a smile. "I sold it. Two months ago. I couldn't handle living there anymore. Every time I walked into that damned placed, you were everywhere. Some of your stuff is in a storage shed, but a lot of it's gone."

Ryan breathed out, slumping back against his pillows.

"I'm sorry."

"No, it's okay," he took her hand. "Seriously, it's just—everything's different."

"I know," she reached out and placed a palm on his cheek. He closed his eyes, appreciating the warmth of her skin. "Listen, Ryan, when you're ready, if you're able to walk, let's go out to the dining room and I'll make you something to eat. Then I'm going to have to call a doctor and he's going to come talk to you for a while. Try to figure out what happened."

"A psychiatrist?"

"Yes," she rolled off the bed.

"Jesus," Ryan shook his head in disbelief. "Did you ever think I'd need a shrink?"

Erin laughed. "No. Never in a million years."

"As for food," Ryan let Erin help him up. "Pancakes, bacon, hashbrowns, eggs—over easy—and some country fried steak sound really good right now. After all, since you're actually making me food for a change, I figure I better play the pity card while I can."

Erin smiled, the first true smile he'd seen since the hospital. She turned away abruptly. "Eggs, toast and a glass of orange juice? Okay, if you insist."

THE NIGHTMARE RETURNED that night, forcing Ryan awake a little past 3 a.m. The sheets were soaked with sweat, and he spent the rest of the night watching television on the couch.

Erin had looked concerned when he woke up screaming. Then again, she'd worn that expression all day. She wasn't just worried about his current state, but where he'd been, what had happened to him and what was going to happen to him—and them—in the future. Nothing was certain, not anymore.

Still, as his heartbeat lowered and his breathing returned to normal, she'd held his head in her hands, telling him everything would be okay. He stared into those mesmerizing green eyes of hers as if for the first time. Everything about her felt different, but he knew she wasn't the one who'd changed—he had.

As the glow from the television flickered across his pale face, his eyes dancing with the monotonous imagery, he thought about those months after he had disappeared. It had only been six months, but with him dead, that was a long six months. Perhaps it happened after a night out with friends—a man had gotten through to her, into her, his body pressing between her legs. He pictured her body coiled around this man, her head arched back in delight, her throat moaning 'thank you' for taking her mind off the one who had abandoned her.

Ryan flipped the channel, his jaw tense. An old Looney Tunes was playing. Bugs Bunny was hiding behind a tree, waiting for Elmer Fudd to turn his back. Bugs Bunny grabbed Elmer Fudd's gun from his shoulder, swung it around, and returned it to its original position.

Ryan blinked. It was suddenly morning. He was still sitting upright, but Looney Tunes had been replaced with paid programming. Yawning, he stood up, feeling chilled. He was wearing nothing more than his boxers, and his skin felt dirty from the dried sweat.

Ryan shuffled into the kitchen. He grabbed a glass from the drying rack and poured himself some water, his eyes focusing on the construction site across the parking lot. A new condominium building was being erected, but so far it was nothing more than steel girders and scaffolding.

"I swear they never make any progress on that place," Erin suddenly appeared behind him, her arms slipping around his waist.

"Morning," he said, putting the glass to his lips.

"Get any sleep?" she swung around to his side, her fingers still lingering on his back.

"A little," Ryan looked her over. "Bugs Bunny did me in."

"Have to watch out for Bugs," she smiled, her eyes not leaving his. "I'm so glad you're back."

Suddenly, she was in his arms, kissing him passionately. Shocked at first, he just stood there, his arms instinctively wrapping around her but otherwise not reacting. Her lips, while as sweet as ever, felt different, her touch and movements foreign. Her hands squeezed his shoulders, then his neck. Her fingers slid through his hair. He felt dizzy, put off by the sudden attack. He tried to kiss her, but it didn't feel right.

"What's wrong?" she asked. The room stopped spinning, and he looked her in the eyes. That look of worry had returned, but he knew that she wasn't thinking about his well being this time. Had those six months driven him away, she was thinking. Had something between them died?

Nothing, he told her without speaking, the taste of her lips still lingering on his, the smell of her skin swirling in his nostrils. Whatever was wrong with him, he had to overcome it. He'd never connected with anyone like he had with Erin. Had never felt the way he had for her before.

She kissed him again, this time more cautiously. He tried to respond, tasting her trembling bottom lip, but then she pulled away, frustrated by his apparent disinterest. He grabbed her shoulder, wanting to pull her to him to prove his desire for her. She looked away suddenly, taking him off guard. "It's okay. It's going to take time. Besides, I've got to head to the office."

There was something else. Something she wasn't telling him. She quickly disappeared around the corner.

"Let me come with you," he called out, but Erin didn't respond. He walked to the hallway, repeated her name and stopped, horrified by what he saw.

Erin was standing in front of the bathroom mirror, holding an open prescription bottle. She tossed her head back and took a couple pills, not bothering to chase them with water. It had always been her habit to swallow pills dry, but that's not what bothered him. Starting at the base of her neck, the light pink patches of deformed skin snaked to some point below her shirt line. The skin appeared warped, stretched in some places and shriveled in others.

Ryan felt something welling in his chest, a heavy, uncontrollable fury he'd never felt before. For a split second, he could picture the cabin Erin had told him about exploding, taking with it the flesh from her back. Christopher Morgan hadn't killed her, but he had caused her immense pain and permanent damage. The man would haunt her forever.

"The burns go down to the midsection of my back. It's less noticeable on my calves. My ass healed," Erin watched him in the mirror, downplaying the scarring.

"Why didn't you tell me?" he growled. He did not understand how he hadn't noticed earlier.

"It wasn't important. It isn't important, not to me," she looked down at her feet. She wasn't a good liar, not right now. "You'd see it soon enough."

"*He* did this to you, that son of a bitch."

"Yeah, and he's dead," she spat, brushing by him to the bedroom. He followed her inside. She looked at him, apprehensive, and then removed her shirt. She turned her back to him, revealing the full effect of Christopher Morgan's sadism. The burns covered much of her upper back, her skin twisted and red where it had once been smooth and golden. Grafts had been applied in areas, but the damage was still evident, Morgan's brand permanently stamped into her flesh. "There's not a night I don't think about what I would do to him if I had my chance, if someone hadn't done the job for me. But I can't."

Neither can I, Ryan thought. Never had he wanted revenge more.

THE TRUTH WAS that Erin did think about Christopher Morgan every night, but it wasn't of revenge. She'd dream, just before drifting into a deeper sleep, of Morgan standing in her doorway, his stocky frame a silhouette, his cold, gray eyes glowing. He came after her, his body always dark, his eyes glowing, the monster chasing her around the house in slow motion. She never escaped. He always caught her.

That part of the dream was always the same. The nightmares that followed vary. Some nights he would stab her with his butcher knife; others he would shoot her from afar, having watched her for minutes in his scope before pulling the trigger. He'd throw kerosene on her and light her on fire. Sometimes he would simply lick her face, her breasts and her legs with his grotesque tongue.

All of this she told no one, not her mother or even the therapist that had been assigned to her following her kidnapping. She had said all the right things to get back on duty as quickly as possible; her mind, according to the official analysis, had healed much faster than her body.

It was the physical scars she had to convince people were no longer an issue. They were what people saw, what people could relate to. They hurt. Every damn day they hurt, sometimes so bad the pills couldn't even numb the throbbing. But she could overcome the pain. It was the thought of Christopher Morgan lurking around that next corner that stabbed at her every second.

She was a big girl, though. She could handle it. She could handle anything. And she had to prove it to others. She'd done it with dozens before Ryan. He might be more challenging to fool, but she could do it.

Erin dressed quickly and returned to the hallway where Ryan was waiting for her. She kissed him on the cheek, silently telling him goodbye. Her lips hovered in place for a moment, just inches from his face, and then with a bemused smile on hers she turned toward the front door.

"I'll just be here doing nothing," he said jokingly, the rage that had consumed him twenty minutes earlier seemingly gone. She was flattered by the way he had acted and yet stunned at the same time; his outbursts were so unlike him that they took her off guard each time. His therapist had told them emotional ups and downs should be expected given his situation, but nonetheless they marked a significant difference in his personality. She didn't like it.

She left her condo, saddened that she had to leave Ryan, and skipped down the stairs toward the parking lot. It was a pleasant albeit overcast morning, though it looked like the sun would break through soon. Her mind on the weather, Erin was completely unaware of the army of reporters swarming toward her until it was too late.

12

BURSTS OF LIGHT. An eruption of clicks. Erin Kinsley stared over a sea of rabid photojournalists and television reports as Special Agent in Charge Walter Monroe approached the podium. The large man blinked amidst the steady bulb flashes, then commenced. "We are ecstatic to announce that Agent Ryan Harper, who went missing six months ago in Oregon, has been found alive and well."

Behind Monroe stood Ryan and Senator Richard Chandling, whose near-assassination had eventually led to Ryan's disappearance. Chandling, a tall, white-haired, red-faced man who looked the part of the classic white politician, had the slightest of smiles on his face. Ryan, meanwhile, squinted incessantly as cameras flashed in his face. He did not want to be standing on a stage before the world press.

The flashes continued, causing the camera-shy SAC to momentarily look away. The man, a thirty-year veteran of the Bureau, was a sharp contrast to Chandling. His skin was dark, almost black, which made the white strands in his short, curly hair stand out much more than any man would want them to. His neck was thick, hinting at physical strength, and his voice deep and confident. Like Ryan, however, he was unused to talking to the media.

The reporters were in a frenzy, ever since the rumors had begun to fly. Ryan Harper, the federal agent who'd disappeared while hunting down a ruthless killer, who'd been praised for his heroics while questioned of his loyalties at the same time, had been found alive. Every news agency from every corner of the globe was in Seattle right now, trying to get an angle, trying to make up for the fact that it took them over 48 hours to even land the story.

"I am confident that the truth will be revealed in short order."

The press conference ended with Monroe walking off the small platform. The room exploded in a barrage of questions as Erin slipped out the side door of the press room into a wide, sparsely decorated hallway. The corridor became eerily silent as soon as the door closed behind her. Two people were at the far end of the hallway talking over mugs of coffee, but their voices were muted. Erin leaned against the wall and took a deep breath, knowing this would be the last peace she would have in some time. She had spent six months attempting to figure out what had happened to Ryan and had failed miserably; she now had a second chance and was determined to succeed.

The silence vanished in a heartbeat. The door opened and the chaos from the other room permeated the corridor. Monroe emerged, glanced at her and then continued on his way, walking determinedly back to his office. Chandling and Ryan entered next.

"Erin, I was wondering where you were!" the senator grinned widely at the sight of her, his glistening teeth outshining his frizzy white hair. He took a step toward her and gave her a gentle hug, and she reciprocated the warm reception.

The two had a long history together. She'd known him since she was a little girl; both he and her father had served in the first Gulf War together. Chandling and her father remained friends. She had visited Chandling and his family frequently until her dad had died of cancer during her freshman year of college. Though they didn't speak often after that, Chandling had helped her pay her way through college and law school; most of her family's money had been spent on medical bills. He was also responsible for introducing her to the FBI.

When Chandling was shot and his family murdered, Kinsley vowed to find the killer and bring him to justice. At the time, she couldn't imagine what the senator had been through. As they returned to their car following a movie, Chandling and his family had come face-to-face with Christopher Morgan. His wife of over thirty years received two bullets to the chest and one to the head, while his seventeen-year-old daughter met a similar fate. Ironically, Chandling suffered two serious gunshot wounds but survived. To lose one's family in such a violent, sudden way when he himself was the target would be unbearable for most, and yet, somehow, the senator managed to pull himself back together and return to office.

"I never thought I'd be standing with the two of you again," Chandling placed a large hand on Ryan's shoulder, but kept his attention on Erin. "Happy that he has returned?"

"Can't complain too much," Erin shrugged jokingly, her eyes falling on Ryan. "How was it out there?"

"Like being paraded around at a dog show," Ryan stated grimly, then turned to the senator. "I don't know how you do it day after day."

"You get used to it. At some point you learn to embrace it. *You'll* get used to it very quickly."

"I'd rather not," Ryan looked agitated.

"Erin, do you mind if I talk with Ryan alone for a minute?" Chandling asked.

"I've got to get back to work anyway," Erin spotted John Lancaster walking toward them. She brushed past the two men and headed for Ryan's former partner.

"Nothing," John stated as she approached. "We've been canvassing the area where Ryan was found and nothing. Just like six months ago."

"So that's it?" Erin motioned for John to follow her back to their desks. As dismayed as she was at the news, she wasn't surprised. Whoever had taken Ryan and returned him six months later knew how to cover any tracks, and that combined with the amount of rain that had fallen near Portland over the last week made it extremely unlikely they would find anything of value. She was beginning to suspect that Ryan was returned during the storm for that very reason.

"That's it. We have yet to find any witnesses that may have seen him being brought into the area, and it's unlikely we will. Our only evidence lies in Ryan."

"Thanks for the update," Erin commented as they neared John's desk.

"At least you'll start getting laid again," John chirped as he plopped down at his desk, a tangled web of newspaper clippings, filing cabinets and absolute disorganization. A coworker standing nearby snickered at his joke.

Erin rolled her eyes and continued to her desk at the opposite end of the office. Unlike John's, she kept hers as clean and object-free as possible, save for her computer and a Seattle's Best coffee mug to hold pens and scissors. A calendar that hadn't been flipped in two months and a photo of her and Ryan embracing in front of the Taj Mahal were the only decorations fastened to the fabric walls that defined her space.

Today, however, a small, brown, padded package was sitting on her keyboard. She set her bag down on her desk, switched on her computer and then picked up the package. It was flat and extremely light. She opened the glorified envelope. A DVD in a flat jewel case fell into her hand.

There was a piece of white printer paper folded neatly inside the case. The paper was nearly blank save for the simple note, typed in 12-point Times New Roman:

WATCH THIS. DON'T TELL THE FBI
OR YOUR ALLEGED BOYFRIEND.
I'LL CONTACT YOU WHEN IT'S SAFE. BE CAREFUL.

She set the note down on her desk and looked at the Staples-brand DVD. Yesterday's date was written by hand with a permanent black marker. The handwriting appeared to belong to a male.

Now curious, Erin sat down at her desk and waited for her computer to log into the network. As she did, she studied the envelope. There was no return address, but her name and address had been printed by computer—also in Times New Roman—onto a white label. Several generic American flag stamps—many more than necessary—were plastered carelessly in the upper right.

Her computer finished loading and she slipped the disc into her DVD drive. Nothing happened, so she navigated to the drive, opened it, and found a single file, titled 20130613sp441v7_09:13.avi. It was 1.2 gigabytes in size. The file opened into her video player, and what appeared on screen immediately took Erin's breath away.

"THE FBI ISN'T going to reinstate you," Senator Chandling told Ryan Harper as soon as they were alone. The hallway had emptied, but the typically booming politician spoke in a whisper nonetheless. "At least not anytime soon."

"I'll be back soon enough," Ryan stated. "I just need to rest up for a week or two. Work out a little."

"You don't understand. I'm not talking weeks or a month. I'm talking months, a year. Maybe never."

Ryan began to say something, but then stopped. Chandling was staring at him intensely, waiting for him to react. The senator often spoke like he did on camera, always aiming to stir emotions and elicit a strong response. Though Erin knew the man since she was a girl, Ryan had never fully trusted the senator. It wasn't that he felt the man blatantly—or even intentionally—lied, but simply that he was a living-and-breathing politician. He couldn't turn it off. Every breath of air he took, every word he spoke, was part of an agenda. Even when it was just a conversation in an empty hallway.

Ryan had noticed this the first time he had met the senator, a week after he had been shot by Christopher Morgan. Lying in a hospital bed, weak and faint, his family murdered, he still spoke like every word he said would come back to haunt him at some future time. Erin claimed Chandling had always been like this, and she was probably right; that's just who he was.

"Right now, you're a liability. You're going to be for a long time. You don't remember anything from the last six months —"

"My amnesia isn't going to interfere with how I do my job."

"Who knows when something's going to trigger your memory. You've been through a traumatic experience, and the last thing the FBI needs is an agent flipping out in the middle of an operation. You're a question mark, Agent Harper, and that's not a good thing."

"I've been through a traumatic experience, and you're right, I don't know what that experience was," Ryan felt his voice rise, anger and frustration once again welling up inside him. "Erin's back was burned off her body. I was kidnapped. And who the hell knows what was done to me since. But the FBI isn't going to turn me away because I had a bad couple of months. I'm one of their best agents."

"You *were* one of their best agents."

"Where's this coming from? What have you heard?"

"The decision's been made, but they're not going to tell you right away. They need you for this investigation, and they need you on their side until the issue goes away."

"'The decision's been made', huh?" Ryan shook his head. If what Chandling was saying was true, it was absolute bullshit. He was an FBI agent, and he was a damn good one. It wouldn't be long before he was back to full strength, and a few therapy sessions would appease any lingering doubts. It made no sense for the FBI to throw him away. And yet there was something about Chandling's lecture that rang true.

"The good thing is," Chandling said, pausing for dramatic effect, "you are the man of the hour. You are the most famous lawman since Eliot Ness. At least until the press tires of you. It's not too late."

"What are you saying?"

"We're in this together, Agent Harper," Chandling showed a sliver of a smile, his thick lips spreading, a glimmer of teeth flashing between them. "You've done so much to help me over the last year, to bring justice to the bastard who killed my family. I'm forever within your debt, and I want to help you salvage your career."

"I'm still not convinced my career needs salvaging," Ryan said, though the senator detected his lack of confidence.

"Listen," Chandling eased up, his demeanor suddenly changing to light candor. "I've been in this boat before. Let me help you. We're not talking a lot of effort here, but simply a few choice appearances at the right time to keep you top of mind in the eyes of the public. You're popular—a hero—and the public doesn't want to hear about a hero being stripped of his career before it can truly take off. And the FBI doesn't want to hear about it, either. So let me help you."

Ryan shrugged. "I'm open to ideas. I—"

"There's a banquet coming up in a few days, hosted by Luis Salazar. He's a friend of mine, as I'm sure you know. It's the Fourth Annual Seattle Against Multiple Sclerosis Summer Ball. I'm going to get you an invitation, have you meet a few very well connected friends. Get your picture in the paper."

"I'm not supposed to talk to the press and I intend to abide by my word," Ryan stated firmly.

"Of course. You don't have to talk to the press. Just get your picture taken—it shows the world that you're not huddled in an insane asylum somewhere. Bring Erin, get your picture taken with her. You're back, you want to have a good time and live life again, you have a beautiful girlfriend whom you love and presumably you want to start a family with at some point. You need money, a career, to do that, don't you?"

Chandling must have seen Ryan's bemused expression, for he stopped momentarily and chuckled. "You see my point."

"I do. I just—"

"Good. I'll get you tickets to the event. I'll have them—"

"Ryan!" Erin's voice came from the other end of the hallway. The two men turned to see her waving them toward her, a serious but excited expression on her face. "We just got a break."

13

RYAN HARPER WAS strapped to a metal slab, dressed only in shorts. He was unconscious, though his left arm twitched occasionally. His lips were dry and cracked, parted slightly. A nasal cannula delivered him oxygen, the transparent tubing disappearing under his shaggy hair and reappearing at the base of the neck. He was unshaven. His body was conspicuously less firm, his arms and legs having lost muscle mass. An IV connected his body to a drip bag.

If Erin didn't know him so well, she wouldn't have recognized him right away.

"Jesus Christ," Ryan said, watching himself on the large computer screen before him.

"It looks like he's conscious," John put his finger to the screen. "He's moving his head."

"If he is, he's drugged out of his mind," Yusuf Himayat leaned back in his chair as he chomped on two pieces of gum. "Oh, and don't touch my screen again or I will break that finger."

Erin, standing behind the FBI technical engineer, put a firm hand on his shoulder, which seemed to shut him up. Yusuf, a 27-year old Iraqi-American and technological whiz kid, was more than susceptible to female influence. Darker skinned than most Iraqis, Yusuf had baby-like features exemplified by a large, cartoonish nose. Many of the female employees in the office found him adorable, at least until he opened his mouth. Born and raised in Connecticut, he didn't have the accent most expected and he managed to say all the wrong things more often than not.

"The video is high def, definitely good for extracting detail," Yusuf commented, swatting at John as the agent once again started to point at something. The video showed Ryan in what appeared to be a small, polished room. A metallic table could be partially seen to the left in the video; it was littered with various objects including a laptop computer and cables. Another, smaller table was situated beside Ryan, and on it sat more cords, a stethoscope and other medical monitoring equipment.

"Here comes the scientist," Erin said as a man appeared on screen, shuffling at a slow pace. He was not an old man but moved like one, his scrawny legs seemingly unable to properly support his tall, lanky body. He wore a white lab coat, but underneath, jeans and a light-colored collared shirt. His face was gaunt but not unhealthily so; he had a receding hairline and large ears. He was the stereotypical nerd, except he didn't wear glasses.

Yusuf leaned forward to his keyboard and captured a freeze frame of the man's face.

"Looking up matches now," he said, and then resumed the video.

"How long ago was this taken?" Senator Chandling asked from the back of the darkened room. "This is unbelievable."

"Hard to say," Ryan said. "There's nothing to indicate a time or date, no timestamp visible. But this video had to have been taken months ago, based on my appearance. And I had to have been there for a while, too—you don't lose that muscle mass overnight."

"Yusuf, if you can find anything that indicates when this video was made it would be extremely helpful," John said. "Any kind of meta data that would give us a clue."

"Of course. *That* is my job," Yusuf retorted dryly.

"This was just sitting on your desk when you came in?" John asked Erin in disbelief, ignoring Yusuf's annoyance.

"Sent via the postal service. No return address."

"Postmark?"

"Redding, California," Erin said.

The scientist continued to shuffle around the screen, organizing items on the two visible tables. Ryan twitched from time to time but otherwise remained stationary. Ten minutes passed before anything else happened. The scientist disappeared off screen for a couple minutes, and then returned and picked up a remote control that was connected to the side of the operating table. The group fell silent as they watched the scientist rotate the metal slab, placing Ryan at a 75-degree angle to the floor.

The man walked to the other side of Ryan and checked that his IV was still connected properly; his actions were methodical, not hurried. He then moved back to the far table, picked up the wires and started placing electrode monitors on Ryan's chest, abdomen and temples.

Erin looked at Ryan and took his hand. He squeezed back, but his attention never wavered from the screen.

The scientist, content with his placement of the monitoring devices, returned to the laptop and started typing. He glanced once or twice at Ryan but otherwise kept his attention on the screen.

"Can you pull anything off that screen?" John asked, leaning forward to point to the laptop. It was angled on the table just enough so that only a sliver of the computer screen was visible.

"I know what you're talking about, you don't have to point," Yusuf snapped and

John recoiled. "It'll be tough. I'll see what I can do, but we have about five degrees of visibility to play with—I doubt it."

The scientist pressed a few more keys on the laptop and then returned to Ryan to remove the monitoring devices.

"If we don't find a match, you'll want to distribute his picture to hospitals in the region," Yusuf aimed his index finger at the screen, emphasizing to John how to point without touching. "Looks like he has a broken wrist. See, under his left sleeve." Erin didn't see it at first, but sure enough, the mysterious scientist had a cast on his left arm.

"Good catch," John said.

"That's why they pay me the big bucks."

"They do?"

"No, not really."

The video cut out a minute later, leaving them in momentary darkness. Yusuf switched on a desk lamp and shifted his attention to another screen, which was attempting to find an identification match based on the scientist's facial features.

"This may take a while. I'll make a couple copies and get the original down to forensics for fingerprinting. I suppose I've found my new pet project for the next couple of days," Yusuf grinned. "This is exciting. Our first big break."

Erin nodded, suddenly feeling good about the day. Yusuf was right: three days after Ryan's return, six months after his disappearance, they were finally building momentum in the case. She turned to Ryan, hoping that something on the video had sparked his memory.

As if reading her mind, he shook his head, "No, none of it looks familiar. To me, none of that ever happened."

14

SHARP SPIKES OF pain were shooting up and down Erin's shoulders when John Lancaster arrived at her doorstep with two six-packs of Fat Tire and his wife Kendra standing by his side. She forced a smile, but was already regretting inviting them over.

"The beer has arrived," John held the beer to Erin's face as soon as she opened the front door.

"Gee, thanks," Erin responded, looking past John to his wife, a pretty woman with sharp features and high cheekbones. Of South African descent, the product of a white father and black mother, her complexion was fair, though certainly much darker than John's pasty skin. Erin had always found her gorgeous. "Good to see you, Kendra."

"I apologize for my husband in advance," Kendra rolled her eyes as she followed John inside. Erin shut the door and proceeded down the short hallway after her guests. "John hasn't even started drinking yet."

"Oh my God!" Kendra exclaimed upon seeing Ryan, who was waiting for them in the living room. She brushed past her husband and embraced Ryan, kissing him hard on the cheek. "This is unbelievable! I am so glad you're safe." She leaned back, still hanging onto him, and looked him up and down. "I can't believe—I mean, I knew—but to see you here—oh my God —"

"Good to see you, too, Kendra," Ryan said calmly. Erin thought his reaction was strange until she remembered that to him, he'd seen her just a few days earlier—in December.

"I wish she got that excited when she sees me," John remarked, watching Kendra take Ryan in. "Maybe I should disappear for six months."

"Now I'm getting excited," Kendra winked at John, who playfully grimaced at her.

"Glad you guys made it. The reporters outside didn't attack?"

John responded, but Erin didn't hear him. Her back was throbbing now, consuming her thoughts. She closed her eyes, just for a second so that no one would notice her agony. She forced herself to ignore the pain, but it continued to pulsate into the base of her skull.

"We should start drinking." John had placed himself on the couch.

"Amen to that," Kendra chimed. Erin agreed silently.

"So," John gazed at Ryan as he removed the caps from four beers. "Have you heard the latest rumors?"

"No, what?" Ryan raised an eyebrow.

"Apparently, according to some very reputable tabloids, the mystery surrounding your disappearance has been solved," John paused for effect. "You were never gone. Your beautiful, smart and sophisticated FBI-agent-of-a-girlfriend Erin Kinsley has actually had you locked in a room for the last six months. Sex slave stuff."

"Seriously?"

"Seriously."

"I wish I remembered more in that case," Ryan snorted as he touched her hip affectionately.

"Not funny," she pulled away and retreated to the bathroom. She didn't even remember opening the medicine cabinet or grabbing her pills, but as the two tablets slid down her throat she relished the thought that in a few minutes everything would be back to normal. The pain wouldn't be gone, but it would be tempered. She could deal.

"Change of subject," Kendra, the constant peacekeeper, raised her bottle as Erin returned to the living room. Ryan looked at her, more curious than concerned about her sudden departure, but she gave him a reassuring smile and he returned his attention to Kendra. "To the return of a good friend."

"Here, here!" John exclaimed, drinking half his bottle in one swallow. Erin took an equally large swig. Then another.

"So, Ryan," Kendra touched his arm. "When are you going to get back on active duty?"

"That's a touchy subject," he warned her halfheartedly. "Technically, I can't be reinstated until the investigation closes, and who knows when that will be. I'm also not allowed to actively participate in the investigation in any way, nor talk to the press or do anything that makes me or the FBI look bad. So, in other words, I'm pretty much screwed until someone makes a breakthrough."

"And how is the case coming?" Kendra asked. A school teacher, she was often an outsider to conversations between the other three.

"My dear, the FBI cannot discuss an ongoing investigation," her husband said, squeezing her hand. "But, we did get a small break today."

"I'd say a big one," Ryan said.

"We received—well, I received—a video in the mail today that shows Ryan on an operating table. There's a man—a scientist or doctor or something—who is examining him. The computers are looking for a match as we speak."

"Operating table…" Kendra murmured. "Cut open or anything?"

"No, nothing like that," Ryan grinned. "He was monitoring my body stats. The video didn't show much more than that."

"Hopefully we'll find a match," Erin said. "At the very least, we know that someone wants to help us. Someone out there is willing to talk."

"And what about where you were found? There have to be some clues there."

"Not really," Erin shook her head. "It was raining… tracking the route Ryan took was a lost cause. We found some of his footprints, but most of them had washed away. There're a lot of broken branches— Ryan was definitely moving in a hurry— but after a quarter mile, we lost the trail. Dogs didn't get much further."

"And there's nothing within a forty mile span where I could have been hiding for six months," Ryan shrugged. "The UFO theory is sounding better by the minute."

"There was no UFO," Erin grinded her teeth. "But this is the mystery of mysteries."

"So if you guys are still stretching for ideas, then shouldn't Ryan be given a bigger role in the investigation? After all, he may be the only one who can figure it out. It must be in your head somewhere."

"SAC Monroe was perfectly clear that I am to keep out of the way—and keep my mouth shut—for the foreseeable future."

Erin noted a low grumbling in his tone. The way he'd said Monroe's name seethed with disdain. It was rare for him to show disrespect to superiors, even when he disagreed with them, but she could hardly blame him. He was stranded and helpless, and that's not a position in which he was used to being.

"*The man* gave me some old case files to look at, which basically amount to a whole lot of nothing and a spotty history of Christopher Morgan."

"Well, that's something," Kendra said cheerily. "I mean, Christopher Morgan has to have something to do with all this."

"The man's dead," Ryan said tersely.

Kendra shook her head in disbelief. "Yeah, but he was found hanging from a tree sixty feet above the ground a couple months after you two disappeared. There was no way he climbed up that tree. His death is as odd as your disappearance."

"I suppose," Ryan shrugged. "But the guy was a killer, a paranoid anti-government nut. He certainly had a screw or two loose. He could've killed dozens of people over the years—the only reason he didn't get caught earlier was that he was so disenfranchised with the world that he entirely dropped off the grid. The only reason we caught a break was because his girlfriend turned him in."

"He got cornered and knew there was no way out. He'd just been betrayed by his girlfriend. He had nothing to lose—he was expecting to die that night, Kendra," John chimed in. "He didn't have some grand scheme, but if he did, it sure as hell didn't work out for him very well."

"I understand that, but still…" Kendra said desperately.

"I agree with you," Erin told Kendra. "Everything's connected. It's silly to assume Morgan wasn't somehow connected to the people that killed him and took Ryan."

"Up until today, we didn't even know for sure that someone else *was* involved,"

John argued. "Not for certain anyway. Sure, it was highly unlikely that Ryan just bumped his head and was lying in a coma for six months. But, there was no evidence—absolutely no evidence—that actually suggested Ryan had been kidnapped . There're no houses or cabins anywhere near the location where he disappeared—or reappeared—other than the one that Morgan blew up. Satellites show no low-flying aircraft—or ground vehicles—that could account for his removal from the area. I've decided I'll blame Appalachian hillbillies on the whole matter."

"Yes, John," Ryan said dryly. "I was kidnapped by a bunch of Appalachian hillbillies in the lowlands of the Cascade Mountains."

"You're a very cute guy," John grinned from across the table. "Maybe they saw something they liked."

"John, regardless of what the evidence—I mean lack of evidence—has suggested in the past, you have this video now that tells you otherwise," Kendra said softly. "Ryan *was* taken."

"Yeah, but how?" John asked. "The satellite photos don't give us any clues."

"Then they were altered," she shrugged.

"We've had those photographs analyzed by the best analysts and computers available. No alterations were found," Erin raised her hands in defeat. "I know what you're saying, but—"

"You guys combed the woods for days after Ryan disappeared," Kendra insisted. "You found nothing. You *know* Ryan wasn't in those woods after that night. The whole area was on lockdown for weeks, and yet somehow he got out. The photographs are lying."

John opened his mouth to speak, but he couldn't think of anything to say. He looked at Erin and then Ryan, both wearing the same defeatist expressions.

"The roads were blocked already, so they couldn't have gotten out by car."

"Correct," Erin said.

"You had, what, four helicopters in the air that night?"

"Correct."

"Would anyone on the ground actually notice a fifth one? I mean, with everyone running around, they'd all sound about the same."

"So what you're saying is that someone had a helicopter ready, flew to the exact spot Ryan and Morgan were, landed, took them, left—and then modified the satellite photography to cover their tracks," John looked at his wife with amazement.

"I know you've thought about that exact same scenario before," Kendra told him.

"Yeah, but every time the evidence suggested otherwise."

"Frankly, this new evidence suggests that we've been deceived," Ryan said. "I'd like to see these photographs."

"Sweetheart," John leaned toward Kendra and kissed her on the edge of the mouth. "I think you're in the wrong profession."

15

"MERCY!" RYAN DECLARED, rising from the kneeling position he'd held for the last hour. He remained in place for a moment, body swaying ever so slightly, gazing down at the menagerie of satellite photographs spread across the living room floor. He gave them one last scan and then, frustrated, turned on his heels and disappeared down the hallway. Erin heard the bathroom door shut.

"Well, it was a good idea for about three minutes," John groaned, tapping his fingers impatiently on the corner of one of the photographs. "Maybe two and a half."

Erin mumbled a laugh and leaned back against the base of the couch. She glanced over at Kendra, who at some point had fallen asleep on the couch. Her mouth was agape, but she looked comfortable. Erin was jealous.

Kendra was right, Erin acknowledged. Despite the lack of any evidence, the logical solution was that Ryan had indeed been removed by helicopter and the records altered. It was the only explanation that made any sense. And yet that solution required a combination of unsettling ingredients: a highly coordinated enemy, one capable of extracting him from under the noses of dozens of FBI agents and powerful enough to have access and the willingness to alter government data.

Her eyes flicked over the twenty or so large sheets of poster paper sprawled in front of her. The photographs, each taken five minutes apart, were captured from over 400 miles above the Earth's surface. They were taken at night, but the brightness had been enhanced to the point where almost every tree was distinguishable from the next; the terrain, logging roads and other geography were also as clear as day.

The pictures catalogued the series of events leading up to Ryan's disappearance. The cabin, and the field where the last evidence of Ryan's presence was found, were clearly defined in each photograph. The second photograph showed the cabin shortly after its detonation, the area a white blur. In the third, several agents could be seen lying dead or wounded, others converging on the location. Several helicopters moved into frame as well.

A few sheets later, a speck assumed to be Ryan was shown at the bottom of a rocky hill, not far from the burning cabin. His earpiece was found partway up the hill. By then the FBI were swarming the area and several police cars had tightened the perimeter. Helicopters were scanning the woods for Morgan.

On a subsequent sheet, Ryan could be seen standing in another clearing halfway up the hillside, an old logging truck turnaround. Morgan was with him, standing only a few feet away. By the next frame, both men were gone. Erin didn't know how long she had stared at that single photograph over the last six months, analyzing, assessing, practically begging for it to reveal something that the experts didn't see. A faint dirt road connected the clearing to the nearby highway, but two police cars were positioned only a quarter mile away, blocking any chance of escape. The picture had haunted her dreams, teasing her with a truth that couldn't be seen. The men just disappeared into the woods. Help had been only a minute away.

"So, how're things going?" John asked, his voice suddenly quiet.

"Fine," she said, her eyes closing. When John didn't answer she finally looked at him, and noticed he was watching the bathroom door. "Wakes up having horrible nightmares, sleeps sporadically. He's tired most of the time, falls asleep faster than usual, doesn't eat much, but other than that…"

"Okay," the man nodded, seemingly unfazed by the list of symptoms. "And how is he? I mean, is he—"

She knew what he meant. "He's normal. He cracks jokes at inappropriate times, has been obsessed with the case—like always—and… He's just a mentally drained version of Ryan." She could have told him that there was something off that she couldn't quite place… The way he touched her, the way he kissed her, the way he looked at her when she came onto him. The way he laughed at movies he generally didn't like, or the way he brushed his teeth. But she didn't. Now was not the time.

"I see," John nodded, studying her, trying to determine if she was being honest. Erin thought he would see through her, but John rolled onto his back, perhaps also realizing that now was not the time. "It is good to have him back, though."

She detected hesitation in his voice.

A moment later, Ryan returned to the living room, his face and hair dripping with water. He looked at the two of them—Erin could have sworn with suspicion—and then sat down on the arm of the couch behind Erin. He touched her shoulder and gave it a gentle squeeze. God, that felt good. She closed her eyes, taking in the ad hoc massage, but before she could indulge in it further, she felt her cell phone vibrating in her pocket.

It was Yusuf. Calling at midnight.

"Yusuf, you're still working, huh?" she answered.

"Of course," he said. "You?"

"Yeah."

"Awesome," he said. "I don't have a lot of great news for you, unfortunately."

"Shoot."

"For starters, no match on our mystery scientist dude. He's not in any national database. I've started tapping into local jurisdiction DBs, but it's not a good sign. I really thought that with the high-res capture of his face we'd get a match."

"Shit," she muttered. "So what did you find?"

"Not a whole lot," he said, drawing out his words. "First off, there was no meta data that would help us out—the video file is dated yesterday, but all that tells us is that's when the file was created. When it was filmed, who knows? As for what I could extract from the video itself... I wasn't able to scrape anything off the laptop screen, which was a shame. There isn't anything written anywhere that would indicate a time or date. The room is either underground or has no windows, as the lighting is centrally based and remains constant throughout the video's running time. Let's see, what else... None of the items on display are especially unique or easy to track."

"Any good news, Yusuf?"

"Well, Harper—the Harper in the video, that is—has a wound on his abdomen, on the right-hand side about three inches above the waist. It looks nearly healed, there's no bandage or anything."

"Ryan," Erin turned to look at her boyfriend, her back suddenly reminding her it no longer liked to twist like that. "Lift up your shirt for a moment." He gave her a quizzical look. "Just do it."

She leaned toward his abs, but there was no sign of any wound or scarring. "Nothing."

"Hmm," Yusuf said. "Maybe it's nothing. If Harper still had some kind of mark on him, we might have been able to extrapolate how old this video is, but it could have healed months ago and there's no way we'd know."

"Thanks, Yusuf. Anything else?"

"Nope." She could picture him shaking his head emphatically like he always did. "What are you working on so late?"

"We're going through the satellite footage once again. We were convinced that there has to be something wrong with it."

"Nice," Yusuf hissed excitedly. "I'd be happy to give it another look over if you want."

"I figured you'd never want to look at these photos again. How many times did you go through them? A hundred times? A thousand?" Erin laughed.

"Once or twice at most," Yusuf said. "I gave them a preliminary scan when we first got them, but that was it."

Erin's smile faded. "What do you mean? You were the chief analyst on the project." She felt John and Ryan stiffen, detecting the suspicious tone in her voice.

"No, I was for like a couple hours, but got pulled off it for another assignment."

"Another assignment?"

"Yeah, I can't even remember what it was. It was fairly inconsequential, but urgent at the time. I thought it was weird they'd take me off Harper's case. Of all cases."

"But it was properly analyzed?"

"Yeah. It got sent over to Quantico and passed through the ringer over there. They didn't find a thing, but I would love to take a fresh stab at it. You never know, right?"

"Yusuf, could you find out who signed off on the analysis? I want to—"

"You think someone tampered with the investigation?" the casual tone in Yusuf's voice suddenly vanished.

"I don't know, but I'd like to find out." She hung up the phone. She shifted her attention back to the dozens of photographs spread out before her. Even though she couldn't see it herself, she was now certain that the photographs contained a hint as to what really happened.

16

"AT LEAST THERE'S food," Ryan Harper said, staring wide-eyed at the daunting array of platters before him. The food ranged from the basics—potato chips—to the expected—shrimp cocktail—to the unexpected—duck, alligator, salmon and about two dozen dishes with fancy, hard-to-pronounce names.

"You're hungry? Really?" Erin asked sarcastically, though her stomach was grumbling, too. She knew the Luis Salazar banquet was going to be lavish, but the billionaire's event had exceeded his already grand reputation. The CenturyLink Field Event Center, an unimposing four-story block of a building attached to the southern side of the football stadium, had been transformed into something more befitting of Vegas than the Pacific Northwest. The concrete floors were covered with black wood, the walls draped in black. And yet the room was full of light, the spectrum of colors slowly transmuting one into another, the room's atmosphere evolving minute by minute. A rock band played in one corner; Cirque du Soleil performed overhead.

Neither of them had been looking forward to the event with particular enthusiasm. Socializing with a bunch of rich businesspeople was not their forte. But the allure of Salazar's event was enough to demand an appearance.

As Ryan scanned the food selection, debating where to begin, he said, "If you were smart, you'd find a sugar daddy tonight."

"Why do you think I agreed to come?"

"I assumed it was out of your unquestionable and undying love for me, that's all."

"Yeah, that's all," she rolled her eyes, but couldn't help but smile.

"I make you that happy?"

"It's just that…" she stopped and turned to him. "Well, you're sounding more like your old self. You've been distant ever since you returned—understandably, of course. It's nice to have you back." Erin realized she was blushing, and looked away.

Ryan was silent for a moment, and then she felt his fingers on her chin, guiding her back to him. He looked at her, right in the eyes, and pecked her on the lips. Then, in her ear, he whispered, "I can't wait to get you out of that dress."

That wasn't the response she was expecting, and the way he said it made her blood boil. She smiled again, and he smiled back, pleased with himself for evoking such a reaction.

"Get your food," she said, now needing to get her mind off sex. Damn him, she thought. Just as Ryan picked up a plate, a booming voice spoke their names from a few yards away. Turning, they saw Senator Chandling ambling toward them, a wide smile plastered on his face. Erin could immediately tell he'd had a few drinks.

"Erin, you look gorgeous," the red-faced politician gave her a polite look-over, but before she could thank him he had already shifted his attention to Ryan. "Ryan, I'm so pleased you decided to come. I wasn't sure you would."

"I'd been cooped up long enough," Ryan momentarily glanced at Erin. She had tried to talk him out of the event. The FBI had asked him to stay out of sight and out of mind, and yet he'd been persuaded by the senator's argument to do the opposite. Chandling was looking out for Ryan's well being, but she didn't agree with the man's strategy; the FBI wasn't going to boot Ryan out the door, at least not without provocation. Appearing in public at a swanky event wasn't going to help.

"Come with me," Chandling placed a large red paw on Ryan's shoulder and angled him toward a nearby cluster of people, motioning to Erin to follow suit. The group appeared to be crowded around a single individual whose back was to them. Even before Chandling spoke his name, she knew exactly who it was.

Luis Salazar was in his mid-forties and wore an expensive black suit with a crimson shirt and matching tie. Though she'd seen him on television several times, Erin was immediately taken aback by his presence. He wasn't amazingly handsome, as his dark, bushy eyebrows and full lips didn't quite seem to fit the proportions of his face, but everything about him exuded an unbelievable level of confidence and energy. He was, after all, the founder and CEO of Salazar International, a conglomerate of companies that primarily dealt in the pharmaceutical and biomedical industries. He was one of the richest men in the country.

As stunned as they must have looked to be in the presence of one of the richest men in the country, he reacted equally shocked. At the sight of Ryan, his eyes bulged and, for a split second, Erin thought she saw his hand tremble. The reaction would have been strange if not for the fact that he was staring at a man who up until recently had been presumed dead. Salazar hesitated and glanced at Erin, but then forced a smile and took Ryan's hand.

"I heard you were back," the billionaire's voice was soft but commanding. "I still can't believe it."

"Neither can I," Ryan retorted.

The man nodded gently, his neatly combed black hair bobbing with him. "Is it true you don't remember anything about those months?"

"I'm confident it will come back to me, but no, nothing."

"That's a shame," he said through closed lips. He was acting strangely, Erin acknowledged, but she couldn't pinpoint the reason. From what she had heard, Salazar was neither an elitist nor an eccentric, but he was acting like he wanted nothing to do with Ryan.

Sensing the awkwardness of the situation, Chandling interjected, "Luis, I'd like you to meet Erin Kinsley."

The billionaire's dark, curious eyes jumped to Erin and she blushed as he carefully looked her over, a move that by some would be regarded as offensive but one that she found incredibly flattering coming from him. To Ryan, he said, "I'm so glad you brought Agent Kinsley. She's extremely beautiful."

"Thank you," she said, secretly urging the blood rush in her face to subside. "You can call me Erin."

"You can call me Luis," he said with boyish charm, his white teeth flashing a huge smile. He extended his small, tan hand and she took it, giving it a hearty shake. At first she thought this newfound warmth was directed towards her because of her sex, but she realized quickly that whatever had been bothering him before had vanished. "Both of you, of course."

"Well, my job for the evening is done," Chandling proclaimed proudly. "I believe you and Luis will find you have a lot in common." And with that, the senator vanished into the crowd, already eyeing his next calculated conversation.

"I've been following your case very carefully," Luis motioned to them to follow. "I want you to meet someone." He started to lead them through the crowd, his very presence causing the tides to part. "I've become a huge fan of you and your career. I've read about you. You're a star among agents, Agent Harper. Top of your class, fast advancement through the ranks... I'm a little surprised you chose to station yourself out here in the boondocks that is the Pacific Northwest when you could've had clear sailing back in Washington."

"I like it here," Ryan said. "Better weather."

"Very true," Salazar said. A waiter appeared beside him with a tray of drinks, and they were quickly dispensed to Erin and Ryan.

"So what makes you a fan of an FBI agent exactly?"

He shrugged. "I have a vested interest in what goes on in this community. And the country. That's all." Salazar stopped behind a young woman with long, straight blond hair. She was speaking to a group of drunk men, her back to the newcomers. Even from behind, Erin could tell the woman was a knockout. She had a athletic frame and an ass-kissing black dress to accentuate it. The billionaire snaked his arm around her waist.

"Excuse me," she giggled to the other men before being spun around to face Ryan and Erin. Her smile faded momentarily when she saw Ryan, but then returned just as quickly and grander than ever. The woman, who couldn't have been older than 25, was absolutely beautiful. Erin was certain that she was a supermodel. Her face was slender and perfectly structured, with a petite nose, big eyes and luscious lips. She was wearing a low-cut dress, and for good reason. Had Erin had breasts like those, she would be, too. The girl was perfect. Erin immediately hated her.

"Marie, I'd like to introduce you to Ryan Harper and Erin Kinsley, of the FBI.

They're my star guests this evening."

"I have read so much about you," Marie said with a Parisian accent, shaking Ryan's hand. She turned to Erin. "And nice to meet you."

"To clear the elephant in the room," Salazar beamed. "Yes, I'm nearly twice as old as she is. Love works in mysterious ways."

Marie smiled widely and leaned into her beau, pecking him on the cheek.

"Speaking of love, do you not love the look of this place?" Marie gazed up at the ceiling while Erin listened to each French-infused syllable roll perfectly off her lips. "Luis holds the best parties."

"It *is* quite something," Ryan agreed.

"I try to do things differently," Salazar chimed in. "It's worked well for me so far."

"You never finished explaining why you've taken such an interest in me."

Salazar chuckled and looked at Marie as if to reaffirm that something funny had been said. "You *are* just like your profile, Agent Harper. Very to-the-point."

Ryan shrugged.

"To be to-the-point, I'll say this: you led an assault into the Oregon woods to save your girlfriend and capture a killer who nearly slaughtered the entire Chandling family—dear friends of mine, by the way. Some of your friends were killed in that assault. You then disappear as if someone snatched you right out of the air, and then you reappear six months later to what? A suspension? Doubt? Suspicion?"

"It's not *that* bad…"

"Let me finish," Salazar raised his voice, though his frustration was clearly not aimed toward Ryan. "You've risen through the ranks without a spot on your resume—in fact, more praise than anything else—and then the FBI tries to tarnish your record with this investigation? It's a small minority of people who are actually stupid enough to think you had some nefarious plan—after all, it doesn't make any sense. If you're involved in some illegal operation, why would you sneak away in such a theatrical manner? And how could you have possibly been working in cahoots with the likes of a rightwing nutcase? It *is* a small group of people that think you may have something to do with all of this, but that's all it takes. Every day this investigation goes on, the groundwork is set for suspicion and doubt. The public is overwhelmingly on your side, but if your innocence isn't confirmed soon, what'll happen? They'll start questioning whether there is something to the investigation. Public support—and interest—will fade, and that can only hurt you. You do want to get back on duty, right?"

"Of course," Ryan said.

"So that's why you're of interest to me, Agent Harper. I'm a very rich man and a very powerful one. I get my way."

"I don't need you pulling strings for me."

"I'll use *that* influence if I need to, but I doubt it'll come to that," Salazar laughed, his demeanor relaxing. "But PR is important, and I can give that to you. Your very presence here is beneficial… You'll be on the cover of tomorrow's paper, with a nice picture of the four of us to accompany it."

"I don't need that, either."

"I knew you'd say that," Salazar shrugged. "You're a behind-the-scenes guy. Hell, you've made a career of it. Let's walk and talk for a moment…"

The billionaire slapped Ryan on the back and led him away, leaving Erin alone with Marie. Through most of Salazar's tirade, she'd watched Marie study Ryan. Meticulously. Ryan was handsome and she wasn't surprised that Marie would be interested, but the attention she'd given him was unwavering.

Once the two men had walked away, Marie's eyes finally shifted to Erin. "You must be so happy that your man has returned. I cannot imagine what it was like."

"It was tough, but I'm happy he's back. It's taking a bit of getting used to."

"I hear he does not remember anything? Is he the same as when he left?" Marie asked as if it were small talk, but Erin got the sense that she was actually curious.

"No, not exactly. But he's getting there."

Marie nodded, but said nothing. She glanced back the way the two men had gone, looking anxious.

"So… How long have you and Luis been together?" Erin decided to break the awkward silence.

"About four months," Marie rolled her eyes up as if expressing her love right then and there.

"Wow, that's impressive."

"Impressive?" she asked innocently.

"He has a reputation, that's all."

"Oh," her eyes narrowed, but the edge of her lips curled into a satisfied grin. "I have that kind of power over men. I guess."

"I can imagine." Erin was surprised by how she was treating this girl she didn't even know, but she was just so damned perfect in every way. The girl was beautiful, and young, and French. She annunciated every word, her English very good but her confidence in the language much less so. It was that lack of confidence, that shyness, that seemed out of place for a girl who could get anything with the right glance.

Marie smacked her lips together, but said nothing more on the subject. "About Ryan… What is the last thing he remembers?"

Erin grunted a laugh. "That's part of an ongoing investigation. I can't say anything."

Marie rolled her eyes playfully—again—and touched Erin's forearm with her long, slender fingers. "Erin, I am just asking. I did not mean to…"

"It's nothing personal."

"I am sorry. I just did not know…" Marie trailed off, her eyes dropping to the floor. Her hand receded to her side.

Erin suddenly found herself blushing of all things, embarrassed by how she'd been acting. This girl—and she really was just a girl—was not a bad person. Marie was gorgeous, and perhaps a gold digger, but she meant no harm. And Erin had been a complete bitch to her.

"It's an awkward situation," Erin said cheerily, trying to shift the mood of the conversation. "Everyone wants to know about what happened to him, but everything about him is *the* investigation. Makes for really poor water cooler talk."

"Water *cooler*?" Marie scrunched her nose, not understanding.

"Small talk."

"*Oui*, small talk," Marie smiled, nodding. "Yes, I can imagine it is hard. And with your man not remembering anything. Not remembering you."

"Oh, no!" Erin laughed, shaking her head. "He remembers me just fine. It's just the last several months."

"I understand. So he does not remember from the night he disappeared."

"Well, give or take a few weeks," Erin shrugged. "Well, there you go, getting top secret information from me already."

Marie laughed, a sincere giggle that was both cute and not at all obnoxious. Erin laughed, too. "Your secret is safe with me." The girl smiled, her eyes locking with Erin's as if she were silently reiterating her oath. Erin smiled wider, acknowledging she actually liked this girl. What a change a couple of minutes made; only moments ago she had hated this beautiful creature. There was something about Marie that exuded comfort, as if her very being emitted a natural aphrodisiac.

Marie's attentiveness didn't slacken until the men returned, each holding a pair of wine glasses. Salazar was chuckling loudly, with Ryan in tow. Ryan wore a bemused expression, but when Erin gave him a look, he grinned and winked and then shifted his attention back to the host.

"*Merci*," Marie said, taking her glass from Salazar. Salazar remained focused on Ryan, who was telling one of his training tales from Quantico.

"… and the guy just marched onto the shooting range while guys were still shooting…"

Salazar erupted with a shocked laugh, and Marie followed suit, though her smile was slight, her laughter faint. She was once again staring avidly at Ryan, and Erin felt her affection for the girl fading once more. But as she watched Marie out of the corner of her eye, she realized that the way she was studying Ryan was much more meticulous than any crush; she was taking in every word, every subtle expression, every hand gesture and was processing every moment of it. Erin suddenly had the feeling Marie was smarter than she let on.

RYAN PLANNED TO make love to Erin once they got home, but an evening of food and socializing led to a quick demise of his plans. Both were asleep within minutes. From the sleep came dreams that were nothing more than fractured thoughts and memories, recollections of past events he couldn't remember and friends that had long since faded from memory. A woman wearing a flowery dress, sitting in a chair, her head turned to him, her eyes angry. "We have to stick together. We have to stick together," she said, her voice older than her appearance. A young woman, no older than 20, running down a hallway from him, naked from head to toe, her fiery red hair bouncing with every playful hop. She gazed back at him over a bare shoulder, her eyes luring him to the bedroom.

And then the redhead was gone, and he was sitting in a car, staring at his hands which rested gently on the steering wheel. The car didn't move. Neither did his hands.

He gazed down the street—his old street. Everything was still, and yet something was coming. In the distance, a darkness approached. He wanted to run. He prayed for the ability to run. He prayed until his throat was so dry he could not swallow. He prayed like he had never done before. But the prayers were useless. Something appeared in the darkness, a shapeless, featureless object. It was the Face. It had returned for him once again.

The whispers began.

17

IT WAS WELL into morning when Ryan woke abruptly. He could tell it was late by the way the penetrating sunlight glanced off the closet doors. Through the half-open blinds, he focused on a couple of construction workers chitchatting across the street. One of the men removed his helmet to wipe his brow. It was going to be a hot day.

Something had awoken him—he wasn't sure what—but when he saw that it was nearly ten, he knew he wouldn't fall back asleep. Sleep was relative, of course. He hadn't slept well since his first night back, the Face never far away.

A soft tapping at the other end of the apartment—away from the construction—reminded him of what had awoken him in the first place. Grumbling, he stood up and lumbered into the hallway.

It suddenly dawned on him that Erin wasn't home. She'd left him to continue her investigation. He paused at the edge of the kitchen. It looked just like they'd left it the night before—spotless, with no dishes to be seen. She hadn't eaten breakfast to avoid waking him. She would shrug the gesture off as being considerate, saying he needed the rest and deserved to sleep in. But he knew that was bullshit. She was off doing her thing—both she and John were—and they didn't want him around. He was the only one who could help, but they saw him as a distraction, a magnet, a has-been. A bitch and a son-of-a-bitch, that's what they were. He trusted them with every ounce of his soul and they were off working without him. His partners, and they wanted nothing to do with him. Hell, they were investigating him.

He leaned against the wall with his bare forearm, the veins pulsing down to his clenched fist. He wondered what else they did behind his back, what they had done while he was gone. Erin was a beautiful woman and John was an observant man. A married man, but he and Kendra were no perfect couple. The last six months would have strained things between the couple. John and Erin would have worked late for months. One thing led to another. Love, certainly not, but their frustrations had to boil over at some point.

The tapping came again, and Ryan blinked back to reality. His jaw relaxed and he shook his head at his own thoughts, at their absurdity. He crossed the living room to the front door.

It took a moment for his eyes to adjust to the outdoor light, and another to recognize the young woman standing before him. Then last night came back to him.

"*Bonjour*," Marie said in her cute French accent, the corner of her lips curling upwards. "Luis"—she said the name like "Louie" but with an intentional "s" slapped onto the end for effect—"said I am to pick you up at ten o'clock. You are clearly not ready."

Ryan blinked, not recalling anything about ten o'clock or being picked up, but then again last night was hazy. He remembered her vividly, though. She looked every bit as gorgeous as she had the night before, though her flowing blond hair was tied into a loose, disheveled ponytail and her dress replaced with denim shorts and a T-shirt. The shorts gave way to incredibly perfect, tan legs, and her shirt, a light pink fade with mini-sleeves, was cut partway in the front to reveal that wonderful cleavage she possessed. A bikini strap teased on her right shoulder.

Luis Salazar's toy was a temptation, that was for sure, and she played into it. Her head cocked slightly to the left, her bangs curling slightly across her face, she gazed at him with awkward intensity.

"If you are going to look, I am going to look," Marie said matter-of-factly, her eyes scrolling across his chest and abs. He was only wearing his tuxedo pants, and with all his free time lately, he'd been working out extensively. Before he could respond, she shrugged a nonchalant "so what" and returned her attention to his face.

"I'll get dressed," Ryan said, pulling his eyes away from her.

He quickly threw on slacks and a yellow polo T-shirt and greeted Marie, who looked him over once again, apparently disapproving of his style. But she turned on her heels—and her flip flops—and walked out the door. Ryan grinned and followed, struggling to take his eyes off her alluring figure

"You are to talk business with Luis?" she asked at the bottom of the stairs.

"I have no clue," Ryan said, stopping to admire the black Ferrari 360 convertible parked in Erin's spot. He'd never had much of an affinity for cars, but he knew he was in store for a fun ride.

Marie, unfortunately, was a slow driver.

"The speed limit is 40, just so you know," Ryan commented a minute later as he watched a minivan pass him on the right.

"I just learned to drive last year," Marie scrunched her nose at him, her lips smacking together. "I grew up in Paris. I took the metro everywhere."

"How old are you again?"

"I am 23. How old are you?"

"Thirty-two. How old is Salazar?"

"Luis?" she asked, as if she didn't know his last name. "Forty-three." She kept her eyes on the road, avoiding his disapproving stare. Ryan grunted a laugh and leaned back, feeling the air course through his short hair.

"Do you want to go back to the FBI?" Marie asked after a moment of awkward silence.

"Yes, definitely. I'm just waiting for the word."

"The *word*," she said, processing the statement. Her fingers tapped on the steering wheel as she turned a corner. "So you do not want to work for Luis?"

"Is that what this meeting is for? He's going to ask me to work for him?"

"I do not know. He did not say," Marie shrugged. "He only tells me certain things."

"I see," Ryan paused. "No, I have no plans to work for him."

"He seems very interested in you. He talks more about you than he does me."

"I'm a very handsome guy."

Marie smiled wide and threw him a look out of the corner of her eyes.

"He strikes me as eccentric. Eccentric people tend to get fixated on things."

Marie's smile faded, but she nodded in agreement. The light turned yellow ahead, and Ryan prepared for a quick stop. Instead, she accelerated through the intersection.

"What do you remember from your disappearance?" she turned to look at him. Though he should have expected it by now, the question took him off guard. He straightened in his seat, glanced at a mother and her toddler walking down the side of the road, and replied, "Nothing. Not a damn thing."

"It does not make any sense."

"You're telling me. It feels like I'm dreaming right now."

Marie looked at him again, waiting for him to explain. He realized that she wasn't going to look back at the road until he did. "It's hard to explain. I'm here, but I feel like I'm somewhere else. Or like I'm watching myself from behind a window. Know what I mean?"

"No," Marie giggled.

"Well, that's how I feel," Ryan stated, surprised he was opening up to her. "But don't tell anyone. That's top secret."

"I made the same promise to Erin last night," Marie turned onto the Magnolia bridge. The bridge, a rickety concrete and iron erection that rose quickly from sea level, curled off to the left and into the hilly suburbs. She gunned the engine, finally letting the vehicle breathe. Her attention on the road before her, Ryan watched her hands, how they gently curled around the black steering wheel, barely touching it. Her skin looked soft, inviting.

As she curved around the southern stretch of Magnolia hill, an affluent neighborhood to the northwest of downtown Seattle, Ryan noticed that she was glancing at him every few seconds. The corner of her lips were once again curled into that smirk of hers, too. He had to force himself to look away.

Marie cut the engine in front of Salazar's gated property. Much of Magnolia was a suburban community, but it was also home to steep cliffs that plunged precipitously to small, rocky beaches that grasped at Puget Sound. Salazar's home was situated at the end of a narrow road that housed one mansion after the next, grand structures with large bay windows that took in the majestic views of Elliott Bay.

Salazar's mansion was exceedingly grand, though Ryan could only see parts of it through the bigleaf maples that spotted his front yard. Despite being one of the richest men in the northwest, his security seemed lax; the stone wall that bordered his property was five-feet tall at most, the iron gate unexceptionally standard.

Marie climbed out of the car and as she approached the gate, it opened silently and automatically.

"Thanks for the ride," he came up alongside her.

"*Merci*," she said matter-of-factly, and he got the sense their chitchat was over. She skipped onto the front step and opened the door, gesturing to him to follow. The inside was pleasantly cool, and surprisingly plain. A nondescript painting hung on the wall directly in front of him, but the lighting was so dim he could hardly see it.

Marie disappeared down a hallway to the right, but this time Ryan got the impression that he wasn't to follow. His assumptions were confirmed when, just as quickly as Marie had vanished, Luis Salazar came around the corner with an expression of mild surprise, as if he hadn't planned to run into him at that exact moment. "Ryan Harper! Good to see you."

Salazar motioned to the hallway. Ryan followed him into a large room that could, more or less, be described as a living room. The fish pool in the middle of the room caught his eye, but beyond the ornate sculptures and darkly painted canvases that lined the walls, he found himself drawn to the large bay windows and the view beyond.

Salazar continued through to the kitchen to a vast, red-stained deck at the back of the house.

"I hope it wasn't an inconvenience to come out here?"

"I'm suspended, remember," Ryan replied. "Not much to do."

"How's the investigation going?" Salazar walked between two sets of beach chairs and arced to the right.

"What investigation?"

Salazar laughed, but his smile quickly faded. "You of all people aren't sitting around twiddling your thumbs while your girlfriend does all the work."

"Fair enough. I have a few ideas, but too early to tell."

Ryan thought Salazar was going to press for more information, but instead he stopped and spread his arms wide.

"Impressive view," Ryan commented. The blue waters of Elliott Bay glistened before them, Seattle to the east and Mount Rainer in the distance.

"Amazing view," Salazar corrected. "In more ways than one."

He was right. Marie had emerged from the house, now stripped down to a pink polka dot bikini that left little to the imagination. She tossed a copy of *Us Weekly* on a pool chair and, over her bronze shoulder, threw a glance and smile at the two men.

A streaking pain suddenly shot from one eye to the other. The sky and deck spun. He was in a hallway, the naked redhead running playfully away from him toward a doorway. She nudged the door open with her shoulder and then turned to gaze at him, her large eyes flashing. She giggled, her tongue sticking out between her teeth.

"Agent Harper?" Marie's smile faded. She looked concerned. He realized he was in Salazar's arms.

"Have a seat," Salazar led him to a nearby chair. "I'll get you a drink."

"I'm fine," Ryan straightened up. His whole body burned. "Every once in a while I remember something, ever so brief. Sort of just hits me." He immediately regretted saying anything. He didn't want the FBI to know about his nightmares, let alone a stranger he'd met the night before.

"I hope it was something good," Marie said as she approached, still looking worried.

"It was, I think," he shrugged. "Images come and go so quickly it's hard to tell."

"So your psychiatric records aren't too far from the truth then," Salazar muttered. Ryan shot him a hard look.

"With connections like mine, you shouldn't be surprised that I can get access to just about anything."

"I'm not," Ryan said. "I'm surprised you thought I'd be okay with you looking at my records."

Salazar seemed indifferent to the comment. "I'm trying to help you. I use the assets at my disposable to do so."

"Why are you trying to help me again?" Ryan noticed that Marie had shied away from the conversation and returned to her lounge chair. Though she'd put a pair of earbuds on, her iPod wasn't playing. She was listening intently.

"I told you…"

"I know what you told me," Ryan looked Salazar dead in the eyes. "But I don't buy into that I'm just a charity case, the latest cause for Luis Salazar."

Salazar chuckled and shrugged defeat. "I swear, that is a reason. But sure, I have other motivations as well."

"I can't be bought."

"*Anyone* can be bought," Salazar raised an eyebrow, confident in his response. "But I don't need or want to buy you. You're a respectable man, Ryan. As am I. One of the best in the bureau from what I hear. It's simply a matter of me having the capability to help you, and if you deem that it's worth a favor down the road, then so be it. A friendly favor, nothing else. I'm sure even you have exchanged a few favors for friends." Salazar stepped forward and put a firm hand on Ryan's shoulder. "I'm going to help you get your job back no matter what. You can take it and run or offer a helping hand if need be. It's your call, and I won't think any less of you regardless."

Ryan studied the billionaire. He seemed truly intent on getting his job back for him, and what he asked in return was pennies. Still, it was hard to tell if he was sincere.

"Luis, you have a phone call," came a man's voice, slightly accented. Ryan glanced over his shoulder to see a gray-faced man standing by the edge of the pool. The gaunt figure had thin, purple lips and large bags under his eyes, his sharp features indicating Eastern European descent. Brown, straggly hair was combed straight back, revealing a thinning scalp. As unimposing as he appeared, his calculating black eyes indicated his greatest assets weren't ones that could be seen. As Ryan studied him, the man threw him a piercing stare.

"Please excuse me," Salazar spun on his heels and started toward the house. He stopped a few feet later. "Oh, Ryan, this is Sergey, my close friend and chief counsel. He's been with me for years."

"Pleasure to meet you," Sergey and Ryan met halfway to shake hands. As they approached one another, Ryan had the nagging suspicion that he'd seen Sergey before. He had no memories to back the feeling, but there was something strangely familiar about him.

"Were you at the banquet last night?" Ryan took in his features.

Sergey shook his head. "I was tending to other things."

Just then, an ear-shattering scream rang through his skull, and Ryan threw his hands up to block the sound. The screeching continued, and Ryan gasped, feeling the sweat and tears coming. Sergey, Marie, the pool, the house, the view all vanished. A gunshot went off, but there was nothing but intense whiteness. He felt hands on him—all over him—trying to tear away a piece of him. Then they were carrying him. He struggled, but it made no difference.

He was back in the car, staring at his old house from across the street. The screeching continued, nauseatingly loud. *Make it stop*, he shouted, but there was nothing he could do. He opened the car door and crossed the street, his movements noiseless as he approached the front door.

He looked to the right and could see the darkness coming for him, the abyss consuming everything. He screamed, knowing what was to come. He tried to run, but instead he kept walking to the front door. The darkness embraced him, and the light was gone.

An orb appeared in the distance.

18

THE SATELLITE PHOTOGRAPHS taken the night Ryan disappeared had been doctored. Erin knew, even before Yusuf told them. She could tell by the way he was establishing the scene, explaining the details before getting to the point.

"So the pictures have been altered," John tried to evoke an answer from Yusuf, also well aware of the tech's mannerisms.

"I've had my algorithms pouring over the photos for the last two days," Yusuf ignored John's plea for directness, pacing back and forth in front of his computer. It was rare for him to be out of his chair, let alone not staring at one of his several monitors. "The algorithms look for digital variations in photographs. In other words, pixilation where there shouldn't be pixilation."

He picked up the hard copies of the photographs and placed them on a table in the middle of the room. He immediately began flipping through them one by one. They were in order, each timestamp exactly five minutes after the next. "There are no missing slides, no gaps in the chronology. That would be too obvious."

Yusuf started going through the photos one by one, retracing Ryan's steps to John and Erin. Though they knew the sequence of events better than anyone, they watched intently, drawn in by Yusuf's excitement.

The young man stopped on the photo where Ryan and Morgan had vanished. His eyes danced over the photos.

"What is it?" John asked impatiently. Erin leaned forward, desperately hoping she'd miraculously spot the two between the dark trees. Of course, she saw nothing.

Yusuf flipped to the next photograph. "Nothing. There's nothing wrong with these pictures,"

"Are you fucking kidding me?" John spun around on his heels, throwing his arms up into the air.

Yusuf grinned, and Erin knew that "nothing" was not actually "nothing."

He returned to the first slide where the two men had disappeared. Dozens of people had looked at these photographs and none of them had had any luck finding anything out of the ordinary. Computers had done the same, comparing pixel to pixel. And yet Yusuf had found something.

His finger slid to the explosion. Erin and John leaned in, studying it carefully, the way the flames and smoke swirled upward and then drifted to the northeast. Yusuf flipped through a few more of the photographs, demonstrating how the cloud slowly grew and eventually dissipated. He returned to the slide where they'd vanished once more, and then the photograph after that.

"The smoke hasn't moved. It hasn't grown or shifted direction or thinned."

That wasn't much to go on. Yusuf knew it. "Look at the people," he said.

John and Erin compared the people in the two slides, all of whom appeared as nothing more than ants. The clearing where the cabin had been was well lit, and they could see several agents standing at its outskirts. In the previous slide, they were in the exact same position. Every single one of them.

"If you're still not convinced, it's the helicopters that seal the deal." Erin eyed a helicopter, which had broken into view from the southeast shortly after the explosion occurred. Through the series of photographs, it slowly traveled north, toward where Ryan had pursued Morgan through the woods, but then veered west, beginning a search pattern. She hadn't paid much attention to it, its presence unimportant.

But on the two photographs in question, the helicopter had not moved. It was conceivable that it could have slowed to investigate something on the ground, but it was in the exact same spot in both shots. Even the rotors hadn't moved. She checked the timestamps; they showed two different times, five minutes apart.

"They're the same photograph," Yusuf declared. "No one else noticed, but no one else looked in the right spot. We've all been so focused on the region where Harper and Christopher Morgan disappeared—that's where the point of alteration would have happened—that we didn't look at the most obvious landmarks."

Someone had effectively deleted ten minutes of events from the only reliable physical record available.

Her mind racing, Erin didn't know what to say.

"How could the analysts—hell, the computers—miss something like that?" John asked angrily.

"The simple answer is that we were looking for alterations within the picture itself. The logarithms overlooked something as basic as repeating a photo two frames in a row. It's very old school."

"Jesus," John murmured. Erin was still stunned. "So someone hacked into a government mainframe and modified the data in the fifty hours it took for us to get our hands on it. That's some quick turnaround time."

Yusuf put his hands behind his head and breathed out. "Wait for the complicated answer. Maybe someone hacked into the system. They probably did. But you asked how the computers missed something like this… They shouldn't have. I ran pixilation logarithms first and didn't get anything, but doing a quick variance analysis on the pictures—you know, comparing each one to determine how much changes from frame to frame—returned a red flag in about five minutes."

"What are you saying?" Erin asked.

"Any half-assed analyst would have done that test sooner than later. And yet, nothing. We got back an approved analysis report with no significant findings whatsoever. It's bullshit. We didn't find anything because no one looked at the pictures. Not like what the report says."

"Who's the lead analyst on the report?" John glanced at Erin, concerned.

"Harold Li. He was two years ahead of me at MIT, a really smart guy. I gave him a call, and he never looked at the imagery. The whole report is bullshit. The pictures were never analyzed, and yet an FBI report made its way to us. The hacker who changed the pictures doesn't bother me—it's the person who has the power, and the guts, to manipulate an FBI case like this. Whoever it is had intimate access to our case files and probably access to the imagery to begin with."

"OK," John whistled. "Yusuf, better keep this close to the chest. For the time being."

"I don't want to end up dead," he raised his hands in defeat. "I'll shut up until you tell me otherwise."

"Good," Erin stated, unable to believe what she was hearing. "The report had to come from somewhere. There has to be a paper trail or something."

"I'm on it," Yusuf nodded. He dropped into his chair and started typing.

Erin felt John's hand against her forearm, and she turned to see him close to her, his eyes deathly serious. In a harsh whisper, he said, "Whatever's going on here, we need to remain focused on the real question at hand. We're getting closer to the *how*, but we have to keep asking ourselves *why*? Ryan was taken and returned for a reason, and we still have no clue why. There's an endgame to all this."

He'd said something similar before, but this time she believed him.

19

RYAN AWOKE, GASPING for air. He felt hot and damp, and his head hurt. His vision was momentarily blurred, but when his eyes focused he found himself staring up at a ceiling he didn't recognize. A ceiling fan whipped around gently, its effects minimal given the degree of air conditioning in the room. Though his body burned, the room itself felt cold.

He was lying on his back on a bed. He groaned and started to push himself up, but Marie appeared above him, her face only inches from his. "Stay down," she said, and he obeyed.

"How long was I out?"

"Two hours or so," she paused to think about it for a moment, her nose crinkling.

"Jesus," he sighed. Marie shifted her weight and started dabbing at his chest. "Where are my clothes?"

"You are still wearing your pants," she flirtatiously cocked her head to one side, acknowledging the awkwardness of the situation. "But you were burning up. I thought your head was going to blow up. We brought you in here—one of the guest bedrooms."

"Thanks," Ryan said.

Marie's smile widened, as if she'd just won a gold star in kindergarten. "At one point, I wanted to be a nurse."

He tried to move again, and this time Marie didn't stop him. He sat up, the room momentarily swaying, the pressure immense against his temples. But the vertigo quickly receded and his headache dulled to the point where he could stand up on his own. Marie waited patiently by his side.

"Where's Luis?"

"He had to go back to the office. A meeting. He wanted me to tell you…" she paused, trying to remember. "That he was sorry, but glad you are okay. He said he will have someone call to reschedule a time."

Can't wait, Ryan thought to himself. Marie noticed his expression but shrugged, and then motioned with her head for him to follow.

"What do you dream of?" she asked as they entered a wide hallway. "When you pass out?"

"I don't know," Ryan lied. "I don't remember much."

Marie put one hand on her hip and cocked her body accordingly, casting him a dubious stare. "You don't remember anything?"

"Bits and pieces, really. Nothing of significance." For some reason, he felt guilty lying to Marie. Her child-like nature begged for openness, but he couldn't bring himself to tell her the truth.

The truth was that he remembered every second of his nightmares. Eerily so. The naked redhead running down the hall. Erin sitting in their old house. The wall of black racing toward him, then engulfing him. The whispers. The orb that became the Face. The Face.

He blinked, trying to shake the image. The very thought of the Face had caused him to start sweating again. He didn't know what it was or what it represented. Was it real, or a trick of the mind? Then again, who was the redhead? He had memories of her and yet he couldn't remember her. He wouldn't just forget someone like her. Did it mean something? Did the redhead know about him, about his disappearance?

"You must remember something," Marie insisted once they had returned to her car. "Do the dreams give you clues about where you were?"

Ryan smiled, appreciating her tenacity. She smiled back, her hair bouncing in the wind. "Nothing of use. I'm in a dark room, but it's all warped. None of it really makes sense. I can hear these whispers all around me, but they don't make sense either." He wasn't going to tell her about the Face.

"What do you smell? I was taught to use all senses."

That was the first time anyone had asked him that. "Just a faint smell. Some kind of chemical, but I can't even describe it."

"Hmm," she murmured to herself, pondering the comment. After a long pause, she asked, "Do you feel safe?"

"Safe?"

"Safe," she repeated, annunciating the word as best she could. "Do you think the worst is over?"

"I sure as hell hope so," he laughed, but was surprised by the line of questioning.

"Tell me," she looked at him. "Did you want to meet with Luis? Was it your idea?"

"Definitely not." He wasn't laughing anymore.

"You should be careful…" her eyes returned to the road. The words faded in the wind as if she had committed to speaking them and then changed her mind at the last second. "…around him. He always has an agenda. Always wants something."

She shrugged off her comment as if it were no big deal, like she was some foolish girl giving bad advice, but Ryan knew she meant what she had said. He thought about pushing her to explain but had the feeling she would not indulge him. They drove the rest of the way in silence.

20

LUIS SALAZAR POURED himself a glass of scotch, set the open bottle down on the deck and leaned back. He put the glass to his lips and closed his eyes, smelling the strong musk of the aged whiskey. A pleasant breeze rippled over the deck of his boat, and he breathed in the salty air.

His 75-foot Viking Sport Cruiser rocked gently, and Luis looked around. Puget Sound sparkled in the early evening sun, the water a deep but majestic blue. The water was surprisingly calm even for a beautiful day such as this, and aside from the sound of a jet rumbling miles overhead, all he could hear were the harmless waves slapping against the hull. He was miles from shore, the nearest boat a distant car ferry that glided silently along the surface.

It was days like these that allowed him to forget the shit storms he had to deal with.

Luis drank half his glass with one gulp. Things had been calm for months; the press had grown bored and moved onto other, better things. Chandling's approval ratings were up and his party was in control of the Senate. The man had carried a vital bill to victory, and with it billions in dollars of revenue for his firm. He'd also started fucking one of the hottest women on the planet.

Things had been calm for months, but nothing lasted forever. Ryan Harper had returned from out of nowhere, bringing with him a world of pain and suffering that Luis had hoped was long behind him. When Harper had vanished, the threat of discovery had faded, for Morgan had also vanished. The killer was dead, and there was nothing more to say about it.

Until now. The press had returned, with more fervor than ever. Where had Ryan Harper been? Who was holding him captive all this time? Was that person connected to Christopher Morgan, and in turn the murder of Senator Chandling's family?

The answers to those questions weren't pleasant. Especially not for him.

SHE BOARDED THE boat silently, her ascension to the aft deck slow and deliberate. Every place she put her hands, her feet, everywhere she looked and listened, was planned. There were no missteps, nothing left to chance. With only a faint pitter-patter of water dripping from her wetsuit, the woman strode to starboard and ascended the stairs to the upper deck. Her left palm slid casually along the hardwood rail.

"Who's there?" the billionaire mumbled as if waking from a dream.

Her nostrils flared. She could smell the alcohol, even through the black neoprene mask that covered her face.

Salazar moved sluggishly at first, the scotch weighing heavily on him. He was camped on a chair near stern on the starboard side, wearing nothing but red-and-white swimming trunks. His typically tan chest was a rosy pink, his nose a darker shade. His black hair was windswept.

The man looked over as if expecting a friend, but a friend he didn't see. She was dressed in a black wetsuit, only her hands and feet exposed. Her mask hid her hair, face and neck, save for the oval aperture for her eyes. The plastic, custom-made pistol attached to her belt only added to her ominous appearance.

The billionaire sobered up quickly, but not quickly enough. Startled, he tried to stand, but before he could utter a word she'd crossed the deck, grabbed him by the neck and thrown him to port. The 43-year-old body slammed hard against the base of another deck chair, and he crumpled to the floor in shock.

She took a step toward him and he looked up, his eyes wide with fear. His body trembled.

"Tell me what I want to know," the woman hissed.

"What do you want?" he cried.

"You know," she said softly, easing back momentarily. Then, with amazing intensity, she shouted, "Ryan Harper! What did you do to him?"

Salazar's eyes bulged at the name, and for a moment his lower lip quivered. But then he collected himself, pushed up on his right arm and gazed at her with all the sincerity the liar could muster. "I have nothing to do with that."

The woman growled and kicked out, striking the billionaire's arm. He lost his leverage and collapsed to the deck once more, grunting on impact. Before he knew it, she was on top of him. He rolled to look up at her, and was met with a swiping fist to the face.

"Tell me what you did to Ryan Harper," she growled in his sunburned ear.

He laughed, in shock, blood trickling from his gums. "He just showed up one day. You know as much about him as I do." Impressive, she thought. Though he'd expressed the truth in that first half-second of her attack, he'd taken control of his emotions almost immediately. Even under duress, he was refusing to tell the truth. That wouldn't last long.

"Liar." Though her anger was, for the most part, feigned, she never let this pathetic man see it. She grabbed him by the neck and collar bone, squeezing flesh, bone and sweat to get a hold, and pulled him to his feet. She dragged him a couple meters and then hurled him forward like a rag doll. His body sailed over the deck's windshield and landed with a satisfying crunch on the slanted windows of the lower deck. He rolled clumsily until he lay in a crumpled heap near the bow. He moaned in pain.

The woman took her time. She stepped up and over the windshield, crossed the white roof and then hopped down to the bow deck. The deck, nearly 35 meters in length, was encompassed by a fragile metal rail. Just like before, there was nowhere for the billionaire to go but in the water.

"Tell me, or I'll make you swim to shore," she strolled over to him, casting a long shadow across his torso. Salazar had rolled onto his back and was squinting up at her, his breathing unsteady and painful. He'd broken a rib.

"I don't know what happened to him," he said breathlessly.

"That's strange," the woman stepped over him and kneeled down, raising her right fist to strike him once more. She enjoyed punching him, she realized.

"No! Please, no!" the billionaire whimpered, raising his hands to protect himself. He was wailing now, tears streaming from his eyes faster than blood left his nose and mouth. "Please, I don't know what happened to him."

"What *do* you know?"

"Please don't hurt me anymore…"

"Tell me, Luis." She hissed his name.

"I didn't want him kidnapped. Hell, I didn't want him coming back. I wanted him dead." The truth, she observed.

"Why?"

"He was getting too close to the truth. I couldn't let that happen."

So it was true. Salazar really was responsible for something so heinous. Harper's investigation had taken a dangerous course, so dangerous that he had been cautious enough not to reveal his findings to his own agency, the FBI, nor even those closest to him—his girlfriend and his partner. But Salazar found out anyway, and decided to take matters into his own hands.

"You sick bastard," she sneered. "You sick, sick bastard. So you hired Christopher Morgan?"

"What? No. No! I didn't hire him."

"Who did you hire?"

The billionaire looked up at her with pleading eyes.

"Tell me!" she raised her fist again.

The billionaire looked at her fist with amazing clarity, and then back at her. He shook his head. She punched him quick and hard. He let out a loud gasp, but then shook his head once more. She struck him again. His body trembled worse than ever, and she felt the warmth of urine against her left foot. He shook his head violently.

He wasn't going to say, but she knew enough for now.

She punched him again, this time in the temple. The billionaire blacked out.

A HALF HOUR later and several miles away, the woman with blond hair sat behind the wheel of her boat, the bow rising and falling as she skipped over the water's surface at breakneck speed. Her palms barely on the wheel, hair whipping wildly behind her, she was preparing for what was to come. It had gone on long enough, and the return of Ryan Harper had made things much more interesting. She needed to accelerate things, put things into motion. She'd guaranteed that. The battle was coming soon.

Her headset rang. She killed the engine, the boat lurching to a drift on the crest of its own swell. Two rings sounded before someone answered.

"What's wrong?" Sergey. The lawyer. He was more than that.

"I want him dead," the billionaire screamed. His voice was slurred. The concussion.

"What happened?"

"I was attacked. I want him dead. Now."

"Who?"

"You know who. Ryan Harper. I want him dead."

21

ERIN KINSLEY WATCHED her boyfriend out of the corner of her eye as her 2010 Toyota Prius hobbled along the dirt-and-gravel road. Ryan was focused on the world around him, captivated by the tall Oregon trees and off-and-on underbrush as if he were a child watching his first television show. The only difference—there was no eagerness in his expression, only scrutiny and study. His eyes scanned the area that he'd passed through just over six months ago, looking for something to trigger lost memories.

She parked the car. It was warm, but the trees provided shade. Branches shook from a wind that didn't reach the ground. There was a dustiness to the air, and dandelion seeds drifted aimlessly. Erin couldn't see how any of this would remind him of what happened; it didn't even look familiar to her. She remembered cold air, mud, gas fumes and darkness, not summer greens, sunlight and the smell of pine trees.

Ryan only had second-hand memories of the cabin assault that had almost taken her life. The story was only as complete as what others knew, which meant it wasn't complete at all.

They walked the short trail to where the cabin used to be. Remnants of yellow police tape hung from trees, though most had long since been stripped away. Ryan took his time, stopping occasionally to look into the distance as if trying to spot a memory hiding behind the trees. But then he'd continue on, saying nothing, and Erin opted not to disturb him.

Only the foundation of the cabin remained, a few charred beams and a patch of lifeless dirt. The rest of the structure had been vaporized upon detonation or removed by Forensics.

Erin found herself staring at the spot as well. It was eerie, seeing the place where she'd almost died. She never had seen the cabin intact—not from the outside anyway—but she remembered it vividly. Scrambling through the hole in the floor, the rotting wood crumbling before her. Her body falling into the darkness, her eyes flashing to the grass just feet away. Shouting for her friends to go away. Heat so intense she thought she was going to disintegrate. Screaming—her own screams. Chaos. Pain.

Now, the scene was tranquil, natural, the horror washed away.

She showed him where Radly, Halsbrooke and the others were killed, and he nodded as if his memories were clicking into place. But Ryan soon grew anxious, and she led him into the woods. Though only a few bits of police tape remained here and there to mark his path, she'd walked this stretch so many times in the months following his disappearance that every step was second nature.

As they approached the hillside that Ryan had climbed to nowhere, she realized that he had started to lead her.

"No, I just know it's this way," he said when she asked if he remembered.

They reached the bottom of the hill, a large slope of rock, gravel and dirt. Casings and Ryan's earpiece had been found there. Ryan started climbing, weaving between boulders and shooting toward the southeast edge of the tree line, exactly where the FBI had deduced he'd entered. Erin followed him closely.

Once back in the woods, Ryan paused once more, his hand running over a small tree. The bullet hole in the bark was still clearly visible. He pressed on, and they soon arrived at the clearing where Ryan's trail had ended.

RYAN IMMEDIATELY RECOGNIZED the clearing, even though he had no memory of it. It was larger than what the satellite imagery had suggested, almost the size of a football field, with tall, swaying grass and remnants of tire treads. The ground rose swiftly on the far side, even steeper than the first hill they'd climbed.

"We know you didn't leave via the road," he heard Erin behind him. "We already had its only exit blocked a quarter mile down. There weren't any fresh tire marks to indicate an escape vehicle."

He wasn't listening to her. The ground, the sky, the trees… they were all swirling. He squeezed his eyes shut and then reopened them, hoping it would stop. It didn't. He closed his eyes again, gasping for air, feeling the sweat trickle from his temples. When he tried to open them again, it made no difference.

The sunken eyes of the Face began to take form. He shook, his mind catapulting back to that night six months ago. He fell to the ground, blood erupting from his nose. He felt weight on top of him and turned reflexively to block a blow.

A slit formed across the Face, its lipless mouth moving incoherently. The whispers thundered, as if a thousand voices were shouting at him all at once and yet hardly making a sound. He squirmed, trying to look away, but couldn't. He was drawn to the mouth, watching the wretched gap quiver with each breathless word.

"Then stop talking and shoot me!" he heard his own voice. A gunshot, the kick of the weapon in his hand. An adrenaline rush, a high feeling. The darkness vanished, replaced by dazzling, intense whiteness. The air buzzed, sizzling with electricity.

Figures surrounded him, silhouettes against the nothingness. The brightness hid their true forms, white-on-white ghosts. Someone grabbed his shoulder and he turned to look, but nothing was there, and he was no longer in pain or in the woods. The Face's mouth consumed him, the bottomless gap only inches from his. The whispers were louder than ever, a constant screech. He tried to cover his ears, but his hands couldn't find his head. The noise was unbearable.

And then there was silence and the Face spoke, though the movement of the mouth was out of sync with the faint whisper that was its voice, "Don't tell her."

RYAN SNAPPED FROM his dream, his hallucination, in an instant, unleashing a loud gasp as his body relaxed. He was sweating profusely from head to toe, his clothes soaked, skin burning. Erin knelt beside him, holding him steady where he'd fallen, her hands on his shoulders. He was ashen, as if his soul had been torn from his body.

"It's okay," she told him. "It's okay, you're back."

His breathing calmed, and he began to cry, ashamed and embarrassed and frightened all at once. He could see she was devastated as well. She wrapped her arms around him. He squeezed back, burrowing his face in her neck.

"The Face told me something this time," he said.

"What?" she asked.

"It told me not to tell you. That's all."

"Not to tell me what?"

Ryan shrugged.

"So why'd you tell me?"

"Why wouldn't I tell you?" he withdrew from her and smiled faintly. "No fucking way am I listening to some creepy alien face."

She smiled. "If you don't, they might come back to implant an anal probe or something."

"Hmm, I didn't think about that," he said. "Let's get the hell out of here."

22

THEY CHECKED INTO a small place called the Ashlane Motel, which sat at the base of Mt. Hood about fifty miles east of Portland. The motel, a quaint, unremarkable lodging sitting against Route 26, was the only place to stay in Rhododendron, an eye-blinker-sized community.

Ryan threw their bags on the bed, went into the bathroom and reemerged twenty-five minutes later looking refreshed and wearing nothing but a towel. Erin, who'd spent the time flipping channels, grinned at the sight of him. His straw-colored hair was darkened from the shower, condensation still on his washboard abs. He smiled at her teasingly and whipped off the towel.

"Don't get any ideas, Agent Kinsley," he said. "My stomach is grumbling and I'll have nothing stand in my way, even a sexy woman such as yourself."

"I'd rather have food than you any day of the week," Erin huffed. She switched the television off and turned away, feigning disinterest. "The restaurant across the street?"

"I don't think we have much of a choice."

After Ryan dressed, they crossed the two-lane highway and entered a small diner with a log cabin exterior and faux wood paneling interior. A tall plastic plant and two fold-out metal chairs served as the waiting area. Smoking was no longer permitted, but the air was stuffy. Still, it smelled of food and Ryan was undeterred.

"Sit wherever you like," a young, plump waitress called to them from across the room. They sat down near the front window and waited for her to finish attending to another couple.

"There's something else about my dream," Ryan told Erin. "Right before I snapped out of it—this last time—I saw people. Or at least I assume they were people."

"But 'people,' as in many?"

"I don't know how many. Three, maybe four. And then one grabs my shoulder, so there may be more. Who knows? But they were there with me, in that clearing." He breathed out, then said, "But it's just a dream, so who knows if it means anything…"

"The dreams you're having are way too real for them to mean nothing. If you see people in that clearing, then I believe there were other people in that clearing."

"Which is fine, except there's no evidence of anyone else being out in those woods," Ryan looked up at the waitress as she brought them a couple of waters.

"Had a chance to look at the menu?"

"No, but I'll get the biggest cheeseburger you have. Medium, please."

"I'll get the same," Erin said. The waitress hurried away. "You're wrong about no one else being in the field—we found something in the photos."

Anger flickered across his face. It wasn't the reaction she'd been expecting.

"What do you mean?" Ryan's eyes blazed. "When the hell were you going to tell me this?"

"Yusuf just figured it out," she said defensively. She explained Yusuf's discovery and the possible implications, that someone in the government had altered case files to cover up the truth. "I wanted you to visit Oregon before telling you anything. I wanted to see what you remembered."

"You should have told me," he said venomously. "You shouldn't have kept this to yourself."

"Listen, I want to find out what happened to you as much as anyone," Erin reached across and took his hand reassuringly. "But even if we never figure out what happened, at least you're back. We're together. You're fine."

"I'm not fine," he interjected tersely, his lips pressed tight. "I have nightmares every fucking night, and now I'm starting to have them when I'm awake."

"The nightmares will go away in time… The therapy will help."

"But how long? A month? A year? I don't know if I can handle this for a year. These nightmares… they're like nothing you can ever imagine. It's like being wide awake in some horror movie, only you can't run or defend yourself. And the Face…" He lowered his voice. A couple of patrons were watching him. "It scares me just thinking about it."

"Ryan, I've never seen anything you can't handle. This is just another obstacle you have to overcome." Stay positive, she told herself. Ryan had always been confident of a positive outcome no matter how dire the situation. But he was different now. He was exhausted, frustrated with himself. She couldn't imagine him struggling through a year of constant nightmares and restless nights. She couldn't imagine herself doing the same.

"And I've never lost my temper the way I do every day. Ever. What's that about?"

"Lack of sleep, that's all…"

He laughed, but it was more mocking than anything else. "Don't kid yourself. I nearly punched a hole in the wall the other night over some petty argument. I don't even remember what we were arguing about. That's not normal. That's not me."

Ryan leaned forward, as if to tell a secret. "There's something different about me.

I don't know what it is, but I feel different. We're sitting here, but all of this"—he motioned to the diner— "doesn't feel right. Like *this* is the dream."

"I'LL BE RIGHT back," Erin said suddenly and scooted out of the booth. Ryan knew he had upset her, but let her go. She wasn't angry at him. Just the situation. And why shouldn't she be? He was royally fucked up in the head, and she was the one who had to put up with it. They'd never been an emotional couple, but now they were arguing more than ever and she was running to the bathroom crying like a little girl. They'd always trusted each other, too, but how could she fully trust him now? He could snap at any moment.

"Here's your food, darling," the waitress arrived with two burgers.

"Thanks," he examined his burger. It looked pretty ordinary, but the fries looked great.

He did not really trust Erin either. Not completely. She was reporting back to the FBI on what he said and did; hell, she could be in the bathroom right now calling Monroe about what he'd just told her. Everyone was always talking about him. Ever since he'd been back, that's all they did. Everyone wanted a piece of him.

Shit, he thought. He had to keep his mouth shut. He wasn't going to get better until he got back onto the job and into his normal routine, but he wasn't going to have a chance at that until he was better. He had to feign normalcy, even if that meant lying to Erin. And John.

John. His partner, his best friend, the son of a bitch. What a great partner he'd been. But now, it seemed as though John scrutinized everything he said, trying to decipher a hidden meaning or code. His own goddamned partner didn't trust him.

Ryan gazed out the window. The sky had just a tinge of evening light. Traffic remained sporadic, a few cars whizzing by per minute. A squirrel sat at the edge of the highway, frozen, contemplating. A sedan idled across the road, below the hotel sign. The driver's door was open and two men stood beside it, a map unfolded before them. The men didn't look like casual traveling companions. Neither looked at the map.

"You waited for me?" Erin returned from the bathroom having splashed water on her face. "You're such a gentleman," she teased.

"Always," Ryan said. As he and Erin ate their food, he studied her. She was the woman he loved, the woman he desired, and yet that love, that desire, now felt flat. He was in love with a version of her that didn't exist in his new reality. None of what he remembered existed here. He needed to return, to confront whatever was holding him back. Erin would only remain patient for so much longer.

THE AIR WAS uncomfortably cold when Erin awoke. Lying on her stomach, she blindly pulled the bed sheets over her bare shoulders. She gazed across the bed at the air conditioner beneath the room's sole window, the metallic box humming violently.

For a moment, she convinced herself that something good had happened, but then she remembered the frustration from hours earlier. Shaking his head, Ryan had rolled onto his back, apologizing and then cursing himself to sleep. He still wasn't functioning the way either of them wanted.

A shadow passed in front of the window, another hotel patron. It was still night, Erin realized, the only light from outside the orange glow emanating from the parking lot. She closed her eyes and rolled onto her side, reaching for Ryan's warmth. He wasn't in bed. She sat up to find Ryan sitting at the small desk in the corner, combing through case files.

As much as she needed the pleasure he'd once provided, she understood and was willing to be patient. No matter how many times she told him, he didn't see it that way. He was a wreck and his impotence was just another element to cause him stress.

She found her top and shorts on the floor beside her and then slinked over to Ryan. When she placed her hands on his shoulders, he momentarily tensed, taken off guard.

"What are you doing up?" he glanced at her but his focus remained on the large stack of papers.

"Have another nightmare?"

"No," he said. "I didn't want to put it to the test."

Erin frowned. "You've got to get some sleep at some point."

"I've been reading about Morgan again," he ignored her. "About his military career."

Morgan's short stint in the Army was the last well-documented part of his life. He served for a short while in the Gulf War, predominantly as a sniper. He was considered an excellent shot, but had a reputation for bucking authority and quarreling with fellow soldiers. After he was injured in a skirmish, he spent several weeks in a Kuwaiti hospital before being discharged for psychiatric reasons. What those reasons were remained unclear as most of the documentation had been lost in a fire and the psychiatrist that treated him died years ago, but Morgan reportedly grew increasingly paranoid as the war went on, resulting in "antisocial and counterproductive behavior."

After the war, he worked briefly in Arkansas doing various forms of manual labor before slipping off the grid in late 1993. During that time, connections were established with a variety of underground organizations, including anti-government groups that appealed to his growing resentment of the military. But his dealings with such groups were poorly documented. He never raised serious red flags.

"No credit cards, bank accounts or parking tickets for almost twenty years," Ryan commented. "That's pretty impressive."

"He didn't want to be found and did a good job of it."

During the FBI's investigation into Morgan, evidence was found linking him to several crimes throughout the United States. However, at the time of the crimes he had never been considered a suspect.

"Come on," Erin leaned over him and wrapped her arms around his neck. "Come back to bed."

He reluctantly stood up, turning into her arms. She pecked him on the lips and then withdrew, teasingly biting her bottom lip. He showed little emotion, his face impossible to read, but his hands slid up her thighs and hooked around her hips. She gasped as he picked her off the ground and threw her on the bed. He calmly turned off the lamp, cloaking the room in relative darkness, and then slid onto the mattress next to her, his hands returning.

"Ryan," she said softly as he kissed her at the base of her neck, his hands tugging on her shirt, his body pressing between her legs. She wrapped her arms around his head, urging him on. Maybe this would be it, she thought. Maybe this time would be different.

It would be different, but not in the way she imagined.

The attack came suddenly and without warning. The door swung open, the lock shattering from the cheap wood frame. The orange light from the parking lot swept across the darkened room, the lingering smell of pine trees and gasoline blew in on a gust.

Neither Ryan nor Erin had time to react. Ryan rolled onto his back, but all he could do was stare as a dark silhouette appeared in the doorway. The man was large, with thick arms and an even thicker neck, his features in shadow save for the glancing light off his bulging skull. He didn't hesitate as he raised his left hand, revealing a pistol. He was only fifteen feet away, the barrel of the gun steady as his finger curled around the trigger. No one could miss at that distance.

23

THE INTRUDER AIMED the gun at Ryan's chest. The man didn't hesitate; there was no time to react.

The bullet entered one side of the head and emerged out the other, blasting brain and skull against the hotel room wall. The large man stood silently in the doorway as his arm dropped to his side, the weapon dangling from his hand. Erin watched out of pure shock, unable to move. And then the man buckled, toppling first to his knees and then to the floor, what was left of the inside of his skull seeping onto the carpet.

"Jesus fucking Christ," Ryan screamed as they both rolled off the bed in unison, Ryan landing below the windowsill, Erin on the opposite side of the bed. Within seconds she'd drawn her standard issue from her suitcase, removed it from its holster and switched off the safety. Still crouching, she aimed the gun at the now open door, her forearms resting on the mattress.

For a split second the room spun in front of her eyes, the reality of the situation hitting her. She was breathing so heavily it was the only thing she could hear. The sudden burst of adrenaline was causing her hands to shake. Her eyes darted nervously from the open door to the window beside the bed.

Then second instinct kicked in and everything snapped into place. The man's brains had splattered against the far wall, indicating the second shooter was oriented to the right of the doorway—and likely in line with the window. The shot had come from a distance . The shooter had also saved their lives.

Gunfire—four rounds—suddenly peppered the air. Ryan and Erin ducked, but the gunfire was aimed at someone else. Had come from a different direction. There was a third gunman.

Ryan surveyed the landscape from his crouched position below the window. "Don't see anything." Two more rounds were fired. This time he didn't duck. He shook his head. "Nothing. Coming from our direction. Out of sight."

The hotel was shaped like an "L", with the small leg protruding perpendicularly toward the highway, the majority of the rooms running parallel to the road. Whoever was shooting was in between their room and the end of the building. Eight rooms away at most.

A metal twang. A bullet had hit a vehicle.

"Across the road, in the woods. Right of the restaurant," Ryan reported. The other shooter was using a high-powered rifle. She'd heard it this time, but only barely. The shot had been muffled by a silencer. Silencers decreased accuracy, especially on rifles, but that hadn't stopped the person from firing a clean shot through a man's head a hundred yards away.

"He's not firing at us. Get the gun," Erin moved around the edge of the bed and made her way to the open door. As soon as she was in cover position, Ryan made his move. He scrambled to the dead body, snatched the pistol from the man's lifeless grip and then scurried back to his original position. He checked the chamber and magazine. His silence indicated he was good to go. The entire action had taken two, maybe three seconds.

Erin poked her head out the open door. The air smelled of exhaust and gunfire. The neon lighting that illuminated the plain concrete walkway buzzed incessantly. She could see nothing out of the ordinary, but knew the gunman was there somewhere, hidden behind a car.

She sensed Ryan's presence above her. She darted forward, taking cover between two cars. She dropped from sight just as two more gunshots rang out and the car window above her exploded. Ryan sent three rounds in response.

"Four cars away, between the Volvo and Kia," he whispered to her as she situated herself. Safety glass was strewn everywhere.

Erin was in a harrowing position. Her best move was to circle around the cars away from the building and attempt to flank the trapped gunman, but that would expose her to the shooter in the woods. The marksman had saved their lives only moments before, but she didn't know his intentions: was he truly trying to save them, or waiting to do the job himself?

Two more shots came. Erin glanced over her shoulder to see Ryan retreat into the hotel room, the wood near his head shattering as bullets slapped into the door frame. He waved at her to move further out. He seemed willing to trust the shooter in the woods not to kill her. Then again, it wasn't his life he was risking.

She inched further into the parking lot and threw a glance to the woods near the restaurant. A street lamp illuminated some of the dirt and grass next to the road, but beyond the tree line it was pitch black. Erin slipped around the hood of the sedan and checked the space in between the next two cars. It was clear, as expected. She moved behind the next car and checked the next row. Still clear. She refused to look back at the woods. She was in the open now, a sitting duck. If she had miscalculated, she'd be dead at any moment.

Nothing. Silence. The buzz of the lights, a whine of a mosquito in her ear. The sound of her breathing, slow and steady and yet agonizingly loud.

Erin positioned herself to shoot. She aimed her weapon at the space she assumed the gunman to be, her arms resting on the trunk of the car. At any sign of movement she would fire. Ryan left the safety of the hotel room and started down the sidewalk, his new pistol fixed on the gunman's position. His stride was slow but methodical, his aim steady.

"Throw down your weapon," Ryan shouted, "or I will shoot you."

No response.

"Slide it onto the sidewalk where I can see it."

She heard a squeak and gravel crunching, the sound of a shoe shifting weight and rotating on the asphalt. The buzz from the lights increased in volume. Something was about to happen.

A door opened. Not a car door. Out of the corner of her eye, she saw a middle-aged woman in a white T-shirt and shorts emerge from the doorway adjacent to Ryan's position.

"What the hell is—"

"Get back in your room!" Ryan commanded. The woman looked startled but didn't immediately react.

It was in this moment that the gunman saw his opportunity. Ryan was distracted. So was Erin. Sensing he was in trouble, Ryan dove into the woman's room, taking them both to the floor. The gunman fired three more rounds. Erin saw the top of his head and pulled the trigger, but she didn't have a clear shot. Two car windows erupted into a shower of safety glass. A car alarm went off.

The gunman returned fire, sending two wild shots in her direction. The second bullet struck the tire of the car she was hiding behind. It hissed loudly as it deflated, and the back-right section of the car collapsed. The sudden movement caused her to fall backwards.

She heard footsteps. The man was retreating. A muffled rifle shot crackled through the air. A chunk of brick on the side of the hotel disappeared into a puff of smoke. The gunman dove to the ground, out of sight from the marksman in the woods. A moment later, the man, a dark-haired individual in his mid-thirties, scrambled around the corner of the hotel. Just as he disappeared from sight, Erin heard another rifle shot. The man yelped and contorted as a bullet caught him. He continued running.

Ryan made it to the end of the hotel before she did, running at full speed. As Erin pursued, she caught movement out of the corner of her eye and looked back. A shadow of a person was racing across the highway, his features indistinguishable in the inconsistent light. The woodsman shooter passed out of sight behind the other end of the hotel.

Erin reached the back of the hotel. Somewhere up ahead she heard Ryan running through the woods.

24

RYAN WAS MORE out of shape than he'd thought. He could feel a twinge of pain in his side, a slight strain on his lungs. Adrenaline pulsed through every facet of his body, causing his temples to pound. Despite the cool night temperatures, he was already sweating, his mouth dry. Physically, mentally, he was out of sorts.

Trees blurred by him on both sides. He paid no attention to the twigs and brush he was stepping on with his bare feet. He could see the gunman in front of him, a glimmer of movement in the darkness. He wasn't far ahead, and Ryan was gaining.

Ryan stopped and raised his pistol. The adrenaline made his hands shake, but at this distance, assuming he could see his target, it would be hard to miss. "Freeze!"

The man didn't freeze. He hadn't expected him to. He pulled the trigger, thankful the man hadn't stopped. He'd come to kill him, to kill him and Erin, while they slept. The coward, the bastard. He deserved to die. Ryan would take pleasure in it.

The gunman dropped to the ground and out of sight, but Ryan could hear him scrambling through the brush. Ryan fired again, blindly this time. He stepped forward, squinting in the darkness. Another step, then another. He was running once more, the trees racing by him.

"Pull back," he heard John's voice. "We know he's here. Let's regroup."

He continued on.

"Ryan, don't get lost. If something happens…"

"I'm on him!" Ryan heard himself saying.

Then came SAC Monroe's voice, his stern warning: *"Harper! Stay where you are. That's an order."*

No, it wasn't going to happen like last time.

Another flash of white, another wild shot. Ryan didn't even duck this time. He continued toward the light, but the light didn't disappear. It grew in intensity and width, and soon it consumed him.

"There's no one around to save you, Harper. It's just you and me, and I have the gun." He didn't recognize the voice, but he knew it was Christopher Morgan's.

"Then stop talking and shoot me!" It was his own this voice, distant but clear.

He felt his finger curl around the trigger, a feeling of immense warmth and pleasure pulsing through his body.

He was in a bedroom. The blinds were closed but the room was bright, the sunlight piercing through every possible space. An attractive young redhead lay below him, her mouth parted, her eyes closed. Her large breasts heaved as he fucked her, pressing deep between her legs. She was moaning, but he couldn't hear her. All around him were the whispers, the unintelligible whispers.

He knocked on his own door, feeling elated. He stared at the door, waiting for someone to answer.

The door disappeared in an instant, replaced by a distant orb. It grew in intensity, the Face coming for him.

"Remember," it told him. "Remember who…"

THE WOMAN WITH blond hair struck the hit man in the shoulder as he rounded the corner of the hotel. It wasn't a kill shot, hardly a graze. She silently cursed herself for missing him so many times, but she didn't dwell on mistakes. She dropped the rifle on the blanket where her spent shells had collected and darted forward. At five paces she had reached the other side of the road, at another ten had slipped out of sight behind the hotel.

Her eyes adjusted to the darkness of the forest quickly, for she'd spent the last several hours sitting patiently waiting for this moment to occur. She saw Erin Kinsley enter the woods from the other side of the hotel. Kinsley didn't matter. Ryan Harper was in front; he would encounter the hit man first. Given his fragile mental state, it was unclear whether he could handle the pressure at hand. She had to protect him. He knew what she didn't. He was too important to her. The billionaire wanted him to disappear permanently this time. His attempt had failed so far, but the hit man was still alive. It was dark and Ryan Harper was unreliable. She had to get there first.

An exchange of gunfire. Ryan Harper had told the man to freeze. This was the difference between him and her. He was still bound by laws, trained to obey. She had no limits. She could hear Ryan Harper nearby, his bare feet pounding against the dirt and bushes. She saw him to her right. The hit man was not far ahead; he knew he was losing ground and that he would have to fight back to survive. All he had to do was stop and wait for the FBI agents to come to him.

She exhaled when she saw Ryan Harper collapse. At first she thought he'd been shot, but then she recognized his symptoms as something else entirely. He slumped to his knees, his hands outstretched, reaching for support. He found a small tree and he leaned against it, silent.

The hit man had circled back. He didn't know Ryan Harper had fallen, but he was scanning the darkness. Erin Kinsley was running toward her boyfriend now, more concerned about his safety than hers. She thought he'd been shot. It was admirable, but sloppy. The mission had to be first. Relationships, emotions second. Anything else meant risk of death.

"RYAN!" ERIN CRIED as she approached him from behind. He was hugging a tree so small it was bending under his weight. Even though she couldn't see his features, she searched the darkness for the sight of blood. She dropped to a knee beside him and grabbed his shoulder. He didn't respond.

She couldn't go through this again. He couldn't leave her again. He couldn't have returned just for him to die in front of her eyes. This wasn't how it was meant to be.

He was still breathing. Hyperventilating. One of his nightmares. Erin breathed out. He was going to be okay...

The gunman. She cursed herself for her lack of discipline. She scanned the woods, searching for the hit man. Her ears strained for noises, but all she could hear was the blood pounding in her temples. Then she saw him, straight ahead. Walking toward them. Gun aimed at her chest. There was no way he could miss from that distance. Her pistol was at her feet. If she made a move, he would fire. Then again, if she didn't, he was going to kill her anyway.

His chest erupted. He gave a brief shriek and then crumpled to the ground, lifeless. A figure emerged from nowhere and fired a third round into the back of the man's head.

"Freeze! FBI!" Erin picked up her gun and aimed it at the mysterious person. The figure, no more than a silhouette, turned to face her, but said nothing. Erin rose to her feet, helping Ryan up next to her. "Drop the gun."

The shooter remained silent and made no move to drop his weapon. Erin reissued her order, but knew it was no use. The mysterious figure was not going to yield.

"Who are you?" Ryan asked breathlessly. He took a step forward, then another.

The figure turned, then paused, looking back at them. Seemed to hesitate. "It was Luis Salazar. He hired these men." A woman's voice.

The silhouette moved to the left, briefly ducking behind a tree.

"Don't —" Erin cried, but she'd already committed to not shooting. The woman continued to sidestep and simultaneously back away. Even though she was moving, it was becoming increasingly harder to see her in the shadows of the tree. Then she was gone.

"Marie?" Ryan whispered.

In the distance, police sirens.

25

"WHEN MONROE TOLD you to stay out of the press, I don't think getting into a gunfight and destroying a hotel is exactly what he had in mind," John Lancaster noted as he scratched at an itch on his round, red chin. The senior agent reclined in his grungy yellow office chair and crossed his feet on the corner of his desk.

"Your understanding of public relations defies me," Erin said dryly, running a hand through her matted hair. She hadn't had a chance to shower since the night before. "How you wound up in the FBI instead is just a wonder."

"I know, I know, Kendra tells me that all the time."

"Tell me who the guys are, John," Ryan said testily. He sat in a casual position at the end of the desk, slouched, his legs extended, but he was anything but calm. He'd been on edge for the last nine hours. He looked like he would kill the next person who crossed him the wrong way.

"Wow," John seemed unconcerned. "Someone didn't get much sleep last night."

"Hilarious," Ryan said crisply. "Who the hell were these guys?"

"Hit men."

Erin waited. Ryan's fist clenched.

"Fine," John sighed. "The one with most of his brains souped onto your hotel room floor was Francis Wilkerson, 46. Lived in Vancouver, Washington and worked for a dry cleaning business. He lived in a shithole apartment, but that's a moot point now. In his spare time, he liked to make some extra cash—which he subsequently gambled away. He made this money by killing people. He'd been linked to several hit-like murders but no arrests. Most likely he made a living working for angry wives and husbands who didn't feel the divorce option was the best choice.

"The other one is Hans Anderson, born and raised in Portland. No prior arrests of significance. Still, based on his not-so-shabby living arrangements in downtown

Portland and the lack of a taxable paycheck in the last four years, we can assume that this wasn't his first hit."

"Money trail?"

"Still looking into it. The bank just opened an hour ago or so. We did find fifty large in Mr. Anderson's closet, pretty fresh. Nothing so far at Wilkerson's place, but detectives are still combing through it."

"So they sound like plain vanilla hit men," Erin chimed in. "No mob, gang ties?"

John shook his head and shrugged. "We haven't found a common connection between the two either."

"And Luis Salazar? Any links to him?" Ryan asked in a low voice.

"Do you expect there to be?" John's eyebrow raised in cynical fashion. "If there's evidence tying them to Salazar, I'm sure it's not going to be just sitting on their mantle."

"And yet Marie saves our lives and tells us he's responsible. Hard not to take that seriously."

"But Luis Salazar?" Erin asked quietly.

"It's preposterous, I know. It doesn't make any sense. But Marie…"

"We don't know it was her. And we don't know whose side she's on." The woman had protected them—at least Ryan—for a reason, but whose reason? John had been saying that Ryan hadn't escaped; he had been returned. Someone had invested a lot of time and presumably money into kidnapping him and doing God-knows-what kind of experiments on him. Marie, or whoever she was, could be protecting that investment. In fact, Erin couldn't imagine any other scenario that would make sense.

"It was her," Ryan insisted, but he sensed what she was thinking. "If she was working for the people that took me, then who were the two guys who tried to kill us in the first place?" He was right, at least to an extent. There was a third party at work, one that wanted him dead. But the men who were trying to kill him couldn't be involved in his disappearance, could they? Let him go only to kill him?

"She never shot to wound—she was there to kill. Protect the truth," Erin reasoned, brainstorming.

"You think this woman is trying to throw us off?" John asked.

"No. I don't know. There's no reason we should trust her. We don't know what her intentions are."

Ryan sighed, frustrated. "If she were trying to throw us off, why Salazar? Him of all people?"

"Like I said, I don't know," Erin stated tersely. "I don't know what to make of it."

"Does anyone know what to make of anything involving Ryan over the last six-and-a-half months?" John stood up, brushing away a few crumbs from a breakfast sandwich he'd devoured half an hour before. "Let's get some fresh air."

Erin and Ryan followed John down to the lobby and outside.

"Don't mention Salazar again in the office. Or to anyone else," John said, aiming for a nearby Starbucks. "But you know that. That's why you haven't said anything to Monroe yet." John paused, then continued. "Salazar's involvement may not make sense, but that doesn't mean I don't believe it. In fact, I do."

He paused again, letting the words sink in again. Erin remembered the awkward introduction at Salazar's banquet, the way the billionaire had been almost desperate to get away from the two of them.

"Before Ryan disappeared, he was doing a little investigation on the side."

"What kind of investigation?" Erin stopped, her head spinning to Ryan.

"Don't look at me," he raised his hands in defense. "I know not what I did."

"He wouldn't tell me much," John directed his answer to Erin. "Said he was just looking into something, a hunch, nothing more. He didn't even believe it himself, and you know how he is if you try to press him. He wouldn't tell me, so I let him go on his merry way. From your reaction, Erin, I'm guessing he didn't tell you, either?"

"No," Erin was exasperated. "Why wouldn't he tell us?"

"This is very weird hearing you talk about me in the third person like this," Ryan said.

"None of this is ringing a bell?" John asked.

"No, nothing."

"You started looking into whatever you were looking into about three weeks before your disappearance. A few days before you disappeared, you told me you'd caught a potential break. You sounded excited, as if you expected that things were about to click into place. Somebody had contacted you claiming they had information."

"And did I meet with this person?"

"No. You referred to the person as a 'he,' so I'll assume he was male. But no, you didn't meet him. He never showed for the meeting and never called back. Then the lead came in about Morgan and your attention shifted back to that case."

"Why the hell didn't you bring this up after Ryan disappeared, John?" Erin shouted. "Don't you think this would've been important?"

"Of course I thought it was important. But I wasn't sure," John looked back at Ryan. "After you disappeared, I scoured your files, looking for any notes you may have taken. There was nothing. I tried to track your phone records back to when you'd received a call from this mysterious informant, but there was nothing. Again, I realized you'd never specified that the person had *called* you per se."

"So why didn't you tell me, John? Jesus Christ."

"Erin, I didn't tell you because Ryan didn't tell you. He either didn't trust us or was trying to protect us. I probed you to determine if you knew anything, and I determined you didn't. I decided to keep it that way," John shrugged. "Maybe it was a poor decision in hindsight. I don't know. But I had nothing to go on, and I stayed up countless nights trying to uncover some clue to what the hell he was working on."

"With me gone, you figured the threat was gone. If someone else was involved, they might let down their guard, assuming that no one else knew about my investigation," Ryan surmised.

"Give or take, yes."

"Or you raise the stakes and put the heat on them, force them to make a mistake," Erin argued.

"Very true," John nodded. "But assuming someone else was involved, they'd gone undetected this far. They took Ryan without a trace. This during one of the most massive FBI operations since the Boston Marathon bombings. I didn't feel that heat would bring them out again."

"John, I can't believe this. How could you not tell me about this? Me, of all people? We should have brought the heat… we could have done it. Scare whoever it was into doing something stupid."

"I didn't really need to," John looked at her, his eyes surprisingly cold. "You were on the hit list, too. Whoever wanted Ryan out of the way assumed that you also knew what he knew. You almost died, but didn't. If there really was someone else out there, they would try to kill you."

"You used her as bait?" Ryan interjected.

"Yes, but no takers," John stated firmly. "I'm sorry, Erin."

"Fuck you, John."

"Hey, I did what I thought was right. What's important now is we have a break. At least on a superficial level, it makes sense. Who would Ryan have been investigating that would've made him worried enough not to tell the two of us anything? It would have to be someone powerful, with the resources able to cover up a crime. At the very least, someone with enough political clout to unhinge an investigation should it come to light."

"Salazar does fit that bill," Ryan said. "He's heavily connected in Washington. He's also friends with Chandling. Jesus."

"'Friends' may be a relative term here."

"Based on evidence, we always assumed that Morgan was just some radical who decided to take out a U.S. senator. What if Morgan tried to kill him for an entirely different reason?" Ryan theorized. "The senator gets into a bad deal with Salazar, doesn't pay or doesn't deliver, and Salazar tries to take him out, his family and all."

"Chandling definitely wouldn't have been reelected if a scandal came to light," Ryan shook his head in disbelief. "And Salazar is worried I'll regain my memory and get back on his trail."

"Let's remember who we're talking about," John interjected. "Luis Salazar. Humanitarian of the Year. He's been on the cover of Forbes. He isn't some trigger happy criminal."

The woman says otherwise, Erin thought. She needed to sit down. None of it made sense, and yet it did. Salazar was involved, likely responsible for Ryan's disappearance. But his dealings with Chandling, his blackmail of a U.S. senator, was merely conjecture. To get to the truth, she'd have to confront a man she'd known since she was a little girl, who had been her mentor and helped her become the woman she was today.

26

RYAN STOOD IN the parking lot and scanned the area for anything out of the ordinary. Erin's condo was only a stair climb away, and yet he wasn't certain they would make it that far. Someone had tried to kill them, and failed. Would there be another attempt?

Erin's condo would not be the best place for a second attack, Ryan quickly surmised. There were few places to hide. A couple bushes near the stairs. Several cars. Small trees lined the well-lit road. A shooter could stake out in the construction site next door, but that was unlikely. The attack would be at close range, like it was before; the attacker would look like a civilian, talking on a cell phone or reading a paper. Then *pop!* He's dead and the nightmares end.

It didn't sound all bad.

There were too many people on alert in the area. Since Ryan's return, a police car had been stationed outside the building. There were now two. The neighbors had taken to calling the police anytime they noticed someone sneaking around on the property. Most of the time they were paparazzi. "Celebrity FBI Couple Split After Affair with Alien Revealed" was a popular *Onion* story in circulation.

He and Erin marched wearily up the concrete stairs to the second floor, his attentiveness waning with each step. It was only the afternoon but it felt like he'd been up all night. He had been up all night. The adrenaline had long drained away.

During the attack was the first time in a long time he had felt clarity, if only for a fleeting moment. As he fired his weapon, as he ran through the woods, the world seemed well. Whole. But even as more light was shed on the case, the more certain he became that answers were within reach, it felt as though the walls were caving in around him. His reality seemed more distant than ever; he was an observer, not a participant. He talked and interacted with this movie, but he was disconnected, like he wasn't the one doing the talking. The closer he came to the truth, the more disconnected he felt. Every time he closed his eyes, even just to blink, he now saw the Face, its distorted, sinister mouth talking to him. *Remember*, it told him.

He didn't know if he wanted to remember. He had a growing suspicion that when he did, it wouldn't be pleasant. The revelation, whatever it was, would change everything, and bad things would happen.

Ryan unlocked the door to Erin's condo and froze. The gray sheen disappeared and once again he was in the moment, his veins pumping nothing but adrenaline. There was something different about the place. With the blinds closed it was dark, as expected, but a faint but foreign odor drifted through the air, pleasant but out of the ordinary. There was a stillness, too, a stuffiness.

Someone was there.

Erin drew her weapon. He didn't have to tell her. She stepped inside slowly, her firearm trained down the hallway toward the dim living room. They should call for backup, he thought. It was foolish to go in alone. With the light to their backs, they were sitting ducks should someone unload a few rounds. But this was their home, their job to protect it.

Ryan flipped on the hallway light, waited, then continued forward. The bathroom off the hallway was clear. They approached the living room. Ryan felt useless without a gun. Erin was his sole defense. He could think of worse, but whoever the intruder was, he wanted to be the one to kill him. He wanted to teach these sons of bitches a lesson.

Erin took a half step into the living room, her gun pointing toward every possible position. This was the moment of truth. She was exposed, vulnerable. She had twenty points to cover; the gunman only had to aim at one.

Ryan kept his eye on the shadows of the bedroom. The door was only open a foot, just as he remembered leaving it, and through it he could only see a hint of light from the bedroom window. It was the perfect place to hide, and from which to attack.

"I wouldn't shoot," came a woman's voice. "For my sake."

From the kitchen. Erin spun around and Ryan froze.

He didn't take in her facial features at first. He saw the black shoes and matching cargo pants and dark gray hooded jacket, hood thrown back. A bulge under her jacket suggested she was carrying a weapon. She was tall and slender, attractive.

"What are *you* doing here?" Erin exclaimed, her gun unwavering. She recognized her.

Ryan blinked and the woman's features came into view. He gasped, ever so slightly.

"*Bonjour*," Marie said, her French accent as sweet as ever. "Please do not shoot."

THE WOMAN WITH blond hair, who called herself Marie, observed the reactions of Ryan Harper and Erin Kinsley with some satisfaction. Ryan looked stunned, and his was the only reaction she was concerned about. He had liked her as a simpleton, a French whore, but there was no assurance he would like her still.

Erin was simply perplexed, unsure how to react. She kept her gun aimed steadily at Marie's chest.

"How did you get in here?" Ryan asked.

"It wasn't hard," she shrugged and leaned back against the edge of the kitchen counter, crossing her legs at her ankles. "Please do not shoot."

Erin didn't lower her weapon.

"If I wanted you dead, I would have killed you already. Or let those men do it."

Silence. Silence to indicate, *that was you?*

"Call me your guardian angel. You would be dead if not for me."

"But—" The questions were so predictable.

"I'm not the helpless girl you think I am." She felt strange saying those words. She never said such things, never let people in like this. Doing so betrayed every aspect of her training, her upbringing.

"French Intelligence? What agency?" Erin asked, then demanded. Her gun remained trained on Marie, but not as steadily as before.

"You are assuming Marie Aumond exists. That she went to college. Was recruited by an intelligence agency. Do not assume so much." To explain who she was, what she was, was too exhausting. Too long of a story. She didn't want to waste her time, nor did she feel comfortable revealing that much about herself. "I did not come here to talk about me. Let us talk about Luis Salazar."

"We need to—"

"Know if you can trust me? You cannot. You know what you know, that I saved your life. I am here now to talk to you. I have been working on this case for over six months, since you disappeared. Well, since a man hacked into a secure government database and altered satellite imagery that would have helped you immensely, Erin."

"And forged the analysis of the photographs."

"Yes. The man who changed the imagery was named Gerard Sampre. A former CIA analyst who started outsourcing his services to other governments and private buyers. The CIA does not know about his post-agency career. That is how limited their scope is."

"Where is he now?"

"Dead. I killed him. He was smart enough to delete any trace of the actual project—the original imagery does not exist anymore—but he was also smart enough to keep records of his financial agreements, in case he needed leverage. This led me to Luis Salazar. Funds from several of Salazar's accounts vanished twelve hours after Ryan's disappearance. Two weeks later they were deposited into Gerard's offshore account. The delay reduced the chances that the money transfer would be detected. Large sums of money were also withdrawn in a similar fashion shortly before the Chandling assassination attempt. It was determined that Salazar had suddenly elevated himself to a new, dangerous level of involvement in governmental affairs.

I was brought in to assess the threat, gauge his intent and determine the accuracy of the rumors that Ryan had been kidnapped. And if so, to what purpose."

"And?" Erin asked.

"Progress has been slow. Salazar has something to hide, but I do not know what.

I infiltrated his organization and his home to get into the position I am now. I built Marie from the ground up to match his preferences in women, especially ones he has shown to keep around for a while. But Sergey—who doubles as his chief of staff—runs a tight ship. I have not had an opportunity to gain Sergey's trust, or Salazar's for that matter. I have accessed his home systems, but whatever he is hiding must be on the Salazar International servers. And not in a location most would be able to access."

"So you don't know much?" Erin asked. She meant to say, So you've been fucking Salazar for months and still haven't figured out anything.

"I know that Salazar is responsible. The boat accident he had a couple days ago… That was me. With your return, I wanted to accelerate the process. Kick things into motion. He didn't tell me much, but he ordered the two of you dead. Sergey hired those two hit men to take you out."

"What do you think happened to me?" Ryan asked. He believed her. It was clear Erin did, too.

"I don't know. Not yet," she told him. "But you, Salazar and the politician are connected. Salazar ordered his death for some reason, and the only logical reason is something related to his influence in the senate. The politician sits on the Ways & Means Committee as well as the Foreign Security Council. A large percentage of Salazar International's revenue is generated from numerous government grants and contracts. The company receives over $4 billion a year in black budget funding from Congress. Most of that funding comes from the committees where Chandling presides. It is in Salazar's interest to keep the politician happy. Or keep him motivated to vote in his favor."

"However necessary," Erin commented.

"However necessary," the woman with blond hair repeated. "You have a relationship with the politician. You need to discover what Salazar is using for leverage over him."

"And you?"

"I will keep in touch."

As Marie brushed by them to leave, she already regretted telling them so much. It was a tactical mistake. She worked alone for a reason. Involving them was a risk, a weakness in her armor. And yet she felt compelled to involve them. Ryan Harper was held against his will for six months, his life turned upside down, his body tortured and experimented upon for some program run by the government he so dutifully served. That made her angry, and she never got angry.

27

SENATOR RICHARD CHANDLING lived in a modest mansion just outside Olympia, the state's capital ninety miles southwest of Seattle. The house sat on a not-so-modest thirty acres of wooded real estate, its stucco white a stark contrast to the surrounding green pines.

Even before the house came into view, the forested drive that hugged the Puget Sound shoreline brought back childhood memories. It always did. Erin remembered her parents driving her to the home, excitement welling as she envisioned discovering treasure within its cavernous rooms or hidden in an undiscovered cave on the property. She would feverishly stare out the car window, searching for her first sight of the house through the passing trees.

Upon turning onto Chandling's driveway, she was first met with another view. A gray rock wall now bordered the property, the drive passing through an open black iron gate. The sight of the barrier took her by surprise, but it shouldn't have, she quickly acknowledged. He'd almost been assassinated less than a year earlier.

The gravel driveway immediately opened into a wide roundabout in front of the home, a two-story building with six bedrooms, a front patio and a detached garage. Erin gazed at the house as she parked in front, recalling racing through the hallways of the home in her socks, dropping G.I. Joe soldiers with parachutes off the second floor balcony and exploring the forest, always to her mother's chagrin. At the time, Chandling and his wife had yet to have children; Erin had free reign of the property.

The front door opened and a man emerged, his piercing eyes fixated on her. He was in his mid-forties with jet black hair and a youthful face, muscles rippling beneath his polo shirt. A small headset indicated he was security.

"Come in," he said, serious but cordial.

"Not going to check my badge?" Erin asked dryly.

"I know who you are," the security guard stated, a slight but noticeable Southern twang to his voice. Erin noticed an Army tattoo half hidden under his gray polo. She also noticed his hair had hints of gray at the temples.

"This is Jedison Green, my head of security," Richard Chandling appeared in the entryway. "I've improved security since the shooting."

"From zero to something," Jedison commented before vanishing down the hallway.

Chandling placed a hand on Erin's shoulder and guided her toward the back of the house. The hallway was equally unfurnished, a few photographs and paintings hanging on the wall. "Erin, I've made a few changes since you were last here. Swimming pool, patio… remodeled the bathroom and kitchen." They emerged from the hallway into the kitchen, an expansive space with multiple islands, mahogany cabinets and black appliances and countertops. Large-paned windows lined the eastern-facing wall, granting the kitchen and dining room an unheralded view of the pine forest in Chandling's backyard. Through the windows she could see his freshly minted patio, the wood still bright and virginal, and beyond that a swimming pool that was nearing the end of construction.

"I've had to keep myself busy since… you know."

Erin noticed several framed photographs sitting on top of the grand piano in the corner. Behind them, fresh flowers. She found herself drawn to the vigil, the last memories of Chandling's family. She leaned forward to examine the photos, most of them of the entire family or Chandling's daughter Beth.

"I can't stand having the photos all over the place. Everywhere I'd walk they'd be there, staring at me. But I couldn't just flush them from the place. 'Tough' isn't a strong enough word, but I owe them at least this much. This was their home, too."

Erin gazed outside again, at the pool and deck. He was rebuilding the house as best he could, altering it away from how it was when Kathy and Beth were alive.

"So what's so important we couldn't discuss it over the phone? I've got a flight to Washington tonight so let's keep this quick."

Erin knew it was best to get straight to the point, but she couldn't find the words to begin. She'd recited this moment over and over in her head for the entire drive from Seattle, but still it didn't feel right. Chandling was like a father…

"Erin?"

"It's about your family. And you."

"Oh?"

"Why would someone want you killed?"

The senator chuckled hesitantly, as if waiting for a punch line. "How many times have we gone over this? Every indication suggests that Christopher Morgan targeted me because of my politics. He was a nutcase." He chewed on things for a moment, then said more quickly: "Have you found something?"

"Luis Salazar. Know of any reason why he'd want you dead?"

The senator blinked twice and then laughed loud and hard, the noise echoing off the walls. "Luis? We're good friends. He knew my wife and daughter well. He is *not* involved in this."

She started to say something but Chandling shook his head and raised his finger. "Luis is not a gangster. He doesn't have a violent bone in his body. Why on earth would you suspect him? Even if he were such an evil person, this implies I would be complicit in my family's death as well. I would have to be involved in something that would have resulted in their deaths. And Luis—one of the richest men in the state—would have had to hire an assassin to execute my family and me... This is all preposterous."

"Last night two men tried to kill Ryan and me. I have evidence they were hired by Salazar."

Green straightened, suddenly attentive.

"What evidence?"

Erin looked at Green. He was watching her intensely.

Chandling detected her hesitance. "Jedison is very good at keeping his mouth shut. What evidence?"

"An insider. A reputable source."

The senator gave no reaction. A blank slate.

"Salazar tried to have us killed, and I'm sure he will again."

"Then why don't you arrest him based on this 'evidence' you have?"

"The case needs to be bulletproofed. After everything he's done, conspiracy to commit murder is nothing. I want more. I want everything." She was clenching her fist. "Shortly before the attempt on your life, Salazar withdrew money from his bank accounts to pay for your assassination. He did it again shortly before Christopher Morgan attacked me and Ryan disappeared. Once again to pay off a man named Gerard Sampre to modify the satellite photographs that showed Ryan's extraction on the night he disappeared."

"It sounds like you have a lot of evidence already."

She was stretching the truth. She'd been told this had happened, hadn't seen it for herself. But Chandling didn't need to know that. "If I go after him now, he'll take you down with him. Once that happens, your career will be over, probably worse."

The senator sat silent for several minutes, thinking, his eyes distant. Without a change in his expression, he stated, "You're offering me a chance to come clean in exchange for—"

"I'm not promising anything. This isn't in exchange for anything. But tell me now and I swear I will do everything in my power to help you. I don't know your reasons, but I want Salazar. You've done so much for me. That's what I can do for you."

Chandling's chin slumped to his chest as he pondered the offer. The silence was unbearable. Erin became convinced he wasn't going to talk, that he was done. But then Green leaned forward and whispered in Chandling's ear. Chandling listened intently. At first he seemed resistant to what Green was saying, but then the man retreated to his original position, eyes on her, and Chandling grew motionless once more, considering whatever had been said. More silence. More waiting.

"Erin, I love you like a daughter," he finally said, his eyes watering. He looked at her, trembling. "I hope you've seen me like a father. Don't think of me as anything less. Luis had nothing to do with this. At least I can't comprehend how he would be involved. I never talked to him about this. Haven't talked to anyone about it." He sighed. "Kathy was having an affair. For over a year. I found out about it after a couple months. I begged her to stop it, and she did. For a short while. I begged her again, but she said she didn't love me anymore." He paused, choked. "She promised to stay with me for appearances' sake. I was up for reelection soon and a divorce doesn't cater to the family values vote. I agreed, even though it killed me inside. After everything she'd done, I still loved her."

"Who was the man?"

"His name was David Humphries. They had met at a fundraiser in Portland. I never was able to find out when they started sleeping together. That wasn't all, though. He was an addict. Kathy got into the stuff."

"What kind of stuff?" Erin couldn't believe her ears. Kathy. Using drugs.

"Oh, a variety. Pot. Cocaine. Ecstacy. Some other pills. No meth, thank God." The senator rubbed his wide brow. "I'd noticed Kathy acting erratically for months, but never thought it had to do with drugs."

"So how did Salazar find out about this?"

"He didn't," Chandling said sternly. "After I found out about the drugs, I couldn't handle it anymore. That's when I hired Jedison. I asked him to talk to Mr. Humphries. No physical stuff, but threats. He did. I just wanted to put a scare into him. Kathy comes back to me the next day and threatens to tell the world that she is a drug-using whore. She was high at the time. She continued to use, and use with him. So I asked Jedison to go back again, but this time to rough him up a little. No broken bones, but to inflict some pain."

He waited for Erin's reaction. She blinked, didn't react. She could see herself doing the same thing. In the corner, Green fidgeted, the first time she'd seen any kind of emotional reaction from the man.

"Jedison did." Another pause. "And this time he took notice, but not in the way I had expected. He shows up at my house, bruised and bloodied, and says that if I don't pay him $500,000 he'll tell the world about Kathy. Same threat as she made, only he was going to throw in several hours of pornographic video as proof."

"And you paid?"

"I thought about it. A lot. But no, I didn't. I could tell he cared for Kathy, maybe even thought he loved Kathy. I couldn't see him, as drugged out as he was, doing that to her. So I told him off and said that if he ever sees Kathy again I'll go to the authorities. That was a month before. You know."

"You're saying this David Humphries is the guy who had Kathy and Beth killed?"

"I didn't say that," the senator straightened up in his seat, the first time he'd moved since he'd started talking. "I don't think he had it in him. He was a father himself, a guy who, I hate to say it, got mixed up in one bad thing after another until it had consumed him. He wasn't violent, and certainly wasn't someone who would hire a hit man. Besides, if anything he would want *me* dead, not Kathy and Beth as well."

"Maybe Morgan misunderstood, or ignored his instructions," Erin suggested. She didn't know what to think. If this were true, Salazar had no connection to the assassination attempt. Which meant that Ryan's disappearance was unrelated. Which meant… It made no sense.

Chandling leaned forward, his elbows resting on his desk, his massive hands extending toward her. "Erin, you can see why I didn't tell you about this at first. If this gets out it will destroy Kathy's legacy. I'm telling you because you seem certain Luis is somehow involved. I don't see it, but maybe I overlooked something. Luis is my friend, but goddamn if he's involved then I will strangle him myself."

His face was flush red now. "Look Humphries up. After my threat to go to the police, he stopped seeing Kathy and I tried to get her off drugs. She kept disappearing so I assumed she was still using, but I don't know who with. I had Jedison look him up after the shooting, but he'd died. Drug overdose, I think. Look him up, connect the dots for yourself. That's what I didn't tell you."

28

ERIN WAS ONCE again gone when Ryan awoke for the morning. He shuffled into the kitchen and threw a pan onto the stove. As he waited for it to heat, he checked outside. It was cloudy, but it looked like the sun would break through before too long. The construction crew across the street was already hard at work.

He tossed a couple eggs onto the pan and they began to fry, sizzling loudly. He stared at the eggs, acknowledging he could relate. His head felt like that on a daily basis, a scramble with no room to maneuver. No matter where the eggs went, they could not get out. They were doomed to fry, to be devoured.

He sat down on the couch to eat his breakfast, the living room feeling tinier than usual. He was a man without purpose. Erin was tasked with extracting the truth from Chandling, and Marie, whoever she was, from Salazar. There was nothing he could do. His destiny was in their hands.

The stacks of case files sat before him on the coffee table. He began to flip through page after page, soaking in the details as best he could. Many were administrative—not very useful—but he stopped when he arrived at Patricia Giddy's official report. Without picking it up, he started reading.

Witness initially denied tipping off the FBI to the whereabouts and identity of Christopher Morgan, the report read. She claimed that she was sleeping at the time the tip was provided. Witness stated she had suspicions regarding suspect's income, but she "didn't know and didn't ask."

Following the discovery of Christopher Morgan's body, witness changed her story and said that she did call the FBI on the morning of January 6. Witness said she began to fear for her life in the weeks preceding the raid on Morgan's home. Morgan had become very paranoid and abusive (note: Giddy showed no signs of abuse in her initial interviews) and would disappear for long stretches at a time. Witness said she knew he "killed people for a living", but didn't know the specifics of his crimes. She found this out shortly after she moved in with him; he hid large amounts of cash in the apartment and often purchased new weapons. She feared he would have no problem killing her. She didn't originally say that she'd tipped off the FBI because Morgan was yet to be found and she was worried he would return for revenge.

For some reason, Ryan felt a rage swelling inside him. Had she loved him at one point? Had Morgan loved her? He had trusted her enough to live with her. And yet, she hadn't trusted him back. Instead, the bitch betrayed him, setting everything else that happened into motion.

He flipped to the second page, an addendum. There wasn't much on the page, but it read: Giddy, in the months following Morgan's disappearance, appeared on a variety of interview shows and news outlets. It is reported that she received payment for many of these interviews. At the time of this report, it is presumed that she has made over $350,000.

She betrayed Morgan and made money off the whole ordeal. Only in America.

That was the end of the report. The third page contained a black-and-white photo of Patricia. He stared at it for a minute. She was young and pretty, though her face showed signs of a tough childhood. She had flowing, wavy hair. Her eyes looked weary, old for such a young age.

A bead of sweat splattered on the photograph, across Patricia's cheek. He wiped his forehead. His skin was moist, the air suddenly hot.

He stared at her eyes. He'd seen her before.

"CHANDLING'S BEEN LEADING us on a wild goose chase since minute one," John declared angrily.

Erin moved her phone to the other hand. "He's trying to protect his wife's name."

"He's trying to protect himself." She could hear him pacing. "Why are you defending him? I know why, but why? If he was any other person…"

"He isn't just any other person."

"He lied to us. He told us no one had a motive to kill him. His family was gunned down before his eyes and he lied to us. And then Ryan was taken and he continued to lie to us. He doesn't deserve your sympathy."

Erin sighed, gazing out the car window. A couple crows fought over an indistinguishable lump of road kill cemented to the empty road. The gray skies were beginning to break apart, beams of sunlight filtering through to illuminate the surrounding trees. The window was cracked open an inch, the air seeping through still cool.

"David Humphries. See how he died, find out where he lived. I want to talk to his family." She was in no mood to argue with John, especially when she knew he was right. She wanted to give Chandling the benefit of the doubt. She wanted to believe that everything he had kept private had been for Kathy's sake. But he had lied to them, to her, for the last year, hindering their investigating, leaving Ryan to suffer in some laboratory. He was like family, but he was also a politician. Such news could have destroyed his campaign, and he'd been facing a tough challenger. His numbers had been down. His wife having a drug-fueled love affair would have been disastrous.

He'd been protecting himself. Not Kathy.

"I have to go," Erin stated and hung up. A shiny black pickup truck had driven by her and veered into the gas station across the street. Jedison Green emerged from the cab. She watched the man circle around the rear of his vehicle, eyes never leaving the ground. He continued walking, leaving his car behind. Erin straightened up and looked at his truck. His tank was on the driver's side, facing away from the pumps. Green wasn't pumping gas, she realized. He had stopped for her. His eyes lifted and he looked at her as he casually strolled across the street, his intense stare never wavering.

She rolled down the window.

"You trying to follow me, ma'am? Not a very good hiding spot."

"Not trying to follow you. Talk with you."

He nodded and smiled. It was an attractive, rugged smile. He leaned over and rested his elbows on her door, his head nearly in the car. She smelled aftershave, shampoo.

He continued to look at her. He was attracted to her, she thought at first, the way his eyes searched her, looked her over. But it wasn't that. He was studying her, waiting for a tell, trying to keep her on edge. Making her think about how he was looking at her. Distracting her, a sleight of hand.

"Well?" he said finally.

"David Humphries."

His eyes flickered. "I like my business because I get to protect my clients from the crazies. Sometimes you have to rough people a bit. Not happy about it, not ashamed, either."

"The senator…"

"You're not recording this?"

"No."

"The senator told me to convince the man that he wasn't to come around no more. Told me this Humphries character was threatening to destroy the family. It was a nice family. But you know that."

"So you convinced him."

"I tried to."

"Tell me exactly what happened."

Green didn't hesitate. He seemed unconcerned about admitting a crime to an FBI agent. He knew she cared little about him, about what he'd done. She was focused on the big picture. "I went over to the house. He was home alone, I made sure of that. He opened the door, I let myself in. I don't like wasting time, so we didn't talk much. One punch took him to the floor. After that it was mainly intimidation, a few more punches but mainly scare tactics. You give them a taste, let them know it's just a taste. If you have to come back again, they'll get the full meal."

"What did he say to you?"

"Like I said, we didn't talk much. He denied that he was trying to ruin the Senator, but what would you expect him to say? Mainly he just whimpered and begged for me to stop. I asked him if he understood, and he said 'yes'. I believed him. He understood."

"Do you think he had Chandling's family killed?"

Green leaned back and gazed into the distance, at nothing in particular. He contemplated the question. Then he shook his head, puffing out his cheeks. "No, ma'am. I don't see it." He looked at Erin again. "Humphries was a nobody. A loser. Hell, not even a loser. Just a guy who made some dumb mistakes. He was no killer."

"And yet…"

"And yet you have nothing else to go on," Green shrugged. "I understand. Maybe I'm wrong. Hell, I could be wrong. But if he was responsible, he must have been tripping one great trip to go to the lengths of hiring an assassin to gun down an entire family. It just doesn't make sense."

"No, it doesn't," Erin stated.

"Luis Salazar on the other hand…" he opened his mouth to say something more, then shook his head. "No, he's no mastermind either."

"What were you going to say?"

"He's a smart guy. Thinks very scientifically. He's a savvy business guy. But I don't see him murdering an innocent family and kidnapping Agent Harper. No, just can't see it." He gazed at her, but his analyzing stare had vanished, replaced with concern. "I've spent a fair amount of time with him. Relatively speaking. He and the senator meet frequently. I've always gotten a strange vibe from him. I can't quite place it. Like he's hiding something and is nervous as hell about it. I think you're on the right path there. I don't know what it is, but there's something there."

Green stood up and stepped back into the road. Erin wanted to ask him more but she got the sense the conversation was over. He turned away, started back to his truck. She started her engine.

"Oh, Agent Kinsley," he called out. "I know Salazar's been trying to befriend Agent Harper, right? That strikes me as very dangerous."

RYAN HARPER STUDIED the photo of Patricia Giddy, certain he'd never seen her before yet simultaneously convinced he had. It couldn't be her, he thought. It can't be. It didn't make any sense. It was unlike him. He would never do that to Erin, would never even consider betraying her.

But there were those weeks he didn't remember, the time period that preceded his disappearance. He'd been onto something, investigating the Chandling case behind the backs of John and Erin. What else had he done behind her back?

He was suddenly back in his dream, following the naked redhead down the hallway. She was Patricia and she was welcoming him into her bedroom. He followed her in and she turned to him, gentle and welcoming. She wrapped her arms and then her legs around him, her soft lips caressing his, the tips of her large breasts pressing against his chest. He threw her onto the bed and indulged himself, thrusting harder and harder until she cried. In his dream, she was silent, but he could see her expression, a twisted mix of pleasure and pain that urged him on.

"We have to stick together. We have to stick together," a woman in her earlier forties told him, angry and sad and lonely all at once. Her flowery dress hung from her hourglass frame, fluttering in a breeze from the open kitchen window. He stared up at her from a table, scared and furious. His mum put a revolver to her head and pulled the trigger.

Patricia again. Wearing clothes this time. Screaming, her mascara in streaks down her cheeks. "You fucking bastard," she said, throwing something at him. It was cash. "I can't do this anymore. You. Monster."

The Face appeared, closer than it ever had been before. The whispers were shrieks, hurricane-force winds exploding like percussion bonds. "Remember. Remember. Remember. Remember who you…"

He was back in the living room, the picture of Patricia Giddy in his clenched hand, the paper crumpled and moist from his sweat. He sucked in a deep breath and closed the case file, his world spinning. He stumbled into the bedroom, the walls caving in, and spotted Erin's laptop on the bedside table. He crawled across the bed and flipped open the screen, the computer humming to life. His trembling fingers struggled with the small keys, but he entered Erin's credentials, guessing her password on the second try.

He searched for Patricia's file, mistyping her name several times, his hands clammy, shaking uncontrollably. He couldn't believe it. He refused to believe it. All this time.

Her file loaded on screen. Her details. Her history. Current address. The same picture.

She mouthed her approval at him as he gazed down at her, at the pocket in her neck where a small pool of sweat had collected. She arched her head back.

He had to see her again. Had to know the truth. She had the answers he was seeking and now he knew who she was, where she lived. She would tell him what he needed to know.

The drive to Patricia's home was an agonizing blur. The world around him was crumbling at the seams; he could see it at the corner of his eyes. The houses, cars, roads, people, trees all fell into a creeping darkness, the very sight of them breaking away from reality and vanishing into an endless abyss. He kept his eyes straight ahead, afraid to look around, frightened to death to see the nothingness in the rearview mirror.

He was in his dream, but he was awake. He could hear the whispers, chanting now, screaming at him in their incoherent way. This was purgatory. He'd been dead the whole time. This was his reckoning.

He somehow made it to Patricia's street. She lived to the north, in Shoreline, a quaint neighborhood, the last place he would expect her to end up. The very air trembling around him, he could not read the numbers on the houses, so he parked the car and staggered onto the sidewalk. He blinked, trying to keep the row of houses in frame, but the nothingness tugged at his perception. Everything was twisting out of his control.

He stopped at a small chain link gate, the mailbox perched beside it matching Patricia's address. He looked up at her house, but it was all a haze, a distant, unreachable target.

A sound behind him. Two. He spun to look, seeing nothing but the blackness. Car doors. He'd heard car doors opening then slamming shut. A black town car sat across the street, the driver's side window rolled down. Nobody inside. Two men were crossing the street toward him, their features indistinguishable.

They were coming for him.

He turned to open the gate, his fingers fumbling with the latch. The men's footsteps echoed in his ears, momentarily drowning out the harsh whispers that assaulted him from all angles. The gate wouldn't budge. He glanced over his shoulder, frantic.

The men appeared beside him and seized him by the arms. He fought back but they held firm, tugging him toward the road. He shouted for help.

"Don't make me shut you up," one of the men stated in his ear. "Luis told me to tell you that he'd make it all better. You just need to trust us and get in the car."

He didn't trust them and he didn't want to get in the car, but he had no choice. They threw him into the back seat. He scrambled to the other side, ready to escape, but when he looked outside the world had fallen away, replaced by the deep blackness that had been pursuing him. The car shook and he realized they were moving.

Patricia climbed on top of him, her naked legs coiling around his ribs. She gazed down at him, her eyes filled with happiness, her smile wide. Somewhere in his mind he heard her laughing at him.

ERIN PARKED HER car in front of her building and scanned the parking lot as she climbed the stairs to her condo. Ryan's rental car was nowhere to be seen. He hadn't answered her phone calls, either. She frowned and jogged up the rest of the steps.

She started to put her key into the lock, but paused and then tried the doorknob. The door opened. Panic reverberating in the back of her mind, she nudged the door the rest of the way, letting it drift to a stop against the hallway wall. She drew her gun and entered.

"Ryan?" she called out, already knowing he wouldn't respond. Silence greeted her.

She moved methodically down the hallway, refusing to think about the possibilities. *Secure the room, worry about everything else after.* The living room was empty, her case files spread across the coffee room table. A few had fallen to the floor. She forced herself to look away and went into the bedroom. No one was there. Her laptop lay on the bed, screen open but dark. She put her gun away, finally allowing the gravity of the situation to sink in. Whatever had happened, Ryan had left in a hurry.

She returned to the living room and picked up the files on the floor. Patricia Giddy. Witness reports of the FBI assault. Dead-end tips and leads. As she set them back on the table, Erin noticed something on the couch. It was a crumpled photograph.

THE CAR SWERVED down the ramp, the tires screeching on the smooth pavement. The sky disappeared as the car descended into the parking garage, dropping floor after floor, seemingly to the pits of hell. Ryan watched the floor numbers flash by, ignoring the black tentacles that grasped at the edge of reality.

"Remember," the Face whispered in his ear, the rush of air through its hideous lips a horrendous, agonizing scream. "Remember who you—remember who you—remember who you…"

A security gate opened before them and the car passed through a narrow corridor, coming to a stop in a small room separated from the rest of the garage. The door beside Ryan opened and a pair of hands yanked him from the vehicle. He struggled to break free, but the hands clenched his shoulders, crushing them.

"Let him go," said a voice he recognized.

The hands released him and Ryan stumbled away from his captor. He looked up, blinking away the Face and the approaching blackness.

"Welcome home." It was Salazar. Directly ahead of him. Voice calm, distinguished. It had been him all along. He wanted to kill the man. It would all be over if he killed Salazar. Or they'd kill him if he tried. Either way, it had to be better than his reality, this waking nightmare. Ryan squinted, trying to see him. He saw a figure and lunged at it, grabbing Salazar by the collar with one hand, neck with the other.

"What's wrong with me?" Ryan screamed. The whispers were so loud he was sure Salazar could hear them.

"Everything will be okay soon," Salazar said soothingly. Ryan heard a click and the whispers stopped. The darkness was replaced by light and Salazar vanished, as did all existence.

29

ERIN LAY AWAKE in bed, staring at the dim ceiling. It was nearly midnight and Ryan still wasn't home. He wasn't answering his cell phone—she'd left him five voicemails before giving up—and she feared the worst. Many of countless possibilities came to mind. He'd been driving and blacked out behind the wheel. He was slumped in the corner of a booth, drinking himself into oblivion to vanquish his nightmares. He'd jumped off a bridge, the nightmares too much to handle. He was with Marie.

When the front door opened, she sat up immediately. She exhaled a long overdue breath and raced out of the bedroom, barely trying to veil her eagerness to see him.

Ryan's hair was unkempt. He was wearing jeans and a faded T-shirt, clothes she didn't recognize. It was evident he hadn't showered today. He stank of sweat. Despite all that, he looked more alive than she'd seen him since his return. The way he stood, the way he stared at her was different. His eyes met hers with a sizzling intensity. His chin was tight, one corner of his lips curled into a slight smile.

"Where were you?" Erin declared.

"Worried?" he tossed his keys on the floor. "I needed some alone time. To collect myself."

"You still could have—"

"I'm here, aren't I?" he insisted. The abruptness surprised her. His smirk grew. He was thinking something but she couldn't detect what it was. He came toward her and she couldn't help but smile, still not sure what to make of his approach but amused by how out of character it was.

"You look beautiful," he told her as his eyes flashed across every curve, muscle and ounce of fat on her body. She couldn't help but blush. His fingertips touched her waist, sending electricity up her spine. Something was different about him, like a weight had been lifted off his shoulders. His fingers found the patch of skin between her tank top and pajama buttons and slid across her pelvic bone, then her belly. They curled around her pajama strings and pulled, loosening the bunny ears. She watched him the whole time. He wanted her more than he had ever wanted her before, more than any man had ever wanted a woman. He didn't say it but she could see it in his eyes, a hunger that she was all too willing to satisfy.

Then he kissed her on the lips, a long, hard, passionate kiss that sent shock waves to her core. He tore away her top in an instant, while she worked to remove his shirt. His mouth moved up her neck, his teeth nipping at the soft skin. His hands worked their way down her pants, then her pants were on the floor, and he pinned her against the hallway wall. She gasped, shocked by his ferocity but simultaneously turned on. Her bare legs curled around his waist. He unzipped his pants. She looked at him but his mind was focused elsewhere. She didn't care. She felt him between her for the first time in a long time and he pressed hard, making up for all those long, miserable months.

IT WAS ALL so clear now. The blackness was gone, the dreams, the nightmares. He was here, out of his purgatory, with the scent of Erin Kinsley all over him. He was with her, fucking her against her hallway wall, determined to satisfy her in ways she'd never been satisfied before. He wanted every ounce of her, to devour her over and over again, and he'd get his way. She wanted it. She wanted him.

She panted loudly as he did her, his young, muscular body thrusting into hers. He could feel tears trickling down her face. Didn't know if they were from happiness or pain. Didn't care.

She was beautiful, sexy, and she was his for as long as he wanted it.

Patricia had been sexy, too. Bigger breasts, younger body. But she was a dumb slut, a girl who took off her clothes for a living and didn't think twice about it. She'd do anything, which was great, but there was no challenge or surprise. Ask her to do something and she'd do it. That's no way to live.

The bitch had recognized him at her door. She'd never met Ryan Harper in person, but of course she knew who he was. She wanted him, he could tell. And why not? He was a good-looking guy. Handsome, rugged, intelligent. But she'd probably given that look to countless guys since he'd died. Acted on it many times, too. That was her job, the slut.

She invited Ryan into her home. Of course she did. With the money she'd made from her television appearances and the cash she'd stolen from her dead assassin boyfriend, she'd bought a nice little house in the suburbs, worlds apart from the shithole where she'd lived before. She dressed like a suburban mom, too. Still looked hot.

She asked if he knew anything, and he said no. She told him that she slept better now than she had ever before, now that Christopher was dead. He had beat her. Terrorized her. Made her feel good sometimes, too, but not for long. Gave her money, but she knew where the money was coming from. A businessman cheating on his wife, no problem. A United States senator? Even she was smart enough to know that was bad business.

"Where's the money?" he had asked.

"Don't know what you mean."

"My cash. My money. From all the jobs."

"*Your* money?"

The money was upstairs, hidden in the attic. Typical dumb whore. So unintelligent, so uncreative. She didn't tell him, but he found it after he killed her.

He didn't just kill her, though. He punched her a few times until she was dazed, in no condition to fight back or scream for help. Didn't even break the skin on the knuckles, thankfully. She crawled along the floor, trying to escape, but he knocked her on her side and tore off her pink track suit and sports bra, just so he could see those magnificent breasts one more time. And to make her think he was going to rape her. There's nothing like that feeling that you can do anything, and that the woman knows it, too.

Her trembling lip squirting blood, she asked why. He told her why, told her who he was. She didn't believe him at first, but he made her believe.

Death by toaster. A rather unique way to die, to kill. He preferred a nice, clean, planned kill—especially one he was getting paid for—but every once in a while you just needed a good ol' fuck-you killing. He wrapped the cord around her neck and strangled her. That didn't kill her, didn't even cause her to pass out. She betrayed him so he wasn't going to be friendly to her. He bashed that toaster into her skull so many times her mother wouldn't be able to recognize her from a bowl of oatmeal.

He sat back and admired his work for several minutes, and to collect his breath. Adrenaline pumping through his heart, his entire body was on pins and needles. He wouldn't come down from this high for a long time.

Only a few hours earlier he'd been sitting on Luis Salazar's couch, suffering through his last nightmare. Only this time the nightmare was an awakening. The memories came flowing back to him, that of his mother right after paps beat the shit out of her and the day she decided they needed to stick together, with a good old family murder-suicide. She forgot to kill him before killing herself, though. And the many beautiful days he had watched luscious Erin Kinsley from across the street, the day he walked up to her front door, rang the doorbell and punched the shit out of her. The sight of watching those FBI agents flee for their lives as he gunned them down one by one in the forest.

The Face came to him. It told him to remember who he was, and he remembered. He was Ryan Harper. And he was Christopher Morgan.

PART III
TROJAN HORSE

30

THE ANXIETY HAD passed with a couple of valiums and he found himself sitting on a couch, high as a kite but feeling like the world made sense for the first time in a long time. Across from him, Salazar sat with his legs crossed, a glass of Cabernet hanging precariously from between two fingers. Sergey stood silently nearby, ready to react if he decided to go for Salazar's throat.

He wanted Salazar dead, but he wasn't going to kill him. Not now. Not today. He had a whole new life ahead of him and he needed to see where the pieces fell before making too many rash decisions. Salazar would die at his hand at some point, but he didn't know when. Tomorrow. A week. A month. Years. It remained to be seen.

"Why'd you do this to me?" Christopher Morgan asked, looking at his hands. They belonged to him, and yet they were the hands of Ryan Harper. Younger, leaner.

"I would have thought your first question would have been 'How?'" Salazar sipped his wine.

"Okay. How?"

"Brains are computers. Organic, extremely complex computers, but computers nonetheless. With data that can be copied and manipulated."

"You copied my brain." A statement. A question. Maybe both. "That's impossible."

"The technology exists. We discussed it and adapted it to the human brain. You just need to know how to store it and categorize it, and that's what we did."

"And this?" Morgan raised his arms.

"The brain can hold a lot of data. A lot of data. But a fully developed brain can't just be copied to another. To switch from one copy to the other, or to merge the data of two brains into one, would be too severe. The host brain wouldn't stand for it. You'd have an aneurism and your brain would shut down." Salazar leaned forward and set his glass down, next to the gun and bullets. "But, my company has developed ways to merge multiple sets of data together. Slowly feed the brain new data and eventually convince it that that data, that individual, is the dominant force."

He didn't understand. How could anyone?

"You look like Ryan Harper. You *are* Ryan Harper. You have his memories, his emotions. A full copy. I needed him to be there first so that his friends and loved ones would welcome him back. If he showed up talking and sounding like you, with none of his memories, it would be disastrous. Our program—visualized by the Face that has been haunting you—has been feeding you memories since you returned, convincing your brain that something's not right. We trick the brain into not trusting itself, so that when the switch is made—as it was for you just now—it doesn't shut down."

"What right do you... have?" he shouted angrily, though he suspected his words came out slurred and unintelligible.

"What rights I have are my concern. I gave you a second life. Your face was plastered over every television set in the world. Your days were limited. Even if you escaped you would have spent the rest of your life in hiding. This was your only chance. You're younger, better looking. You have a ready-made life."

"And Ryan Harper—"

"That's his emotions talking. What do you care about him?" He was right. He didn't care about the FBI agent or his friends or that life. And yet he felt a tinge of regret, sadness. He was feeling what Ryan Harper was feeling. "You'll learn to trust your emotions in time. The brain is still sorting things out. Yours is the dominant existence. You have his memories and his emotions, but use them as a resource, not a guide."

Christopher Morgan remained silent. He wanted to kill him. He was pretty sure Ryan Harper wanted to do the same. This man, this egotistical bastard, had taken their lives and conducted a sadistic science experiment with them. He had no right to do this to him. To them.

He would kill him. Not today, but he would kill him. Salazar would pay for what he did.

CHRISTOPHER MORGAN LAY naked next to Ryan Harper's girlfriend, stroking the curve of her back and ass with his knuckles, the same knuckles he had used to beat Patricia Giddy into submission only hours earlier. Erin's skin was moist with sweat. Her body pulsed in rhythm with her rapid breathing. He felt the scars he'd given her, their mere existence turning him on.

She purred at his touch and he liked it. She was a tough woman, but all women were the same. Get them into bed and you could do wondrous things with them.

Erin rolled onto her side and smiled. "I went and saw Richard today. He still denied Salazar's involvement. Told me a story that some guy was blackmailing him in exchange for keeping pornographic videos of his wife out of the news."

"Was it the truth?"

"Don't know. It was a wild story, but not one you can easily make up. I'm looking into it." She sighed. "If he's telling the truth, then everything we've thought is wrong."

"Salazar…"

"Maybe it's not what we think. I don't see how it could be, but I don't know anymore. Marie—if she's telling the truth—has been undercover with Salazar for several months now and hasn't found anything. Maybe Salazar isn't involved at all."

"Maybe," he agreed quietly.

"Your FBI friends are investigating me," Salazar had told him earlier. "I need them to stop."

The billionaire asked for his help to shift their attention away from him. The man who put his mind into another man's body, who had stripped him of his existence and tortured him for months with imaginary faces and splinters of painful memories.

"You were created to be an insider. Be good, act like Ryan Harper would act. You have his smarts, skills and knowledge. Once reinstated in the FBI there's no telling how far you can climb. Director of the Bureau perhaps. It's a win-win for both of us."

"You tried to kill me. Just the other day."

"Ah, yes," Salazar had nodded, once again picking up his glass of wine. "An unfortunate episode. A mistake."

"A mistake?" You don't accidentally hire two hit men to kill someone.

Salazar had shrugged as if it were no big deal. It was a big fucking deal, but he supposed billionaires could shrug off most any situation.

Morgan couldn't, though. He wouldn't. He had no interest in helping Salazar. But he did have an interest in helping himself. Salazar knew who he really was. Sergey knew, too, and surely others. He intended to make the best of his situation, and it only took one person to blow everything. If Erin and John continued to investigate Salazar, they would discover the truth, and once they did, it would be done. He couldn't let that happen. Every one of them would need to be dealt with swiftly and definitively. Only then would he be safe.

ERIN RAN A hand across her chest, feeling her heart pound against her rib cage. She closed her eyes, trying to calm her heart rate, listening to Ryan breathe. Tonight he'd made love to her repeatedly. Not as before, different, a more carnal, violent yet sensational attack. He had touched and held her differently, talked to her differently than what she remembered, but that didn't matter. If every night was like tonight, she could get used to it.

She glanced at Ryan to see if he had more in him, even though she wasn't sure she did. His lips were parted slightly, his eyes closed. He'd already fallen asleep.

Erin inched closer to Ryan and put her arm around him, her body against his. She lay there for a long time, exhausted but unable to sleep. The nightmares would come soon and she wanted to be there for him. She held him, waiting, but the nightmares never came. She was surprised and perplexed. Something great had happened to him today.

31

ERIN KINSLEY DRESSED in the living room, opting not to watch the news as she normally did in the morning. She'd watched Ryan sleep for an hour, unmoving, mouth open, tranquil. She'd never seen him sleep so peacefully, even before he was taken.

Her phone vibrated in her pocket. "I'll be right down," she said in a whisper, carrying her shoes to the front door. He deserved to sleep. After everything he'd been through, after all those torturous nights, he deserved at least one good night of sleep. Maybe the worst had passed, that more good nights were ahead for them. One day at a time.

"Sneaking out on me?"

"I was trying not to wake you," Erin turned to see Ryan leaning against the wall next to the bedroom door, naked. He slowly nodded his head, his expression restrained, and then pushed away from the wall and strode toward her. As he approached, his eyes fell to her body, carefully canvassing every curve. "You look incredibly sexy."

Erin smiled, a wide grin. He came nearer and nudged the front door closed with a fist. His other hand lingered on her waist, his body close.

"John's driving me today. I was just on my way out."

He didn't hear what she said. He kissed her, forcing her against the door. She received him warmly, her palms brushing his chest as he scooped her up in his arms. His hands slid across her body, then up her shirt.

"I have to go," she said reluctantly, pushing them away. He tried again and she laughed, rejecting him once more. He grunted his disapproval. "Later."

"Yeah," he huffed.

"I have work to do. You know, like figuring out what the hell happened to you," she punched him playfully in the shoulder. He didn't look pleased. "We're going to pay David Humphries' family a visit."

"Who?"

"The addict that was having an affair with Chandling's wife."

"Oh. Yeah," he shrugged, seemingly uninterested in anything other than ripping her clothes from her body.

"You want to tag along?"

He remained silent for a moment, then shook his head. "No, I have some shit I have to take care of."

"Like what?"

She'd asked it innocently, merely curious, but Ryan perceived the question in another light. "None of your business," he barked, glaring at her. As if realizing he had overstepped his bounds, he softened quickly. "Just some stuff, nothing of interest." He leaned forward, pecked her on the lips.

"Oh, okay," she laughed it off. Her phone began to vibrate again. Ryan turned away and retreated down the hallway. She stood in the doorway for a moment, perturbed by his behavior, but the intoxicating memories of the night before quickly erased any ill feelings. By the time she reached the parking lot and John's car, she'd forgotten about the minor outburst.

Little did she know it would be the first of many warning signs that the man she called Ryan Harper was not who he said he was.

DAVID HUMPHRIES' HOUSE was a two-story, four-bedroom clone of every other house in view. Light yellow with white trim, it had a small front yard with two Japanese maples and carefully groomed shrubbery. Dark-leafed rhododendrons and yellow roses lined the outer walls of the home. A hose ran across the driveway and onto the lawn, a sprinkler spraying water back and forth in a redundant rhythm. It was a place where bad things didn't happen. Usually.

Humphries had died a week after Senator Chandling's family was gunned down. He was declared dead at Tacoma General, but his verdict was sealed in his home, on the second floor. Paramedics responded to a call from his teenage daughter Emilie and found him foaming from the mouth in the upstairs bathroom, rubber hose hanging from his arm, the needle still stuck in the skin. Crack cocaine. Accidental overdose.

"Daughter said her dad didn't do drugs," Erin read from the report as John pulled into the driveway. "Emilie questioned the cause of his death."

A crisp little woman in her mid-forties greeted them at the door.

"Are you the wife of David Humphries?" John asked.

Her sparkling eyes dimmed at the question, but she didn't react in the way they expected. "Oh. No. He was the former owner. The family isn't here anymore, God bless them."

"Oh," John stated, glancing at Erin. The house was the last known address of the family.

"A tragedy, really. That's how we afforded the home. That's inconsiderate to say. You should talk to Margie next door. She should be home, I saw her out back earlier.

I didn't know them."

They found Margie bent over a row of carrots in her backyard, her legs, arms and face caked with dirt. She was in her late sixties or early seventies, elongated wrinkles streaking from her mouth, eyes and nose like war paint. But she moved around the garden quickly and diligently, her New Jersey upbringing oozing from her every movement and word.

"Yeah, it's a real shame with the Humphries. So much tragedy, how it all happened so quickly. Never would have taken Dave for a drug user."

"Did you know him well?"

"The whole family, yeah. Emilie, the daughter, not so much, but we got along. We'd all have dinner together once a month or so. Real nice family. Who were you again?"

"FBI. Agent Erin—"

"Oh," she looked surprised. "Didn't know you guys investigated this kind of thing. Not much to investigate. Just a horrible tragedy. One minute you're there and another you're not."

"You said you didn't take him for a drug user. You never noticed anything suspicious?"

"No," she shook her head. "Seemed like a good family. Dave liked washing his car. I'd see him every day out doing something. Even if it was pouring. He liked to jog, too. I have some pictures if you'd like to see. A few boxes I collected afterwards. I don't think Dave's parents could bear walking into that house. Some movers came and packed stuff up, auctioned off everything. I figure they'll come by eventually for what I have, but I understand why they haven't."

"We'd like to see the pictures, sure."

Erin liked putting names to faces. And not just a mug shot or yearbook photo, but candid photos that showed the person in their natural demeanor, with family or friends or animals or even alone. They revealed a lot about people. A serial killer could look just like any other dad at a family barbeque. A wife beater no different than his college buddies. A drug abuser could have the seemingly perfect life. But there was always at least one photo or relic that revealed that person's true character.

"Off with your shoes," Margie said as she slipped off her Crocs. "Don't want mud schlepped all over the place." She led them up carpeted stairs to a nicely decorated guest bedroom. She opened the closet door and started lifting and tugging several boxes into the open.

"Let me help you," John leaned over to help, but she swatted him away.

"I have it perfectly fine," she huffed. "And if you call that assaulting a law enforcement official, I'll swat you again."

Erin snorted a laugh and John stood up, red-faced but equally amused.

Margie opened each of the boxes and started removing picture frames, handing them one at a time to the agents. Many of them were of Emilie Humphries, documenting her growth from a button-cute toddler to a good-looking, raven-haired teenager. *She looks much like I did at that age*, Erin thought, placing the frames on the bed as Margie continued to pull more photos from the boxes. There was a picture of all three Humphries, including David's wife Gienna, somewhere in Africa, beaming next to a tribesman of some sort. Another showed them at Disneyland when Emilie was six or so.

"Here's the one I was looking for," Margie handed them a postcard-sized photo. It wasn't framed and had "Happy Holidays from the Humphries" printed at the bottom. "Gave this to me the previous Christmas. I couldn't bear to look at it myself so I put it here."

"Emilie. How old is she?" Erin asked.

"Oh, she must have been 17 in that picture, but turned 18 before that Christmas." Margie dabbed at her eyes with her earthy fingers, though there were no actual tears. "Poor girl."

"Where are the mother and daughter now?" John asked.

Margie stopped, her eyes darting up to John. "You are FBI right? As in law enforcement?"

"Yes…"

"I would have thought you'd done your research. The whole family is gone."

"I'm sorry... Gone? Dead?"

"Yes, dead. God wanted nothing to do with them, wiped them off the face of the planet. This does put things in a different light, yes."

John looked befuddled. Erin imagined she did, too.

"Gienna was so distraught after Dave's death. Poor thing didn't know what hit her. Drunk driver. That's what hit her. She had taken to walking by herself around the neighborhood at all times of the day. Since Dave's death, that is. Was out one night and some drunk kid—an illegal from Mexico—smashed right into her not two blocks from here. Killed the Mexican, too, so he got his punishment. That was a week after Dave died. Can you imagine what poor Emilie must have felt? I can't. Poor girl found her dad's gun—wouldn't have figured him for a gun owner, but I didn't see him as a druggie either—she shot herself in the head the morning before her mother's funeral. Thank God I was out in the morning. Probably would have been me who found her."

Erin couldn't believe her ears. A wave of death had swept over the family. One family gunned down, another family, lost in a series of seemingly freak incidents.

"Ever see Dave with anyone else? Frequent visitors, strangers…"

John's phone rang. He excused himself and stepped into the hallway.

"God, no. He loved Gienna. At least I assume he did. Never can tell these days. Clearly I didn't know him as well as I thought. Never can tell these days, even with people you think you know so well."

John reentered the room, his face flushed. "We have to go."

Erin knew something was wrong immediately. She thanked Margie for her time and allowed John to lead her outside, his hand on her arm. "That was Monroe. Patricia Giddy was just found murdered in her home."

32

"**YOU MURDERED PATRICIA** Giddy," Salazar looked up from his desk as Sergey led Morgan across his expansive office. It was simultaneously a statement and question, calmly made. Morgan could see the anger simmering just below the surface. Amused, he took in the details of the room, admiring the paintings and suits of armor that adorned the walls, the bird's eye view of Seattle before him.

Morgan slouched into one of the two chairs in front of the desk. "With a toaster."

"Ryan Harper wouldn't sit like that," Salazar snapped, but Morgan didn't move. Instead, he chuckled. Salazar looked worse than before, his facial bruises faded but his eyes tired, hair disheveled. The man was in over his head and knew it. Should have thought about that before you brain-fucked two men who could shoot you dead from 100 yards out. "I give you new life and the first thing you do is go and kill your ex-girlfriend? Are you fucking stupid?"

Give you new life. Salazar thought he was God, a manipulator of men. Maybe he was, but he wasn't going to get any respect. Not from him. "You get what you paid for."

"This isn't funny. This could jeopardize everything."

"Don't worry. I bleached the whole place down, removed finger prints, blah blah blah. If there's one thing I know how to do, it's kill people. Get away with it, too."

"We should be trying to let everything surrounding your case resolve quietly. Not attract more scrutiny. Your new friends are turning over rocks I'd rather they didn't turn over, and you're out giving them more ammunition to keep looking."

He had a point, but killing Patricia felt too damn good.

"Luis," Morgan smiled a toothy one, letting the "s" slide from his tongue nice and long. "I fell into some sorry groups of friends in my youth. After I left the Army. Real bad people, the lowest common denominator. There was this guy named

Gabby, a real tough guy who liked to call the shots. He was a well spoken fuckhole, probably went to a really nice school and thought he was going to be the shit at some point. Most of these 'friends' listened to this guy for some reason or another, most of all because he gave orders and sounded like he knew what he was talking about.

"One day he gets this idea to kill his son-in-law because he's beating the shit out of his daughter. So Gabby starts hatching out this intricate plan to take him out. Gabby is tough, but he's never killed a man before. He thinks he knows what he's talking about, but he ignores the simple stuff. How to make sure no one sees you dragging the husband out the front door. How to hide the body so no one ever finds it. Cover up the evidence. I point these things out and offer to give him some tips. I then start getting worried he's going to get me in big trouble, so I offer to do it myself. He says, 'No no no, this is my plan and I'm in control. Do what I say and we'll be fine.' Fine! I want things to go better than fine, and I don't want some fuckhole telling me what to do. I tell him, 'Fuck you and your plan.' He says, 'You're in on it already. You're part of the group.' If he gets caught, he's going to take me down with him.

"So I blow his brains out."

Salazar stared at him, wide-eyed.

"Let me clarify. You're Gabby in this situation. I'm me. Be careful who you give orders to."

"I see," the billionaire grimaced.

"I'm a killer. You took me and put me in a pretty face. That doesn't change who I am. Maybe you should have experimented with a prom queen or class president instead."

Salazar remained silent for a while longer, then said, "Maybe we got off on the wrong foot."

"Maybe."

"How can I make you happy?"

Morgan straightened in his chair and crossed his legs. "Money. We can talk about the full amounts later, but I want $100,000. Today."

"I figured you'd bring up money. Is that all?" Salazar was surprised.

"We can talk about the full amount later," he repeated. "That's what I need now. You probably have that in your wallet."

"I'll get you the money," Salazar glanced at Sergey. The pale figure nodded and slipped out of the office like a ghost.

"Where did you keep me?" Morgan changed the subject. "You know, when I was away."

"I don't know. One of our facilities."

"Where?" Morgan insisted.

He shrugged as if he didn't know. "That's not your concern."

"I want to know."

"I don't want to tell you."

"I have a million more questions. You going to play dumb on all of them?"

A bead of sweat had formed at Salazar's hairline. He was nervous, especially now that Sergey had left him alone. "Most of them. You have a new life. New opportunities. Why's it matter?"

"Curiosity," Morgan sneered, then stood up and spun away, leaving the billionaire at his desk. The man was a walking disaster. He was playing bad guy but didn't really know how to play. He could see it in his eyes, a deer blinded by oncoming headlights. Only in this case, the car would keep coming and the deer wouldn't move. Before he was done with him, he'd have a whole lot of money, a new life and a dead billionaire lying at his feet.

33

"CHRISTOPHER?"

Her swollen lips parted, bloodstained eyes widening.

"—A woman connected to the deaths of Senator Richard Chandling's family last year was found brutally murdered in her home today. Patricia Giddy, the former girlfriend of killer Christopher Morgan, was responsible for tipping off authorities this January—"

The toaster whistled through the air, striking the side of her skull. *Thwunk*. Blood erupting from her ears.

Christopher Morgan replayed Patricia's death in his mind. He pictured her teeth shattering from her mouth, her nose caving in as she gurgled for mercy.

As the adrenaline rush from the killing had faded, he acknowledged he'd been as reckless as Salazar had said. This was no time to attract attention to himself or the case, and no matter how much he made it look like an unrelated incident, people were going to link the crimes. He didn't regret it, but the death had been messy, too. Not his normal style. Maybe that was a good thing—a bullet to the head would have looked too much like a hit—but amidst the blood, brains, cartilage and everything else he could have missed something. Left evidence behind. A fingerprint or hair. He was thorough, but his mind had been on overdrive that day.

"—No official word has been given yet by either the Seattle Police Department or FBI—"

Morgan cranked up the volume, then leaned back in his seat. He closed his eyes, Patricia no longer a silent dream. Her desperate whimpers regurgitated in his head like Beethoven. He rolled down the car window, tapped the outside of the door with his fingers. A soft breeze swept through the vehicle.

"—neighbor discovered the body, but few details are available. Speculation is that

Giddy confronted an intruder in her home. Still, her connection to the assassination attempt on United States Senator Richard Chandling, which claimed the lives of his wife and daughter—"

After killing Patricia, he had trashed the house. Went through drawers, stole jewelry and ransacked her medicine cabinet. He'd been searching for the cash she stole from him, but mainly he wanted to cover up the true intentions of the crime.

"You change your rental car?" Erin snapped him back to reality as she hopped into the car. "Thanks for picking me up—John had to run out early and get Matthew from daycare. Lily…" He didn't care. Stopped listening. Patricia gasping for air. He felt Erin's hand on his. He rolled his eyes to look at her. Erin leaned over to peck him on the lips. *Now we're talking*. He grabbed her by the back of her skull and gave her a long, sensual kiss, which she warmly accepted. "I can't wait to get home either."

He smiled but said nothing as he pulled the car back onto the street.

"Wait, did you buy this car?" she placed her hands on the dash. No dust, brand new. New car smell and everything. A black Ford Mustang. A little flash, a little sexy, but not expensive. Nothing that would stand out, attract attention to him. Or his money. "I like it!"

She was so much more relaxed, so much happier. Now that he'd shown her a good time. Now that he was a new man.

"You heard about Patricia Giddy."

"Listening to it now," he switched off the radio.

She told him the details she knew, which were exactly what he had wanted her to think. He'd been smart about covering up crime scenes in the past, but now he had firsthand knowledge of how law enforcement approached evidence. It would come in handy for years to come. "The killer bludgeoned her to death with a toaster. Parts of her brain are stuck to the kitchen ceiling."

"The FBI taking over the case?" Morgan took a right and noticed that the car behind him, a white Ford Focus, did the same.

"No. We're letting the SPD take the reins with an FBI liaison. Initial analysis suggests it's a coincidental crime, and we'll treat it as such until the investigation suggests otherwise."

"What do you think?" Morgan took a left, and the white car did, too. It was following them and not even trying to hide it.

"Where are you going?" Erin asked. "The analysis is sound, but it's all too convenient. Seems to be a theme lately."

"What do you mean?" Morgan took a hard right onto a straightaway and gunned it. The white car did the same. He eased up, letting it approach. The driver was a ballsy son of a bitch. The car gained ground until it was nearly on his bumper. Then, suddenly, it veered into the opposing lane of traffic and accelerated. As it passed them, the beautiful blonde in the driver's seat threw a sideways glance at him. Then she swerved in front of him, nearly forcing him to slam the breaks, before zipping through the next intersection.

"Is that who I think it is?"

He didn't say anything. Erin already knew the answer.

He followed Marie, driving south. They entered the Sodo district, just south of downtown. An unappealing blend of industrial and commercial properties, Sodo was a flat landscape of warehouses, train tracks and fast food restaurants. All but devoid of residential property, the district emptied in the evening, the only activity commuters passing through on their way to greener pastures.

Marie parked in a small, vacant lot outside a dark warehouse and Morgan pulled up alongside her.

"Salazar is rattled," Marie said, remaining in her car. Her voice was once again different, deeper and firmer than the ditzy, sprightly one he'd grown accustomed to. "That's good. He likes things going to plan. As soon as his plans break down, he starts making mistakes."

"Good to see you, too," Erin said dryly, but could tell Marie meant business. She told Marie what Chandling had told her and what she'd found out about the Humphries family.

"I agree, they didn't die by accident." Marie said quickly, taking only a moment to process what Erin had said. "Nor Patricia Giddy, by a drug addict. Someone in a psychotic rage doesn't bleach the entire house of evidence. Very staged. How do Salazar and Humphries tie together?"

It was strange watching Marie like this. The cute little girl with a sweet French accent was no such thing. Dressed in a sexy summer skirt and T-shirt, her hair exactly the same as it should be, she had changed nothing about her appearance. But the way she moved her body, her head never tilting flirtatiously or her torso tipping forward to flaunt that amazing cleavage, combined with her deeper voice and hardened, determined stare, made her look entirely different. She looked tough, serious and most of all intelligent. She was dangerous.

"John Lancaster and I are still looking into it."

"We need to find that link. You've told him about me?"

"As much as we know, yes. Which isn't a lot."

"Okay," she nodded, then turned to Morgan. "And you, Ryan." *Ryan*. She still said his name the same sexy, flirtatious way.

Morgan shrugged. "I've just been sitting around doing nothing."

"And you? Marie?" Erin asked. Morgan knew Erin hated being left in the dark about Marie's affairs. About the woman's true identity. Then again, so did he.

"Since we last spoke, Salazar's team has revised the company's security protocols. They put special emphasis on a small internal network that I have so far been unable to access. I am certain that the information I need is there."

"So, same progress as last time?" Erin remarked. Morgan detected the faintest of smiles form on Marie's face. She found Erin's frustration amusing.

"Up until now, I didn't know precisely where to look. Now I do. I will access that network even if it means breaking into Salazar International headquarters to do so." Marie's smile remained, though it was no longer pleasant. She was deathly serious about what she was saying. "It's only a matter of time now. Salazar is on the verge of breaking. I will succeed."

He suddenly became aware of the sweat that had collected between his fingers and the steering wheel. The tightness in his chest, the onset of panic. He exhaled through his nose. *Calm. Always be calm.*

Morgan scanned the area. There were no security cameras, no people in sight. A car drove by, but only one. A train was chugging past on the far side of the building, its pistons hissing, thousands of tons of steel clanking and creaking along rusted tracks. It was enough noise. He threw a glance at Erin. Her gun protruded from underneath her jacket. He could easily seize it and put a slug in both women's heads. He leaned back in his seat, his right hand shifting to the space between the two seats. *Do it*, he told himself. *Rid yourself of two problems right now.*

He gazed at Marie. She stared back at him, her large eyes studying his. The bitch was smart, smarter than him. She could see right through him. Did she know what he was thinking? Could she see him processing the next move? She remained unmoving, on guard without appearing on guard. She had to have a gun in her car. It could be in her hand right now. He'd seen her in action before, seen how fast she reacted. How good of a shot she was. As soon as he'd make his move, she would be prepared.

Morgan put his right hand back on the steering wheel and forced himself to look away from Marie. Now wasn't the time. It was too risky. It was also too soon.

Both women were too valuable to eliminate. Erin would defend him to the end, even as he was choking the life from that pretty face of hers. And he needed Marie. She wanted to know what Salazar knew, and so did he. He was confident that she'd get it, and share it with him first. But he needed to learn more about her. Who she was. Where she came from. How he could use her to his advantage.

34

CHRISTOPHER MORGAN WATCHED the woman who called herself Marie emerge from the jewelry store, multiple shopping bags swinging from her bronze arms. She casually scanned her surroundings, her eyes hidden by a pair of designer sunglasses, and headed north toward the Belltown district.

Morgan exited the café across the street and started following her. She walked at a casual pace for several blocks before turning out of sight. He was certain she hadn't seen him, but when he rounded the next corner, she had vanished.

"Shit," he muttered. She could have gone either left or right. Entered a building. Jumped into a car. He continued to walk, searching for any sign of her. He saw an alleyway to the left. Hadn't noticed it before due to a truck that had been in his line of sight. He jogged across the street and entered the alley, a narrow slit in between two buildings. He stopped at the next block, looking in both directions. He saw something out of the corner of his eye. He looked but it was gone, vanished around another building. A shopping bag? He wasn't certain. He ran diagonally across the street and turned the corner.

There she was, walking briskly away, her shopping bags swinging at her side.

He followed her, gaining ground. She didn't look back. She had lost the cute girlfriend gait. She moved with purpose, having adopted a more serious, determined stride, her long, muscular legs taking her somewhere in a hurry. After several more blocks, Marie crossed the street, a residential strip shaded with large maple trees, and entered an apartment building. Morgan ran after her, praying the door wasn't locked. The apartment complex had six floors and if he didn't catch her soon, he might not at all.

The door was unlocked. He entered. A small hallway ran away from him toward the back of the building, and a large wooden staircase rose to the second floor. There was no elevator. He stopped and listened, waiting to hear Marie's footsteps above him. He heard nothing. He went toward the stairs anyway. Higher apartments had better security and provided a safer vantage point to see possible threats. She would not reside on ground level.

He didn't know she was there until it was too late. He'd put one foot on the stairs and the next thing he knew Marie was behind him, a gun to his neck, his arm twisted painfully behind him. She'd come out of nowhere.

"*Bonjour*," she whispered in his ear. "What are you doing here?"

By the time he turned around, the gun was nowhere to be seen, presumably hidden in one of her bags. She wasn't happy to see him. Not in this place.

"You saw me coming," he stated.

"Since you were sitting at the café 12 blocks back," she said icily. "What are you doing here?"

She was good. Damn, she was good.

"If you didn't want me to find this place, you wouldn't have led me here," he said, a gamble but one he assumed to be true. He'd followed her for blocks and she hadn't looked back. She knew he was there the whole time.

She relaxed just a little, pondering her own intentions. Then, without saying a word, she started up the stairs. Her apartment was on the third floor, facing the street. A studio, it looked more like a poorly furnished hotel room, with a queen bed, a small desk and not much else. There were no decorations, family photographs or anything else that would betray her identity—or slow her down if she had to pack in a hurry.

She double-locked the door and flipped on the overhead light. The blinds were closed, offering little sunlight.

"Nice place," he muttered.

"It serves my needs," she said, making no effort to lead him further into the apartment. They remained standing in the short entryway, extremely close to one another. "I cannot offer you a drink, other than water." There was no refrigerator in the tiny kitchenette in the corner.

"I'm fine," he looked her over. He realized he was sweating profusely from his pursuit, but she showed no signs of perspiration. "You're good at what you do."

"I am the best," she flashed her eyes at him. Flirtatious Marie was back. It kept him off his guard, kept him thinking about other things. Everything about her was an act, one calculated moment after the next. The mystery excited him.

"Who do you work for exactly?"

"I will not tell you that," she ran a hand through her long hair.

"What's your real name?"

She smiled at him but said nothing.

He felt his nostrils flare. He didn't know whether he wanted to kiss her or punch her. Maybe both. He had to know who else was involved in her investigation. She had to report to someone, and if she went missing, that someone would come looking for her.

"What *can* you tell me?"

"What *are* you doing here?" she asked. She'd asked the question before, but then it had been threatening, cold. Now she was curious.

He reached for her, a couple fingers touching her waist. She reacted instinctively, her hand grabbing and twisting his wrist. He winced, the pain excruciating, but he pressed toward her anyway. Her eyes widened, not sure about his intentions. He reached for her with his other hand and she acted defensively again. She was strong, much stronger than he could have imagined, but he was strong, too. Her back hit the wall. She stared at him again, unsure how to react. She didn't like being out of her comfort zone, not being in control. He knew how that felt. He leaned forward, kissed her on her closed lips. She didn't accept the kiss but he could feel and hear the warm air rushing in and out of her delicate nostrils. He drew away, just an inch or so, and waited for her reaction.

She stared at him for a moment, irritated and dumbfounded. Her eyes were as wide as a deer in headlights. She turned her face and took a small step away from him, but at the same time loosened her grip on his wrists. He wasn't ready to give up. He took hold of her waist, firmly. She didn't fight, not really. She turned to face him again, her expression unchanged. He kissed her again.

THE WOMAN WHO called herself Marie lay on her bed, a bed she rarely used let alone shared with anyone. Ryan was behind her, his body against her. He was perspiring heavily.

She didn't know what to think. She'd never made love to a man before. Sex, plenty, but she had never enjoyed it, never been with someone who she actually cared about.

She didn't know why she cared so much about Ryan Harper. She barely knew him. But there was something about the man that drew her to him. Her undercover mission had been a failure so far. Months wasted. Ryan's return had changed everything; the cracks were taking form, the dam about to break. She could see the stress in Salazar's face. But it was more than that, more than just the mission. Somewhere along the line it had become personal.

She was attracted to Ryan, she acknowledged. He was handsome, strong-willed, kind. She was designed to complete missions, not to develop feelings for others, but she had nonetheless. No matter how hard they tried, the ability to feel something for someone else couldn't be eradicated from a person's genetic structure. It was only natural.

And yet it was something more. Six months of Ryan's life had been taken from him, his body a living experiment. People did things to him that he could not control. Without memory or motive, he was still at their mercy. She could relate. Her entire life had been an experiment, always at the behest of someone else. She too was a lab rat and while she appreciated the gifts she'd been given, her life had been laid out for her, fate determined at birth.

Few people could understand that, but Ryan could. At least he would be able to once she got to the truth.

"What's your real name?" he cooed in her ear, his lips so close the hair on the back of her neck stood on end.

It was a loaded question. She didn't have a real name, and she had many. She was every person she'd ever been, yet she was no one. She didn't exist as herself, only as the characters she played to complete her mission. She never told anyone her real name, but she would tell him. "I operate under the codename Dolphin."

"Okay. But what's your real name?"

She rolled onto her back to look at him. He put his arm around her. "That is my real name. Dolphin."

He watched her for a moment. He didn't believe her at first, but then laughed and shook his head in acceptance. "Okay, Dolphin. You called that for a reason?"

"I'm the best swimmer you will ever know." Another loaded question, one she wasn't prepared to discuss.

"Must be. And what agency do you work for?"

"Just because I slept with you does not mean I am going to now tell you everything," she exhaled loudly, an attempt at playfulness. She wanted to tell him everything and yet feared doing so. It was against every protocol and instinct engrained in her head. To tell him even a few things would lead to more questions, many of which she would not answer. But it would make things so much easier, bring them closer together.

"But the French?" he asked, nibbling at her neck, his left hand caressing her chest. "Why do the French have an interest in all this?"

She closed her eyes, loving his touch. She giggled, not Marie's giggle but her own. She hadn't even known she was capable.

He was seducing her to get answers. She knew it. She couldn't blame him. She was a mystery and it was his job to solve such things. It was as natural for him to ask questions as it was for her to protect secrets.

She pushed Ryan off her, using her strength to pin him to the bed. She crawled on top of him, her bare legs straddling his sides.

"Why do you like me?" she asked in her hardened French accent. "My body?" He nodded. "My personality?" He nodded. "My accent?" In Marie's sweet accent. He nodded. She already knew the answers, but she wanted to hear from him. Marie was designed to be enticing, to be attractive and sexy to every man who encountered her. Even the toughest of men could be taken off guard by nice cleavage and a killer smile, even if just a little. That little distraction paid huge dividends.

Her accent went away, and with it a weight off her shoulders. Marie was gone and only Dolphin remained. "I'm not French," she said in an American accent, her own voice. She'd forgotten what it sounded like. "I'm assigned to cases the normal agencies can't handle. Top secret. Major damage control. Sovereignty protection. Foreign government restructuring. You name it, I will do it. You have to report to a director, the public, the President. I don't. I'm told to do a task or gather information, and am permitted to make decisions in the best interest of the United States."

As she expected, this left Ryan speechless. It was a lot to process. She was a super spy, paid for by black budgets signed off by senators and congressmen who knew nothing of her existence. She worked outside the structure of government, not bound by political motivations or public discretion. Few people in the world had access to her file. She did not exist.

"Wow," he exclaimed eventually. "Didn't see that coming. So… why are you so concerned about Luis Salazar?"

"Remains to be seen. My job is to determine what exactly Salazar is doing and assess the implications his actions have on the government. If he is a legitimate threat to the sovereignty of the United States, then I am to eliminate that threat."

Ryan remained silent, his eyes growing distant. She waited for him to process what she'd told him. No, she wasn't Marie. She wasn't innocent or harmless or stupid or anything else he had thought. She was dangerous. A killer. Tough-as-nails.

It was a quality she knew he desired. Erin Kinsley wasn't so much different than she, in many ways. She was more dangerous, more deadly than Erin, smarter, but not that dissimilar. But Ryan's demeanor changed as she hovered over him, the faintest of twitches in his expression. It unsettled her. Distrust. Fear.

She climbed off him, equally perplexed by her own reactions. She was disappointed, but she understood. She'd betrayed his trust. She'd lied to him. He'd fallen for a woman who didn't exist, and she'd pulled the rug out from under him. She'd been naïve for thinking he'd react any other way, for thinking that he would fall in love with her. And it wasn't love. He had lusted after her. Marie was young, pretty and as dumb as a brick. Men lusted after women like that. Ryan was no different.

"I'm going to take a shower," she said, suddenly furious at herself for letting her emotions get the best of her. Ryan made no attempt to follow. She crossed her tiny room, entered the bathroom and closed the door two-thirds of the way. Switched the shower on, didn't wait for it to get warm before getting in. Lowered her head, letting the water course through her hair and streak across her streamlined face.

She laughed. To be emotional was to be human. She shouldn't be upset for feeling things, for feeling conflicted. It was a sensation she wasn't used to, but there was something satisfying about it. Maybe her emotions were misleading her, making her overanalyze Ryan's reaction. Isn't that what emotions did? Confuse the mind, dilute the truth?

Dolphin remained in the shower for a while longer. The water burned her skin, but it felt good. She hoped Ryan would join her, her ears straining to hear the door creak open further, but he never did. Maybe he had taken the opportunity to leave, to return to Erin Kinsley, or maybe he was still lying in bed, waiting for her. It didn't matter, she realized.

She finally turned off the water and stepped out of the shower. The air felt cool. She dried herself, listening for Ryan's presence. The floor outside groaned. He was still there. She smiled to herself, lazily wrapping the towel around her body.

She emerged from the bathroom to find Ryan standing next to her desk, her pistol in hand. He was pressing the clip back into the grip of the weapon. His eyes flicked up to her. He turned to face her, the gun falling to his side. She stood watching him for a moment, and he did the same. Her instincts told her to react. He was armed and she wasn't. But this was Ryan Harper, standing naked before her, holding her gun. He wasn't a threat. For once her instincts were wrong.

"Interesting weapon," Ryan said softly, motionless.

"It doesn't fire for anyone but me," she looked around. He'd gone through her other desk drawers and looked in her closet. Most people wouldn't have noticed, but she wasn't most people.

He noticed her discovery and said, "I'm sorry. I was curious. You make me curious." He raised the gun, aimed it at the bed and pulled the trigger. There was a soft click but the chamber didn't fire. He nodded with approval, threw her a look and then set it down on her desk. "Come here."

She went to him, suppressing the warning signs that were sparking in her brain. He tugged at her towel and it fell to the floor. She felt his body on hers, his lips on her neck.

"We have to take Salazar down," he said in her ear.

"I know." Quietly, not wanting to think about Salazar right now.

"What you need is in his office."

"I know."

"Then get it."

His mouth moved across her cheek and he kissed her, long and hard. She grasped at his back, urging him on, but then he pulled away, shaking his head. She watched him dress and leave, confident that she would see him in this capacity again, completely unaware that he was already plotting her death.

35

THE BITCH HAD to die. Marie. Dolphin. Whatever the fuck her name was, she had to die.

The woman was more dangerous than he'd ever imagined. She would discover the truth about him and then it would be over. He had to kill her as soon as possible.

Christopher Morgan chose to walk back to his car rather than catch a cab. Evening had arrived, but the sun still hovered in the west. Lost in thought, he mapped out scenarios. Each plan was risky, downright reckless, but he had no option. He had to act quickly or wait for the inevitable.

Dolphin's scent lingered in his nostrils as he envisioned her death. He pictured her naked in his arms, his right hand around her throat. He should have killed her then, squeezed until her esophagus was crushed. But killing her wouldn't have been as easy as that. She was tough, deadly. She would have snaked out of his grip and gone straight to that snazzy gun of hers. Put a bullet between his eyes. No hesitation. She said it herself. She did what it took to accomplish her missions.

Still should have tried. Still should have figured out a way. Get your gun, return to her apartment and finish her off.

No, he urged himself. There was too much at stake, too many players in the game. She had to die, but so did Salazar, Erin and John. And he didn't want to just kill Salazar. He wanted to take down the whole house of cards, but he wouldn't be able to do that without her help. It was a risky gamble to let her burrow closer to the truth on her own, but the information could be invaluable to him. He could kill her then, if Salazar didn't do the job for him first. He had to play the two against each other.

The plan had formed in his mind by the time he reached his car. It wasn't perfect, it wasn't without its risks, but it was the best he could come up with. It had dawned on him how much he needed to know the full truth. Everything that had been done to him. What Salazar's plans were for him. Just killing him, and killing Dolphin, and killing anyone else who was a threat would not satisfy his needs. He rarely asked questions, but this time he had so many.

He called Salazar on his cell. It redirected to Sergey. The gruff security man begrudgingly informed him Salazar was out to dinner, said he'd be free later in the evening.

Salazar was a creature of habit. Only ate at half a dozen restaurants for dinner if he had any choice in the matter, which he almost always did. After two failed calls he found Salazar was dining at a place in West Seattle, overlooking the harbor.

The billionaire was seated in the corner at a small table, an open of bottle of wine in the center, a candle flickering in between him and his dinner partner. She was a young little thing, even younger than Dolphin, also blonde. Her face was unmemorable, but her body was to kill for.

"Marie not enough for you?" Morgan said as he strolled up to the table. Salazar's face reddened.

"Variety," Salazar brushed away the comment with a wave of the hand.

"Need to talk to you. Now."

"I take it it's urgent."

"You'll want to hear it."

"Excuse me," Salazar glanced at his date, who nodded understandingly. Only she didn't understand that he wanted her to leave. When she finally got it, her cheeks flushed, eyes angry, and she stormed away. Morgan took her place at the table. "What is it?"

"Marie. I fucked her."

Salazar didn't blink, but it was a forced reaction. The billionaire didn't like being screwed. Definitely didn't like his girlfriend getting screwed. "You came here to tell me that?" He played it cool. Impressive. If he was Salazar he would have lunged across the table and buried his knuckles into his face. Or at least he would have tried.

"She fucked me because she doesn't care about you. Not the way you think at least." Morgan picked up the girl's wine and put it to his nose. It smelled expensive, but he wasn't much of a drinker. It diluted the mind, caused him to make mistakes. He hadn't taken a sip since his boot camp days.

Salazar remained silent, struggling for composure, unable to respond.

"Oh. Sorry," Morgan grinned, amused. "She's a spy."

More silence. Then Salazar broke a smile. Even laughed. "You had me going there for a moment. Why did you really come here?"

"Her name isn't Marie. She's not even French," Morgan said, deadly serious. "She's an American spy. That woman on the boat. Y'know, who attacked you? That was her. She was trying to get a reaction out of you and she got it. She tapped your phone while you were unconscious and listened to you ordering a hit on me and Erin. She knows you're behind my disappearance and it's her job to figure out why."

The table cloth was now choked in Salazar's right hand.

"Luis, she is dangerous. She will take you down. And me with her."

Oh, the anger was simmering now. He wasn't even trying to hide it. His face was near purple, the veins on his neck and forehead bulging. His eyes looked like they were going to pop out of their sockets. Salazar suddenly jumped from his chair, knocking it to the floor, and flew across the restaurant. Morgan followed him across the room to the "Employee Only" door through which Salazar had fled. A large maintenance closet. Salazar was leaning against a set of shelves, hanging precariously over a splatter of vomit on the floor. Most of the food had yet to be digested.

"Feel better?"

"Not really," Salazar grumbled, but he straightened up and wiped his mouth. "You're telling the truth."

"I am."

"You hate me. You could just be fucking with me."

"That's why I didn't kill her myself. Knew you wouldn't believe me. You've got to see for yourself."

Salazar stared at him, looking ten years older. He'd missed a bit of puke on his cheek.

"It wasn't supposed to be like this. This isn't what I wanted—"

"You fuck with people's lives like this and what do you think was going to happen?"

"You don't understand," Salazar started to say something more but stopped himself.

"She wants access to some protected files you have in your office. She's been trying to get to them for months."

"Sergey told me to never take women in there."

"Smart man. Tomorrow night you're not going to listen to him. You're going to go out on the town, get a little drunk and demand a little one-on-one time somewhere kinky. You take her to your office."

"I'm not going to let her in there! Not after what you just—"

"Sergey will have a team waiting to take her out. She'll show her true colors to you, and then you'll know. And she'll know that you know, and trust me—there's nothing more satisfying. She's tough, but you see what she'll do to stay alive."

Salazar gave a feeble nod. For a man who had carried out the most elusive kidnapping in history, he was showing little gumption. But it did not matter. If Salazar succeeded, then Dolphin would die and he'd have to do some sleuthing himself. But they would underestimate her. She would get what she needed and escape, maybe even killing Salazar in the process. Then she would come to him.

36

THEIR FOOTSTEPS AND laughter echoed in the expansive lobby, the only other noise that of a bubbling fountain at the front entrance. The empty space, typically full of people and energy, felt surprisingly claustrophobic, the dark of night pressing against the tall windowed walls, the interior lighting reduced and television displays black.

A security guard sat by himself off to the left, watching them while trying to look inconspicuous. Dolphin wondered whether she would encounter him again later tonight.

Luis Salazar fondled her as they zigzagged to the elevators. She would trot away from him giggling, and he would chase after her like some pathetic lap dog, his hands outstretched. He would grab her by the hips and pull her into him, his fingers teasing where he wanted to go, and then she'd jab him in the ribs and squirt away from him once more.

Neither of them had drunk much, but both acted otherwise. Alcohol did not affect her—it was all an act—but even Salazar seemed overly flirtatious. No matter. He was taking her, for the first time ever, where she wanted to go.

"Where are we going, Luis?" Marie asked innocently, nestling her head into his as he held her from behind. He kissed at her neck, cupped her breasts and urged her toward the elevators with his pelvis. She knew where they were going. She'd been dropping hints all night. He only took his hands off her to press the button. As soon as the doors before them slid open, he pulled her inside. She rotated in his arms and kissed him long and hard, her hands fumbling with the buttons on his shirt.

"You bad boy," she said mockingly. "You never take me here."

"Thirty-seven," Salazar spat as her lips touched his neck, then his chest, then his abs. The voice-activated elevator rose as she went down. He awkwardly grabbed her by the chin and led her back to a standing position. "Not in here. Cameras."

"Are there cameras in the conference room?" she asked. "The break room? Your office?"

"No, no, and no," he gazed at her, a strange smile forming on his face. His nostrils puffed out as if he were angry.

The elevator doors opened and they stumbled into the hallway of the executive floor. She'd been here several times, but never outside of working hours. The main hallway remained lit, but the surrounding offices were dark. Empty. They were alone. It was perfect.

They stumbled into Salazar's office, a long, rectangular room with mahogany-paneled walls and décor that fit the billionaire's preference for international cultures: a knight's armor, paintings from the Persian empire, Chinese jade work, a Samurai sword. A wooden sculpture of an African warrior. It was a mismatch of items, but the arrangement worked nonetheless.

They left the lights off. Moonlight shone through the large windows behind the desk, painting the room in multiple shades of pale blue.

"I want to give you a treat," Marie took Salazar's hand and led him to his desk. She undid his belt. He gripped the side of his desk, letting her do the work. She unzipped his pants.

"Birthday came early," he muttered.

"Hold on," she took a step back. She opened her small purse and pulled out a vial of Chapstick. She grinned seductively at him, her eyes sparkling as she applied it to her thin lips, and then went to him once more. He kept his hands on the desk as she kissed him on the lips, soft and slowly. He closed his eyes, taking her in, but made no move to hold her. He wanted one thing and she wanted another, and tonight, for once, she'd get her way.

He emitted a slight groan and collapsed in her arms. She laid the unconscious body on the floor, her mind already on her next task. She sat down in his chair and activated his computer. The screen flashed on, revealing a password dialogue. The security protection would be state-of-the-art, but she'd spent six months hacking into the same systems. Different network, same weaknesses.

She inserted a USB drive and a moment later a small black popup appeared in the lower right corner, white symbols flashing by too quickly to read. The program she'd developed months earlier processed for just over six seconds, and then the password box filled itself in and submitted. His desktop appeared.

She began to copy the contents of his computer to her drive. The computer only contained a few gigabytes of valuable content, but a quick search of the drive indicated what she was looking for wasn't there. Using another, simpler program she had coded, she quickly tracked down the network drives to which he was connected. One stood out to her immediately, its name alarmingly blunt: //t_horse.

She clicked on the network drive and a second password prompt came up. Her program loaded immediately and began analyzing the network's defenses, searching for a hole. It took longer this time—nearly thirty seconds—but the password screen disappeared and was replaced with a large batch of files. She began copying.

Dolphin began clicking on folders and files, at first at random but then more systematically as she identified patterns in the naming schema. Simultaneously she put in a search for "Ryan Harper" and it began to process.

Numerous files contained biological records and test results, information she'd be able to understand given the time to read through them. But Salazar's office was not the place to do so. The billionaire would be out for hours, and they would probably be left undisturbed all night, but she would leave nothing to chance. Tonight was on her terms. She would be out of the building and away from this monster of a man in less than fifteen minutes.

Ryan Harper's name blinked on the screen. Dolphin moved her mouse to bring up the search matches. Dozens of files had been returned, all containing references to the FBI agent. She clicked on the first one. A diagram of a brain appeared, with different areas colored like a heat map. The second was another diagram, but the colored regions had expanded or contracted. The third was a log:

Patient 16 v2 (alias: Ryan Harper) development status, age 1, 3 weeks, pass
Patient 16 v2 development status, age 4, 4 weeks, pass
Patient 16 v2 development status, age 5, 4 weeks 1 day, pass
Physical progress pass
Patient 16 v2 development status, age 6, 5 weeks, pass
...

The log file continued for another 200 lines. Dolphin closed it. She started a search for 'Patient 16'.

The search returned results immediately. One file caught her eye, an executable. She clicked on it. 'Connecting' flashed for a moment, and then the screen went black, a search dialogue box at the top. Next to the search box was a dropdown containing the options 'Patient', 'Facility', 'Program' and 'All'. She left it on 'Patient' and typed '16'.

The screen filled with text. The patient's name was redacted, but every other piece of information, from hair color to body build, matched Ryan's description. The 'Original Date of Birth' was redacted as well. His intelligence rankings, from IQ to cognitive scores, were also listed.

The word 'Location' caught her eye. Next to the label, it said 'CA Facility'. The words were hyperlinked. She clicked on them and a topographical map of California loaded. A yellow marker indicated a point to the north, not far from the Oregon border. Her eyes widened. Dolphin stared at the dot for several seconds, processing its importance. She knew of the property. The marker indicated a piece of land that was owned by Luis Salazar. He had a summer cabin there. The land was otherwise uninhabited.

She froze. Her eyes left the computer screen for the first time in what seemed like hours and fell on the two large doors at the far end of the office. She'd heard a noise, ever so faint. A creak in the floor. It could be nothing. It could be something. She waited, not breathing, tuning out the hum of Salazar's computer. It came again, so faint she could barely hear it. A footstep. Was that it? Had she heard a footstep?

She removed the USB drive and placed it in a small pocket she'd built into her dress. She turned the computer monitor off.

The noise came again, more pronounced. She slipped out of her heels. Not a security guard. An entire team, moving into position. Her heart beat louder. It was a trap. Dolphin reacted immediately, darting for the door. The double doors burst open and four armed guards—three men and a woman—entered the office. Two held semi-automatic machine guns, the others pistols. All four wore vests.

The first three didn't fire a shot. She caught the first man in midstride, the full force of her body toppling him over and knocking the wind from his lungs. Before he hit the ground Dolphin made her move on the woman. Dolphin caught her in the face with an open palm before she could even process the attack. The impact broke her nose. The woman grunted and recoiled, but Dolphin grabbed her by the shoulder to hold her steady and punched her once more in the head, knocking her out cold.

Dolphin caught the second man in the waist, lifted him into the air and slammed him against the door frame. He cried out, but managed to elbow her in the temple. She felt the sensation of pain ripple down her spine, but the blow had little force.

Silently, breathlessly, she up-ended him and threw him on the ground, then delivered a single well-located punch to the head. He blacked out. Out of the corner of her eye, she saw the fourth guard raise his gun. He was young, scared, way out of his league. He hadn't signed up for this.

She grabbed a gun from the floor and lunged out of the office. The young guard fired three times, but in his haste his shots went wide. She didn't wait to return fire. Shooting blindly, she sprayed several rounds toward the guard. She heard an anguished scream. A body crumpled to the floor.

Her threat neutralized, she observed the young man she'd shot. He was lying on his back, his hand to his neck, blood squirting out from between his fingertips. He might live. He might die. His survival was irrelevant to her.

She looked back toward the elevators. Tranquility had once again returned to the office area. She'd expected more people to be lurking in the shadows, but nobody came. They'd only sent four after her. If they had they known who she really was, they would have sent an army.

But she still had 37 floors to go. The stairs were not an option, not anymore. The elevators were even more problematic. More guards would be arriving soon. She had 30 seconds max.

Her plan was still on track. She had what she'd come for and now she simply needed to get out. Salazar was her ticket home. She lifted Salazar up by the collar and slung her arm under his shoulder. She dragged the unconscious body across the room and into the hallway. One of the guards was beginning to stir, but it would be minutes before he could think—let alone see—clearly enough to do any damage. She reached the elevators and pressed the down button. There was a pleasant chime and the doors opened.

She ordered the elevator to descend to the lobby. The car began moving, but as she expected, it stopped moments later. No panic, no concern. She thought only of the steps necessary to complete her task. Dolphin sat Salazar down in the corner farthest from the overhead camera, his head rolling to one side, swollen lips parted wide. Then she peered up at the surveillance camera, knowing Sergey was watching her, his eyes beaming with satisfaction that he'd been right all along. She was trapped, or at least he would think so.

She had a hostage. The one hostage that mattered.

"Take me to the lobby or I will kill him," she said with a hard French accent.

She waited, listening. Ten long seconds dragged by and nothing happened. Dolphin backed away from the camera and put the gun to the billionaire's head. For a split second she thought of the long months they'd spent together. She had no desire one way or another to kill the man. If that's what it took to complete the mission, then so be it. Her job was to get the truth and she had it in her pocket.

"Five seconds," she stated to the camera. She knew Sergey was staring back at her, thinking.

Five seconds passed and her finger curled around the trigger. But she couldn't squeeze. If she killed him, she was done. Sergey knew that. That's why he didn't bite. And maybe he didn't care. Sergey had been in Salazar's employ for years and was rich as a result. If Salazar died, he could just move on to the next gig or retire to a beach somewhere.

But…

Dolphin knelt down beside the billionaire and buried the weapon between Salazar's legs. The muzzle nestled up against the base of the penis. A single bullet would tear it to shreds. She gazed up at the camera again, her cold, emotionless stare establishing that she would do it. Words were unnecessary. Sergey would be frowning now, processing his options. He had none, other than to play by her rules. There was no skin in the game if she killed his boss, but if she just removed his dick, that was more skin than Sergey would want to deal with. No man would forgive another for letting his penis get blown off.

The elevator began to lower.

"When the doors open, I do not want to see anyone. I will walk out of the building without seeing a soul," she growled, hoisting Salazar onto her shoulders. He was heavy but she was strong. Her shooting arm remained steady.

The elevator doors opened.

"SWEETHEART, I'LL BE home soon," Christopher Morgan told Erin Kinsley, then laughed at her response. "What do you mean I never call you 'sweetheart'?" He repositioned his cell phone between his shoulder and ear, knowing exactly what she meant. Ryan Harper never used the term, but he did.

Erin didn't push the issue, but insisted he come home soon. "I will, I'm just wrapping up a few things," he reassured her, wondering if she were waiting at home in some skimpy lingerie.

The thought didn't excite him nearly as much as the situation at hand, however. As Erin continued to yammer on, he gazed down at the crumpled body of his unwitting host, who lay just a few feet away. Smashed-in nose. Broken neck. The death had been quick, nearly painless. And most importantly, silent.

Now he sat in the man's home, the only noticeable noise the muffled sounds of the neighbor's television through the walls. A pet cat meowed somewhere in the other room, the refrigerator buzzed and churned as refrigerators do. The place was tranquil, the perfect spot to wait and watch.

Across the street, on the same floor directly across from him, was Dolphin's apartment. The lights were off but little did she know that the blinds, the ones she always kept closed, were open, giving him a full view of her home. As soon as the lights went on, hers would go out.

"I've got to go," he said hastily as his phone indicated another call coming in. He hung up on Erin and answered the other line. It was Sergey. "Well?"

"She escaped."

Morgan was unsure how to react. He'd been looking forward to this moment since the previous night, the chance to kill Dolphin himself. And yet the fact that she'd escaped spoke to her survival skills. She was a warrior who would fight to the end. Not unlike him. Would it be as easy to kill her as he expected? He wasn't so sure.

"Then I'll have to do your work for you."

"She's not what I expected."

"Salazar?"

"Unconscious but alive."

Morgan hung up and picked up his M24 sniper rifle. The last time he'd used one of these, he'd blown a hole in the skull of the female FBI agent he now knew to be Agent Halsbrooke. With luck, tonight, he would do the same to another woman.

Time seemed to slow to a crawl in the subsequent minutes. The rifle sat quietly by his side, waiting to be called to duty. It would take him just under three seconds to lift the weapon, aim it and find his target. He'd practiced many times in the last hour and at this range, the weapon was overkill.

A half hour passed. He began to doubt Dolphin's return. She was intelligent. Why would she come back here? It was foolish, naïve even. But she was confident in her abilities. She trusted him, and he was the only person who knew about her place.

He blinked, sat upright. A woman was crossing the street toward the front door to Dolphin's apartment building, her back to him. He leaned forward and snatched up the rifle. He centered her in his sights, the 10x magnification of the scope providing him a close-up view. Even magnified, he wasn't sure it was her. She was the right height and build, but was wearing a black hooded sweater that covered her hair and face. He couldn't kill the wrong person, not here.

She walked to the front door and put her key in the lock. His finger slid over the trigger, but he wasn't sure it was her. She slipped inside and was gone.

He shifted his aim to her apartment windows. The room was dark, but as soon as the lights went on he would know it was her. He waited, his lips smacking together in anticipation. He felt the contours of the rifle against his shoulder, cheek and hand, the resistance of the trigger to his finger. Dolphin had only moments to live.

37

"YOU NEED TO clean your place," was the first thing Erin said after Yusuf Himayat let her and John into his apartment. The one-bedroom unit had a couch, television and coffee table, but otherwise lacked decorations. A long-dead plant sat in the corner, its brown parched leaves hanging uneasily from the stem, and stacks of newspapers lined one of the walls. A few pizza and Chinese takeout boxes lined various crannies of the living room.

"Too busy," he blinked but seemed unaffected by the comment. "How come you didn't call me back sooner? I said it was important."

"Surprised you read newspapers," John kicked at one of the stacks. It swayed for a moment before coming to a rest against another stack.

Yusuf shrugged. "My mom got me a *Seattle Times* subscription. I told her I read all the important news online before they publish it, but she thinks I'll go blind if I stare at a computer screen all day." As if on cue, he rubbed his swollen eyes. "I should cancel, but I keep saying I'm going to at least scan through them."

"Good luck," Erin said dryly.

"This way," he waved for them to follow. They navigated through the mine field and entered Yusuf's dim bedroom, where it was clear he spent most of his time. They meandered around more pizza box stacks. The sheets on his twin bed hung halfway off the mattress. What Yusuf lacked in cleanliness he made up for in electronics, however.

"You have a better set up than at work," John stated with sincerity.

"Not quite, but I have to live up to my hacker reputation," Yusuf sat down before his electronic monstrosity and tapped a few keys.

Erin noticed a still frame from the mysterious video they'd received several weeks back, zoomed in on the scientist's face. Yusuf noticed her looking at it. "Still no luck. I haven't had any luck tracking down that guy. I searched every database I know and… nothing. On the plus side, I do have some good news for you."

"We're all ears."

"David Humphries," Yusuf stated. "The guy who allegedly died from a drug overdose."

"We know who he is."

"Right. You asked me to find a connection between him and Luis Salazar."

"What'd you find?" John asked impatiently.

"I didn't find any direct links. But I did find a guy named Darren Todd. Young guy, just out of college by a year or so. Worked as an aide for Senator Chandling."

"Go on," Erin sat down on the edge of Yusuf's bed but quickly reconsidered. The smell was worse closer to the sheets.

"As you know, Senator Chandling is instrumental in many of the grants provided to Salazar International. But he deals with big budget issues on the congressional floor. The details are worked out between Salazar's lobbyists and, among other people, Chandling's aides. It's all a little sketchy to begin with, but that's another story. Bottom line, Darren Todd's main responsibility was working with Salazar's team—and Luis Salazar directly at times—to produce the thousands of pages of legalese necessary for the grants to go through. Darren Todd reported to Senator Chandling but worked side by side with Luis Salazar."

"You think Todd was spying on Chandling for Salazar?"

"I bet if you ask Chandling whether Darren Todd knew about his wife's affair with David Humphries, he'd say 'yes.' Chandling had taken him under his wing. Too bad he's dead."

"How?"

"Darren Todd was run off the road near Olympia four days before Harper disappeared. Car went into a ditch and the impact snapped his neck. No suspects were ever identified. Some black paint was found on the bumper, but police were unable to link it back to a make or model."

"So he got rear-ended and—"

"Where the accident occurred there were no traffic signals, stop signs or crosswalks, so it was an odd place to have a fender bender. It also happened at night when there was little traffic," Yusuf stated. "I think this is the guy who contacted Harper. The reason he never showed was because he was dead."

Erin looked at John to see his reaction. "So Salazar finds out about Todd talking with an FBI agent and has him killed, but starts questioning how much he told Ryan already. He then orders Morgan to go after Ryan and me, because he assumes that I would know what Ryan knows."

"I just thought of something," John shook his head angrily. "Todd wouldn't have emailed Ryan, because he knew emails leave a paper trail. He probably did call Ryan, but not directly—he would have called the FBI and asked for him. The switchboard would have sent him to Ryan's cell, but in Ryan's phone records, the call would have shown up as coming from us. How could I be so stupid?"

Erin ran both hands through her hair. More pieces were beginning to fit, ever so slightly. The truth was close. As much as she wanted to discover it, she feared it, too. Ryan had gotten in over his head and Salazar had destroyed numerous lives to protect the truth. When revealed, things were going to become incredibly messy.

38

NO ONE HAD followed her. She was certain. She'd taken her time, meandering through the streets of Seattle, catching cabs for short rides, entering bars and exiting through the rear doors, blending in with strangers. She was safe, assuming her home was safe.

As she walked up the stairs to her apartment, she weighed her options one final time. Salazar had discovered that she was not who she said she was. It was unlikely he knew her true identity. Salazar intended to kill her right then and there; he hadn't thought about safe houses or backup plans. He had never considered the possibility that she'd escape. No one knew about this place. No one but Ryan Harper.

Dolphin reached her floor. She paused, listening for noises. Nothing. She brushed back her hood and went to her door, key in hand. She inserted it, rotated it and felt and heard it click free. She pushed the door open.

She knew immediately that she'd made a huge mistake. Her eyes fell on the window directly across from her, on the open blinds. The same blinds she'd closed months earlier and never touched since. The ones she would never open.

Dolphin spun away, her shoulder rotating up as she let her body fall beneath her. She felt a tearing sensation in her chest. She hit the floor hard, halfway in her apartment, halfway in the hall. The pain was intense. She'd been shot. Blood was splattered on the hallway wall.

Training and instinct took over immediately. She was still in the shooter's line of sight. *Move now.* Grimacing, she pushed herself to a kneeling position and crawled out of view. She closed her eyes against the pain. She could hear her blood splattering on the floor. She'd made a mistake. Too many mistakes. *Don't dwell on the past. Open your eyes.* She did and looked down at her shirt to see a large, red splotch on her chest, a couple inches from her shoulder. The wound was serious, but it had missed her heart.

She stood up, willing the pain away.

CHRISTOPHER MORGAN ABANDONED his rifle next to his dead host and ran toward the front door. He'd hit her, he knew, but hadn't killed her instantly. She would try to escape, even if she bled out in the process. He clambered down the stairs of the building, taking three steps at a time. His movements felt slow and heavy; every second he wasted he feared was another opportunity for her to weasel out of his grasp. She wouldn't make it far, but the thought of her escaping lingered in his mind.

He reached the ground floor and burst onto the street. It was quiet, deserted. He drew his sidearm, ran to the entranceway to Dolphin's building and shouldered his way inside. He started up the stairs but paused after a few steps. Next to him, on the railing, was a bloody handprint. She'd already made it downstairs. He backed down the stairs and followed the dim hallway to the rear of the building. He kicked open the exit door and cautiously stepped outside, gun at the ready. He scanned the alleyway. No fire escapes or dumpsters, only a few parked cars and a couple dampened cardboard boxes.

He spotted her, already a block and a half away, headed west. Even at this distance he could see she was in pain. He started running once more, pleased more than ever with his youthful body. Ryan ran fast and breathed well, an asset not to be underestimated.

Dolphin must have heard him, though, for she looked back and increased her pace. At her first opportunity, she cut to the right and disappeared.

HER SHOOTER WAS gaining ground. She only had a few more blocks to go, but it would be close. She was beginning to feel lightheaded, even though the bleeding had slowed considerably. The wound throbbed with every step, but the pain wasn't what worried her. Pain was a sensation, a distraction, and there was nothing she could do about it. Survival. Safety. Success. These were attainable, within her control.

She crossed Second Avenue, noticing how she was beginning to stagger. The loss of blood was starting to affect her, but she just needed a place where she could be safe. She clutched at her wound with her right hand, afraid to remove it, while she kept her other hand buried in her sweater pocket. She had no gun, but her pursuer didn't know that.

She rounded the corner, once again headed west. First Avenue was just ahead, and with it traffic and people. A popular and trendy block with restaurants, bars and nightclubs, she could hear the chatter of barhoppers and the steady beat of dance music. Her pursuer would be more hesitant to attack her here, but she couldn't dwell in the area. She was injured and would draw attention.

No one noticed her as she crossed the street. The intersection was alive with people, laughing and shouting and talking. They reeked of alcohol and sweat and perfume. The girls were all painted up as cute little things, the admiring men all looking the same with their white collared shirts and toothy, vacant grins. How nice it was for these people, she thought disdainfully, that they could live their lives in such ignorance to the world around them.

Dolphin glanced back. Beyond the crowds she could see the man—it was definitely a man, though she couldn't make out his face—approaching. His head moved back and forth determinedly, searching for her. She continued forward, the street dropping sharply as the city descended toward the cold, dark waters of Puget Sound. She didn't look back again until she'd reached the next intersection, but when she did she saw him at the top of the hill. He could shoot her from there if he were any good, but there were still too many people around. He began to jog down the hill.

Dolphin veered to the right and forced herself to run. Her pace felt sluggish. Each step she took aggravated her wound, but she pressed on. She was so close, so close to safety, but the man was only a block behind her and gaining.

She descended another block, the sounds of the bars, people and cars long gone. Buildings rose up on either side of her. The city continued to slant downwards as if carrying her toward inevitable reprieve. Or death. She could hear her pursuer's footsteps behind her, gaining ground, but she didn't look back. Fifty meters, maybe forty-five. As long as he was running he wasn't shooting; if he stopped, she was dead.

She barreled down the hill, nearly losing her footing at one point. She could see the water ahead of her, no more than a hundred meters away. Her pursuer was now 35 meters behind her.

She wanted to stop, to exhale, to just give up and let him approach her. Maybe he'd be cocky and come too close. But there was a reason why he'd shot her from afar. He knew she was dangerous at close distances. If she stopped, even momentarily, she'd lose her slim advantage.

She crossed the dual set of train tracks that split downtown from Puget Sound. A traffic signal—its red light casting an ominous glow on her surroundings—swayed gently under a late night breeze. The four-lane road beyond the tracks was quiet, not a car in sight. Gentle waves splashed against the wooden dock supports, the smell of salt water and gasoline pungent.

Dolphin darted across the road. Her vision was blurring, her limbs weak. The man was only twenty meters back. Did he see what she was about to do? If he knew about her, then he had to know where she was going. But he didn't know, not everything. He was close enough to shoot her. She didn't hear the footsteps anymore. He had stopped, and now was collecting his breath. One, two, maybe three breaths at most. Then he would raise his gun, steady his arms and fire. He wouldn't miss.

She was ten meters from the water's edge.

CHRISTOPHER MORGAN SUCKED in a deep breath, his lungs screaming at him, his body shaking. Calm yourself, he instructed his body. He took in another heavy mouthful of air and held it, his left hand taking his right and the pistol embraced within.

The bitch was his. She had nowhere else to go except over the edge and into the water, and what good would that serve her? She'd be a sitting duck.

He steadied the gun and brought the bloodied, frantic woman into his sights. At that moment nothing else existed in the world. He could see only her and the large target on her back, feel only the weight of the gun. He pulled the trigger.

She shifted to the left, just a couple of feet, a side-step that was so quick he had no time to adjust. It was as if she'd anticipated the exact moment he would pull the trigger.

He got her in her sights again, but it was too late. She threw herself over the wooden railing and vanished from sight. As he approached, he heard a heavy splash as her body toppled into the water. He reached the railing and peered over the edge. There was no space to hide beneath his feet, no dock to cower under.

He waited patiently, ready to pull the trigger as soon as he saw that blond mane of hers appear. But it didn't. She didn't.

As he stood there, the truth dawned on him. He knew what kind of woman she was. She was relentless. She didn't do things by chance. Not once in his pursuit had she shown the vaguest interest in throwing him off guard or losing him in crowds. She'd been headed to this spot this entire time. She had always intended, from the moment he shot her in the chest, to jump into the water.

39

ERIN KINSLEY FELT something heavy pressing down on her, the weight excruciating. Whatever it was ground its mass into her upper back, twisting until her skin split and burned.

She gasped loudly and awoke from the sound of her own agony. She slid off the couch, ignoring the papers piled on her lap, and staggered down the hallway to the bathroom, her mind numb with pain. It hadn't hurt this bad in months. Her flesh was on fire all over again, Christopher Morgan's stamp branding her once more. She found her medication, twisted the cap open and popped a pill into her mouth. She needed two. Wanted two. She took another.

Erin hunched over the sink, attempting to find a position that eased the pain. She splashed water over the once-boiled skin, attempting to soothe it, appease it like some angry God. She wanted to cry, but she refused to give in to misery.

After a few minutes, the medication kicked in and the searing pain transformed into a distant throbbing, never gone, but no longer debilitating. She straightened up and examined herself in the mirror. Her attack had sculpted itself into her face. She looked like crap, her eyes red and puffy.

She heard the front door open, the familiar sound of keys jingling in the lock. Ryan was home. He was just getting home. She wondered what time it was, realized that it had to be the middle of the night.

"Where were you?" she asked when he appeared in the doorway. He stared at her for a moment. Ice prickled up her spine.

"You should be asleep," he said finally.

"Where were you?" she repeated, a little more forcefully. He wasn't drunk. Didn't even looked tired. But she could smell the sweat on him, even see the stains on his collar.

"It's personal," he muttered, turning away.

She grabbed his arm. He rotated quickly, instinctively, and for a split second she thought he was going to hit her. It was an absurd thought. His body relaxed a moment later.

"You've been out late the last several nights. Hard to reach during the day. What's going on? Where have you been going?"

"Personal matters," he repeated calmly. Too calmly.

"Ryan—"

"Drop it," Ryan leaned forward and looked her straight in the eye. She stared back at him, at those eyes she'd known for so long. "Trust me," he said, and pecked her on the lips. "I love you."

She knew those eyes, but something was missing. She couldn't put her finger on it. He said he loved her but the statement sounded cold. It had sounded that way for weeks, if not longer. Was she just realizing it now?

She returned to bed and Ryan collapsed next to her, not bothering to change out of his clothes. She rolled onto her side and watched his profile, listening to his soft, calm breaths. She willed herself to go back to sleep but couldn't. She watched him for what seemed like hours, not sure whether he was awake.

"Yusuf found something today," she finally blurted out. "Evidence. Circumstantial, but it's a huge step in the right direction."

She told him about Darren Todd and the connection between him and Salazar. Darren Todd, young, lots of potential, killed tragically in an unsolved hit-and-run the same night Ryan was to meet with his mystery informant. "Chandling is unavailable until tomorrow afternoon. I didn't have a chance to confirm with him. But I looked at the police report. It's spotty at best, a real rush job."

"Hmm," Ryan murmured a response.

"This is about you, Ryan," she insisted, frustrated at his disinterest. "Salazar is the person that connects everything. He holds the answers. We just need to find the right leverage. We're close."

Ryan rolled onto his side to face her, his features masked in shadow. She suddenly felt pressure on her cheek and realized Ryan had grabbed her, his hands squeezing her skin. She gasped, shocked by how quickly he had seized her. Her heart beat louder. She wanted to push his hand away. He wasn't hurting her, but she didn't like his touch.

"Find the truth. Take down Salazar. But I can't be a part of it," he said, his voice low, unsettlingly calm. "I have too much stuff going, too much shit to figure out, to deal with it. To even think about it right now. You understand?"

She didn't. She couldn't comprehend. But she nodded anyway.

"I have to live the way I am regardless of what the truth is," he said, his grip softening. "I'm here, alive, with you. That's what matters to me." He kissed her, hard, his teeth knocking against hers. It was passionless, forceful, as if he had gathered all his strength to commit the act. She wasn't having it, not tonight, not the way he was treating her.

Ryan let go of her and returned to his side of the bed, to the very same position he'd been in moments before. He didn't speak again and neither did she, but she continued to watch him for a while longer. It was as if the last few minutes had been a dream, a blip of consciousness that hadn't really occurred.

She couldn't go to sleep. She had too many questions. But then it was morning, and she had indeed fallen asleep.

40

IT WAS STARTING to rain as Morgan parked in front of Luis Salazar's home. The sky was a light gray, the rain nothing more than a haze. The forecast had it getting worse before it got better.

The mansion, as Morgan soon discovered, was on lockdown. Even before he climbed out of the car, he eyed several guards. Two leaning against the short stone wall that bordered the property. Another two near the front entrance. A fifth milling around the property. Not rent-a-cops either. Private security, high end. Large heads, thicker necks, even thicker arms. Their muscles bulged, even through their parkas. Ex-military for sure. They weren't afraid of violence. Hell, they were thirsting for it. Not unlike him, Christopher Morgan thought as he approached the gate. These men just wanted a reason.

The two near the entrance had already gone on alert the moment his car entered the vicinity. They watched him warily as he walked toward them, eyes twitching with anticipation. Hands on holstered pistols.

Before they could intercept him, Sergey, more pale-faced than usual, emerged from the house to greet him.

"Where the hell have you been?" he snarled. "We thought you were dead. You didn't answer your goddamned phone all night."

"I wasn't in the talking mood," Morgan stated, brushing by Sergey.

"Well?"

Morgan walked through the front door and waited for the lawyer to follow. Sergey hustled inside and Morgan closed the door, preventing the guards from eavesdropping.

"She got away," Morgan said, his eyes adjusting to the dim interior lighting. Sergey grimaced. "Got her real good, though."

"How good?"

"Fifty-one mil through the upper chest. But she's a tough cookie."

Sergey put a radio to his lips. "Put eyes on nearby hospitals."

"She won't go to a hospital. You know that."

"How'd you let her get away?"

"I hit her from across the street. By the time I got there, she was two blocks away. Chased her through Belltown, almost got to her, but she jumped into the Sound near the Edgewater."

"Jumped into the Sound?" Sergey threw him a sideways glance. The look was almost comical, except Sergey wasn't smiling.

Morgan shrugged. "Don't know if she drowned or what." He wanted to say he was sure she was dead. That she hadn't gone far, that she had to be somewhere down there, gray as a ghost. But she'd already pulled off so much he'd be a fool to underestimate her. She'd jumped into that water. Hadn't even come up fighting for breath. *I'm the best swimmer you've ever met.* That's what she'd said to him.

"She has to be dead," Sergey reassured himself. As if not wanting to even think about the possibility of her survival, he changed topics. "She was alone with Luis for only twenty minutes or so. It was quiet the whole time. At first, that was normal. But when things didn't get heated, I realized something was up." A pause. "You were right."

"I told you not to underestimate her," Morgan commented. "You should get someone over to Third and Cedar, by the way. Her blood's all over the place. Maybe we can find out who the hell she really is." She'd told him. Had she told him the truth?

Sergey spoke into his radio again, delivering orders.

"Cops have gone through the scene by now, but I'm sure you're resourceful," Morgan muttered. He realized Sergey was leading him down a flight of stairs to a part of the house he hadn't before seen. The stairs descended to a plain hallway, the white walls decorated with nothing more than a few old photographs. Unlike the rest of the house, there was nothing ornate or fancy about it.

Sergey stopped in front of a door and reached into his pocket, withdrawing a chain of keys. A guard, a big black man with thick lips and a wide nose, stood idly by, muscular arms folded in front of him. Sergey and Morgan entered the room. As Sergey locked the door behind him, Morgan's eyes fell on a pale figure seated awkwardly on a couch in the corner. It was Salazar. His lips were chapped, face gray, eyes bloodshot, a crimson red. A pistol sat on the cushion next to him.

"You look like shit," Morgan stated.

"I feel like shit," the billionaire spat. "I want that traitorous bitch dead before noon."

"She's dead," Sergey said. "Harper shot her and she fell into the ocean."

"Good." The word was icy, venomous.

"She *jumped* into the ocean. I didn't say she was dead." Morgan looked around the room. It appeared to be a storage room, with boxes and dusty metal shelves lining the walls. There weren't any windows.

Salazar's eyes widened. *"What?"*

"Did she get what she wanted?" Morgan wasn't interested in Salazar's hysterics.

"No. Absolutely not," Sergey braked testily. "She was in there for twenty minutes. There's no way she was able to hack her way in."

"She knew how to get into your systems already. She's spent months preparing." Salazar tilted his head to look at his lawyer.

"There was no network activity coming from the office. And even if she did have access to your computer, she wouldn't have been able to break into the secure databanks."

"'No network activity'? None?" Morgan growled. She had gotten in. She had gotten what she wanted. What he wanted. "Even if she never got past the login screen, you would have seen activity. She covered it up. Don't doubt what she can do."

Sergey opened his mouth to say something but changed his mind. Salazar detected his hesitation. "Sergey, find out what she accessed. I don't care if it takes all goddamned day. We need to know."

They were worried. On any other day he would have loved to see Salazar shitting himself, but he too was worried. He'd made a mistake. He thought he could control the situation. Use Dolphin to his advantage. But that had been foolish. He had failed to kill her and she'd gotten away, perhaps with evidence that proved he was not who he said he was. He never should have let her get close to that information.

His only hope was that she was indeed dead. That her body would wash ashore somewhere. If she was still alive, he was fucked.

A SLIVER OF light extended across her cheek to the corner of her eye. She blinked but otherwise lay motionless. Even before she became aware of her surroundings she could feel her body, the soreness in her legs, tightness in her chest. She shivered. It was cool in her sanctuary and she was still wearing her soaked pants, her feet in small puddles of water. She was topless, her skin caked in dried salt and blood. Her right hand rested lazily on one of her breasts, holding a thick pad of bloodied gauze. It was no longer pressed against her wound as it had been when she'd fallen asleep the night before.

Dolphin winced as she shifted, straightening her legs and torso from the awkward sitting position she had, over the course of the night, slumped into. Breathless, she looked down at the bullet hole in her upper chest. It was already partially healed, thick, dried blood circling the wound. The bullet had gone in one way and out the other, she remembered. It had been a matter of stopping the blood loss. The rest would work itself out.

She was in a confined basement, gray dawn peeking through dirtied ceiling windows. She'd purchased the modest rambler six months earlier, shortly after the previous owner had died. She'd kept the mildewed furniture as it was, along with the old man's tool collection he kept in the basement. She'd barely touched the place since for she had no need to do so. Her very presence in the house spoke volumes of the mistakes she'd made over the last forty-eight hours.

Bloody gauze littered the concrete floor, the contents of a small medical kit sitting off to one side. Her soiled shirt lay crumpled beside her, cut and torn beyond repair.

Dolphin peeled off the rest of her clothes and walked to a set of dimly lit shelves in the corner. She dropped to her knees and reached into the shadows of the bottom shelf. She withdrew a black plastic bag and tore it open. She dressed quickly, the dry sweat suit an instant relief. She pulled the shirt's hood over her head and slipped into a pair of thin wool socks.

She quickly consumed two energy bars.

Reenergized, she looked around the room. A laptop, cell phone and pistol lay on the ground next to the spot where'd she fallen asleep. She barely remembered traveling to the house other than a blurred patchwork of moments stumbling along residential sidewalks and backyards. She didn't recall entering the house or the basement, let alone booting up her backup laptop and connecting the flash drive containing Luis Salazar's stolen files. In her dazed stupor, as she applied bandages to her wound, she had simultaneously started analyzing the files.

Dolphin picked up the laptop, phone and gun and placed them on a workbench. She booted up the laptop and began to take in the thousands of files at her disposal. As the machine processed, the extent to which she'd been betrayed overwhelmed her.

She had put her full trust in Ryan and he had betrayed her. He'd been working with Salazar all along. She hadn't seen it. Somehow. Salazar had recruited Ryan Harper and in return the FBI agent had told him everything about her. She'd made love to him; he had simply seduced her. He'd beaten her at her own game. And almost taken her life.

Erin Kinsley. Dolphin couldn't help but think of her. She was unknowingly investigating her own boyfriend. It was only a matter of time before she broke the case, and then what? Ryan wouldn't let her get that far. He was just waiting for the right moment. He had to see the guise crumbling away. He would kill her.

She had to warn her. She picked up the phone, typed Erin's number. Her thumb hovered over the Call button. But Erin wasn't her concern. Dolphin was close to completing her mission and nothing could stand in her way. Who knew how much Ryan watched her. Her phone could be bugged. Calling her would put Erin in greater jeopardy. It would also confirm to Morgan that she was alive. Dolphin cleared the phone and set it back down on the table. It was a risk she couldn't take. Not now.

A map appeared on her laptop, a topographical layout of the west coast of the United States. A yellow spot pinpointed a location in northern California, the latitude and longitude of her next destination displayed beneath.

She once again had the upper hand. She had Salazar's files. She had the evidence she needed to take him down. And if the malware she'd programmed was working as planned, Salazar didn't even know she'd succeeded.

41

"ANOTHER DEAD END."

Erin didn't flinch as John dropped a stack of paper in front of her. He circled around the conference room table and plopped into a chair, sighing heavily.

"It wasn't going to be that easy," Erin slid her index finger across the top sheet, barely looking at it.

"No abnormalities," John leaned forward and pulled the stack to him. He started flipping through them. "If Darren Todd received any compensation for spying on Chandling, he didn't put the money in the bank."

"The kid was a Yale grad. He wasn't stupid."

"Yeah, but he was a kid. They make mistakes. They buy cars, spend a shitload of money on strippers. Throw some cash around to impress a girl. Something," John stated. "Darren Todd didn't do that. He was perfect."

"According to his financial records," Erin didn't look up. "It's not the whole picture."

John opened his mouth to say something but refrained. He leaned forward, resting his elbows on the table. "What's wrong?"

"Didn't sleep well."

"Oh come on," John rolled his eyes. "Yesterday you were fired up about Darren Todd. You were convinced this guy was the key." There was a momentary silence. She didn't look up, not right away. But when she did, John was glaring at her with those suspicious eyes of him. She knew what he wanted to ask. He knew she was sick of him asking.

"He's fine."

She said so reluctantly. John picked up on her hesitancy immediately. Even with her eyes on the pad of paper in front of her she pictured him leaning forward, his chair squeaking as he changed positions. She waited for him to ask the question, knowing it was inevitable, wondering if she'd purposely shown her hand. She had to tell someone. John was the only person in whom she could confide.

"What's going on?"

"Ryan's just pissing me off right now. It's nothing."

"I know you better than that."

He did. She gazed up at John. He was concerned.

"I don't know what it is. I can't put my finger it on."

John's cherubic face crinkled. "I've barely spoken with him in weeks. He seems like a different person."

"He *is* a different person," Erin stated, her fists clenching. "Whatever happened to him changed him. And not for the better. I don't like what he's becoming." She pinched her lips shut. She'd vowed not to talk to John about this. He was already suspicious about Ryan and she loathed him for it. John, Ryan's best friend, had never fully trusted him since his return. She'd never been able to figure it out, his reasoning. But maybe it was just obvious and she'd ignored the signs. Refused to see them.

She realized he was waiting for her to continue. "He's been a complete asshole the last few nights. Like he's tired of me all of a sudden. But it's not that. It's like he has something on his mind so pressing he can't think about anything else. He comes home at all hours of the night, too. Don't ask me doing what. I don't know."

"You've always been open with each other."

"That's the scary part. Whatever he's hiding from me, he doesn't want me to know. But what could that be? What could that possibly be? We're trying to find out what happened to him and he's completely disinterested. I don't get what is more important than that."

"Another woman?"

"No," Erin shook her head defiantly. "Not that."

John raised an eyebrow, dubious.

"It's not that," she insisted. "It's something else. Bigger."

John's gaze drifted away, to no place in particular. He nodded to himself as if contemplating what Ryan could be up to, as if he had any way of knowing.

"I don't know where he was the day Patricia Giddy got killed." The words hung in the air for what seemed like minutes.

"What are you saying?" John didn't blink.

Erin laughed, reclining in her chair. "I don't know. I don't think he killed her. He didn't kill her. But it's been nagging at me."

"You must have said it for a reason."

"Like I said, something's just not right. I don't know what it is."

Maybe he had remembered something he'd forgotten. For a couple days, he had seemed more relaxed than she'd ever seen him. His nightmares had gone away. The sex had been amazing. Everything had been all right. But then he'd begun to distance himself, hiding whatever he was doing. Had he remembered something he didn't want her to know? He'd hidden things from her before, from before he disappeared. What if he was hiding those same things again?

She realized John hadn't weighed in on what she'd said. He noticed her gaze and stated, "Ryan didn't kill Patricia."

"I feel he knows more about it then he's letting on."

"Have you asked him?"

"No." She was scared to. Scared how he would react. Scared of the truth.

John scratched at his chin. "When was the last time you heard from Marie?"

"A while," Erin muttered. Her mind suddenly went in a different direction. Could it be that simple? Could it be Marie? Not Marie, the super secret spy, but Marie, the hopelessly gorgeous girl that Ryan drooled over every time he was in her presence. Maybe he *was* cheating on her. Sleeping with Marie.

"I've never known Ryan to be a cheater," John read her mind. "Never saw it in him."

But he's different now. He was a changed man.

She began to speak when the door opened and Yusuf poked his head inside. "Monroe wants to see you. Right away."

It was a thankful reprieve. A part of her was relieved that she'd been able to share her concerns with someone, but it would only feed John's suspicions about Ryan. There had to be a logical explanation for Ryan's actions, one that didn't involve murder or cheating. She just couldn't picture it.

She and John walked down the hallway, headed toward Monroe's office. She slowed as they approached. Standing outside Monroe's closed office door was Jedison Green.

CHRISTOPHER MORGAN SAT silently in the corner of Luis Salazar's sanctuary, watching the chaos around him. The room, devoid of sunlight, appeared smaller by the minute. The stagnant air grew thicker. The temperature was a few degrees beyond comfortable. Sergey had been on the phone talking at a feverish pace with the security team and his IT staff. He stabbed at a laptop with his index fingers. Salazar paced nervously back and forth, chewing on his fingernails. Every few seconds he threw a glance at the television screen in the corner, rotating security feeds appearing every few seconds. As if he expected Dolphin to emerge in the hallway, gun in hand.

Morgan's hands rested calmly in his lap, his body unmoving. To anyone else, his demeanor would appear tranquil, even unconcerned. In reality, he was as far from calm as one could get. He only gained satisfaction from seeing Salazar run around like a headless chicken. Dolphin had been right. The billionaire liked being in control. As soon as he lost that control, his armor disintegrated. The billionaire was a businessman first and foremost. He had overextended his reach, and to what end? To play mad scientist by toying with human experiments? He was in a mess that was continuing to get worse.

But Morgan was in that mess, too. Hell, he was the mess. He was the proof, the final product of everything that had gone wrong. Dolphin's survival meant that shit had just exploded. Had hit the figurative fan.

Dolphin was alive. Morgan knew it. And Salazar had tried to kill her. She would come at the billionaire with everything she had. Then she would come after him.

"Initial blood work came back," Sergey's voice caught Morgan's attention. He looked over to see the gaunt lawyer reading something on his laptop. Salazar stopped mid-step, waiting for more information. "Nothing so far."

Of course not.

"How's the scan going?" Salazar circled around the desk to look over Sergey's shoulder. "I'm less concerned with who she is than what she gained access to."

Sergey frowned. "She definitely got into the system. I'm processing the logs from last night, line by line. I'm finding some blips in activity, but nothing substantial. She covered her tracks well. At a glance, you'd never know she was there."

"She got in," Salazar stated vacantly. His skin managed to drain of even more color. "What did she look at?"

"Still working on that."

"Sergey—"

"I'm working as fast as I can. She's good. She didn't want us to see what she was looking at."

"Could she have gotten into..."

"No. No, I don't think so. It would have taken time just to crack through our normal security protocols, let alone the other firewall layers to get to those files."

"Keep looking."

"What exactly is in these files that you're so worried about?" Morgan asked, still seated in the corner.

Salazar looked at him icily. "Files you should hope never see the light of day. Proof that you aren't who everyone thinks you are. Information about our procedures, algorithms. I should never have gone along with this. This is not good."

"Calm down, Luis," Sergey gazed up at his boss. Salazar's behavior was even making Sergey nervous. "She's dead, and if she isn't, she's near death. And she didn't get into those files."

"You better be right, because if you're not we're all dead."

42

ERIN SUCKED IN a breath when she saw Jedison Green in the hallway outside Special Agent in Charge Monroe's office. He seemed to hear her for he looked up immediately and grinned ever so slightly. "Agent Kinsley," he acknowledged.

"Jedison, nice to see you."

"I believe they're waiting for you two," he motioned to the closed door.

She threw John a nervous look. He gazed back at her, masking his emotion. He was as nervous as she was. She turned the doorknob.

"Sit down," Monroe said as soon as they'd entered. Erin's eyes fell on Senator Chandling, who turned and looked at her over his shoulder. He frowned, then returned his attention to Monroe. The SAC was already tapping his dark fingers together. He was angry.

John and Erin seated themselves beside Chandling. She felt like a schoolgirl who had just been caught smoking in the restroom.

"The senator was in the area and decided to stop by. He wanted to get an update on your investigation, see if you had found any evidence that links Luis Salazar to his family's death."

Erin threw a sideways glance at Chandling, but he continued to stare straight ahead.

"We're making progress on the case, but it's still too early—"

"Why don't you explain to the senator the progress you *have* made." He wanted to know, too. She and John had left him in the dark, and he hated surprises.

She outlined what they had discovered; Chandling remained silent, unmoving, his stare focused on nothing as if he'd slipped into a trance. He took the news hard, she deduced, though she had expected a more emotional response. He was an emotional man, not one to stand cold-faced behind a podium, let alone in private.

But she understood his shock. Up until now so much had been conjecture, thinly related ideas and pieces of evidence that could be molded a dozen different ways. Darren Todd changed things. He solidified the idea Erin had proposed to Chandling, that his family, Luis Salazar, David Humphries and Ryan Harper were all connected.

"Darren Todd knew about your wife's affair," John chimed in. "He told Salazar. Salazar convinced Humphries to blackmail you, knowing that you didn't have the money to pay him off. You would go to Salazar for help, and in return he would be owed a favor. But you didn't bite and the plan imploded, forcing Salazar to clean up the mess he created. Ryan figured this out but didn't have any evidence. Darren Todd, frightened by the violence, went to Ryan for help, but Salazar found out and had him killed as well. Fearing what Ryan had already learned, Salazar arranged for his demise."

"I trust your analysis," was all SAC Monroe had to say at first. "But is there any evidence?" Erin could tell from the expression on his face that their discovery had piqued his interest.

"We're still working on that."

Monroe frowned, but redirected his attention to Chandling. "Senator, what do you think of all this?"

"I didn't want to believe it," Chandling said flatly, his eyes finally flicking up to meet Monroe's. "It's ridiculous. Preposterous. But what they say makes some sense." He dabbed at his eye with his knuckle. "My family." Lip quivering. "They were taken from me. And all this time it was my friend. Friend." Laughter, not at all pleasant. "*Friend!* He murdered my family."

Monroe appeared to mull everything over for a moment, and then looked at Erin. "I want to know more about this Darren Todd. Dig up what you can. Then bring Salazar in for questioning."

"Is that wise?" Chandling asked. "He's covered his tracks so well. If he finds out you're investigating him, he'll wipe out any remaining evidence."

"And probably hide behind an army of lawyers," Monroe muttered. "But if he has the only remaining evidence, then that's where we go. We can only tread carefully for so long. If he's responsible—and I trust Agent Kinsley and Agent Lancaster— then we need to put him in his place. Show him that the FBI is not to be messed with."

"I just don't know—"

"Thanks for coming by, senator," Monroe focused on a piece of paper on his desk. "You're always welcome, but thanks to these agents' hard work, my day just got a little busier."

"Of course," Chandling stood up and, without looking at Erin or John, strode out of the room. They rose to follow.

"Don't even think about leaving," Monroe walked around his desk and closed his door, trapping them inside. "What the hell was that?"

She told him about the altered satellite photographs, leaving out Yusuf's involvement. "The technical analysis was forged as well." Someone on the inside was involved.

"And what? You thought I was that person?" he barked, one of his eyebrows rising to his scalp.

"We wanted to keep things off radar," John stated.

"You still don't have any evidence. All of it, you've just strung together stories. I'll admit they fit. At least sort of. But there's no evidence."

"We will find it. We're getting close," Erin said.

Monroe breathed out heavily, his anger receding. He returned to his desk and sat down in his chair. "I want you to talk with Luis Salazar. But don't persecute the man. Ask him about Darren Todd. Interview him, don't interrogate him. Don't make him feel like he needs a lawyer, or needs to start watching his back. You need a lot more than what you have before you can go after him with the big guns."

"Thank you, sir," John stated.

"When you do bring him in, you better make sure whatever you find sticks. Even if you're right—and I trust you, Agent Kinsley—a shit storm will rain down on us and none of us want that. Politics aside, though…" He sighed nervously. "Be careful. I have trouble believing that someone in the FBI, let alone the government at large, participated in Agent Harper's abduction. But you seem to think otherwise. Whoever's responsible won't hesitate to lash out again."

A STORM HAD rolled across the Sound. The surrounding mountains had vanished, replaced by an impenetrable grayness that sucked away all color.

Christopher Morgan was oblivious to the storm, seated in the dungeon where he wasted away with his unintended allies. He wondered why he remained with them, stranding himself in this false fortress of solitude. He should be out there, hunting. Not inside, waiting.

Waiting was all Salazar had left. The billionaire now watched the security feed without interruption, consumed by paranoia. His body tensed every time a person as much as twitched. He'd felt so safe here, in his home, making big decisions that seemed so inconsequential from a distance. His decisions were catching up with him.

Morgan wondered if he saw the end. It was near, but did he realize it? The man's face, no longer handsome or charming but strained and pale, manifested the stress he was experiencing. He was a confident man, a proud man. Proud men could overlook the obvious writing on the wall.

Salazar's cell phone rang. The noise broke the dead silence that had permeated the safe room.

"What do you mean?" Salazar gasped into the phone. "You were supposed to take care of it."

Morgan straightened up. Salazar had stiffened, like a cat on alert.

"This is your Goddamned mess. No. No, what else can I do? This is your mess." A long pause. "You were supposed to protect me. You said it would be OK. It's not OK. You were supposed to protect me."

Salazar hung up. His arm, phone in hand, drooped to his side.

"Who was that?" Morgan asked earnestly.

"The FBI is still investigating me. It's heating up. Most of what they have is bullshit, but they're on to me." He sighed, a pitiful noise. It looked like the man's head was about to explode.

"Who was that?" Morgan repeated. Who else knew about him? How many others were there?

Salazar ignored him. The billionaire crossed the room and collapsed into the couch against the far wall. He buried his face in his hands.

Another cell phone rang. It was Sergey's phone. Sergey looked at the Caller ID, hesitated, then answered. He said nothing at first, listening. Then he jumped to his feet. "There's still time."

There was more silence as the person on the other end of the line spoke. Morgan watched intently, straining to hear but unable to. Salazar ignored the conversation, his thoughts elsewhere.

"I understand. It needs to be done."

Sergey hung up the phone, slipped it into his pocket. He looked at Salazar, watching the pitiful man cower on the couch. Sergey's expression had changed, Morgan observed. He didn't know what the man was thinking. Sergey was frustrated, angry. Sad even. Worried. Sergey glanced at Morgan as he crossed the room but said nothing. Morgan rose from his chair, sensing something was about to happen. The way the man moved, something was up.

"Luis," Sergey knelt in front of Salazar. His voice was soft, soothing. The billionaire raised his head to look at his right-hand man, the man who had been loyal to him for so many years. Sergey took Salazar's hand and guided it to the pistol sitting beside him. Salazar took it, his fingers curling around the grip of the weapon. He was like a zombie, unaware of what he was doing, unaware of what Sergey intended. "I'm sorry. It has to be this way."

Salazar's eyes flickered, the realization of Sergey's actions—of his own—finally settling in. He gasped, ever so slightly, his body stiffening. But it was too late. Sergey seized Salazar's hand and forced it upward, toward the billionaire's neck. The muzzle of the weapon disappeared against Salazar's throat.

43

LUIS SALAZAR'S FINGER hooked around the trigger and pulled it, guided—forced—by Sergey's hand. A gunshot rang out, the piercing bang magnified in the isolated room. The bullet entered his throat and passed into his cranium. Skull and brains exploded onto the off-white wall behind him.

"Holy shit," Morgan leaped backwards, drawing his own gun.

"Put your gun away," Sergey said calmly, his attention still focused on the man he'd just murdered. Sergey grabbed the gun by the barrel and placed it on the floor, then applied his hands to the oozing hole in Salazar's neck and the pulverized mess that represented what was left of the billionaire's brain. "Luis, Luis, Luis!" he screamed over and over again.

Morgan watched, stunned at what he was seeing. Blood squirted from between Sergey's fingers, staining his hands red, but there was no chance of saving Salazar. He was dead, killed instantly.

"Your shirt!" Sergey shouted, his face flushed red.

"He's dead."

"Give me your goddamn shirt!"

Morgan unbuttoned his shirt and handed it to Sergey. Sergey placed it behind the billionaire's head, trying to keep the brains from leaking onto the sofa.

"I just bought that shirt."

The door burst open and the heavyset guard entered, gun drawn. His eyes fell on Luis Salazar's corpse and he froze, jaw hanging open.

"He just shot himself!" Sergey cried, looking over his shoulder.

"I'll call 911," the guard said.

"You do that," Sergey said somberly, carefully letting Salazar's body fall to its side. "Tell them not to hurry. He's dead." The guard stepped into the hallway to call 911.

The performance was Oscar-worthy. The guard believed Sergey. Hell, if Morgan didn't know better, he would've believed him, too. Sergey stood up, Salazar's blood dripping from his fingers. He sighed, gazing down at his victim. Morgan envied him. He could nearly smell the adrenaline pulsing through Sergey's veins. Sergey's body was shaking uncontrollably, his breathing rapid. What he just did could never be undone. Morgan had wanted to be the one to do it, but to see it happen in front of him, inflicted by the last person Salazar would ever have suspected, was a sight to see.

"He was going to ruin everything," Sergey told Morgan. "He would have confessed. We were all at risk."

Morgan didn't know what to say.

"We were in the hallway when it happened. He confronted you, asked whether he was suspected in your kidnapping. You refused to answer, but you asked him if he was responsible. It was careless of you, but you asked. He became irate. I led you into the hall where you continued to ask me questions. That's when we heard the gunshot."

"The guard—"

"I'll take care of the guard. He's worked under me for years. He'll do whatever I say."

"Just like Salazar expected of you."

Sergey grimaced. "Luis treated me well over the years. I didn't want to kill him. But he was going to ruin everything. I couldn't let that happen."

"And now you're the boss man."

"Luis never was the boss man to begin with."

ERIN TURNED DOWN the narrow drive that led to Luis Salazar's mansion. It descended quickly along the cliff side, the massive houses to her right barely visible through the thick-leaved trees.

"What the hell is this?" John asked, leaning forward in the passenger seat. Up ahead was a police car, blocking the one-lane road. Its lights were on, flashing incessantly. Several other emergency vehicles were parked further down the road.

They stopped the car and flashed their badges at the nearest police officer.

"There was a shooting," the man said, motioning behind him.

"At Luis Salazar's home?"

He shrugged. "A suicide from what I hear."

They jogged the rest of the way to the house. The gate was open, as was the front door. A team of medics stood in the yard next to an empty stretcher, chitchatting with one another, seemingly unconcerned with the situation at hand. John and Erin entered the home, following the tracks of muddy footprints down a hallway to the right. A door sat open, revealing a staircase that led to the basement.

"What happened?" John asked the police officers who were lingering in the downstairs hallway.

"Luis Salazar committed suicide," one of the cops pointed down the hallway. "He's dead."

They entered a windowless room with shelves and boxes against one wall, a couch against another. A stain of blood and brains plastered the wall above the couch. The lifeless body of Luis Salazar lay outstretched on the floor, the back of his skull gone. But Erin wasn't interested in the corpse.

"Look who's here," John elbowed Erin, unaware she'd already seen Ryan. He was in the far corner, talking with a plain-clothed detective. He was wearing jeans and a white T-shirt; the shirt he'd been wearing in the morning was wrapped around Salazar's head. He turned to look at her as she approached, dismissing the detective.

"What the hell are you doing here?"

"Erin," he said, surprised at first. "I was right outside when it happened. Heard the gunshot and everything."

"But what are you doing here?" she repeated.

He told her he'd come to talk with Salazar directly. He wanted to see how Salazar would react if he started asking sensitive questions. But Salazar asked him first, interrogating him about whether the FBI had opened an investigation into his involvement. Ryan told him he didn't know, but Salazar continued to press. Ryan asked him point blank whether he was involved. Salazar became upset and asked him to leave. He and Sergey were talking in the hall. They were only outside for a minute or so when the gun went off.

"You shouldn't have come here. Alone. Why didn't you tell me?"

"You would have said I shouldn't have come," he stated wryly.

She frowned. She didn't like that he was here at all. Salazar had tried to kill him only weeks before. Going into the lion's den to confront the lion, alone, was too dangerous, too unpredictable.

"I would have said the same thing," John said.

Ryan ran a hand through his short hair. "I know it was stupid. I know I should have told the two of you. Everything's just been so insane, I couldn't handle it anymore. If Salazar was really responsible for my disappearance, I had to know."

"Now we may never know."

"I know," Ryan's gaze shifted to Salazar's corpse, his voice lowering. "He killed himself because he knew it was only a matter of time. He did it. He was the one. I'll be honest, too. I'm sorry he's dead." Ryan's face had twisted into an angry snarl. "He took the easy way out. I would have liked to kill him myself."

THAT EVENING, CHRISTOPHER Morgan lay in bed, feeling the warmth of Erin Kinsley against his body, under his arm. Her back to him, his nose buried in her hair, he was unable to sleep. He watched the window, observing the light around the closed blinds. The window was ajar, the relaxing sound of rain steady.

He replayed Salazar's death over and over, the way his eyes flashed realization the moment before Sergey pulled the trigger.

He'd thought about killing Salazar so many times in so many ways. None of them involved involuntary suicide or the element of surprise. He'd wanted to taunt Salazar, to make him know death was coming for him long before it actually arrived. Make him piss his pants, shit himself. Make him cry for mercy.

But there was more to consider. Salazar was not in charge. Not now, and not before. Morgan had never been able to picture Salazar carrying out the deeds he allegedly committed, even though the evidence suggested otherwise. He had the money. He had the means. He had the motivation. The pieces fit, but the man didn't. He'd always been frightened, too nervous about everything that had been happening.

Sergey, meanwhile, also knew the business. He had access to the resources and the funds. Was he the wizard behind the curtain?

Morgan carefully unwound himself from Erin's body and climbed out of bed, grabbing his phone from the bedside table. He paused at the bedroom door to make sure she was still asleep, then went into the living room.

"Do you know what time it is?" Sergey growled.

"You were sleeping?" Morgan glanced at the clock on the cable box. It was 1:15 am.

"Could've been," he stated.

"I want to know what's going on. Everything. And I want to know who told you to kill him."

44

SENATOR RICHARD CHANDLING brought the fork to his mouth, the slimy scrambled eggs—peppered with seasoning—sliding through his lips and down his gullet. A piece broke away and dribbled down his prominent chin. He reached across his plate, took a big gulp of skim milk to wash the egg down, and then wiped a cloth napkin across his face.

Across the table from him, Christopher Morgan sat silently, his food untouched, disgusted by what he saw. Chandling wasn't the man everyone knew. What they thought they knew. It was an act, a thin mask of deception. People believed he was a man who cared for their well being, their lives and careers and relatives, their cats and dogs. People believed he became a public servant to serve them, to represent their best interests. Everything he did was false, a means to the end.

Morgan saw it so clearly now.

Richard Chandling wanted power. He had power and he wanted more. His greed had gotten him this far, but it would be his downfall. He didn't see it, though. He was that deluded, convinced of his own invincibility.

He ate his breakfast without care, slurping down his plate of food. He wouldn't eat like this in public. For once, he was in a place where he could be himself.

The InterContinental in downtown Seattle. The top floor, the penthouse suite. It was morning, but still dark. The building sat in a cloud, the rain now slapping hard against the massive glass windows that encased them.

"I didn't want you to know," Chandling said after he was done eating. He folded his napkin over three times and then placed it on the table top. The man's empty eyes shifted to Morgan. "Not immediately, anyway. I need to protect myself. I'm an elected representative of this country."

Morgan wanted to rip his throat out.

"You're a dangerous man, Christopher Morgan. You wanted to kill Luis for what he did to you, I'm sure. I didn't think you'd actually do it, but I wasn't certain. That's why I had him do my bidding." Chandling pushed his plate away from him. "He was doing my bidding, you know. Luis. He wasn't bold enough or innovative enough to think of this plan himself. I did this to you. I can understand if you're angry."

"You have no idea."

"No, I suppose not," Chandling nodded. "There are sacrifices we all must make. Some of us have to make bigger sacrifices than others." Chandling spoke as if he were conducting a Fourth of July speech. He gazed at Morgan and smiled. It wasn't a pleasant smile, more of a rictus of muscles and skin stretching to evoke a smile, with no sincerity to the expression. "But you got off easy. Men and women die every day serving this country. Somewhere in the world there's an American soldier putting himself on the line. Right now, to defend us."

"Save me the patriotic bullshit, Dick."

Chandling feigned insult, but then his expression returned to its previous, emotionless state.

"There is a project I've overseen for years. Not publicly, of course. A top secret, for-your-eyes-only program that few in the government know about. If word got out the project would be doomed. Our allies can't know. Our enemies certainly can't know. In this case, the idiom is true: knowing is half the battle."

"Get to the fucking point." There was one honest attribute about Chandling that held true: he was a talker.

"The program is called Trojan Horse. Frankly, it's an overly obvious name for such a critical project."

"You put a person's mind into someone else's body to infiltrate their surroundings," Morgan stated.

"Exactly!" Chandling slammed his fist on the table. A rare flash of emotion, or something akin. "Think of the possibilities. You can't overthrow governments with bombs and missiles. Not anymore. We can't just go storming into North Korea and expect everything will go our way. Or Iran. Think about Iran! The solution is Trojan Horse. Instead of trying to coerce leaders by force or diplomacy, why not just make them one of us? Who better to represent American interests in Iran than an American?"

"Sorry to inform you, but I'm not the Shah."

"You're a test case, clearly. There's nothing overwhelmingly special about you."

"Billions of people in the world and you choose me?" Morgan raised his arms in disgust. "Us?"

Chandling grinned mischievously and leaned to one side, as if preparing to scratch an itch up his ass. "This is where Luis and I differed. The government has funded our experiment for years. All black budget of course. Enormous sums of cash you can't possibly fathom. And for the last three years, we've been experimenting on homeless people and runaways. People that won't be missed. That's all fine and good—we managed to work out a lot of kinks with them—but we needed to test in the real world. With someone we could observe in a civilized setting, see how they interact with their friends, how others accept that person."

"And Ryan Harper was the best choice for that? An FBI agent?"

"You're not the first, Christopher. You're not the first. One of many experiments we're running simultaneously. Hell, you weren't on some target list. You—well, Ryan Harper, really—were convenient."

"Convenient?" Morgan wasn't exactly upstanding citizen number one, but Chandling was on a whole different level of psychopath. It was so clear now, he wasn't sure how he'd overlooked it before. How everyone in the goddamned country had overlooked it.

Before Chandling could continue, Sergey entered the room, wearing a rain jacket. His skin looked ghostly white.

"Sergey!" Chandling waved him over as if Sergey needed his permission. "I was just explaining to Christopher here our little plan."

"Why was Salazar killed?" Morgan interrupted.

"He was a little frustrated with me. A lot, actually. Luis didn't exactly know all of the circumstances surrounding your disappearance. And return. He thought you were dead—well, that you were hired to kill Ryan Harper, and managed to succeed. He would have never condoned you being a candidate for the program. I'm sorry, I'm talking about Ryan Harper again. 'Too visible,' he would have said. 'Too risky.' Luis was risk adverse. He didn't like risk."

Morgan watched Sergey throughout Chandling's rant. The man kept his eyes on the floor, his body unmoving. He was visibly upset by what he had done the day before.

"… but it had to be done at some point. You were convenient and we needed to test with someone prominent. I figured if things went badly you could just get shot while on duty. Be done with it…"

Morgan's eyes narrowed. The man spoke as if he were brilliant, as if he were infallible and a mastermind above reproach. He had survived this long on his lies, but the truth would kill him. He had no idea the hell that awaited him.

"Luis was a genius. He designed the program. He had the money to keep it running. But he lacked the willpower." Chandling seized Sergey by the arm. "Sergey is another story. He sees the promise as I do. And he had access to the same funds Luis did. When you returned, however, we of course had to get Luis up to speed. He didn't take it… well. But he didn't have much choice at that point. I thought it would all work out, but he became increasingly agitated. When I found out the FBI was opening an investigation into him, I knew he would break. For all our sakes, I couldn't let that happen."

"So you had Sergey do your dirty work for you."

"Sergey knew it had to be done," Chandling stated. "Now tell me about this bitch who broke into the computer system."

"She's dead," Sergey said quickly. "Morgan shot her through the chest."

"Is that so?" Chandling's eyes sparkled, an illusion from the angle of his face to the overhead lighting. "But there's no body?"

"Not yet. We're still looking."

"I'm sure she'll turn up soon enough. Bitches like that can't stay hidden for long. And dead bitches float to the surface."

45

THE DARK WATER boiled then broke, a silent, unnoticed ripple amongst the small waves that lapped against the nearby shore. Dolphin rose above the surface, her face and hair hidden by a black neoprene mask.

It was going to rain. The air smelled of it, the thick, invisible clouds churning overhead. There were no stars or moon tonight, only a low, ominous ceiling as if the sky itself was collapsing. It was a good night for her. The world was a shadow and so was she.

She jetted across the small, rocky beach and into the foliage twenty meters beyond. Her movements were silent, unnoticeable. She crouched at the base of a pine tree, taking sanctuary in its impenetrable shade. She waited and listened some more. Leaves rustled as a soft but steady breeze blew up from the cool water's surface. The trees moaned as they swayed ever so slightly. But there were no human sounds.

The only sign of civilization was a dock a hundred meters to the north. A single speedboat was moored to the creaky, twisted wood. It was an old dock, long overdue for repair. But the speedboat was new and not cheap.

The land belonged to Luis Salazar. Ten square kilometers of beachfront, forest and farmland. It was undeveloped land, the only manmade structure a small caretaker's house. The land was intended for vacation property, county documents stated. Salazar planned to build a vacation home on the beach and leave the rest to nature. That was fifteen years ago. He hadn't touched it since.

Or so it appeared. Dolphin had overlooked the property, hadn't thought twice about it. Salazar owned real estate around the world. Interestingly, the property was surrounded on two sides by military territory, once used for World War II defense and later for combat training. The land wasn't actively used anymore, but the Army still maintained a small compound just off the Coastal Highway. And yet, electrical poles and cables threaded the military zone, despite the lack of maintained buildings.

It began to rain. Soft, barely noticeable, but there. As she moved further inland, she could hear it on the leaves. The rain steadied, if only a little, the pitter patter erasing all other noise. The dark woods, flat and easy to traverse, the tall, thin trees canopying the sky, brought with the rain a supreme sense of tranquility. The smell of bark and sea salt permeated the air.

It would soon smell of blood.

The property seemed innocent. A small house. An old couple tending the land. Undeveloped ocean property. But she knew in her heart this was the place she'd been searching for. This was the place Luis Salazar didn't want her to find. The key was here.

The house was a couple kilometers inland, a small structure, no more than a one-or-two-bedroom unit. Slate gray paint coated the walls, evident under a naked orange light bulb that protruded from above the home's back door. The house was not a picturesque farmhouse with a grand porch or multiple floors, but a wooden rambler with an exposed concrete base, aluminum doors and dirtied windows. Light flashed from within, a television. Someone was home.

Dolphin scanned the surrounding area. The house sat in the middle of a large dirt-and-flattened-grass clearing, only the trunks of a few sawed-away trees remaining. There was no cover other than a gentle bulge in the ground fifty meters away, hardly a proper hiding spot. Better than nothing, though. An old rusted pickup was parked out front, its bed empty. Twenty meters back, surrounded by chicken wire fencing, was a satellite dish. Not for DirecTV.

On the other side of the house was a small animal pen. Made of mesh wire, wooden posts and an aluminum roof that provided partial protection from the elements, the pen contained six sheep and a few goats. The animals were asleep, so far undisturbed by the increasing rainfall.

It took only a moment to detect the house's security. She counted five high-powered LED lights fixed to the overhang of the home's roof, and that was just what she could see from her position. When triggered they would turn the whole clearing into day. Further from the home, spaced at exactly ten meters from one another, was a series of tall, narrow black posts. They circled the entire property. Motion sensors.

She would have to trip the alarm to get into the house and then disable whoever was inside before he or she relayed an alert up the chain of command. There could be only two or three people at most. Easy to kill. It was the reinforcements that would be challenging.

Dolphin remained in place for over an hour, unmoving. The rain continued, turning the ground around her to mud. At ten past five, the sun began to rise. By 5:30 the sky had turned to an endless gray. A light turned on in the back room of the house. One person watching TV, another just waking up. Two on rotation. At 5:43 a man emerged from the house. He wore cargo pants and a white undershirt. No visible weapons. He was thick, all muscles, a bread-and-butter jarhead. Crew cut, pulsing neck, Army tattoo peeking from under his sleeve. He was 35 at the oldest. He was no retired sheep farmer. He smoked his cigarette, the rain not bothering him in the slightest. It burned to a stub and he flicked it into the mud. Turned on his heels like a true soldier.

"Beautiful fucking day," he muttered as he closed the door.

It was getting lighter by the minute. She had to act soon. Her eyes followed the motion sensors around the property. A meter-and-a-half tall, they were too high to jump.

The sheep pen. She should have seen it sooner. The motion sensors ran against one side of the sheep pen, the posts practically beside the wood-and-chicken-wire fence. A weakness. A glaring weakness. Her way in.

Go. Now. She took one last momentary glance at the house, unable to see through the windows. If they were watching, she'd be dead, but they weren't watching. Why would they? These people didn't see action, hadn't seen it in a long time.

Then she ran. Two seconds, three at most. She crouched behind the sheep pen, out of sight from the house. She waited. There was no response.

Two of the motion sensors were positioned a few meters in front of her, placed at the corners of the sheep pen. She recognized the design. It would be challenging to disable the sensors, especially without the right tools. She'd have to trip the alarm.

There was less than a half meter of distance between the sensors and the pen's fence. A few of the sheep were tall enough to stick their heads over the top of the fence. It was a fundamental flaw in the security, a hole that for whatever reason had been overlooked.

Dolphin leapt over the fence, careful not to leave any noticeable footprints in the mud-and-sawdust pen, and scurried behind the animals' drinking trough. A few sheep shuffled away from her, startled, but otherwise paid her no heed.

A few seconds later, the door opened and the man walked toward the pen. He approached from the opposite side, stopping to look at his animals. Dolphin heard the squawk of a walkie talkie, and then he said, "I don't see anything, over."

The soldier cursed as he circled the pen slowly, headed for the two sensors that had lit up. Hidden behind the trough, unwilling to peer out for risk of being seen, Dolphin was unsure how seriously he was taking the alarm. She imagined he had his gun holstered, too bored to feel threatened.

"I don't see anything, over," the man repeated with the exact same tone as before. "Damn sheep must have bumped the sensors."

"That hasn't happened before," a woman's voice came through the walkie talkie.

"Well, there's nothing here," the man stated, frustrated.

Dolphin heard the footsteps retreat. She rose from behind the trough. The man had circled the pen, his head down. He wasn't on guard. Wasn't prepared for her.

Two steps, over the fence, two more steps. The soldier warily glanced over his shoulder. Her fist sliced into his throat and he gasped, choking on his Adam's apple. He dropped to his hands and knees. She took his head in the crook of her arm. One twist and he was dead.

SHE ENTERED THE house, gun drawn. The interior was as quaint as she expected, the yellow wallpaper from another era. A hodgepodge of portraits and small paintings lined the walls of the living room; there were no recent photographs. The couch and coffee table looked new, however. So did the large-screen television in the corner. A standard-issue rifle was propped against the wall.

A commercial was playing on the television, but the volume was turned low. There was another sound, too. Running water. A faucet. The kitchen was off to her left—she could see the sink—but the noise was coming from elsewhere.

A woman emerged from the nearby hallway, toothbrush in mouth. She was well built, also military. A brunette, she was around 30 years of age, though her hard jaw and brow lines made her look older. She had bags under her eyes—she'd had the night shift.

The soldier did a double take when she saw Dolphin standing in the living room. Dolphin raised her weapon to fire, but the woman was fast and disappeared from sight. She sidestepped to get a better angle, but the soldier had already fled to the other end of the hallway.

All the woman had to do was get on the radio and the mission would be over. Dolphin had seconds, nothing more.

46

"YOU ARE THE future of this nation's defense," Richard Chandling stood before the massive glass wall that separated him from the storm outside, his large, lumbering arms angled behind his back, hands intertwined. Whether he was watching daytime arrive or his own reflection was anyone's guess, though Christopher Morgan guessed the latter.

The deluded politician was still talking about the importance of what they'd done to him, convinced that he was convincing Morgan that it was a national imperative. To him, Morgan was but a cog in the machine, a means to an end, and that end was national supremacy. The senator was unable to see that Morgan thought it all bullshit. He didn't care about national security. He didn't care to be a part of it, let alone some guinea pig.

He was already beginning to imagine how he'd kill the politician.

A heavy gust of wind slapped against the side of the building, bringing with it a sheet of rain and a crunching blow that rippled along its exterior. Chandling ignored it and continued talking.

Morgan looked over at Sergey, who was sitting in a leather recliner, one hand curled awkwardly against the side of his flushed face, the other hovering near a half-drunk glass of vodka. The once-confident minion looked devastated. Unlike Chandling, he could see the walls caving in. And Morgan could see that Sergey understood just how crazy Chandling was, that he had partnered with the wrong man.

Sergey reminded him of his mother. Weak, pathetic, unwilling to fight back. He'd killed the man who'd given him everything on the request of a psychopath. He had the means and the motivation, but not the courage or willingness to take control of the situation. He would go down with the ship and not even try to swim to the surface.

An audible gasp caused both Morgan and Chandling to turn toward Sergey in unison. Sergey had shaken from his static pose, a frantic look on his face. He was hunched forward, staring at his computer screen.

"She got into the files."

"What?" Chandling exclaimed. He bolted toward Sergey.

"All of them. She accessed the Trojan Horse mainframe approximately three minutes after logging into our standard systems," Sergey said breathlessly. "She had access to everything on the server. I didn't think she could break into our systems that easily."

"The systems you designed, that you oversaw," Chandling spat. "That you told me were secure."

"They were secure."

"Clearly," Morgan stated. Dolphin had done what he'd wanted; she'd accessed the files that held the truth and the leverage he so desperately sought. But she had escaped with the truth, with his future.

"She left here… how long until she showed up at her place?" Chandling asked, his brain processing.

"An hour, maybe a little longer," Morgan told him. More than enough time to pass on the data.

"Any word on who the hell this woman is?" Chandling said. "Who she works for?"

"Every database has reported back negative. No records of her anywhere."

"Even the best of spies…" Chandling murmured, seemingly to himself. His voice faded, but Morgan could tell he'd latched onto an idea. The senator sat down on the couch beside Sergey, lost in thought. After a few seconds, he jolted back to attention. "I need you to access a private network."

Sergey loaded a VPN client on his computer and entered the IP address, username and passcode for the network that the senator whispered in his ear. The computer processed for a moment and then confirmed a connection had been established.

"What database is this?" Sergey asked as the computer loaded another login screen. Other than a small United States government seal in the right hand corner, there was no indication of what system the senator was about to access.

"There are dozens of covert agencies operating under the authority of the government," Chandling said softly. "Even the President doesn't know about all of them."

The screen flashed to a dull gray and a nondescript entry form appeared, allowing for various attributes to be searched or browsed. Sergey loaded Dolphin's DNA file into the system and it began to process.

"How do you have access to this?" Sergey asked.

Chandling ignored him.

It took less than a minute for the search to complete. A single match had been returned. Sergey clicked on it. Morgan ventured closer. A profile appeared on screen. No photo, but the description matched. Sex: Female. Hair color: Blonde. Height: 5'10. Weight: 125. Codename: Dolphin. Project classification: EB.

Chandling put a hand on Sergey's shoulder. "Look familiar?" No response. "It should. Your company helped create her."

47

DOLPHIN NEVER PANICKED, but she knew her mission was on the verge of failing.

Her sneak attack had been spoiled. The female soldier had retreated to another room and at any second would call for reinforcements. As soon as she did, whatever secret she was protecting would be locked down and Dolphin's assault exposed.

There was no time to waste. Dolphin darted down the narrow hallway, hoping to take the soldier off guard. Shoulder down, she burst through the door into a bedroom. The soldier looked up as she frantically tried to load a magazine into her pistol. Who knew how long she'd been on duty here, a thankless, boring and undemanding post. She was rusty. Scared.

"Don't," Dolphin told her. She wanted her alive.

The soldier didn't listen. She raised her gun, but Dolphin was faster. She shot first, hitting the soldier in the chest.

Even before the woman had crumpled to the floor, Dolphin had scanned the room. It was an ordinary bedroom, twin beds at opposite ends. Two dressers and two small desks, too. A man and a woman's side. She searched the floor for a walkie talkie. There wasn't one in plain sight. The woman, a true grunt, hadn't had time to call for reinforcements. Dolphin knelt beside the dead body and removed a security card clipped to the woman's belt. There was no insignia, only a washed-out photograph, barcode and name. Sandra Davis.

Dolphin crossed the room and opened what appeared to be a closet door. It was a small room, once a bathroom. The rusted outline of a sink and mirror still lingered on the far wall. Unlike the rest of the house, no effort had been made to decorate the room. It was gray and barren and stripped of wallpaper and paint. A small window that had once sat above the toilet was boarded shut. In the toilet's place was a desk, and a computer monitor the size of a large television. The monitor showed six simultaneous security feeds—three from the house's exterior, one at the dock, another of the hallway outside the bedroom. And one that appeared to be subterranean, looking down at a steel door and a dimly lit space with concrete walls and industrial cables.

Dolphin returned to the living room and turned into the kitchen, another quaint room that looked like something out of a different era. There were no other doors or corners, nothing to signify a basement.

Her eyes fell on the kitchen table. There was nothing special about it. A cereal bowl, glass of water and empty vase were all that decorated its surface. Two matching chairs sat opposite each other. Beneath the table, a thick rug. With four small holes cut out around the legs.

She reached forward and applied pressure to the underside of the table. With incredible ease, the table rose up and away from her. The bowl, glass and vase shattered against the floor, the chairs tipped backwards and a stairway appeared before her, leading down to a steel-framed door eight meters below.

Dolphin descended the staircase, the early morning light at her back. She examined the heavy door, then the security scanner to her right. She looked at Sandra's security badge, wondering how far it would take her. She scanned the card and the little light bulb flashed green. The door clicked open and she entered the next stage of her mission, unaware of the discovery she was about to make.

48

"JESUS CHRIST. WE are screwed."

The tone of Sergey's voice sent shivers down Christopher Morgan's spine. There was no panic, no hysteria, only a calm acceptance of their fate.

Codename: Dolphin. Not a spy. Not a secret agent. Not even a person. She was a weapon, made to topple governments, assassinate leaders, infiltrate the most ruthless of regimes. Corporate espionage, computer hacking, seduction. A master of all things. She was a genius, designed to calculate complex plans in real time. Manipulate her surroundings to get her way. She did not fail.

Chandling ran a hand through his thick white hair. Even he looked dismayed by the realization of whom they were dealing with. That made Morgan even more uneasy.

"This can't be real," Morgan said defensively. "It's like out of some kind of corny sci-fi novel."

"You exist, don't you," Chandling gazed at him with his chilling eyes. "Genetic manipulation has been around since the beginning of agriculture. Only recently has it begun to show its true form. Countries wage war over the technology. Maybe not with tanks and troops, but they are fighting every day to protect, or steal, this technology from each other. It's what will define warfare in the future."

Morgan had shot Dolphin through the chest with a .51 millimeter bullet. Even though he missed her heart, a normal person would have bled out in a matter of hours, if not sooner.

But she wasn't normal. She was designed to be better than normal. To be superior.

"The EB program... Luis was involved with it over a decade ago," Sergey said softly, his gaze on the floor. "It was a super soldier program. 'Extraordinary Beings' is what it stands for. They're born in the womb, but the government owns them. We played with their genetic structure to remove impurities and enhance other attributes. Luis was only involved for a short while. He saw greater financial opportunities elsewhere."

"But it says she can breathe underwater!" Morgan pointed to the screen. "That's not just an enhancement."

"I'm not familiar with her specific model," Sergey said. "But we need oxygen in the blood to survive. Why do we have to get it through the lungs? Maybe she has gills."

"She doesn't have gills. I would know." He shook his head in disbelief. Breathing underwater wasn't her only "special" trait. *Accelerated regeneration of damaged cells. Fucking Wolverine. Maximum efficiency of muscle strength. IQ estimated at 240.* That was beyond genius level. *Speaks 16 languages. Capable of learning new languages, dialects and cultural mannerisms in minimal time.*

"Sergey," Chandling said quietly. The lawyer looked at the senator. "We need to assume she's alive and healthy by now. She also has access to extremely damaging information. We should assume that she has identified the Californian plant as a target. Inform security for possible assault. Also, implement the abandonment plan immediately."

"Yes, sir," Sergey nodded, turning away to make his phone call.

"You have him wrapped around your little finger, don't you?" Morgan watched Sergey disappear into another room. "Fucking brainwashed idiot."

"Sergey's a very smart man," Chandling said quietly. "There are leaders and there are followers."

"And you're a leader."

"I've made all this possible."

"Well, with Salazar's money. And his work. His resources. I'm not quite sure what you've done exactly other than fuck everything up."

"Luis was a creator. I give him that. But I brought his work—his experiments—to life. I took it to the next level." Chandling gazed at him, an indignant smile simmering at the corner of his mouth. Morgan returned the favor, refusing to let the man see his disdain. There was no getting through to him, no reasoning with him. Not at this stage. He had deluded himself into believing that he was a god. He fed off anyone who thought otherwise, fed off their fear, their hatred, their ignorance of the one real truth.

Sergey returned to the room, his face ashen. "I just called Security Station One. They aren't answering."

"What?" Chandling spun on his heels, his smile fading instantly.

"She's already inside," Sergey stated.

There was a moment of stunned silence. All air seemed to be sucked from the room. Chandling looked like he was about to explode. Sergey was already on the phone again, trying to reach someone. Anyone.

"What exactly is in this Californian plant?" Morgan asked.

Chandling blinked. Sergey shot a look at Chandling. "The original isn't still there, is it? You destroyed it, right?"

Chandling remained silent and Sergey had his answer. From his reaction, all Morgan knew was that whatever Dolphin was about to find, it wasn't good for any of them.

49

HEAVY, HUMID AIR engulfed Dolphin as she entered the chamber beyond the steel door. Gun at the ready, she moved cautiously into the room, prepared for an onslaught of guards. There were none. The only sound she heard was the roar of an industrial fan somewhere out of sight.

The chamber appeared to be a retrofitted natural cavern, with uneven rocky walls and a curved ceiling, supported by a web of steel beams. The floor, however, was paved and even. A few boxes and canisters were stacked in the corner and collecting dust, but what interested her were four white golf carts parked along one wall.

The golf carts were activated by button control and started silently. Dolphin cautiously drove beyond the room and into the corresponding corridor, where it soon became clear why the carts were necessary.

The corridor seemed to go on forever. Unlike the entry chamber, the corridor was purely manmade. The floor was paved with dark asphalt, a yellow line drawn down the center like a regular road. The gray, concrete walls were lined with electrical cabling that powered the intermittent lighting. The corridor was wide—there was more than enough space for two carts to pass side-by-side—but the low ceilings still made the environment seem compressed, as if the structure could collapse at any moment.

Dolphin accelerated to 30mph—the fastest her vehicle would go—and drove north for more than 10 minutes before the corridor made a 20-degree angle to the west. Though it was hard to tell, she was certain the road was slowly descending. Another five minutes passed before she caught glimpse of something on the horizon. She eased off the accelerator, dropping the cart to under 10mph, and drifted the last kilometer to her destination. She entered a new chamber, larger than the other and fully manmade. Powerful LEDs overhead filled the entire chamber with light, leaving little place for shadow. Several more golf carts were parked on either side of the room. Directly before her was another door. And above the door was another security camera.

Dolphin, still wearing her muddied black fatigues, looked out of place. She suddenly regretted not taking one of the soldier's outfits.

The chamber was empty, the only sound the steady beat of exhaust fans as they attempted to maintain airflow in the enclosed system. Dolphin parked the cart and proceeded to the door. She waved the card in front of the scanner. Nothing happened. The light remained red. Dolphin felt her chest tighten. She tried again, but still to no effect.

Get out now, her mind screamed. There was still time to turn around and retreat. A third scan could trigger a lockdown, if her two failures so far had not done so already. She scanned the card once more, this time more slowly and closer to the machine. It chirped and blinked green.

The door led to a small room with white walls, fluorescent lighting and gray carpeting. A used car commercial played softly on a television that was out of sight. A woman was talking. A man chuckled in response.

Dolphin stepped inside. A soldier, dressed in fatigues, was reclined in his chair, his boots crisscrossed on the surface of a small desk. He was an awkward-looking young man with a slender face and an oversized nose. Leaning against the edge of the desk was a female, dressed in a white lab coat, slacks and T-shirt. She was obviously flirting with the soldier. The two appeared to be having a good time. Enough to distract the soldier from watching his security feed, which was playing on a monitor to his left.

The soldier looked over first. He tensed at the sight of her, but there was little he could do. His pistol was holstered, and his holster was lying out of reach next to the security monitor.

"Don't," she told the soldier. She glanced at the woman, who had begun to whimper. "You. Shut up."

The woman shut up. They both raised their hands.

"Take off your clothes," Dolphin ordered the soldier. She motioned with her gun and he started removing his fatigues. The woman was too small; her clothes wouldn't fit. Besides, Dolphin wouldn't pass for a scientist in this place, whatever it was. A guard, just another grunt, could blend in.

The soldier tossed his boots and fatigues to Dolphin.

"Now, take one of these," Dolphin reached into her breast pocket and removed a small Ziploc bag. She tossed it to the soldier. He looked sheepishly at the gray pills inside. "It'll knock you out for a few hours. Either take the pill or I'll knock you out myself. Option One leaves you without a concussion."

Once the two were out of commission and she was dressed, Dolphin snagged the security card from the unconscious woman and swiped it against the next security lock. It flashed green and she pushed the door open.

Instantly, the temperature dropped. The air became fresher.

She emerged into yet another corridor, this one wide and carpeted, with ample lighting and clean, sterile walls. The corridor curved away from her in both directions, appearing to form a tight oval. Before her were large bay windows, slanted outward as if overlooking some great vista. But the windows were tinted white, almost opaque. She could make out a few lights a floor below, but not much else.

A man, also wearing a white lab coat, passed her. Suspicious. Curious. Interested. He grinned at her and she smiled back, but then he looked away and continued walking in the other direction. He continued on his path.

Keeping the tinted windows to her left, she circled what she presumed to be a large, central room. A series of offices and conference rooms lined the perimeter, most of them dark and empty. There seemed to be few people in the facility; she passed no other people in the hall and saw only two, both men, in offices. Neither of them paid her any attention.

She continued past an elevator shaft that obtruded into the central room, opting to complete the circuit of the upper facility. But there were only more offices, so when she reached a second elevator shaft, she decided to check it out. The elevator required security clearance—her card gave it to her—and the car immediately descended.

It stopped moments later, the doors opening to an ice rink-sized room. What she saw froze her in her tracks.

Among the machines, laboratory counters and cleaning stations were several stretchers—at least 30 of them—lined up in rows of five. As meticulously arranged as they were, the people lying in each bed looked just as prepared, all white-skinned and peaceful, naked arms positioned gently at their sides. White sheets were drawn up to their chests. None of them moved. At first Dolphin thought they were corpses, but then she noticed each was hooked to an IV drip.

Dolphin put her hand on her pistol, resisting the urge to draw it. She inhaled, tasting the rawness of the air, the unnatural chemistry of her surroundings. No scientists were in sight. They were too busy studying the results of their experiments to worry about their patients. Their specimens.

This is where Ryan Harper had been changed. Changed into a traitor. They did something to him here to destroy everything he stood for. Were these people in the process of having their minds and bodies manipulated to suit Luis Salazar's twisted goals? To accomplish whatever cruel experiment the government had paid him to do?

The people surely hadn't volunteered to be here, to be kept underground, drugged and comatose, in some military research facility. They were not given a choice, just like she hadn't had a choice in her creation. The Salazars of the world could play and play and play, press and press and press, modify and modify and modify until what they were left with was less human and more an abomination, creatures that looked human but that could never fit in with normal society. They thought they were God.

Years earlier, she'd felt their god-play firsthand. She'd thought nothing of it at the time. She'd been trained not to. The lessons—how to fight, how to manipulate others, how to kill—all came with a price. The tests were what she remembered most. Drowning her—trying to drown her—making her breathe her last breath and then some to test her limits, breaking her bones, methodically, deliberately, to make her stronger—that's what they said—but really just to measure her healing time. Her

reaction to electricity, chemical agents. She survived. Not everyone did.

She ventured further into the room, passing in between the rows of bodies. She glanced to her left to see two scientists talking, their words silent behind a closed glass door. There were additional laboratories on the outskirts of the center room, each designed to do more tests on the human specimens. Several appeared to be in use.

The anger welling inside her, Dolphin began to plot her next move. She'd come here to find the truth. She'd found *a* truth. She couldn't take these people with her; even if they were able to wake, there's no way they would be able to escape. But if she left them, they were as good as dead. By the time she returned with help, they'd be gone. Moved to another facility. Or exterminated. After all, they were nothing but lab rats.

And then she stopped, her eyes falling on a body three stretchers away. Her eyes widened, her nostrils flared. She staggered to one side, catching herself against one of the beds. She breathed in but there was no air to breathe. The room began to spin.

Dolphin drew her gun, her finger sliding over the trigger.

50

YUSUF HIMAYAT RAN his forearm across his face, wiping away the sweat that had formed on his brow. He stared at his living room with admiration, impressed by how much he'd cleaned over the last three hours. The pizza boxes, beer cans and empty two-liters were in the garbage. His dirty laundry was already in the dryers downstairs. He'd even vacuumed most of the floor and wiped the coffee table clean.

When his mom arrived in a few hours, she'd be so impressed.

His eyes fell on the stacks of newspapers that lined his one wall. He sighed, wondering how many trips it would take to put them in the recycle. Was there even enough room in the bins for all of them? He had to have several hundred pounds worth of newsprint.

"What a waste," he muttered, bending over to pick up the first stack. A dolly would have been great, he thought. Or a few friends to help him carry things out. But it was too early to call anyone—everyone he knew was still asleep.

He'd stayed up all night working on a new operating system he was developing, but had decided to switch gears around 3am and clean for his mother's biannual visit. They were going to go to breakfast, but first she was going to see his place. And he was sick of the disapproving look she gave every time she visited.

Yusuf returned a few minutes later, arms burning just from the first load. The stack of newspapers didn't appear to have shrunk in his absence, unfortunately. He bent down, picked up another stack of papers and quickly decided that he could carry more. He set the stack down on another, bent over and lifted.

"Crap!" he cried, but continued to lift. He could make it. It was only three flights of stairs. The stack swayed. He sensed the inevitable before it happened. Newspapers went everywhere, spreading across his floor.

Cursing, Yusuf bent over and started stacking the papers once more. An article jumped out at him: "Oregon Cheerleader Arrested For Running Brothel. " He chuckled, tossed it aside and looked at the next paper. "Republicans Fight Over Debt Ceiling." Another one. "Flooding Traps Family in Home."

He grabbed another edition, glancing over the front page headlines. He tossed it aside, disinterested. But domething had caught his eye. He swiveled on his toes and picked up the newspaper. Just above the fold read a tragic but unremarkable headline:

Scientist, Daughter Killed in House Fire.

Yusuf scanned the article, not sure why his interest was sparked.

An award-winning scientist and his handicapped daughter were found dead among the burnt ruins of a California home Saturday evening.

Firefighters say Jasper Reynolds, 53, a respected bioengineer and Washington native, was found alongside his daughter Sarah, 12, in their house near Redding, CA. Teenager Ophilia Brown, 17, was also found dead.

The fire appeared to have started when a faulty oxygen tank exploded. No foul play is suspected, said police.

Brown's body was the only one immediately identified. She appeared to have died of asphyxiation.

Continued on page A7.

Yusuf flipped to page A7 and started reading the rest of the article.

How the oxygen canister exploded has yet to be determined. The fire department is investigating.

Just a week before, Reynolds was hit by a car in a hit-and-run incident. Other than a broken wrist, however, his injuries were minor.

Yusuf stopped. The newspaper included a small picture of Jasper Reynolds. He was a nerdy looking man, with gaunt cheeks and a bald head. The picture was at least five years old, but Yusuf recognized him immediately.

He frantically flipped back to the front page. The newspaper was published two months ago, just a few days after the DVD of Ryan Harper's captivity was delivered to the FBI offices.

"Thank you, mom," he whispered, then jumped to his feet and ran to his computer.

51

RICHARD CHANDLING LUMBERED across the suite to the bar, searched the cabinet for the perfect sin and poured himself a glass of George T. Stagg bourbon. He didn't take a sip, as if the need for alcohol was merely an act to show distress.

"Security Station Two isn't answering either," Sergey reported. "She's accessed the facility."

"That means she's seen everything. Including him." As ominous as the statement sounded, Chandling spoke with no sign of emotion.

"Who is 'him'?" Morgan asked. They were keeping something from him. Something he needed to know.

"You did this to us!" Sergey suddenly snapped, crossing the room to scream at Chandling. The senator frowned but otherwise didn't react. "You got me into this mess! All of it!"

"The project needed to continue. You saw the value, too. Its importance. You didn't even need to make the hard decisions. I took care of it for you."

"The hard decisions?" Sergey exclaimed at the top of his lungs. He pointed to Morgan. "This hard decision never needed to be made. This was some insane fantasy of yours. That you were just going to swap out Ryan Harper with a violent killer and think everything was going to work out? That's not what I signed up for! That's not what the government is paying us for!"

Chandling laughed. Heartily. That just drove Sergey even madder.

"You're insane. You're fucking insane. And—"

The senator finally took a sip of the whiskey. "Sergey, I asked for your help and you agreed. You barely hesitated. You saw the mistake Luis was making by shutting down the program. Don't blame me now for the choice you made."

"Had I known what you—"

Morgan grabbed Sergey by the arm. The physical contact seemed to snap Sergey from the spell that had taken hold of him. The gray-faced man stared down at his arm, eyes blazing, then slowly looked up at Morgan. "We haven't lost yet. We know where she is. There's still time to fix this. If she's still inside the facility, that means she still has to get out of the facility. Box her in and kill her."

Before Sergey could respond, his phone rang. He answered it immediately. "'Bout damn time you called back. Deploy a team to Plant 12 stat. It's been infiltrated." He paused, waiting for a response. "Both checkpoints have been compromised. Seal it off. She can't escape. No, I don't know if she's still inside. You're supposed to know that. We're talking minutes here."

Sergey looked at Morgan. "Army's deploying force now."

"How long will it take?"

"Five, six minutes to deploy, another five to get in position."

"Sergey, what is in there that's so important? What does this plant do?"

"I'll answer that," Chandling said, knocking back the rest of his drink. "What Luis told you about... you... isn't exactly accurate."

He paused. Morgan waited for him to continue.

"You are Christopher Morgan first and foremost. And yet you're also Ryan Harper. You are both men, psychologically. You share his memories, his emotions."

"Get to the fucking point."

"The brain isn't designed to have two different personalities, two sets of data. Especially not matured brains. The program floundered for years as we tried to load memories into the minds of other men, only to see them go insane. Eventually they'd go brain dead. The experiments were failures."

"No communication. I can't reach any of the scientists—" Sergey interrupted.

"We were on the verge of killing the program. It didn't work. But then one of our scientists had a child. Started reading all those baby books, you see. It dawned on him that the brain is most malleable at a young age. We started loading data into babies. They seemed to accept it. But we had no way of knowing whether that worked because it would be years before they could communicate with us. Besides, it's hard to infiltrate regimes with children.

"Our goal was to copy an American mindset into the brains of dictators and subversives. We couldn't do that, though. It was impossible. The recipient would go crazy and die. But we knew it was possible if the recipient was young. So instead of replacing the dictator's personality, we would replace the dictator."

"I'm sorry, what?"

"We would clone him. Load both his memories and those of his American counterpart into the fetus' developing brain, then age him rapidly to where he was, identically, that person. Remove the original, replace him with a copy."

Morgan looked at his hands, his arms, his chest. "So I'm not Ryan Harper?"

"You are," Chandling chimed in. "You are exactly him. DNA, appearance, health... You are Ryan Harper. You're just not the original Ryan Harper. You must have noticed you were missing your childhood scars..."

"And the original Ryan Harper? What did you do with him? You killed him, right?" As he said it, he realized those were the same questions Sergey had asked Chandling only moments ago. The same questions Chandling had refused to answer.

Ryan Harper was still alive.

PART IV

RYAN HARPER

52

HIS HEART FELT like it was going to explode. A thousand nails were racing through his veins and arteries, seeking a way out. His body convulsed. He cried out, but his voice was lost. Something was in his throat, blocking his airway. He gagged, rolling to one side. He felt himself dropping, then hitting a hard, cold surface. He grasped at his mouth. His fingers curled around a tube. He pulled, slowly, felt it sliding up his throat. He gagged again. Then it was free and he sucked in, the air excruciating against his ravaged esophagus.

Ryan Harper opened his eyes, blinking several times. At first all he could see was bright white light, but then shapes formed, gray blurs in purgatory. Tears welled and ran down his cheeks. He tried to blink them away. The shapes turned into objects. Hands grabbed at his bare shoulders. He didn't know who they belonged to. He struggled to fight them away, but they kept coming back.

He heard his name. Over and over, a soft whisper. A woman's voice.

"I'm here to help you."

She said it again and her touch was so soft. He rolled onto his back, his flesh against the cold surface, and stared up at whoever was talking to him. He could see the silhouette of a person, a faint shadow. He continued to stare at her, concentrating on nothing else. The silhouette slowly faded, replaced by human features. A small nose. High cheekbones. Blond hair.

"Who are you?" he tried to say, but the words stuck in his throat.

She seemed to know what he was trying to ask. "I'm a friend of Erin's," she smiled. "I'm here to take you home."

Home. He tried to think of what that was, but he couldn't process the word. What else had she said? Friend. No. Friend of Erin's. Erin. Erin Kinsley. He knew that name.

214

"We can't stay here," the woman said. "It's dangerous."

Ryan felt the woman's arms curl under his. This time he didn't fight back. He let her lift him to his feet.

"Can you walk?" she asked.

He didn't know. He blinked again, the room swimming. He recognized the room. It was a laboratory. He'd been here for some time, but he didn't know how long. He was on drugs. He was always on drugs. They wouldn't let him leave. This was his prison. His new life.

"I gave you a shot of adrenaline to offset the sedatives. Can you walk?"

He looked down at his feet. His toes were curled in, just hanging there as the woman held onto him. Concentrate, Ryan. Concentrate. He put one foot on the floor, then the other. The woman continued to hold him, but her grip relaxed. He moved his left foot in front of the right, his first step. His legs were shaky, his body wanting to collapse, but he remained upright.

"Good," the woman with blond hair told him. "Let's go."

"Danger?" he managed to rasp.

"Yes. They'll be coming for us."

She led him across the room, his feet scraping along the cold floor. He still relied on her for support, but the more he concentrated on his footwork the more confident he became. By the time they reached the elevator, he was halfway walking on his own.

As the elevator doors closed, he looked out upon the room in which he'd spent so many nights. Much of it was a blur, but he had memories of the people, the experiments. Being hooked to machines, wires attached to his body. He didn't know why or how he got there, but he was thankful he was leaving.

As they exited the elevator the next floor up, he realized things were returning to normal. His surroundings were no longer spinning. He was in a corridor and walking faster with every step. The woman was leading him with determination, her head swiveling in short bursts like a cautious bird. She was beautiful, he acknowledged. The most beautiful woman he'd ever seen. Was she really his savior, or was this all some kind of dream?

They passed an office. Ryan saw it out of the corner of his eye and turned to get a better look. Red paint was splashed haphazardly against the far wall. No, not paint. Blood. A man lay slouched in his chair, his head bent backwards, mouth gaping. A bullet hole between the eyes, blood and brain splattered behind him.

"I killed them," the woman said. "For what they did to you. For what they represent."

He didn't know what that meant, but it didn't matter. This wasn't a dream. This was reality.

SHE HAD A new goal. She needed to save Ryan Harper. Luis Salazar had experimented on him, cloned him, copied his mind. He had toyed with what defined humanity more so than even what she represented. She'd been a freak from birth, but Ryan... He'd been a normal man. The billionaire had stripped him of that and in doing so destroyed the lives of those around him.

The government had paid him to do it. Her government.

But they didn't know, did they? They wouldn't have assigned her to the case if they knew it would lead back to them. Salazar had overstepped his bounds. He had gone to that next level, crossed the blurry line of morality. But the government had to know. They were investing tens of billions into the program to obtain the technology Salazar had created. They might not know about Ryan, but they knew about all this.

Dolphin dragged her frail companion into the security entrance. The scientist and guard were still unconscious. For a moment, she considered killing them, too, but her rage had passed. Every second they were down here was another opportunity for Salazar to fight back. She'd seen no indication an alarm had been triggered, but that meant little. If Salazar didn't know she'd gotten in, he would soon.

She placed Ryan in the passenger seat of a golf cart and fired up the engine. She accelerated quickly, nearly striking the edge of the tunnel as she drew to full speed. Ryan was now fully awake and alert, repeatedly looking over his shoulder to ensure no one was following them.

He didn't look like the Ryan Harper she knew, and yet she had recognized him immediately. His hair was shoulder length, his face covered with a light beard. His arms were thinner, his chest and abdomen less muscular, cheeks gaunt. He wasn't malnourished but had the muscle mass of a man who had been more or less comatose for the last eight months.

"Where are we?" Ryan croaked.

"Northern California. You were in an underground laboratory."

Ryan began to ask another question, but it was no time for questions. They arrived at the end of the corridor. She stopped the cart and helped Ryan to the stairs. She left him at the bottom and ascended first, listening for activity. Nothing. She reached the top, reemerging in the kitchen. Ryan crawled up the stairs, his breathing labored.

"Come on," Dolphin grabbed Ryan by the arm and led him through the house. She halted at the front door and peered out the window. It was no longer raining. More importantly, there was no army. Nothing out of the ordinary. No footsteps or tire tracks that hadn't been there before.

Her eyes fell on a set of car keys hanging from a nail to the right of the wall. She grabbed them, opened the door and descended the three steps to the muddy ground.

"I'd forgotten," Ryan said to himself, tasting fresh air for the first time in eight months. He looked around, taking in his surroundings.

Dolphin could only imagine how beautiful the scene looked to him, but there was no time to waste. "Come on," she ordered, and he did.

The pickup truck had a full tank of gas. Dolphin started the engine and it purred to life. Ryan put on his seatbelt and looked at her, waiting for her next move. She returned his stare and paused to think for the first time. He hadn't been a part of the plan. She was to infiltrate, retrieve any evidence or additional information she needed, and get out. She'd never considered that the evidence would be human.

"Hear that?" Ryan rasped. She was amazed he heard it over the truck's engine, but sure enough it was there. The heavy beat of helicopter rotors. Military grade.

They were coming.

53

THE TRUCK BOUNCED and trembled as Dolphin gunned it toward the Pacific Ocean, loosely following the dirt tracks that wound to the coast. The road, if one could call it that, was poorly groomed, and the truck reminded them of that every time it hit a pothole. The engine screaming, the frame shaking madly, Dolphin was unable to hear the helicopter or its trajectory.

They leapt over a shallow hill and the ocean came into view. It was less than two hundred meters away. Dolphin glanced in the rearview mirror, expecting to see the helicopter approaching from the east, but it was still out of sight.

A hundred meters.

"We're going to get in the boat," Dolphin stated. "As soon as I stop, start running."

Fifty meters. The dock was just ahead. The speedboat she'd seen earlier still moored. She spotted the key box at its base. It was locked.

She checked the mirror again. Still nothing in view. The rain had helped them; the truck wasn't stirring up any dirt. The helicopter would go to the cabin first. The soldiers would surround the house, then go in. It gave them a little extra time.

Dolphin braked, killed the engine. Ryan jumped out and began limping down the dock, one leg functioning better than the other. Dolphin went to the key box and with a single swipe smashed the padlock with the butt of her pistol. The keys to the boat were inside.

She caught up with Ryan and helped him the rest of the way. He stumbled into the boat, collapsing on the deck. She quickly unmoored the craft and leapt aboard. As she started the engine, Dolphin scanned the massive ocean before her. Even though the rain had passed, the ocean's three-foot swells would slow them down. The craft could reach 30 knots, 35 knots max. Not fast enough to outrun the military.

The wind whipped at her face and hair, the refreshing smell of salty water filling her nostrils and teasing her lips. Water was her security, her safety plan. All she had to do was submerge and she'd be safe. They'd never find her, never get her. But that wasn't an option.

She looked at Ryan Harper.

RYAN HUGGED HIS arms and ducked behind the boat's windshield, trying to stay warm. His body was weak, his arms frail. He hadn't noticed until this point. He'd been on drugs for so long that hours had blended into days, days into weeks. Reality had been a blur, a freakish nightmare from which he couldn't escape. But his body suggested he'd been in there longer than he thought. Even his fingers were thin.

He glanced back at shore. They were hundreds of yards away, but still way too close. He couldn't see the helicopter, but any second it would appear above the tree line and come for them. Kill them on sight, maybe. Or take him back to his dungeon. He wasn't sure which would be worse.

Where they were going, he wasn't sure. The woman with blond hair was taking them due west, to nowhere. He scanned the horizon, searching for another vessel, but he could see nothing. She wanted to get as far away from land as possible, he realized. His captors would try to follow their escape route. They'd check the roads, the forest, the coast line. They would search the ocean, too, but miles out at sea would be the last place they'd look. The woman was simply playing the odds. It was a long shot, but it was probably the best she could do.

The woman glanced at him. He was not sure what to make of her. She looked concerned, but that wasn't it. She was angry.

"Who are you?" he asked, but the boat's engine was too loud and his voice too faint for her to hear. She saw his lips move, but instead of leaning closer, she directed her attention ahead.

Ryan swallowed hard, nearly gagging on the rawness of his throat. He was in a bad state. If his captors caught up with him, he would be unable to put up much of a fight. And as he looked north, he saw the fight coming. Two blips on the horizon speeding toward them. Boats. On an intercept course.

He pointed. The woman cocked her head, saw the pursuit. There was no reaction, no sign of fear or concern. She turned the boat south in a gentle curve, making sure not to lose any speed. Ryan turned around in his seat to watch his enemies approach. Squinting, he prayed they would remain at a distance, unable to catch them.

He quickly acknowledged that wasn't going to happen. Their pursuers were faster. The woman glanced over her shoulder and immediately assessed the same.

"Search for guns. There might be guns," she shouted over the roar of the wind and engine.

Ryan nodded and dropped to his hands and knees, unable to walk on the bobbing surface. He frantically searched the various compartments of the boat, anywhere where a gun would be stored. But there were none to be found, not even a flare gun.

When he looked up again, the boats were even closer. The crafts were sleek and gray, marginally larger than theirs. But theirs seemed to slice through the waves like Ginsu knives, gaining every time the boat rose and fell over a crest. As they approached, he could make out the men more clearly. Each was dressed in military fatigues. They looked like American soldiers. Three to a boat. Short hair, save for one woman. Armed with rifles.

"Take the wheel," the woman ordered. Ryan did as he was told, happy to contribute. While he oriented himself, the woman moved toward the back of the boat, crouching on the floor. She pulled a magazine from a belt pocket and reloaded her pistol—it was a model he didn't recognize. She then holstered the gun and waited for the boats to get close.

And they were close. Only fifty yards back and gaining. One of the drivers stood up and raised his palm, as if requesting for them to stop. They had American flags stitched on their shoulders. They were U.S. Army.

Ryan didn't let up. Whoever they were, they were there to take him back to the hell he'd been in for God knows how long. They weren't there to save him.

"Drive for another 20 seconds," the woman rose to her feet, her eyes on him. "Then kill the engine and jump overboard."

"Huh?" Ryan asked. She couldn't hear him but she saw his shocked expression.

"Do it. Drive for 20 seconds. No longer. Jump overboard."

And then she disappeared over the side of the boat.

Ryan gasped, his heart sinking. His one hope for survival had faded. The woman who'd helped him escape had left him. And to where? They were still miles from shore. Was she giving up? Didn't want to get shot? There were better ways to surrender.

The boats were only 30 yards away and closing fast. They'd seen the woman jump off, but hadn't trailed off in their pursuit of him.

How many seconds had passed? What had she said? Twenty seconds. At least ten had passed. Maybe twelve. Thirteen. Fifteen. The soldiers were close, rifles in hand. Ryan killed the engine and the boat lurched to a stop, riding a huge swell caused by its wake. His pursuers split, looking to box him in, surprised by the sudden surrender. They slowed around him, giving him a wide enough berth. Ryan stared down at the icy waters of the Pacific Ocean, questioning the sanity of what he was about to do.

He jumped overboard.

54

RYAN SLAPPED AT the water's surface, fighting with all his might to stay afloat. The water was cold, breathtakingly so, and his body had little insulation to protect him. As soon as he submerged the cold stabbed at him from a thousand directions, forcing the air from his lungs. It was only a desperate surge of survival instinct that kicked him to the surface, allowing him to take a half-breath before going under once again.

The black waters engulfed him, pressing on him, weighing him down. He kicked and splashed but no matter what he did, he couldn't find his way back to the surface. He looked up, at the shimmering wall above him, wondering if that would be the last time his skin would ever feel air again.

Then there was shadow and a hand extended to him, grabbing him by the wrist. He reached up, desperate to take hold of anything. The hand slipped away for a moment and panic once again ensued, but then the hand returned, this time with helpers. Two hands, three hands, four hands. They were all in the water, pulling him to safety.

His captors.

"What the hell are you doing?" a man said, but Ryan was too busy gasping for air to notice who said it. He collapsed to the floor of the Army boat, the air stinging his wet skin. As his heart rate slowed and his breathing returned to normal, he finally looked up at the three soldiers in the boat. All three were armed, and none of them looked to be in a very good mood.

Ryan glanced over his shoulder. The other boat was a few hundred yards away, circling the body of water where the woman with blond hair had jumped. She had yet to surface.

"Please," Ryan stammered, raising his hands. He realized he was shaking from the cold, his already voiceless words cut short by his body's reflexes. The soldiers lowered their weapons. They weren't going to kill him. They probably didn't even know what he'd done. They were just doing their jobs. They would take him back, only this time there'd be more security. He'd never escape.

DOLPHIN TORQUED HER body so she could see the dark hull of the speedboat fifteen meters above her. It was stationary, drifting with the waves that smacked against its starboard side. She could make out Ryan's silhouette. The other boat was hundreds of meters away.

They'd never make it in time.

With an incredible burst of energy, she kicked upward, her strong arms propelling her skyward. And then she was above the surface, rising through the air, her toes clearing the boat's siding. Before she even hit the deck she had the nearest hooked in her left arm as her right fist struck him in the kidney. The man crumpled to the floor, in too much pain to even scream.

The second soldier managed to turn his head just in time to see her fist rifling at his face. He took it hard, the blow concussing him immediately. He didn't black out, but his arms rose along with his M-16 rifle. Dolphin reached out and took it, the man's grip easy to break, and rammed it into his stomach. He buckled over, the wind knocked from him.

Only the third man put up any kind of fight. It wasn't much. He raised his rifle to shoot, but she deflected his aim and threw a glancing blow to his Adam's apple, temporarily choking him. The man gagged, his eyes bulging, fingers clenching. He fired a single round.

Dolphin heard shouts from the other boat. She grabbed the soldier by the collar and threw him overboard, followed by the other two. The man, still gasping for air, frantically reached for his comrades, neither of whom was in swimming shape.

The boat began moving. She nearly fell over. Dolphin looked over to see Ryan at the wheel, his eyes on the quickly approaching second boat. They were only forty meters away and closing.

"Go, go, go!" the man she'd thrown in the water shouted, waving his fellow soldiers on. They slowed momentarily to toss life jackets to the people in the water, then accelerated once more.

Dolphin walked to stern, knelt down on one knee and put the M-16 to her shoulder. She switched to semi-automatic and fired three bursts, which harmlessly struck the bow. The boat continued and she fired three more, this time hitting the center of the windshield. The boat suddenly veered away, its bow rising high. For a moment she thought it would capsize, but instead it crashed into the side of a wave, losing half its speed. It renewed its pursuit.

"Head towards shore," Dolphin ordered over her shoulder.

They had to be at least six kilometers from shore by now, she calculated. If not more. The remaining boat crew had to have radioed in their position. The helicopter would be upon them soon.

RYAN NO LONGER felt the cold. Or the wind. A renewed level of adrenaline raced through his veins, clearing his vision and making him acutely aware of their situation. Even if they were able to outrun the other boat—and that was a big *if*—what separated them was a matter of seconds. Backup had to be in the area and moving in on their position.

Out of the corner of his eye, he saw the passenger seat next to him explode. Six bullet holes appeared in the console next to his hand. He ducked instinctively, the boat momentarily wavering. He looked back to see the woman with blond hair hunched over but unharmed. She fired back, but the boat kept coming.

It dawned on Ryan: the soldiers would beat them to shore. He and the woman had to go on the offensive. "Hold on!" he croaked, turning the boat hard to starboard. The craft listed to the right, just shy of capsizing. The other boat slowed and turned to compensate. Ryan felt the tug of gravity beckon him toward the black waters, but he didn't deviate from his plan. He kept the boat in its sharp arc, exposing both he and the woman to the remaining soldiers. They were no more than thirty yards away. It would be easy to take the two of them out.

Except their pursuers had fallen into the same semi-circular race, their advantage suddenly erased. They too were exposed, the deck at the same acute angle. The woman fired first, sprinkling the span of the craft with bullets.

The soldiers broke from their pursuit, but it was too late. The woman continued to fire burst after burst. Now to their aft, she fired several rounds into the craft's stern. The boat sputtered and died, its motor obliterated by the 45mm bullets. Ryan slowed, guiding them closer. The woman dropped her weapon's magazine and reloaded in a heartbeat. She continued to shoot.

Two of the soldiers leaped overboard to avoid the onslaught. The third fell to the floor and out of sight.

"Get us out of here," the woman barked. She laid down more suppressing fire as he turned back toward shore. As soon as they had separated from the disabled boat, she pushed him aside. "I'll take over."

Ryan sat down on what remained of the front passenger seat, rubbing his arms to keep warm. Looking forward, he caught for the first time in what seemed like eternity sight of the coast. It wasn't far, a few minutes at most. As they neared, beach houses began to emerge from the mist, mere smudges against a gray backdrop. There was something about the sight of them that reminded him of what once was. They were a blip of normalcy.

"The helicopter's coming."

Ryan heard nothing at first. He searched the skies, but it was beginning to rain and visibility was low. But then he heard it. He couldn't place its location. Not close—but the heavy beat of the rotors added an ominous tone to the atmosphere. Other than the wind, rain and smell of seawater, they were alone, still more than a mile from shore. The gray skies seemed to thicken all of a sudden, extending tentacles to the ocean's surface until there was nothing that separated one from the other. The world was collapsing in on them, threatening to swallow them whole.

Thwump. Thwump. Thwump. The helicopter was getting closer.

Ryan found himself squeezing his own arms, the cold forgotten. They were so close—he could fully make out the houses now, each looking as warm and comforting as the next—and yet they still had a ways to go.

They were a half mile from shore when the boat's engine sputtered and died.

55

THE BOAT FELL silent and Ryan's heart sank. The craft slowed and then became one with the ocean, a piece of driftwood among the waves.

The woman's eyes widened, if only for a split second. It was the first emotional reaction he'd seen from her. She frantically tried to start the engine again, but nothing happened. Flushing it did nothing. She darted to the stern and looked over the side. The way she straightened up told Ryan everything he needed to know. A bullet must have penetrated the gas tank.

The helicopter was louder than ever, the very air sizzling with the sound of its rotors. It was somewhere to the northwest of them, but he still couldn't see it.

"We need to move," the woman grabbed Ryan by the armpit and pulled him to the edge of the boat.

"I can't swim," Ryan said. "Not in my condition." He'd never been afraid of the water, but the thought of returning to the ocean frightened him now. He knew what he needed to do, but his body resisted.

"Now," she gritted her teeth. She grabbed his arm, overpowering him.

"…a life jacket," he managed to say, but she shook her head.

"I'll keep you safe," she said, her grip loosening. She moved her hand across his chest and onto his shoulder. The touch was soothing, reassuring. She smiled, ever so softly, though he sensed it was only for his benefit.

The water punched at him immediately, just like before, but this time the blows weren't as hard, its suffocating effects not as extreme. The woman instructed him to climb onto her back and put his arms around her shoulders. He did as he was told. She began to swim, her slender arms cutting into the ocean with precision.

Their pace was steady and faster than he expected, despite the drag he provided. When he looked back after what he thought were mere seconds, the boat was already a hundred yards away.

Long minutes passed, the sound of the nearby helicopter continuing to threaten. But the woman never once faltered nor stopped to look up. In fact, she didn't even raise her head to breath. Waves splashed over them, causing him to gasp as the salty water stung at his throat, but she seemed unaffected. She just continued to swim, her powerful legs kicking beneath his body.

The shore was close, only a couple minutes away, when it appeared, the low clouds swirling in a frenzy as its rotors sliced through the air. The UH 60 Black Hawk seemed to materialize out of nowhere, 20,000 pounds of force suddenly real, suddenly close, suddenly upon them. Ryan had never seen anything scarier in his life. He squeezed the woman's shoulders, and though she didn't respond, he knew she had gotten the signal. She began to swim just a little faster.

The helicopter approached, but not at the speed Ryan anticipated. It could clear the distance in twenty seconds, but the pilots didn't yet know where they were. Instead, it stopped, its tail swinging outward as the pilot circled their abandoned speedboat. It wouldn't take long for them to realize the boat was empty, and there was only one direction its former passengers would go.

Ryan looked away. He could see the rocks on the beach, could hear the waves crashing against sand. He spotted several trees and shrubs that would serve as cover. They were so close. He could feel the pull of the waves, now drawing them to shore in long, steady bursts. The woman worked double time, swimming faster than ever.

The Black Hawk began to close its distance.

Ryan squeezed the woman's shoulders again, this time harder. She had to hear it, the blades cutting wickedly through the air. She didn't look up, didn't attempt to breathe. She just continued to swim. They were less than a minute away from reaching shore, another ten, fifteen seconds from the tree Ryan had determined would shelter them, save them.

If the pilot or the men leaning out the bay doors had seen them, they gave no indication. Their approach remained slow, zigzagging in a shallow pattern. But it was only a matter of time. They were on a direct intercept course.

Ryan could feel the wind from the helicopter on his back, the sting of the salt flung into the air. They were out of time. He closed his eyes, preparing for his fate.

"Take a deep breath," the woman raised her head momentarily, the first time she'd done so since they left the boat. Before he could react, one of her hands grabbed his wrist firmly. He managed to suck in a mouthful of air just as she plunged beneath the surface, taking him down with her. Almost immediately, his lungs began to scream, panic rippling through every muscle in his body.

He fought to return to the surface, knowing it held a fate worse than death, but instinct was stronger than fear. The woman held on, taking him deeper. He swallowed the last air in his mouth, wondering how long it would sustain him.

A shadow passed above them. The water itself seemed to tremble. Ryan looked upward, trying to distract himself from the lack of air. His lungs screamed, at him, at the woman, at the helicopter directly above. It seemed to stay there forever, for minutes, hours. Had it seen them? Was it waiting for them to resurface?

He tried to break free again. Maybe they wouldn't see him. Maybe he'd be okay. He would die if he stayed under any longer. The woman readjusted her grip. She was too strong no matter how hard he fought.

Blackness began to creep into the corner of his eyes. For a moment he saw Erin, sitting on their couch, smiling at him. He saw his mom, and his father, standing side by side. He saw himself, as a child, in the mirror. Then blackness descended.

56

SEAWATER WHIPPED THROUGH the air, swirling around them as Dolphin dragged Ryan to shore. Ryan hung on her like dead weight, his legs moving out of instinct more than by volition. He was coughing loudly, throwing up mouthfuls of water. She'd kept him under longer than she'd intended, but at least he was breathing.

The air quivered, the rocks on the beach trembled with every rotation of the helicopter's rotors. It was still upon them, no more than fifty meters away. Dolphin glanced back over her shoulder, her hair flapping in front of her eyes like wet rags. The helicopter was moving away, back toward deeper waters, but they weren't safe yet. All one soldier had to do was to look back to shore.

Dolphin's feet escaped the water's grasp, her eyes settling on a large bush and low-hanging tree not far away. The beach was rocky and uneven and her legs felt like they were about to give out. Every muscle screamed, and now Ryan's dead weight had magnified the strain.

Every step seemed to take longer than the last, but then she and Ryan were beneath the tree, behind the bush. Dolphin dropped Ryan on the dirt and collapsed next to him, breathing nearly as hard. She'd never been so exhausted, but then she'd never carried a man on her back for a kilometer, either. Her eyes rolled back to the ocean to watch the helicopter. Waited for it to turn, to return to them. But it continued farther out to sea. They'd made it.

She let her head rest against a rock, closing her eyes. For a moment everything vanished. Ryan's coughing went away, the sound of waves crashing against rocks, the drumming of the helicopter. Her own breathing, her accelerated heartbeat.

Dolphin returned to consciousness. She didn't have time to rest. They had to find cover. She had to get Ryan warm.

The nearest house, a sky blue cottage with large bay windows that faced the ocean, was empty. The gravel driveway was vacant, the interior dark. Dolphin easily broke into the house and led Ryan down the hallway to the bathroom. Though extremely weakened, he had regained full consciousness and was once again walking on his own. She sat him down in the shower stall and turned on the hot water. She undressed him. He was shaking, but within a few minutes the pink began to return to his flesh and his lips stopped quivering.

"You'll be fine," she said reassuringly, rubbing his arms. He held up his hands, which were white and wilted, and told her he couldn't feel his fingertips. "Put them in your armpits." He did so obediently. As the warmth began to penetrate his body, Dolphin glanced around the bathroom. A sunroof above provided most of the light; white-and-yellow striped wallpaper made the room glow. Aluminum cutouts resembling fish lined the walls, along with a few store-bought watercolor paintings.

"Who are you?" Ryan asked finally. His voice was weak.

"My name is Dolphin. I've been working with Erin. Trying to learn what happened to you." She grabbed some soap from next to his head and began scrubbing him. He needed to get warm, but then he needed to get clean.

Ryan shook his head. "Erin's dead."

"She's not. She survived the explosion."

He didn't believe her. She grabbed his chin, forced him to look her in the eyes. "She's alive. Erin's alive."

Ryan studied her. Even now, in his state, she could see his intellect working. He was processing what she'd said, trying to read her. And then, all at once, his defenses failed him. Even in the shower she could see the tears welling in his eyes, his bottom lip once again trembling—this time not from the cold. He let out a low wail, a shriek. It was a sound that even surprised him, but he couldn't control it.

"I thought she was dead…" he whispered. "I didn't have anything to live for. Trapped down there."

"What do you remember? What did those bastards do to you?"

"How'd she survive?"

"She found a hole in the floor. Climbed out just in time. What do you recall?"

"I don't know," his gaze drifted into the distance as he tried to remember. She hoisted him into a standing position as she continued to clean his body. The warmth had given him back some of his strength. "It's all a blur. I remember being on a table. They were always giving me drugs. I only remember the times when I woke up, never when I fell asleep." He paused, thinking. "They put me in a room every few days. Let me run around, had me do puzzles. I thought they wanted to keep me alert, but they were doing tests. But I don't remember much else. It's all a blur."

"We need to cut your hair and get you shaved," Dolphin turned off the shower. She gave him a towel. She found a bathrobe behind the door.

"How long has it been?"

"Eight months."

Ryan didn't react at first. Finally, he said, "I thought it was weeks. Maybe a month."

She tried not to think about it. The very notion made her angry. Furious. She turned away until her anger had dissipated. She had to control herself. Emotions just got in the way. Caused her to make mistakes.

Dolphin found shaving cream and a woman's razor in the medicine cabinet, an electric razor under the sink. After she was done cleaning him up—he looked much more like the man she knew, albeit with thinner cheeks and exhausted paler complexion—she ordered him into the kitchen. "Find what you can eat. Stay away from the windows."

He shuffled away and she quickly stripped down, happy to be out of the waterlogged fatigues. The hot water felt surprisingly good. Her body was designed to handle sustained lower temperatures, but even it couldn't defy the laws of physics. The ocean had drawn much of her body heat away, but she hadn't noticed until the shower burned at her flesh.

When she entered the kitchen a few minutes later, wrapped in a kid's towel, she found Ryan sitting on a stool at the counter, eating what looked to be his fourth Pop-tart. He looked like a kid who'd just been caught with his hand in the candy jar.

"You need to have energy. We have to leave soon."

"We should stay here. Stay low for a while."

"No," she shook her head. "They'll be locking this whole area down. We need to get out before they get their act together."

Ryan nodded. "I couldn't find a phone. We need to call Erin. She can help."

"You can't call her," Dolphin said. "It's too dangerous."

"She can help us. And I need to tell her I'm okay."

"You don't understand. They'll have her phones tapped. John's, too. Anyone else they think you'll call. They've spent eight months keeping you a secret. If they even think you might have gotten in contact with one of them, they'll react… harshly. They'll remove your friends from the equation."

If they weren't dead already. She didn't want to tell him, but the logical course of action would have been to kill his friends the moment she escaped from Salazar's office. She knew too much, had too much information, and now the real Ryan Harper was on the loose as well. Their only chance at containment was to destroy everything that could expose the truth. That meant Erin Kinsley, John Lancaster and any other friends or colleagues Ryan might call upon… There was no reason to hesitate. They'd killed so many. Why stop now?

Ryan processed what she'd said, then asked, "What the hell is going on?"

"We don't have time. Not yet. We need to get moving."

"I have a right to know."

"You do," Dolphin said. "But we need to get out here. Go somewhere safe for a while."

Dolphin found some clothes in the bedroom. A pair of jeans, a dark blue hooded sweatshirt for Ryan. Even some sneakers that fit his feet relatively well. She was harder to dress, but managed to find some track pants and a faded yellow T-shirt. She donned a black San Francisco Giants cap to hide her hair. Grabbed a light rain jacket to hide her sidearm and store her remaining ammunition.

They crossed the gravel driveway to the road, an unmarked strip of faded asphalt that ran along the coast for miles. The road was empty. It was only eight o'clock; most vacationers would still be asleep, especially on a day like this. A quarter mile south was the town of Bedford, a beach town that thrived heavily on tourism. A collection of bars, family restaurants, motels and not much else, it was a place where very little happened.

But that would change in a hurry. It was only a matter of time before the town was swarming with military.

RYAN GLANCED OVER his shoulder repeatedly, expecting soldiers to appear at any second. The town was quiet, tranquil. Not a person in sight. Dolphin led him through the misty streets and straight to an autobody shop. It was as if she had grown up in town and knew it like the back of her hand. He followed her to the back of the building. She picked up a brick that was lying nearby and, with a single swipe, knocked away the doorknob to the rear entrance.

The auto repair shop was deserted. It was small, with only two car bays, a front office and a storage area in the back. The interior smelled of oil and engine grease. She went to the key drop at the front of the building and picked up two envelopes lying on the floor. She read the first and tossed it aside. She glanced at the second, tore it open and removed the car keys.

"'Car is making funny sounds,'" she told him, leading him back the way they came. They circled the building and Dolphin motioned to a minivan parked in front. "It's Sunday. No one is going to check on this car for a full day. Come on, we haven't much time."

He climbed into the passenger seat as Dolphin started the engine. She turned out of the parking lot and drove back through town, making sure to obey the low speed limits and stop at all intersections. Ryan remained silent until they were far from town.

"You still haven't told me what's going on," Ryan finally asked.

"You went missing eight months ago. You and Christopher Morgan," Dolphin responded, her eyes unwavering from the road. "Your friends looked for you for six months."

"And...?"

"And they stopped looking for you two months ago. When you returned."

"What?" Ryan snorted a laugh.

Dolphin still wouldn't look at him. "You returned. You're back up in Seattle right now, going about your day."

He didn't understand. She wasn't making any sense.

"He looks like you, talks like you. Has your memories. He is you by any definition," Dolphin stated tersely. "Only he isn't you, is he? He's someone else. A clone."

Ryan slouched in his seat and laughed. He didn't think it was funny. He believed her. But it didn't make any sense. Cloning. It was science fiction. It didn't happen. His laughter faded. It had happened. All of it. He'd been held prisoner in a laboratory for eight months. When he was first taken, they'd hooked him up to machines. He had cables running from his head for days. They drew his blood, but only once. Had that been it? Had all of this been for that one vial of blood?

He'd been cloned and that clone had been released back into the wild. Into his life, with his friends. With Erin.

"He nearly killed me a couple days ago. Shot me through the chest." She tapped the area between her left breast and shoulder. "He has your memories, but he isn't you. He's someone else."

"Morgan? Do you think it's Morgan?"

"Yes I do."

Ryan tried to breath but couldn't find air. He leaned forward, suddenly feeling nauseous. Dolphin's hand touched his back, trying to comfort him. He knew it was Morgan. As much as he didn't understand it, he was certain. And Morgan was with Erin, had been for two months. She'd seen through him, hadn't she? She'd know better. She was too smart to be fooled by Morgan.

But why would she question him? If he looked like him, sounded like him, she'd have no reason not to trust him. He'd been missing for six months and then miraculously reappeared—there was only one way she would react. She would be elated, just like any loving girlfriend would be.

"We have to get back there as soon as possible," Ryan said. "Immediately."

"It's not safe. They'll be waiting for us. We're going to drop off the grid, wait for the opportune time." There was no emotion in her voice.

"What would you do in my shoes?" he snarled, suddenly hating her calculating approach.

Dolphin finally turned and looked at him. Her eyes looked sad, he realized. Then she simply nodded and returned her attention to the road.

Ryan straightened up, trying to force his thoughts away. Every time he blinked he saw Morgan's gray eyes staring back at him, smiling, laughing. He was cradling Erin, the way Ryan used to, his arms snaking around her, hands on her body.

That didn't matter. Not right now. The moment he escaped, he had signed Erin's death warrant. Now that he was free, Christopher Morgan only had one option. The question was whether he would kill her immediately, or keep Erin alive long enough to use her as bait.

57

SERGEY OMITOV'S FACE was ashen. He lowered his cell phone, his arm drooping to his side. He blinked, looking from Chandling to Morgan as if he'd just woken up from a bad dream. Woken up to a worse one.

"They," he started, but was too shaken to complete his sentence. He swallowed, collected himself, and began again. "She got away."

"What?" Chandling gasped. "We have the goddamned U.S. military as security."

"She managed to steal a boat and head to sea. Two units engaged her, but she took them both out. They found her boat about a mile from shore, abandoned."

"She could stay under for as long as she wanted," Chandling shook his head.

"Not exactly," Sergey added. "She took something with her."

"What?" Chandling leaned forward. Sergey glanced at Morgan. It was immediately clear what he meant. Chandling laughed. Not at all amused. "Ryan Harper is on the loose, too?"

Morgan frowned. He was no longer alone. There was another Ryan Harper, the real Ryan Harper, out there somewhere. Morgan pictured what he looked like, not the man he saw every morning in the mirror but the one he faced on the hillside, the night everything changed. The determined FBI agent. The man who would stop at nothing to get his revenge.

"Why'd you have to keep him alive? Him of all people?" Sergey shouted at Chandling.

"It was protocol," Chandling shrugged. "We have to study the effects of the treatment on both the original and duplicate. Luis was the one who came up with the policy."

"You broke protocol the moment you took Harper for your experiment!" Sergey declared. "You should have killed him like you said you would."

"It was supposed to all work out okay…"

Christopher Morgan walked to the window, looking south. The clouds were darker than ever, the rain coming down in sheets. But in the distance, over the mountains, there was sunlight, just a sliver. There was still an opportunity.

"I'll kill them," Morgan said.

"And where will you find them?" Chandling snickered. "They're two states away. They could be anywhere. They'll disappear."

No, they won't, Morgan told himself. Ryan Harper knew there was an imposter with his girlfriend. Holding her. Fucking her. Preparing to kill her. He wouldn't waste a moment with Erin's life on the line. They would attempt to return immediately, and he would be waiting for them. He would finally get to kill Ryan Harper.

But first, he'd have to remove his friends from the equation.

58

ERIN PICKED AT the damp label of her Bud Light, her fingernails digging under the paper until the entire thing peeled away from the bottle. She crumpled it into a ball and set it down on a coaster.

"This is some celebration, huh?" John Lancaster mused from across the table. He finished what was left of his beer with a final gulp.

"If you can even call it that," Erin's attention drifted to a group of college students who had just entered the tavern, talking and laughing loudly. Aside from a couple of guys playing darts in the corner, the place had been empty. Quiet. Hollow. A complete hole-in-the-wall. The perfect place to celebrate the death of their prime suspect.

"Luis Salazar is dead. The man responsible for Ryan's disappearance is dead."

"Yeah, the man who had all the answers is dead. He took the easy way out. Never told us why."

"The answers are still out there," John said optimistically. "Sergey Omitov—he knows more than he's letting on. You don't work that closely with someone for so long without learning some secrets. Or orchestrating them."

"You think Sergey is that involved?"

"You don't?"

"I didn't say that," Erin rolled her eyes at him.

"Salazar wouldn't—couldn't—have done all this by himself. Sergey's his right hand." John yawned. "I have to go home. I'm exhausted."

"You deserve some sleep," Erin glanced at her cell phone. She'd thought it vibrated, but the screen was still dark. "It's been a long year."

"For both of us," John slid out of the booth. "Still no word?"

"No. Nothing." She'd called Ryan at least twenty times throughout the day and he hadn't picked up. She hadn't seen him since the previous morning. "I'm starting to get worried."

"I've been worried for a while," John muttered. Erin stood up silently and followed him into the parking lot. She scanned the near-deserted lot, watching for movement. The sun was setting, the large pines that lined the perimeter drawing shadows, places to hide. As they approached their respective cars, she continued to assure herself that no one was there waiting for her. "You have it, too."

"What's that?"

"That feeling that something's going down. Something bad is happening. Even now."

"No," she said as she unlocked her car. "The worst is behind us. The threat is gone. But I'm worried for Ryan." As she said it, she acknowledged she did have the feeling, too. After more than half a year of stagnation, their investigation had finally kicked into gear. They had been closing in on Salazar a little every day. He'd chosen to take his life, but had that been his only decision? He'd been a proud man, one who'd grown desperate as his life caved in around him. Even though he was gone, his legacy remained. His legacy could be controlled, if the evidence could be controlled. He would have tried to wipe any remaining traces of his crime from the world. He knew that they'd connected the dots, but he also knew they had no way to prove it. The evidence was sparse. Erasable.

Had Salazar acted, a dying wish? Ryan would be the first to go. He was the reason why things had fallen apart for Salazar. Salazar had tried once before to kill him. Maybe this time he had succeeded.

"Call me when you get home. Maybe Ryan's back by now," John opened his door.

"I'm not going home. I'm going to visit Chandling."

"It's late."

"I only was able to talk with him for a minute or so yesterday. After everything, I owe him this."

"You don't owe him anything. The guy lied to us. Interfered with our investigation."

"Goodnight, John," Erin climbed into her car. She didn't want to argue. Didn't want to think about all the extra baggage, all the loose ends. Salazar was dead. That was enough for now.

She started the ignition but didn't put the car in gear. She waited for John to drive away, leaving her alone in the parking lot. *Salazar was dead. That was enough for now.* She gripped the steering wheel, acknowledging the pain that was once again spreading across her shoulders. It wasn't enough. Salazar didn't matter. Ryan mattered.

As she merged onto Interstate 5 and headed south toward Olympia, a feeling of dread overwhelmed her. She imagined coming home later that night, walking down her hallway and turning the corner to find Ryan lying dead on the kitchen floor. Or worse—that he'd disappeared all over again. The thought had crossed her mind several times throughout the day. Had he simply vanished again? And this time for good? Had his return been a temporary occurrence, a ghostly encounter to tie up loose ends before drifting away into nothingness?

She accelerated, trying to escape her fears.

DESPITE HIS BEST efforts to stay awake, Ryan Harper slipped in and out of consciousness for much of the day, the morning's events finally taking their toll on him. When he finally awoke, he felt more rested than he had in years. With the sun hovering near the western horizon, he watched Dolphin through half open eyes, feigning sleep. She kept her eyes on the road, never taking the vehicle above 65 mph. Fewer cars were on the road, increasing their odds of attracting police attention. Despite her patience, Ryan could see the urgency in her eyes. She wanted to get back as much as he did.

She was not normal—he'd determined that much—but what was normal now? She was beautiful, young and not particularly muscular And yet she'd swum almost a mile without taking a breath. She'd singlehandedly taken down six soldiers and God knows how many more before she took him from his dungeon. And she seemed to have no fear of their precarious situation.

"You said you were shot through the chest," he finally asked.

"Yes. I healed," she stated calmly.

"In a couple of days?"

"I'm not like you. Not exactly," she understood what he was asking. "I was engineered to breathe underwater. I can also heal more quickly than regular people. I'm designed to survive. And I was made to look like this for a reason."

As crazy as it sounded, he believed her. He had no reason to doubt her. He'd already seen her swim without taking a breath. He himself had been cloned, his memories copied. Genetically enhanced super soldiers were no longer that unbelievable.

"Do you have parents?"

"I was born from a womb, so yes. But the woman was a vessel for bringing me into the world, nothing more. I was raised by people who trained me to do what I do."

"And that's to do what?"

"I'm trained to do whatever needs to be done. Assassinations. Stop terror threats. Infiltrate gangs, the mafia… corporations. Whatever."

"How do you breathe underwater?"

"This is like that game… what's it called? Twenty Questions?" she smiled. "In layman's terms, my body absorbs water through the skin and my cells break down the water at a molecular level. Then the oxygen is fed directly into my blood stream, circumventing the lungs."

Ryan didn't know what to say. He simply nodded, which caused Dolphin to laugh again.

"Why are you here?" he asked. "Why are you helping me?"

She looked at him, and though her expression didn't change, he sensed sadness, if only for a moment. Then she started from the beginning.

"The case was never about you. I was brought in to determine who hacked into military servers containing sensitive satellite footage, what was altered and for what purpose. Infiltrating Luis Salazar's organization took some finesse but wasn't challenging. I studied the other women he had relationships with to determine what character would be able to maintain a sustainable relationship with him. It was easy to develop Marie and a sound history that would hold up to background checks.

"As soon as I had access to the periphery networks, I began hacking through firewalls and developing AI scripts that could overcome new, unforeseen obstacles instantly. There were various levels of security, but they were all developed by the same security team. They shared similar weaknesses and properties, all faults I could exploit.

"Then you returned. That accelerated everything. Up until then, I'd heard rumblings about a project called Trojan Horse. Not much, only vague references. Few in the government know what they're funding. From what I could collect, the politicians are throwing money into a black hole with expectations that something revolutionary is going to come out the other end."

"But you began to suspect that everything was connected."

"At first I was merely curious. But once you returned, there were just too many pieces that didn't fit. Trojan Horse had to be the solution. It was what connected everything, even if I didn't know what it was. One of the politicians throwing money at the project was Richard Chandling."

"Chandling!"

"Chandling is a key player in the program's budgeting. What your friends and I pieced together was this: Chandling decided to cut the cord and Luis Salazar, a close friend, didn't like it. Salazar discovered Chandling's wife was having an affair. He tried to use that as leverage over Chandling to make him change his mind, but it didn't work. So Salazar opted for a more drastic solution."

Ryan redirected his attention to the road. It was not yet dark, but all he could see was the stretch of road immediately in front of them. Somewhere ahead was Portland, and beyond that Washington State. Only a few more hours. He was beginning to feel it in his stomach, the sense of hope that had abandoned him more than half a year ago. Even this morning, he'd had no illusions of escape or even survival. But now they were racing north toward Seattle, back to the woman he loved and friends who could help him. It wasn't going to be easy, but now they had the upper hand. No one knew where they were, where to find them. They were on the offensive.

His mind flashed back to the case. Chandling was nearly killed for refusing to cower to blackmail demands. That made sense. But Luis Salazar was responsible for everything? Something wasn't clicking for him, a nagging thought, a redacted memory somewhere in the recesses of his mind refusing to accept that truth. He tried to concentrate, recalling his investigation into Chandling's near assassination. There was something there they were overlooking, but he couldn't remember what it was.

"So Luis Salazar hired Morgan to kill Chandling? And then became concerned Erin and I were getting too close to the truth..." Ryan theorized out loud. "Why not just kill us? Instead, he snatches Morgan and me from under the noses of a hundred federal agents. Why risk it?"

"The billionaire has always shown affection for theatrics. He built a fortune on risk-taking and innovation. The military is financing his experiments—the project has to be worth tens of billions. If he saw that potential slipping away, maybe he thought he needed some proof that the project could work in the real world."

"That just doesn't make sense. Why me? Why not a school teacher, and why not while walking down the street one night? Why take someone that would cause a massive manhunt? It's not logical."

"Most people aren't logical. Not all the time."

"It's not right," Ryan shook his head. Dolphin was wrong. He was sure of it.

59

THE BLACK IRON gates to Chandling's estate sat ajar, a sign that the threat had passed. Erin stopped her car short of the house and climbed out, instinctively searching the shadows for anything suspicious. Chandling's house was well lit, as was the driveway, but the forest that dotted his property was impenetrable. Her hand fell to her holster, ready to draw at a moment's notice.

The front door opened. Senator Chandling emerged, Jedison Green directly behind him.

She removed her hand from her weapon, trying to hide the fact it had been there in the first place. She'd become paranoid, fearful of a threat that was no longer there. She could tell by Green's blazing stare that he had noticed.

"What are you doing here?" Chandling frowned. "Erin, you don't need to be here."

"I wanted to come down here and talk to you in person."

"You're a young woman. Shouldn't you be out with your boyfriend, enjoying the evening?" Chandling waved her toward the door. "But knowing you, I won't be able to talk you out of it."

"Richard, the man who had your family killed is dead. You know that."

"Yes, I know," Chandling closed the door behind them. "Trust me."

"Where are the other guards?" Erin followed the two men down the hall to the kitchen and living room. The house was deathly quiet, not even a clock ticking. Despite the men's presence, it felt empty, too, an uneasy serenity masking something underneath. There was something different, something not quite right, but she couldn't put her finger on it.

"Easy, Agent Kinsley. I've wired the house and the grounds. Like you said, Salazar is dead. The threat is over." Green was confident. Too confident.

"Congratulations on a job well done, Erin," Chandling glanced at her, then just as quickly looked away. She couldn't place it, but he seemed unnaturally tense, even agitated. "Too bad he took the cowardly way out."

"Something I should know, Agent Kinsley?" Green asked.

Erin looked at Green, then scanned the house. She sighed, shaking her head. "No… Everything's fine."

"I need to make a phone call," Chandling announced and quickly disappeared into another room. She watched him go, the light reflecting off his shiny, red forehead. He was sweating. Erin shifted her attention to Green. He was gazing back at her with studious eyes.

"You should go home, get some sleep," Green leaned against the counter.

"How 'bout you show me your security setup."

He shrugged and nodded. He motioned to a side hallway, the one that once led to Chandling's daughter's bedroom. She followed him, memories of the slain teenager coming back in full force. Beth had been such a smart girl, plenty of promise. Was always questioning the order of things, the perception of the truth. She could never have followed in her father's footsteps—she was way too sincere for a life in politics.

Green tapped on the door once and then entered. The room no longer resembled a teenage girl's bedroom, nor a bedroom at all. The only hint of what was once there were a few torn corners of the posters that had adorned the walls. Green had outfitted the room with a desk and four large television screens, each of which possessed a different feed. Erin recognized them immediately—the backyard, the beach, the boathouse, the front drive—all of them were places she'd spent extensive time as a child. A guard sat alertly focused on the screens.

"Along with the cameras, I have motion sensors set up throughout the property. No one's getting in here without permission," Green declared. "You think someone's going to try."

Erin forced a smile. "No, I don't think that."

"But you have a gut feeling."

He barely knew her, but he read her well. "Yes. I don't have anything to go on beside that."

"Between Sam and I, we can handle anything that comes at us," Green stated confidently.

"It's just the two of you?" Erin frowned.

"Agent Kinsley, trust me—we'll be fine," Green insisted.

YUSUF TYPED FURIOUSLY at his keyboard, running a series of searches simultaneously. Browser tabs popped up like fast-growing weeds and his eyes twitched as he scanned for the missing piece. Jasper Reynolds. Darren Todd. David Humphries. Three men, all unique and separate, yet all having met a tragic fate over the last year.

The analyst didn't know what he'd find, or even exactly what he was looking for. Reynolds was the man who had held Ryan Harper captive, who had conducted experiments on him. That was the focus of his search. There was more to the story.

Darren Todd was a nobody. Even David Humphries was an inconsequential player. But Reynolds… He was integral to the truth. He was there, with Ryan. He knew the whole nine yards, the truth about what was done to Ryan, why he was taken and why he returned.

But whose side had he been on? He was killed just like the others, a freak explosion from his daughter's oxygen tank. Puh-lease. Easy to make it look like an accident when no one's looking, not so easy cast among a series of other murders. Yusuf was sure he was killed for leaking the video recording.

The man had been a respected scientist at one point. Hell, when he died he still was. The problem was he hadn't had a meaningful job in ten years. At least on paper. He worked for a food manufacturer, trying to develop new grains of corn or wheat or something. All pretty boring, at least compared to the work he'd shown interest in as a student.

Except the food manufacturer didn't exist. It was a front, a cover. Jasper Reynolds went to work every day, but he wasn't working on corn. His identity had been erased from the world. Even the DMV's photo was corrupted. That's why Yusuf hadn't been able to find a match when he searched for the guy's face two months earlier. The *Times* had published his photo in its newspaper but not online—it only existed in hard format.

Yusuf sighed. He was missing something. There was more to this secretive company Reynolds was working for, but that isn't what interested him. There was something simpler. It was right in front of his eyes. He knew it but couldn't see it.

Reynolds' note had said he'd contact Erin when it was safe. *Be careful.* It never was safe for Reynolds again. Not at all.

Watch this. Don't tell the FBI or your alleged boyfriend.

There was a leak in the agency. Someone covering up Ryan's disappearance. Yusuf knew that. Reynolds must have known that, too. *Alleged boyfriend.* What did that mean?

Yusuf cursed at his computer. He knew the truth was within his reach.

60

JOHN LANCASTER PULLED into his driveway and turned off the engine. It was late and he was exhausted. The last eight months had torn him apart. He switched on the overhead light and glanced at himself in the mirror. The bags under his eyes had only gotten worse recently. There were more wrinkles, more gray hair. His eyes were weary, those of an old man's.

His work had taken a toll on Kendra and the kids, too. Kendra was on edge. She'd been supportive of the long hours, of the phone calls between him and Kinsley in the middle of the night. But the investigation was unspooling their marriage. She wanted him to stop, to just accept that Ryan had returned and was safe and that whoever or whatever took him was in the past, something that could be forgotten.

He wanted to believe it himself. He'd thought about it many times over the last few months, of just calling it quits. Hell, even retiring from the FBI. Ryan, his former partner, his best friend, was back.

But was he? He was there in body, but he was an empty shell of his former self. The man had been through a traumatic experience, one that neither he nor anyone would ever be able to fully comprehend. He was permitted to act differently, to be different. Those kind of things change a man.

But there was something else, something that continued to gnaw at him. He'd built a career on instinct and his instincts were telling him something was amiss.

He climbed out of the car. The air was cool. He looked toward his house. The living room light was on. He took a single step, longing for his bed. He heard a noise behind him. He glanced over his shoulder, saw a figure on the sidewalk at the end of the driveway. John spun around, instinctively reaching for his sidearm. The person's face was hidden by the shade of a tree, but he knew who it was.

"Ryan," John breathed out. "Thank God."

"You were right about me, John," Ryan said coldly.

There was a flash and a loud bang. John retreated, his back slamming into his garage door. He gasped, the wind knocked from him. Another flash, another bang. John curled to one side, the gravity of the situation setting in. He dropped to his knees and stumbled behind his car. The pavement spun beneath him, his vision blurring.

Footsteps approached. He reached for his gun. His hand was shaking, his fingers struggling to grip the weapon. Still, he drew it from its holster and, using both hands, turned off the safety. He turned to see his attacker, but the world turned with him, his house, his driveway, his car, the trees all spiraling away. He had seconds at most, and no time to think. He pulled the trigger.

The man... Ryan... retreated. John rolled onto his stomach, his body, his limbs, heavy. He blinked away the blurriness to see his partner duck behind the pine tree at the end of the driveway. He inched forward, extended his arms before him and gripped his pistol with his other hand, trying to steady himself. His adrenaline was on overdrive, blood pounding in his temples. His whole body was shaking.

John's chin touched the pavement. He raised his head, but a moment later his chin was on the ground again. He stared into the shadows where Ryan waited. Blackness crept into his line of sight, but he blinked it away again. What was wrong with him? He couldn't focus, couldn't steady himself. He was losing consciousness.

John looked down and saw blood pooling beneath him.

MORGAN STOOD BEHIND the tree, knowing he needed to act soon. He'd made a mess of the situation. John should have been dead before he hit the ground. He'd shot the bastard twice in the chest and still he was alive. He should have been driving away by now. But he had no choice but to stay.

John fired a second shot. The bullet missed whatever he was aiming at. He was desperate.

Morgan's phone rang. The Caller ID said it was Chandling. He dropped the call but Chandling called back again. This time Morgan answered.

"She's here," Chandling hissed. "Get down here immediately."

"I'm in the middle of something at the moment," Morgan said calmly.

"I need you to take care of this situation now."

"Why don't you take care of it?" Morgan winced. He wanted to be the one to do it. He wanted to see her loving expression fade as he crushed the life from her gorgeous neck.

"I can't be directly tied to any of this. Luis is the one behind it all. Get down here right now."

"Keep her busy. I'll head down soon."

"Leave what you're doing right now. What can be more important than her?"

Morgan surveyed the street. Suburban. Empty. A light turned on in a house across the street. A porch light in another. He spotted the silhouette of a neighbor peering out of a second-story window. Chandling was right, and he had little time to waste. Morgan stuck his head out from behind the tree. The motion-activated floodlight had turned off, leaving the driveway in darkness. John was still behind the car, he knew. He hadn't fled. Probably couldn't even if he wanted to. Morgan left his sanctuary, his Colt Anaconda aimed at the front of the car.

He took another step toward the car. The floodlight activated. John fired a third round, but again it missed. He was firing blind, Morgan realized. He took another step, then another, giving the car a wide berth. John was there, beneath the grill, lying in wait. Another few feet and he'd be able to spot him. Shoot him.

The front door opened.

"John?" Kendra appeared in the doorway. He shifted his aim and fired twice. Too hastily. Kendra screamed and retreated into the house.

"Kendra! Stay away!" John shouted, a shrill tone to his voice. "Stay away!"

More gunshots rang out, three, four in a row. Morgan fell backwards as he heard one buzz by his ear. He rolled onto his side, breathing hard, gun trained on the spot where John was hiding. For a moment there was silence, and then he heard sirens. Not far away. There was no more time. And he only had two more bullets in the revolver. He had to do it now.

He jumped to his feet and ran the length of the driveway. He saw John's legs, then his torso. He aimed, ready to fire. John didn't move, didn't react. His body was crumpled against the car grill, his arms extended awkwardly in front of him. His face was slumped between his arms, a pool of blood slowly expanding beneath him. He was gone.

One more between the shoulder blades, another in the head, Morgan thought. *Just to be sure.*

Before he could act, a police car screeched to a halt at the end of the driveway. Morgan looked over at the vehicle. The driver's door opened and a portly man climbed out, staring straight at him. He began to draw his weapon, but it was too late. Morgan fired the last of his two rounds at the officer, one ricocheting off the windshield, the other catching the man in the cheek. Morgan dropped the empty revolver beside John and retreated into the shadows as the sound of additional sirens filled the air.

61

"YOU OKAY?" ERIN watched Richard Chandling from across his kitchen table.

"You sure you don't want anything to drink?" Chandling smiled his trademark smile.

"No, I'm fine."

"Okay," he looked even more nervous than before. He glanced at the clock on the wall to his left, then looked down at his lap.

"Darren Todd…" Erin said. Chandling coughed. She continued. "His mom said you two were close."

"You spoke with his mother?"

"Earlier today. She said you took a liking to him."

"He was a smart kid. Full of energy. Did what he needed to do to make things happen. Reminded me a lot of me." Chandling put his heavy mitts on the table. "I saw a bright future for him."

"But he betrayed you."

"Yes," Chandling nodded slowly.

"Why would he do that? I read his college thesis, spoke to a few of his professors. All he ever wanted to do was serve in office. Hell, he wanted to be president. Why would he go and tell things to Salazar?"

"Why do most people do things? Money. Luis is rich, Erin. If he wants something he simply needs to write a check and it will happen for him. It's as simple as money."

Maybe he was right. He *was* right. Darren Todd betrayed Chandling and his family for money. He was young, right out college. Had debts to pay, women to impress. Money could help both. Even help launch his own political career.

"I apologize if I'm acting strange, Erin," Chandling said. Erin realized her attention had drifted. She looked at him to see he was staring back at her. It was the first time he'd looked at her tonight. "Everything around me is falling apart. Luis, my friend, killed my family. I find out my employees were spying on me. It's all… just so much. Please forgive me."

It sounded like a speech. It was a speech. He'd given it a thousand times before. She wasn't in the mood to hear it. Whatever he was feeling, whatever he was going through, he was incapable of expressing it. All he could do was spout out the things people wanted to hear, even to her who had been like a daughter to him. She'd bought into it for so long, had grown up with it. She'd never thought twice about it. But he was a liar. A perpetual liar who only did and said things that benefited him.

Ryan was missing for six months. Ryan went missing trying to capture the man who killed Chandling's family. And yet when it was Ryan who needed help, Chandling said nothing. Did nothing. He had more information to reveal, more facts that could have been used to take Salazar down. The case could have been solved long before Salazar ever considered taking Ryan.

Pain suddenly rippled up her back. "Excuse me."

Erin made it to the bathroom, closed the door and bent over the sink, willing the pain away. She looked at herself in the mirror. She hadn't noticed until now, but she could see the pain etched in her face. She thought she hid it so well, but maybe she didn't. Maybe everyone just chose not to say anything. That Christopher Morgan had permanently branded her.

There were several family photos scattered throughout the bathroom. Several on the wall, a few propped up in frames on the counter and toilet basin. Erin looked at each, acknowledging the happy family that once was. Each picture was of the three of them—Kathy, Chandling and Beth—smiling at the camera, looking so perfect. Kathy looked genuinely happy, but then again so did Chandling. Was it all a show? Were these pictures all lies?

Erin picked up a frame of yet another photo. She couldn't imagine that the family could fake it so well. They could hide their imperfections to the public, to the media, but Erin knew them. Kathy was a kindhearted woman, someone who loved her daughter more than anything else and would do anything to keep her safe. Maybe she loved Chandling, maybe she didn't, but her daughter's security was of the utmost importance. Kathy wouldn't cheat on Chandling. She wouldn't risk losing everything.

She picked up another. It was of Chandling, Beth and one of her school friends. They were bunched together, standing in front of a lake. Chandling, the tallest of the three, was in the center. They were smiling. There was nothing remarkable about the photo.

And yet it was the only photo where Kathy was absent. It was recent, too. Beth appeared to be sixteen or seventeen.

Erin froze. The friend… the friend was Emilie Humphries. David Humphries' daughter. Chandling had never mentioned her, merely mentioned David as some guy that his wife knew. Both girls were wearing the same T-shirt—softball uniforms. Chandling's right hand was on Beth's shoulder, his left just above Emilie's waist. It was an innocent enough photo, except it wasn't. Chandling had been hiding things from Erin from minute one, and yet she'd accepted each secret withheld as merely an act of embarrassment. Chandling had never mentioned that his daughter was friends with Emilie, nor that he knew her personally.

Chandling didn't want people to know what really happened. And yet he hadn't destroyed the photograph. He kept it. A keepsake, a memory. A reminder of the truth.

ERIN'S WHOLE BODY trembled as she returned to the kitchen, where Chandling was waiting for her. She'd been wrong about everything, played as a fool from the beginning.

"Kathy wasn't having an affair," Erin stated.

Chandling's expression feigned surprise. It was a guise, an act. "I told you she did."

"You lied. You were the one having an affair. With Emilie Humphries."

Chandling laughed, shaking his head. "I don't know what you're talking about."

"You had your family killed because they found out. Your blackmail story... I don't know how I could fall for that! Your family found out. They were going to leave you. The press would have found out the truth. Your career would've been ruined."

"Erin, please," Chandling rose to a standing position. "Just calm down for a moment. I don't know where you're coming up with these things."

"Stop bullshitting!" Erin screamed. Chandling took a step backwards. She drew her gun. Her body was trembling but her aim was steady. He froze, raised his hands, still smiling. Smug bastard. "For once tell the Goddammed truth!"

She had to call for backup. She reached into her pocket, found her cell phone. Speed dial John, he'd have the necessary authorities on this place in a matter of minutes. Three rings, four rings. Voicemail. It wasn't like John not to answer.

"Erin, you know me. You know I would never do anything to hurt Kathy or Beth."

Erin couldn't help but laugh. Everything made sense now. Well, almost everything. "And Darren Todd... he wasn't spying on you for Salazar. He realized you were responsible for their deaths. He went to Ryan. You had him driven off the road to keep him quiet. Only you weren't sure if he talked, so Ryan—and me—became liabilities. You had to kill us, too."

All of this. *Over an affair.* It couldn't be that simple, that basic. Too much had happened, too many people had died.

"I'm sorry, Erin." His look of shock had faded. He almost looked elated.

But Ryan's disappearance. His return. That didn't factor in. And Luis Salazar. Marie couldn't have been that wrong about the billionaire—he was connected.

"Salazar financed it all. He paid Morgan to commit the murders. In exchange, he got your political support."

Chandling took a step toward her. She reaffirmed her aim. "What are you going to do, shoot me?" he boomed. He was mocking her. Like he'd been this entire time. The man she thought she knew, that had raised her and treated her like a daughter...

he wasn't that man.

"You're under arrest."

"That's not how this is going to end." He took another step toward her.

Erin heard footsteps in the main hallway. She glanced to her left to see Jedison Green entering the kitchen, his pistol aimed at her head.

"Agent Kinsley," he said fiercely. "You have two seconds to lower that weapon."

62

RYAN HARPER WATCHED the freeway inch by, the mile markers ominous reminders of how far they had yet to go. They'd entered Washington State, Interstate 5 carrying them along the Columbia River through Longview to Centralia, an hour and a half to Seattle. He could see nothing but the road ahead and the dots of lights that represented the farms and small towns that were scattered throughout the region. They were close, but not that close.

Erin could be dead. The thought continued to gnaw at him. Morgan would go after her—he was sure of it—but would he kill her outright? Or would he toy with her in front of him like he did before, making him watch her die.

"We need to call Erin," Ryan looked at Dolphin.

"No," she said quietly. They were driving faster now, nearly 90mph. The engine wailed softly under her foot.

"We should have called her back at the gas station."

"They'll be listening—"

"They're going to kill her tonight. And John. Whether we call or not. We can help them."

Dolphin glanced at him. She said nothing.

She was used to doing things her way. She was used to being alone. No emotional connections, no limitations. No one to hold her back or be used as bait. She couldn't understand his position.

"Dolphin, please," Ryan grabbed her arm. She flinched, but didn't pull away. She stared at his thin hand for a moment, finally contemplating his request.

The car lurched to the right. Ryan grabbed the door for support, afraid the entire vehicle was going to disintegrate under the torque. They zoomed off the freeway toward a large gas station, its bright lights a beacon in the darkness. Dolphin took a sharp turn into the lot, finally slowing as she approached other cars.

Nearby, a teenager with a goatee and a bright white baseball cap was leaning against the side of his car, talking rapidly on a phone through a wide, toothy grin.

Dolphin stopped the van, walked over to him and ripped the phone from his hands. She shoved the stunned kid over the hood of his car and silently returned to the van. Without looking at Ryan, she tossed the phone to him and accelerated quickly. The teenager was still picking himself off the ground when Dolphin hit the on-ramp.

"Wow," Ryan said with amazement. He could have sworn he saw Dolphin grin.

"Are you going to use the phone or not?" she said testily. "After I went through all that trouble for you."

He was pretty certain she hadn't wasted an ounce of energy obtaining the phone, but he didn't bother arguing. He quickly dialed Erin's number.

It rang, but no one answered.

"She always answers," Ryan said quietly.

"Try her again."

Still nothing. He tried John. He too didn't answer.

Dolphin threw him a sideways glance. He couldn't accept that they were dead. They couldn't be. He'd come too far for them to just be dead.

He dialed John's number again.

"Hello?" a woman's voice cracked on the other end.

"Kendra, it's Ryan. Where's John?"

"Ryan, oh my God," she cried, her words nearly indistinguishable.

"What's happened?"

"It's John. He's been shot."

"Jesus. How badly?"

"I don't know. He's lost a lot of blood. They're not telling me anything. They're not telling any of us anything. I found him… was shot in our driveway, Ryan. At our home."

"Kendra, where's Erin?"

"I don't know."

"You don't…"

"Wait, yes. John said something… before the paramedics arrived. He said something about Erin. About her going to Senator Chandling's."

Ryan had to grab his wrist to keep the phone from shaking out of his hand. She was still alive. Erin was still alive.

"Ryan, I have to go. I can't… not right now."

"Kendra, wait!"

"Ryan? You okay?"

"Erin's in danger. I need your help. I need you to get help to her immediately. Someone is going to try to kill her, too." At least she was with Chandling, and his security staff.

"Oh my God," Kendra sobbed. "Yes, of course. Oh my God. Do you know who did this? To John?"

"The man who you think—you're just going to have trust me on this, no matter how crazy it sounds—the man who you think is me… he isn't me. It's Christopher Morgan. He's going to kill her."

There was a long pause on the other end. "You're serious."

"He's a clone."

"A clone."

"A clone of me, yes. But he's really Christopher Morgan. You have to—"

"Ryan, I'm going to get help. But they're not going to believe me. I don't know how to…"

"Just tell them she needs help."

"Okay, okay…" Kendra stammered. "I'll call you back."

The line went dead. Ryan thought about calling her back immediately but his hands were shaking so bad he couldn't even hit the redial button. He leaned forward, unable to think, to breathe, to do anything. A day's worth of emotion and chaos and danger had just exploded inside him, overloading the senses.

"Well?" Dolphin asked anxiously.

"Erin's still alive. And she's in Olympia." Not far away.

Dolphin accelerated.

At that moment, two other words came to mind, two he hadn't thought about until that very moment. "Darren Todd."

Dolphin remained silent, waiting for an explanation.

Ryan felt his heart beginning to knot all over again. "Darren Todd," he repeated. Memories suddenly began to pop in his mind like fireworks, synapses working on overdrive. "He was an aide to Senator Chandling. He called me, said he knew something about the assassination attempt. He was nervous, didn't want to talk over the phone. I assured him that it was okay, but he refused to talk. We agreed to meet but he never showed up. That was just a couple days before we found out about Morgan. I was going off a hunch. I didn't want to tell Erin—she would have talked me out of it, at the very least would have hated me for it. John would have said don't touch it. But I knew. I knew what he did."

Erin wasn't safe. She had walked into the lion's den.

"Senator Chandling murdered his own family."

63

SENATOR RICHARD CHANDLING stood just feet from the woman who had looked up to him like a father for so many years. She had loved him, even. But that love was gone. Her eyes were filled with venom, a ferociousness stirring just beneath her fair skin. She hated him, he was certain of it.

Love. Hate. They were merely words to him. Ideas. Concepts he had studied and mastered over the years to become the man that he was. A respected U.S. Senator. A man with power. A man who could get his way. People were moved by these concepts in a way that fascinated him. He long ago realized he would never understand; he just had to accept.

People were the way they were.

Each motivated by goals. Not unlike him. He was made for office, to rule over others, to make the decisions others were too afraid to make. That was his goal in life, to get to a place where he could help better the masses. And yet there was so much vermin in the world dedicated to preventing him from achieving his goals. Reporters always questioning his every move. Other politicians fighting over every inconsequential word. His family denying him simple pleasures.

"I need a minute alone with her," Chandling stated calmly to Jedison Green.

"Sir, she just pulled a gun on you." Green looked confused by the turn of events. He didn't understand what was happening, why it was happening.

"I'm calling the cops," the other guard, a man with red hair and a red goatee, said. Sam was his name. He never forgot a name.

"No!" Chandling barked, catching the two men off guard. Green looked at him suspiciously. Chandling breathed out, told himself to relax. "I've known Erin since she was a little girl. I need to know why she betrayed me. Betrayed her country like this."

"I didn't betray—"

"Leave us," Chandling yelled at Green. "You've taken her gun and phone. Handcuff her to the oven and leave us. I just need a few minutes."

Green nodded nervously and bound Erin's wrist with Flexicuffs and then looped another set around the oven handle. He tugged on her arms to make sure she was secured and then motioned to Sam to leave the kitchen.

"Jedison, don't leave me with him! He's under arrest! He killed…"

"Shut up, Erin!" Chandling hollered, his face reddening. "Haven't you done enough damage? You conspired with the man who killed my family and then… what, try to blame it on me?"

"Jedison, he's lying…"

"You come into my home, you pull a gun on me, you say you have to kill me because Luis paid you all that money! How dare you! I raised you like one of my own!"

Erin's eyes widened with fright as Green left the kitchen, leaving her alone with Chandling.

"Erin," he said softly, cupping her warm cheek with his hand. She pulled away, screamed for Green again, but he grabbed her face, made her look at him. She locked eyes with him. "I've always loved you like a daughter."

"You killed your family." A statement. A question. "Make me understand."

"It was the only way it would work," he told her. Her expression flickered. Did she not understand? How could she not understand? "The country needs me. They were going to ruin me. Over something so trivial. You see, I first met Emilie at Beth's softball game. She was third-base, Beth played first.. She and Beth became close friends. She was around the house a lot—showed interest in my career. She said she wanted to major in political science and go to American University. I wrote her a letter of recommendation, offered to become her mentor. She ate up my every word.

"She said she wasn't a virgin but that was a lie; she cried the first time. She was so young and smooth, not like Kathy. Emilie was full of energy, too, and she began to like it. What we did together. I would invite her to come over and she would. I would ask her to do things and she would."

He smiled, caught up in his story. "The affair lasted for just under a month. The sex was incredible, the best I'd had in years. I needed my wife for my career, but she no longer brought me any pleasure. Emilie did, any way I asked."

"But then one day her dad showed up at my office. He said he knew the truth. David Humphries was on the verge of losing his job; he'd lost most of his savings. He was going to lose his house. He wanted money to keep quiet, more than I had. But Luis Salazar had the money, and he needed me. His experiments were controversial, his projects costing the government billions. I could get the votes to keep the faucet running; Luis merely had to supply me with the appropriate funds. I was prepared to pay, but I needed to see Emilie once more. She agreed to see me, to do what I wanted—but this time she asked for the money. 'I'll do anything you want, baby, but only one last time. And only after we get what we deserve.'

"*We*. After what *we* deserve. She was just as bad as her father, trying to take advantage of a U.S. senator, trying to ruin my career, ruin my life. I didn't deserve that, the country didn't deserve that. And they didn't deserve the money."

"Richard, give it up. It's over," Erin stated.

"I didn't deserve this. I'd done nothing but protect my name and the power I rightfully deserved. And yet person after person, my closest friends, my family, wanted to tear me down until I was nothing. The Humphries died for a good cause. So did my family. They were becoming suspicious and the turmoil was affecting my campaign. The reporters didn't see it but I did; I could see the cracks forming. Every time my daughter looked at me I knew that she knew. She was just another obstacle. It's not over."

Chandling's large mitt slid away from Erin's cheek to her neck. He placed his thumb against her throat, his index finger under her ear. Her neck was so soft and warm, so fragile. She sensed what he was about to do, tried to scream, but was too late. He squeezed, cutting off her air.

64

FLASHES OF WHITE shot from the corner of Erin's eyes as Chandling choked the life from her. Erin tried to scream but nothing came out. She pulled at her restraints with all her strength, acting on pure instinct more than anything else, the plastic cuffs cutting into her wrists.

She had seconds before she blacked out, before she was dead.

"What are you doing?" she heard someone say. Chandling released her and backed away. Erin gasped, sucking in air. She looked up to see Green walking toward her, concern in his eyes.

"I… I don't know what came over me," Chandling stammered. "She killed my family. I couldn't control myself."

"He killed them…" Erin rasped.

"Stay away from her," Green pointed a finger at the senator, who had retreated several steps. He raised his hands in defeat.

"He killed them."

She didn't know whether Green believed her, but she sensed he did. He reached into his pocket, pulled a knife and opened it with a flick of his thumb. He cut away her left wrist, which was now dripping blood. He was dumbfounded, confused by the turn of events, even by his own actions.

"Agent Kinsley, we're calling your pals and are going to get this squared away," he said. He knelt down beside her, preparing to cut her other wrist.

And then he was on his side, eyes rolled into his skull, blood and saliva bubbling from his lips. A few specks of blood splattered against her face. The metallic twang Erin heard was that of a frying pan striking Green in the side of the head. Chandling loomed over him, holding the heavy pan in both hands. Erin gazed up at the monster, the soulless creature who had killed his family, as he swung a large leg over Green.

His emotionless eyes watched the body twitch, studying it like a curious child.

Erin's eyes fell on Green's knife. Chandling wasn't watching, wasn't, if only for a moment, even aware of her existence. The kill was his sole focus. The knife was only a couple feet away, just behind the senator. She reached for it with her free hand, her fingers wrapping around the blade. She pulled it toward her.

She could sense Chandling's energy. He was going to beat Green to death. He showed no sign of satisfaction or enjoyment—not in the way others feel such things—but raw electricity crackled from his very person. He was enjoying it in his own, twisted way. Chandling slowly raised the pan over his head.

Erin cut herself loose. Chandling turned and realized what was happening. She scurried backwards, looking for separation. Chandling, broken from his spell, came after her.

She rose to her feet, kept moving away. Chandling swung at her and missed by the smallest of margins. Erin spun on her heels, knife at the ready, but Chandling swung back the other direction. The pan struck her hand, flinging the knife across the room. She barely felt it, her only thought on survival.

Erin charged Chandling. He was large but not agile, not trained in combat. And yet in the heat of the moment she didn't take his mass into account. She struck him hard, knocking him backwards, but he stayed upright and twisted violently to the right. She bounced off him and stumbled away. The frying pan fell to the floor.

She regained her footing, ready to go on the offensive, but Chandling's attention was to her right, to the counter top where her gun and cell phone lay. He was closer to the weapon than she was, but she was faster. His large hands reached for her gun; she flung herself over the counter for it. Their hands touched the weapon at the same time, but neither got a grip on it. Erin dropped over the far edge of the counter and landed on her side, the wind knocked from her lungs.

Even breathless, she searched for her weapon. The gun had slid to the base of the refrigerator, just under ten feet away. Still gasping for air, she scurried to it, switched off the safety and spun around. Chandling was coming toward her again, reaching for her. But when he saw the gun in her hand, he froze.

No one would question her if she shot him. Not after he nearly killed her. But she couldn't pull the trigger. He'd stopped, and there were too many questions to which she needed answers. He was the only one who could explain the strange events of the last year.

"Erin, I lost myself. I didn't mean to…" he said, sounding defeated. It was all an act.

"Get down on your knees and put your goddamned hands on your head."

He did as he was told. She made a wide circle and approached him from behind. She grabbed her handcuffs from the counter and shoved his thick wrists as far up his back as possible without breaking his arms.

"You sick, sick bastard," Erin spat, flattening him against the ground. Once he was incapacitated, she realized help was not far away. Flashing red and blue lights reflected off the walls of the front hallway. The police had arrived.

"I needed to, Erin. You must understand."

"You needed to what? Kill your family because you were fucking a high schooler?"

"They threatened to destroy everything that I've worked for. It's not about me, it's about the country. Think about that."

Chandling was delusional. She'd known him for thirty years and only now saw him for what he truly was. He disgusted her, but then she was disgusted with herself. The answers all along had been with him, yet she had overlooked his collusion for what? Friendship? Some false sense of parental bond? Because she took him at face value?

"Ryan—what did you do to him? Where'd you take him?"

"You shouldn't worry about that," Chandling stated icily.

"Tell me, goddamit!" she pressed his arms deeper into his back, tempted to snap both of them. He gasped in pain, his body tightening.

"He wasn't the intended target. But he was someone I could keep an eye on."

"What did you do to him?" she screamed, but he said nothing more. She wanted to beat him until he talked. Anger pulsed through her veins. Her good hand shook she was so furious. But she knew better. The answers would come, she kept repeating to herself. They would come, and it would all be over. It was over.

"What happened here?" a familiar voice penetrated her concentration.

Erin jumped to her feet, gun at the ready. A man emerged from the front hall. He looked at Erin, unconcerned by the weapon she had aimed at his chest. He grinned and she lowered her gun, happier than ever to see Ryan Harper.

65

"HE DID THIS. He did this to you," Erin said breathlessly at the sight of Ryan Harper, the only words she could muster. Her pistol slid to her fingertips, now too heavy to hold. Her legs wobbled, her balance wavered. The air itself seemed to be electrified, overwhelming her senses and control.

Ryan took three steady steps to her and embraced her, squeezing her. Erin gasped, a high-pitched shriek that erupted from the deepest area of her soul. She fell against him, unable or unwilling to do anything else. His chest was warm, his arms comforting. She realized she was trembling, but couldn't do anything about it. Didn't even want to try, not anymore.

Suddenly, everything that had happened over the last 24 hours, the last several months, didn't matter. Ryan's strange behavior, his late night excursions, John's suspicions, Senator Chandling's betrayal... his attempts to kill her. None of it mattered. It was over and she could no longer contain her emotions.

"I was worried about you," Ryan whispered in her ear. He squeezed her even tighter, telling her everything was going to be all right. His right hand caressed her back. His left softly removed the gun from her hand and placed it on the countertop.

Erin couldn't speak. She closed her eyes, feeling his touch.

"Christopher—" Chandling murmured.

Ryan grabbed her cheeks and kissed her hard on the mouth. "I've been an ass the last few days. Had to work out a few... personal issues. But I'm back. I want you more than ever."

She kissed back, not worrying about whether he felt more like the new Ryan or the old one. It didn't matter. He was here, at the right time.

Chandling said something, but she couldn't hear him. She could only see and hear Ryan, feel his touch.

"Green," she said aloud, suddenly remembering the security guard who'd saved her life. She dropped to the floor beside the man. He was still alive, if barely, gurgled breaths bubbling from the corner of his lips.

"Paramedics are on the way," Ryan anticipated her request. "Everything will be all right."

"Stop playing around!" Chandling suddenly snapped. "Why prolong things?"

"Shut up, you crazy fuck," Ryan shouted. He kneeled beside the senator and pulled the man's head back by his hair. Erin watched, not fazed by Ryan's vitriol. "I should kill you for what you did to me." Ryan was furious. He deserved to be. Chandling only smirked.

A phone rang. Ryan shot to his feet, seemingly on edge. He looked at her. It was her phone. She scanned the kitchen, spotted it at the base of the refrigerator. Ryan watched her intently as she picked it up.

"Who is it?" he asked.

"It's Yusuf."

"Do it now," Chandling hissed.

"Shut up."

Erin answered the phone, looking at Ryan. He stared back at her, his entire body tense. She'd never seen him so nervous and simultaneously alert.

"Thank God! Are you with other people?" Yusuf said quickly.

"Yes, I'm here with Ryan at—"

"You need to do exactly what I say. Casually go into another room, get alone."

"Okay," she chuckled, rolling her eyes at Ryan. A forced smile appeared on his face. She started to wander away, toward the dining room.

"If Ryan is near you, you can't react to what I'm about to say. Got it?"

"Yusuf, what is going on?"

"You're in danger—"

"Yusuf, it's taken care of."

"Ryan isn't who he says he is. That isn't Ryan Harper."

Erin froze midstep. "What?"

"Be casual," he stated. She'd never heard him so serious, so straight-to-the-point. "That man—he is not Ryan Harper."

"This isn't funny."

"Erin, you need to get away from him now. Would I make this up?"

No, he wouldn't. But it was absurd. It didn't make any sense. It was unfathomable. Sure, he'd been acting different. Some of his behavior was suspicious. But Ryan Harper was Ryan Harper. There was no question. He was Ryan. She would know.

"That video of Ryan we received—" Yusuf started, frustrated. "The filename was dated. We thought it was the date the video was copied—it was the date the video was made. It was taken after that man near you came back."

The words didn't resonate. She heard them but couldn't process them.

"The scientist, his name was Jasper Reynolds. He had a cast on his left wrist. He broke that wrist a day after Ryan returned. The video was taken after Ryan returned."

Erin couldn't help it. She glanced over her shoulder to look at Ryan, who she could still see through the dining room doorway. He was watching her, arms at his side. His expression, his stance, frightened her. It was as if he was preparing to attack.

"I can't say for sure, but Reynolds, back when he was in college—his thesis was on the advancement of cloning. Do you hear what I'm saying?"

Erin couldn't respond. It couldn't be. It was impossible. She would know.

"Erin, get the hell out of there right now."

She heard movement. Out of the corner of her eye she saw Ryan charging toward her. Instinct took over. She ran into the living room, eyes on the small hallway that led to the foyer and the front door. The room was awash in the flashing blue and red lights from the police car parked outside. She was only seconds away from safety, but Ryan—taller, stronger, faster—was gaining on her.

Erin veered into the entryway and reached for the door. She grabbed the knob and twisted—the door opened—but she'd been too slow. The man who looked like Ryan was upon her, only feet away. He came at her low, ready to take her to the ground, but she clasped both hands together and swung with all her might. Her fist caught the lookalike in the face and deflected him away, his momentum carrying him several feet further.

Pain rippled up her arm and into her skull as her hand reacted to the blow, but she turned to face her attacker. She stepped toward him, but he was already scrambling to his feet, gun in hand. He looked up at her, a toothy smile painted on his face, blood running from a crack in his lip. Suddenly, he didn't look like Ryan at all.

Had it been him all this time? She'd let him make love to her. Convinced herself that Ryan was back. She'd let him take her gun from her. He'd unarmed her and she hadn't even noticed.

Erin ran outside. The floodlights were still on, illuminating the large driveway. The police car was parked just a few yards away, its lights painting the surrounding house and trees with neon blues and reds.

"Help!" she cried, stumbling across the gravel to the car. She slammed against the hood of the car, trying to get the officers' attentions. But the men inside the car didn't respond. Even before she ran to the driver's side window she knew help was nowhere close.

It had taken two bullets, maybe three. Both officers had been shot in the skull, killed instantly by the man posing as Ryan.

Instinct once again kicked in. Even if the men were no longer alive, they were still armed. Erin tugged at the door. It was locked, but the window was rolled down. She reached inside, unlatching the driver's holster. She withdrew the gun, switched off the safety with her thumb.

A hand grabbed her by the shoulder and pulled her backwards. The man threw her to the ground. She landed on her back, the impact stunning her. She gazed up to see the silhouette of her attacker looming over her. She raised her gun to fire. The man kicked the gun away and she watched as it slid to a stop several feet away.

Erin rolled onto her stomach and crawled toward the gun. She didn't make it far. A shoe came down on her shoulder blade and pressed her to the ground. Erin screamed as the man ground his sole against her ravaged flesh, inflaming the pain that had haunted her for the last year. And then she found herself on her back, the man's weight against hers. She punched at him with all her effort, but he had the upper hand. He caught her wrists and twisted them to the ground.

"The other guard is dead, too. In case you're wondering." He looked happy to be telling her. Excited, even.

"Who are you?"

"I'm Ryan Harper," he leaned toward her and licked her lips, then her neck. "Mmm, the sweat of a dirty woman."

"Tell me!"

"You've been a dirty whore, you know that. Letting me do those things to you, letting me inside. You had to have known. Somewhere deep down. I know you did. Every time we fucked you had that look. That I was different, that I wasn't the same person you thought I was. You convinced yourself that you were sleeping with Ryan Harper, but you knew better."

He looked her over, aroused. He bit at her breasts through her muddied T-shirt. She squirmed, trying to break free, but he didn't let her move. "You are one good-looking bitch, I'll give you that."

Good-looking bitch. She'd heard that term before. Every night when she slept. In her nightmares. It couldn't be. She refused to accept it. He was dead, a terrible memory but nothing more. The sky spun above her. Everything was spinning. Chaos.

The man noticed her panic. He smiled, his teeth red from his own blood. "You've figured it out now, haven't you. You dirty little whore. I said before that I wanted you. Well, I got you. Say my name."

She couldn't. It was impossible. It couldn't be him.

"Say it, or I'll knock every Goddamned tooth from your mouth and still make you say it."

"Christopher Morgan," she said breathlessly.

66

CHRISTOPHER MORGAN DUG his thumb into Erin's burnt skin, admiring his handiwork as he pushed her back through the house. She didn't say a word, didn't cry, but he knew he was causing her immense pain. Her shoulder drooped. Walk staggered. Muscles tense. She was being tortured and was at his mercy.

He was elated on many levels. He'd wanted her to know who he really was before killing her. The look on her face when she realized it had been priceless. He would live with that memory for the rest of his life. Her death would be memorable, but nowhere as unforgettable as that expression, that combined look of pain, shock and utter guilt.

They reentered the kitchen, where Senator Chandling and Jedison Green were awaiting them. The politician was still lying on his chest on the floor. If he'd made an attempt to right himself, Morgan couldn't see it. Green was as antisocial as ever, bloodied and unconscious.

"Kill her already!" Chandling spat as they approached.

"No need for impatience," Morgan said. There was still much to be decided. The biggest threat was Dolphin; Erin could once again serve as the perfect hostage. But he'd made that mistake before and paid dearly for it. Still, in the back of his mind, the thought of killing the real Ryan in front of Erin—or vice versa—was alluring. To find their way back into each other's arms only to have them torn apart…

"Erin, it didn't have to be this way," Chandling chided, even as he strained to see her. "But you had to keep digging."

Erin said nothing.

"Christopher, uncuff me."

Morgan ignored the man on the floor. "Up until Ryan and I, he and Salazar were stealing bums off the street. Prostitutes and runaways. People no one would notice.

Cloning them, fucking with their minds. Paid for by the military. But Little Dick here needed to know if it could be done in the real world. With real people watching."

"Christopher, please! Kill the bitch and let me free. It hurts."

Morgan snorted. He looked down at the pathetic figure, aimed his gun at the man's head and fired. Then again. Chandling would never speak another one of his lies.

"The guy was insane," Morgan returned the barrel to Erin's lower back. "He deserved much worse for what he did to me. To all of us."

Erin blinked but said nothing.

"If you're going to experiment in the real world, why the two of us? It makes no sense. Never did. It was bound to end up this way. A cluster fuck with way too many people dead. Mental problems, too. If you were to survive now, think how many years of therapy it would take to get past this." Erin looked away. "I'm going to kill you, you know. Soon."

She kept silence. No reaction, nothing. His nostrils flared. He wanted her to be afraid, to quiver at the very thought of him.

"You know, of the two of us—Ryan and myself, that is—I really got the better deal. He got locked up in some lab, I got to come home to you and fuck your brains out." Morgan pressed behind her, his free hand falling to her ass. She tensed, but only a little. Not the reaction he was looking for.

His eyes fell on something nearby. That was it. The way to make her respond. His hand drifted past her, fingers coiling around the knob to the kitchen stove. It was a beautiful, big, black and expensive-looking gas stove. He turned the knob. A flame hissed to life.

He felt her body go rigid. He smiled, smelling her sweat. Her sudden fear. He ran his hand up her back, feeling her moist skin through her shirt, beneath her bra strap. She shifted uneasily, her breathing intensifying. He grabbed her shoulder and forced her over the stove. Her hands flattened against the countertop on either side of the flame, trying to resist.

"Bend over," he ordered.

He grasped her left arm, twisting it behind her back. She whimpered like the pitiful whore she was as he applied the weight of his body against hers. Her body hovered precariously over the flame, her chest and neck only a foot away.

"I've never cooked a woman before," he whispered in her ear. He licked her neck. "Tastes like chicken." Erin cried out, thrashing from side to side, trying to land an elbow. He was too close and too strong. He pressed his pistol into the back of her neck to calm the bitch down.

"Christopher, please."

Begging. For her life. For beauty. He laughed, pushed her closer. Her right arm was beginning to buckle. She had to be feeling the heat, the inevitable burning sensation of fire on flesh.

"You're finally going to look the way I'd always intended."

A noise. Toward the front of the house. Morgan stopped and listened. It had been faint, so much so he was surprised he'd heard it. He strained his ears. It came again. A car door closing.

Suddenly, a hard object struck Morgan in the cheekbone. As he buckled away, he realized it was Erin's elbow. He felt the taste of blood, a loosened tooth. Erin spun around, looking for better leverage. The bitch was a fighter. But he was a killer. He punched her in the face and blood erupted from her nose. Her head snapped back, stunning her. He grabbed her by the shoulder, bringing the pistol up to her chest. *Kill her. Now.*

"Help me!" she screamed.

No one can help you, bitch. His finger curled around the trigger.

"Erin!" someone cried. A man's voice. All too recognizable. It was his own voice. No. Ryan Harper's.

They were here. Morgan couldn't help but smile. Once again Erin had baited his adversaries to his location. Erin looked at him, hope flickering in her eyes. Smugness. Her Ryan had returned to save her. It was a fool's hope. He raised the gun above his head and struck the bitch in the forehead. She crumpled in his arms, then to the floor.

He couldn't kill her just yet. He had to let them share their final moments together.

67

IT COULDN'T BE too late. Ryan Harper repeated the words over and over in his head as he followed Dolphin up the two steps to Senator Chandling's front door. To have come this far only to find Erin dead… It couldn't end this way. Two cops dead in the driveway, the engine still warm. Wounds fresh. Morgan had been here. Or he was still here. Would he find Erin inside?

He switched off the safety of the police-issue pistol. The weapon felt heavier than usual. His arms—his whole body—were weak. And yet his mind was as strong as ever. He felt like his old self, perfectly aware of his surroundings, well aware that the situation could explode at any moment.

"Help me!" a woman screamed. It was Erin.

He shouted her name, ran forward. Dolphin raised an urgent hand, cocked her head just enough so he could see her fury. He stopped, blood pulsing to his face. Erin was alive—he had to save her—but he'd also blown their element of surprise. Morgan was inside and he now not only knew someone else was there—he knew *who*.

Dolphin entered the house, her pace quickened, and he followed, scanning the second floor. He saw nothing, could hear nothing. A few specks of blood were splattered on the stairs. Dolphin motioned toward the hallway to the left, which led to the living and dining room. She started down the main hallway, which went directly to the kitchen. Ryan sidestepped, entering the living room. Dirty footsteps on the beige carpet were the only indication something was amiss.

The living room—and connected dining room—was empty. Ryan moved forward quickly, trying to keep his steps quiet. Wherever Erin was, she had minutes at most. He peeked into the kitchen. Pots and other kitchenware were scattered on the floor, signs of a struggle. Blood speckled one of the countertops. Two feet protruded from behind a nearby counter, unmoving.

He rounded the corner and entered the kitchen. His eyes immediately fell on a mirror. He looked at his image—a smiling image. Only he was not smiling. It was Christopher Morgan, standing against the wall next to the main hallway. His doppelganger had already seen him, was aiming his gun right at him. Ryan had no time to compensate.

Just then, Dolphin emerged from the hallway. She didn't see Morgan. He was only a few feet from her. Ryan opened his mouth to warn her, but everything happened in an instant. Morgan's eyes flashed, surprised yet pleased by the woman's sudden appearance. He turned his aim to take her out. Dolphin saw Morgan out of the corner of her eye. She reacted quickly, her right arm exploding toward Morgan to deflect his aim. Her fingers struck the barrel, but it was too late. The gun went off— the gunshot deafening—and there was no question Morgan had hit his target. A spray of blood splashed on the wall next to Dolphin. The woman who had rescued him, who'd saved him from an eternity of misery, crumpled to the floor, lifeless.

Morgan returned his attention to Ryan. Instincts taking over, Ryan fired first. The bullet caught Morgan in the right shoulder. Morgan grunted and staggered backwards, but didn't go down. The killer fired back quickly, but his first shot missed, striking the dining room chandelier.

Ryan dropped behind the kitchen island as his lookalike fired again. Another gunshot. Another and then another. Morgan was enraged, careless. He was wasting bullets without a clean shot. Ryan heard footsteps approaching. He heard the click of a trigger, the metallic twang of an empty chamber.

Ryan rose, ready to fire, but Morgan was already upon him. He caught Ryan in the stomach and slammed him against the wall. Morgan hurled him back toward the middle of the kitchen. Ryan hit the edge of a counter and crumpled to the floor, the impact forcing him to lose control of his pistol. He gasped, tasting blood in his mouth and feeling acute pain in his side.

Morgan, sensing his opponent was severely injured, walked past him, toward Dolphin's still body. At her feet, his pistol. Ryan coughed, tasting more blood.

And then, in the corner of the kitchen, he spotted Erin. She was propped against the wall, her head slumped to one side, her arms and legs sprawled before her. Her face was covered in blood. She was motionless. He watched her for what seemed an eternity, waiting for movement, but she didn't stir.

He was too late.

A surge of anger rippled through him. Ryan pushed himself to his feet, turned on his heels and charged at Morgan. He wanted nothing more than to kill the man. He'd do it with his bare hands if he needed to. Morgan wouldn't survive the night, no matter what it took.

A BANG. SOMEWHERE in the distance. And then another, closer. A third, seemingly right next to her ear.

Erin's eyes fluttered, the weight of her eyelids painfully heavy. She looked up, blinding light burning into her retinas. She turned her head ever so slightly. It felt like a freight train was trying to burst through her right temple. Her mouth tasted like blood. Her nose was blocked. She could barely breathe. The light faded, returning her to the kitchen where she'd been knocked unconscious.

Yet another gunshot rang through the kitchen. She looked over to see two men struggling with each other. They were fighting over control of a gun. One was Christopher Morgan. He held the gun. The other was of similar height, but skinnier, paler. His clothes hung from his body. He looked considerably weaker than his counterpart, but was fighting with a ferocity that kept him in the game.

"Ryan," she said aloud, though her voice was barely audible.

Suddenly, Morgan's non-shooting arm broke free and he struck Ryan in the chest with his elbow. Ryan staggered backward, giving Morgan the separation he needed. The killer turned his gun on Ryan, a sickening smile washing across his face.

"Erin's all mine now," Morgan said, trying to get one last reaction from his victim.

But Morgan failed to get off the shot. In an amazing burst of speed, Ryan surged forward and slammed into Morgan with all the momentum he could muster. Morgan stumbled backwards, Ryan in his embrace once more, and struck the bay window behind him. The large glass pane shattered around them as they fell onto the outside patio.

"Ryan!" Erin screamed, pushing herself up with her good hand. She rose quickly, but just as quickly fell against the wall. The room spun, her swollen brain drumming against the confines of her skull. She closed her eyes, trying to will away the dizziness. She lurched forward, grabbing the kitchen table for support. She looked around, the room moving in and out of focus. Everything seemed to be so distant. She staggered onward, the shattered bay window only a few feet away.

Even before she saw them, she could hear them struggling. Shoes on broken glass. Heavy breathing as they fought for the upper hand. She peered outside, saw them about twenty feet away, once again locked together. Their movements seemed unreal. Erin blinked, knowing her mind was playing tricks on her.

Ryan's foot slipped and he stumbled backwards, spinning away. Morgan went after him. He was no longer holding the gun. He reached for Ryan and grabbed him by the right arm, then twisted it behind his back. There was a loud snapping sound and Ryan screamed in pain, his arm or shoulder broken. Ryan spun around and struck Morgan with his good arm.

"You punch like a girl," Morgan barely reacted to the blow. Ryan collapsed to the ground, wincing in pain.

Erin took a step forward, prepared to help, but as soon as she let go of her support the world began to spin once more. She fell back against the wall to regain her balance.

Morgan leaned over Ryan, reaching for his good shoulder. "I'm going to break you piece by piece. Then I'll make you watch as I do the same to your girlfriend."

Erin focused on Ryan. He looked destroyed, his face wrought in anguish. This was it, she realized. She was so close, but couldn't help. And Ryan, on his hands and knees, was at his end.

But she hadn't seen his left hand fold around a shard of broken glass. Ryan plunged the glass into Morgan's neck. Morgan gave no audible reaction, but his face grimaced with pain as Ryan twisted the shard in his flesh. Morgan stumbled backwards, grasping at the glass. Meanwhile, Ryan scrambled across the patio. Erin followed his path and saw he was going for the gun.

Morgan noticed the same thing. He jumped to his feet, calculating his plan of attack. He didn't have time. Ryan would get to the gun before he could make up the distance. He turned and fled towards the woods.

Ryan's broken arm, his shooting arm, hung useless, but he grabbed the gun with his left, aimed and fired. The bullet went wide. Morgan was already too far away.

"Morgan!" Ryan shouted, awkwardly rising to his feet. He started after the man.

"Ryan, no!" Erin hollered, reaching for him, but it was no use. Ryan didn't hear her, his brain focused on a sole purpose. *Let him go*, she wanted to say. *Come back here. Come to me.*

Erin left her perch, staggering onto the patio. The woods and sky swirled, the ground twisting and tilting beneath her. She looked down at her feet, moved one and then the next.

Morgan disappeared into the woods, following the trail that led to the water. Ryan followed, his body vanishing into the darkness like a ghost. Just like that, both Ryan Harpers were gone.

68

RYAN'S FEET CRUNCHED against the gravel path, his hoarse breathing drowning out all other sound. He didn't care. Christopher Morgan was somewhere ahead. He would find him and kill him, erase him from this world once and for all.

Someone screamed his name, or at least he thought so. He couldn't be sure it was real. It was Erin's voice, in his head, saying his name, speaking to him. The voice faded. Christopher Morgan had to die. That's all that mattered.

Chandling's house far behind, the dark woods engulfed him. With the stars and moon cloaked by clouds, there was little light to go by. And yet the gravel path seemed to glow, guiding his path. Maybe God was making it just a little easier for him.

The trail rounded a bend, began to lead down a hill. Ryan could hear the sound of gentle waves crashing against the shore. He saw the faintest of lights ahead of him. The trees began to thin. He could see the water, light reflecting off its surface.

Ryan arrived at a wooden staircase that led to a rocky beach below. The beach was minute, a sand-and-rock bank perched in between the steep hillside and obsidian waters of Puget Sound. The tide was in, leaving no more than a few yards of dry land.

Off to the right was Chandling's boathouse, a small gray structure elevated above the water. The building was small and unimposing, less so than the lengthy dock that extended far into the water. A small sailboat, its masts down, was moored at the dock. A light at the end of the platform flickered as it rocked gently with the waves, but the boat itself looked untouched.

Another dim light buzzed above the door to the boathouse. The door was ajar.

Ryan crossed the uneven beach and stepped onto the dock. The wood creaked beneath his feet as he approached the small building, which wasn't much bigger than a large storage shed. The boathouse had a few small windows, but each was dark and speckled with dirt and salt.

He paused outside the door, listening for sounds, but all he could hear was the groaning of wood and water sloshing against support beams below. Ryan kicked at the door—it slammed into the wall—and peered inside. The boathouse was indeed a storage unit, the walls lined with tools, rope and fishing and boat gear. A small speedboat was docked inside, elevated a few feet above the water's surface.

Months ago he would have tried to reason with Morgan. He would have called for him, try to get him to surrender. But not now. Not today. Morgan deserved to die.

Ryan stepped inside, scanning the dark recesses of the boathouse. There was little room to maneuver—five feet at most on either side of the boat, ten at the bow. There was also little room to hide.

Footsteps ran toward him. Ryan looked to his left but saw nothing. He tensed, searching the darkness, but no one was there. He realized too late the footsteps were outside on the dock, running along the exterior of the boathouse. He looked over his shoulder to see an oar swinging at his face. He ducked and fell backwards, twisting to get Morgan in his sights. His back struck the edge of the boat and he nearly fell through the gap between the floor and the hull, but caught himself with his left arm.

Morgan came at him, swinging wildly. Ryan had no time to take aim. He moved his arm away just as Morgan's oar slammed into and shattered against the boat's hull. As Morgan approached once more, Ryan, no longer in a position to shoot, kicked at his legs. He struck Morgan in his knee and the man collapsed sideways, moaning loudly. He dropped the oar.

Ryan lifted the gun once more, but Morgan, aware of it, lunged forward and tackled him. The gun flew from Ryan's hand and into the water.

Morgan laughed, pressing his weight into Ryan's sternum. "What are you going to do without your gun? Overpower me?" He punched Ryan in the face. Blood filled his mouth. "I'm you, only better. Did you really think you could win?"

Morgan's hands slid around Ryan's neck. Ryan's eyes bulged as he felt his airway collapse under Morgan's superior strength. He dug his fingernails into Morgan's wrists, but to no avail. He only had one good arm, and there was no way Morgan was going to let go.

His vision began to blur.

ERIN STOPPED AT the doorway and peered inside. Two figures were lying on the floor, one strangling the other. She couldn't tell which was which—in the darkness they looked the same. She approached cautiously. The man on top laughed, but still she couldn't tell who was who. And then he shifted positions ever so slightly and she saw light reflect off his neck, off the glass shard.

Christopher Morgan was strangling the life from Ryan. She shot forward and wrapped her arms around Morgan's head and neck, pulling him backwards with all her might. She tore him away from Ryan and he landed on his back. Her momentum carried her further, but she regained her footing and came at him again. He was still getting to his feet, bewildered by the surprise attack.

She jumped on his back and put him in a headlock, trying to twist him to the ground.

"Fucking bitch," he cried, thrashing beneath her. She held steady, but Morgan wouldn't go down.

"Erin…" Ryan croaked, rolling onto his side.

"Get the fuck off me," Morgan backpedaled, slamming her against the wall. A searing pain rippled through her body but she refused to let go. He rammed into the wall once more. Forced to let go, she stumbled away, Morgan now behind her. She spun around, but Morgan had the upper hand. He lifted her into the air and threw her to the back of the boathouse. She landed hard on a workbench. The shelf collapsed under her weight and she toppled to the floor, its contents falling on top of her.

Morgan came at her once more, grinning.

"I'm going to kill him in front of you, Erin. He'll be out of our hair. Well mine. Yours… I'm going to burn off."

Erin searched blindly for something she could use as a weapon. She was lying in a pile of tools and fishing supplies—surely there had to be something she could use—but her mind was fractured. She was processing her surroundings too slowly, her motor skills reduced.

A pungent smell filled her bloody nostrils. Gasoline. She looked for the source and quickly spotted a red gallon-sized jug not far from her right hand. The lid had popped off when the container had hit the floor. She curled her fingers around its plastic handle, ignoring the pain from her broken hand.

Morgan grabbed her ankle to pull her toward him. She lifted the gasoline jug into the air, its contents splashing away from her. The liquid struck Morgan in the face. He staggered back, wincing as the gasoline stung his eyes.

"You fucking whore," he muttered, dabbing at his eyes with his shirt. Erin dropped the jug behind her and tried to will herself to her feet. Her body was unresponsive. She was too exhausted, her brain failing her.

Morgan blinked, his eyesight returning. He glared at her and she stared up at him, unsure what she'd do next.

"You're not going anywhere," he muttered, turning his back on her. Erin looked past him to Ryan, who was now on his knees, trying to regain his footing. He sensed that Morgan was approaching and looked up, but made no attempt to fight as Morgan grabbed him by the hair and dragged him across the room.

"This is the last time you'll see your girlfriend, Harper," Morgan declared. Erin locked eyes with Ryan for the first time. He stared back at her affectionately, but was in too much pain to say anything. She wanted to smile but couldn't muster the strength.

Morgan shoved Ryan toward the bow of the boat. His head struck the hull and he disappeared into the black waters below. Erin felt her chest tighten. For a moment there was silence, but finally she heard splashing and knew Ryan had risen to the surface. Though she couldn't see him, she heard him gasp for air.

Morgan bent down to one knee and stuck his right hand into the water. Ryan began to flail his arms, fighting for the air that Morgan refused to give him.

Do something, Erin told herself. She tried to lean forward, but her body resisted every inch. She collapsed against the broken shelf once more. She looked down, running her hands along the debris that had piled around her. Fishing wire. Hooks. Buoys. A rusted anchor. Rope. A hammer.

Ryan was still fighting, but the splashing had subsided. He only had a few seconds left.

Erin's eyes fell on something, a round cylinder protruding from a cardboard box. It was several feet away. She wasn't even certain it was what she thought it was. She leaned to the side, extending her reach. Her fingertips touched the end of the cylinder, but she couldn't get a good grip. She leaned further, every bit of energy focused on this one task. Her fingers curled around the tube and she pulled it to her. She looked down at it, suddenly aware of its power.

A flare.

"We'll soon be alone," Morgan said softly.

Erin tore off the flare's cap, brought it down against the exposed tip. A spark, but nothing else. She tried again, but to the same result. And again. Frantic, she readjusted her grip and tried lighting the flare once more.

The flare exploded, its tip bursting into a fiery red flame.

Morgan looked over his shoulder. His eyes widened at the sight of the flare. Erin tossed it onto the floor. The gasoline-soaked wood lit up immediately. Morgan started to rise, but the flames came too quickly. The fire jumped up his pants legs to his shirt, then engulfed his neck and face. He screamed. His arms flailed helplessly as he tried to douse the fire, but his flesh was already burning away.

Morgan jumped toward the water, but instead his body toppled into the front of the boat. Erin could only see his kicking feet after that point, but from his fading screams and the stench of burnt flesh she knew that Christopher Morgan's time in the world was done.

Erin dragged herself to the edge of the water. Ryan was holding onto the edge of the dock by his fingertips, struggling to stay above water. She reached down and grabbed him by the collar, pulling him above the surface. Ryan tried to break free, his arms swinging at her, but she didn't let go.

"Ryan, it's okay… It's okay…"

It took him a moment to process her words. Then he blinked and gazed up at her.

It was the first time she'd been able to see him clearly. His face was thin, his skin pale. His cheekbones looked like they wanted to burst through his flesh. His eyes were sunken, large bags under his eyes. His lips were thin and chapped.

But it was him. It was Ryan Harper. This time she was sure of it.

She smiled at him, too weak to say anything else. He reached up and touched her face. His hand was cold and wet, but it was Ryan's. She felt his fingertips slide across her cheek, his thumb brush the side of her mouth. She refused to close her eyes out of fear that he'd disappear.

He didn't.

EPILOGUE

SERGEY OMITOV SHIVERED. The room was cold, and not just in appearance. The walls and ceiling were an unremitting gray save for a few chipped-away sections near the floor. The fluorescent lights overhead didn't flicker like in the movies, but they emitted an endless nerve-grating buzz. The overhead vent croaked air-conditioned air like a sick dog.

It felt like he'd been sitting in there for an hour. Alone, with no water, no food, sitting at this damned table, chained to his chair like some convict. After everything he'd been through, he didn't deserve this.

But he did. Deep down, he knew it. He had allied with the wrong man. Richard Chandling was a sociopath, a man who wanted power above all else. Sergey recognized the man's lust for power years ago, but had seen it as a positive trait.

He had followed Chandling blindly, misinterpreting his depravity as cunning foresight. The man had sold him on a false reality, convinced him to do things of which he never thought himself capable. It hadn't been his decision to kidnap Ryan Harper. To clone him and merge his mind with a known killer. And he didn't know Chandling had gone through all that effort to, in part, cover up the fact he had hired Christopher Morgan to murder his own family. The senator had overstepped his bounds, driven be the absurd notion that he could play God and get away with it. His decisions had led to his own death—and to Sergey's incarceration.

The FBI had little to go on, however. They were holding him for the murder of Luis Salazar, but they knew their case was weak. They hadn't checked his hands for gunpowder residue. And forensic experts had determined that Salazar had been holding the gun that killed him when it was fired. The evidence pointed to suicide. He would walk free.

But the government didn't want him just for murder. They wanted him for everything else. They knew, by simple matter of deduction, that he was involved with everything that had transpired. But they had little evidence to prove it. The California facility had been shut down, the tunnel collapsed. The rest was linked to him only through conjecture and circumstantial information. There was a money trail, but nothing definitive enough to overcome reasonable doubt.

Sergey was confident he would be set free.

The door behind him opened. He started to look back but decided against it. He didn't want to show that he was anxious, that he was sick of sitting in this uncomfortable chair waiting for some interrogator to show up.

"I won't talk with you unless my lawyer is present," he murmured.

The door closed. The person's shoes tapped against the tiled floor. Heels. Sergey glanced to his left as the woman walked by him. She was slender. Had a great body. She was wearing a black business skirt and matching blouse. She sat down before him, her forearms resting on the table. She stared at him through thick-rimmed glasses, her blue eyes piercing. Sergey sucked in a breath. His chest tightened. A bead of sweat formed on his brow.

"Help me!" he hollered, twisting to look back at the door. There had to be a guard outside, someone who could hear him. He repeated his plea, then focused on the camera positioned in the corner. He screamed again.

"Help isn't coming," the woman with blond hair stated. "No one can hear you."

She had to be lying. He continued to shout. Minutes passed. The woman waited patiently. Finally, it dawned on him. He was alone. No one was coming to his aid. No one was here to protect him from her.

"Good, I'm glad that's out of your system." Her voice was different. She no longer had a French accent. She no longer sounded adorable. Or sweet. Or innocent.

"Marie… Dolphin… please."

"I expect you to beg," Dolphin leaned back in her chair. "But it won't do any good."

"You're here to kill me."

"I'm here to get answers. The government… they funded this little project of yours. I want to know names. Locations. I want to know everything."

"Yes. Yes, I'll tell you everything," he nodded.

"Good," she stated.

He told her everything. Everything that he knew. She seemed satisfied. More than pleased with what he'd given her.

"Thank you, Sergey," she said, standing up. She walked around the edge of the table, her fingertips dragging along its surface. Sergey watched her move closer, unsure of what to think. She disappeared behind him, her hands dragging up his arms and across his chest. "You've been very helpful."

"What happens now?"

Dolphin's hands circled around his neck, cradling his head. "I thought it was obvious the moment I walked in the room."

ABOUT THE AUTHOR

Erik Samdahl is a world traveler, marketing executive and founder of FilmJabber.com, one of the most popular entertainment websites in the Pacific Northwest. Erik's articles and movie reviews have been read and shared by millions of readers, and he has been ranked as a top digital influencer on a variety of subjects.

In his limited spare time, Erik is an avid Seattle sports fan, loves to camp in the beautiful northwest and lives to experience new cultures and environments around the world. Erik resides in sunny Seattle, Washington.

Follow Erik:

@eriksamdahl
Facebook.com/eriksamdahlauthor
Eriksamdahl.com